The

Queenslander

To William Henry Macklin

Angus & Robertson Publishers
London ● Sydney ● Melbourne ● Singapore
Manila

First published by Angus & Robertson Publishers, Australia, 1975

©Robert Macklin 1975

National Library of Australia card number and ISBN 0 207 13253 4

Printed in Australia by Watson Ferguson & Co., Brisbane

The Queenslander

Robert Macklin

ANGUS & ROBERTSON PUBLISHERS

AUTHOR'S NOTE

While Queensland, of course, is a real state, Brisbane a real city, the *Courier-Mail* a real newspaper, and J. C. Williamson's a real theatrical company, the characters in *The Queenslander* are real only in the sense that I can persuade the reader of their reality, their authenticity. They have no independent existence.

Brolie's Story
I

I AM still afraid, but I will do it. In a way it's like entering the confessional, a long moment of truth where only pride stands between an endangered soul and a state of grace. Humility is the most difficult test of all and only a Catholic knows how difficult. Though I have had much practice, I doubt if I can confess it all. But I will try.

I loved Pal Lingard. Palmer Albert Lingard. I loved him and I married him and I bore his child. I have not seen him now for nearly five years, yet he is still there. And it's easy for me to remember the beginning, the first time I met him.

When I was a child, a black-haired, blue-eyed child like my mother had been in Ireland, I went to St Theresa's Convent, St Lucia, a Brisbane suburb. My two sisters were in lower grades and they waited for me after school so that we could walk home together. The arrangement suited us. I enjoyed their company. They could do their homework before they went home and since we had to pass Ironsides on the way they were grateful to have me along.

Some of the Protestants at Ironsides were like Protestant children everywhere. They thought they hated us and they threatened us whenever they had the chance. We were "Catholic frogs" for some reason I never understood. It might have been that "frogs" rhymed with so many derogatory words. They would gather round us—boys and girls—as we passed each other on the footpath and chant: "Catholic frogs/Stink like dogs" or "Catholic frogs/Live in bogs" or "Catholic frogs/Lie like hogs."

The words meant nothing to us then except as expressions of hostility. If anything, that made it more frightening than if there had been some rational meaning. Usually the ragging remained verbal but occasionally one of the Catholic boys would reply in kind and then stones would be thrown or punches exchanged.

But that happened only rarely. Looking back, I suppose the whole thing was quite mild, even harmless in comparison with some of the things which have happened since. Northern Ireland for example.

But we weren't to know that then. When it happened I would take Mary's hand on one side (we called her Misty because of some infant malapropism which I forget) and Connie's on the other and we would walk quickly down the footpath looking straight ahead. We would never run.

It was so long ago. Misty was only six, Connie was twelve and I was

1

fourteen. Yet now, twenty years later, when I think of it I can still feel the wet trembling of their palms. And I can still feel the anger I felt then after we were safely home and Misty had stopped crying. She would never cry until we reached home, never in front of the Protestants.

It was on one of those occasions that I met Pal. I had seen him in his parents' store and I knew quite a lot about him even though he was a year younger than I and wouldn't sit for the Scholarship until the following year. I'm certain about the date and every detail of the occasion but when I reminded him of it after we were married he had a completely different version. He said he didn't even have a bike that year. But it was the bike that I remember most clearly. The bike and then the boy.

Connie was on my left nearest the road when the Bells came over from the other side. Godfrey Bell was one of the biggest boys at Ironsides that year, a fat loudmouth always with his face distorted by penny jawbreakers which he sucked loudly through teeth that even then looked gappy with cavities. With him, as always, were the twins. I forget their names if I ever knew them. They were in Pal's class, a boy and a girl, equally scruffy, equally smartalecky and tough. Their father owned an old dilapidated dairy farm down in Long Pocket but the children were never on it. They hung around the shopping centre or simply prowled the streets looking for trouble. Convent kids were fair game any time.

This day they were boisterous and disgusting and insulting but no more so than at other times. We had taken up our position of bold retreat, hands firmly gripped, when suddenly Connie staggered against me. I didn't see it but I assumed the Bells had pushed her. Then my hand was empty and there was a resounding thwack as Connie struck the girl twin on the face. The next instant the two boys were around her, pushing her and keeping her off balance while I tried to go to her aid and shield Misty at the same time. There were squeals and taunts and shouts and then the bike, the skidding of the back wheel as a red and white Malvern Star broke into the ring of bare legs knocking Godfrey Bell into the gutter.

Pal jumped off it just as it reached us and the bike skidded around wildly in the gravel between the bitumen road and the footpath. But the Bells were diverted only for a moment. The twins were at him immediately, the girl just as proficient with her teeth and fingernails as the boy with his fists. For a few moments he held them off but when Godfrey threw his weight into the scuffle Pal was out-gunned. Connie jumped into the thick of it, her fingers tangling in the girl's hair pulling her away from the centre of the fight. For a few seconds I was torn with indecision. I wanted to get away, to get Misty and Connie

2

safely home but I didn't want to leave him and I wasn't sure I could extricate Connie. But I didn't want to fight either. I was fourteen, a young lady. So I just stood there shouting at Connie.

Then I saw Godfrey Bell's thumb whitening as he pushed it against Pal's Adam's apple while the boy twin hit out at him, his stomach, his face, anywhere he could find an opening. Without another thought I dashed at them, my hands grasping for the thumb. But as I reached out Pal twisted away breaking the grip and almost simultaneously buried his fist into Godfrey Bell's face. The blow made a soft sound like a quick squeeze on a water-filled sponge and the bigger boy staggered back with his nose gushing rich red blood. It all happened in my flash of movement towards them and in the same moment I turned towards Connie and the girl who was struggling vainly to reach behind her to break Connie's grip on her hair. Her face was towards me and in instant imitation of the punch I had just seen I closed my fist and swung. I think I closed my eyes also because I don't remember seeing it land, but I felt the pain as my hand struck hard bone. When I opened my eyes she was sprawled on the ground with Connie standing over her.

Pal's struggle with the boy twin was quickly over. His fists cut the air between them, striking face and ribs as the boy retreated back across the road. Then he turned and all three of them were running, stopping only to shout the vilest language I had ever heard. Connie was screaming back at them, making up for her paucity of vocabulary with Gaelic enthusiasm. Then they were round a corner and it was quiet again except for the ringing in my ears. We three combatants just looked at each other, chests heaving, red faced, our systems wild with adrenalin. Then, simultaneously, Pal laughed aloud and Misty began to cry. I was watching him and I saw his face fall.

"Hey, come here." He knelt in front of her. "We won, didn't we?" Misty sniffled and nodded her head.

"You bet we did." Connie was glowing with triumph.

"Right." He looked at me with adolescent seriousness. "I'm very sorry about that." Already he was assuming responsibility for the Bells, not for their Protestantism but because they went to his school, to Ironsides.

"That's all right," I said. "Thanks for what you did."

He grinned. "You better hurry home and put some acriflavine on your hand."

I looked down. My knuckles were dripping blood. I must have hit her in the teeth. "Gosh." It looked horrible.

"Come on," he said to Misty. "I'll give you a doubler home on the bike."

Misty shook her head. "I think she's frightened," I said. "We'd

3

better walk."

"I'd like a doubler," said Connie.

He smiled again. "Okay," he said. "Hop on."

He looked at me very quickly as Connie climbed on to the bar of his bike from the kerb. Then he grinned and pushed the bike away down the slight grade.

There are times, very occasionally, when intimations of the future flash subliminally across the emotional spectrum. I don't say it happens to everyone. Perhaps you have to be half Irish and all Catholic. Perhaps you have to be a woman. But it happens to me and it always has. This was one of those times.

There is a film, *The Pawnbroker*, where Rod Steiger as an old Jew is mentally driven back to Belsen or Auschwitz by the horror that remained with him. The flashbacks always started with a graphic still photograph flashed at subliminal speed as the camera bored in on his watery, pained eyes.

The moment was like that for me, but in the other direction of time; the first flash of something I was destined to look upon and hate, a memory yet to be recorded. But it was a feeling rather than a picture, a mixture of anger at myself and biting jealousy of another woman. I would come to know it well.

Yes. It is easy to remember the beginning. I wish so much that there was no need for me to say anything more. I wish I could let it all go. I wish I could simply say, "I, Bronwyn Lingard loved this man. I love him still." If only that were enough.

Pal's Story
I

IT WAS a damn nuisance; a criminal waste of time.

What other kid had to deliver grocery orders after school along the dull suburban streets of Taringa and St Lucia? Who else had to leave early from footy practice in winter and, like today, from the cricket oval better than halfway to a half-century. (The ball was as big as a pumpkin and his square cut was working like a dream; Bradman himself would have been proud.) And who else was kept from the Toowong baths on non-practice days and from the Milton reach of the river on bright, steaming Saturday mornings when all the other kids were out in their trainees?

No one, that's who. No one. Just Palmer Albert Lingard, son of a bloody grocer.

Pal Lingard bent to lay newspaper at the bottom of the little two-wheeled canvas wagon he pushed and pulled along the wide bitumen streets and concrete footpaths. He loaded the groceries in the storeroom at the back of the shop where the reserve stock was kept. On most days, Joyce or Barbara, the two married women who worked part-time at the store, had the wagon packed for him by the time he arrived home from school. But Fridays were always busy and he had to do it himself. Actually, he preferred it that way. The women were often interrupted by customers as they put the orders together and frequently made mistakes, left things out or put in the wrong sizes of cornflakes or baking powder. At least when he did it he knew it was right. He knew the big storeroom intimately and went automatically to the right shelf for each item. Also, he prided himself on knowing the prices of all the groceries in the shop and this helped him keep up to date.

For a while, when he was serving, he had mentally added the prices of items as he brought them to the counter and the moment the customer reached the end of his list he would tell him the total cost of the order.

He was never wrong but sometimes they took some convincing. He particularly enjoyed it with Professor Halstead, a prissy, pedantic, old-womanish lecturer in mathematics at the university. Halstead was great sport. He squeezed half a case of tomatoes to a pulp before choosing one—one tomato—and picked over a pound of beans which Pal had selected for an interminable time until he found one

7

with a little brown mark or one which sagged when he bent it instead of snapping in half like a good crisp bean should.

When that happened, Halstead would take the offending bean back to the display and choose another, all the while staring at Pal through cocker spaniel eyes as though the boy had set out to wound him, not cheat him but wound him, in a deeply personal and unforgivable way.

Halstead's list was always a long one though seldom did any item top two shillings. Pal had no difficulty carrying the progressive total in his head and, as in their last and most memorable contest, springing the grand total as the final item left Halstead's parched, old maid's lips:

"Fourteen and tuppence ha'penny."

The reaction was inevitable. Halstead took a tenpenny biro from his inside coat pocket and a little notebook from his shopping bag (a string bag, for God's sake): "Could I have that itemised, please."

"Certainly, professor: saveloys, one and nine; Maxam cheese, two shillings; two tins of sardines, one and eightpence; a quarter of a pound of butter" (Halstead had insisted on cutting the half-pound pack himself; Pal had made sure he got the smaller piece) "one and a penny; beans, ninepence ha'penny; two pounds of sugar, one and six . . ." He rattled off the list faster than Halstead could take it down and had to repeat most of the items ". . . grand total, fourteen and sixpence ha'penny."

The trap was set. Halstead bent to his addition.

"Yes, that's what I get also, but," he paused, a flush of triumph enlivening his parchment features momentarily, "didn't you originally say 'fourteen and *tuppence* ha' penny'? I'm sure you did. You were robbing yourself, or rather your father. A little time and care is all that's needed, you know . . ."

The trap was shut tight around him and the silly old bugger didn't know it.

"I did say fourteen and tuppence ha'penny. You're right, sir. But you did bring back two Tristram's bottles and we normally give tuppence a bottle. I didn't realise you didn't want the refund."

Caught. Now what? Does he demand the refund and surrender the triumph or forgo the fourpence for victory? No contest.

"Oh, I hadn't realised you gave a refund on soft drink bottles." (Like hell he hadn't. He probably picked them up from the tall grass along Gailey Road where the kids fooled around in the afternoons.) "Of course, if you charged me a deposit, I must take the refund."

Halstead was a worthy opponent but he lacked imagination.

Lately however Pal had stopped the practice. His father had made a fuss but that, very definitely, was not the reason. His mother said the customers didn't really appreciate it. They couldn't be sure he was correct, and though she had every confidence, it was best to pander to them a little and give them a list. Besides, they now had a new cash register with a built-in adding machine and that was a useful way to double-check. That made sense.

But, no matter which way you looked at it, shop work was a chore to be endured.

Delivering orders was a terrible waste of time compared to cricket or football or sailing. If it weren't for the compensation—and this had nothing to do with the miserly five shillings a week his father paid him—he would definitely find some way to duck out of it. He might even refuse, point blank, and then see how the old bugger got on.

But there was the compensation and he had to admit it was a big one. It almost made the wasted hours worthwhile. Of course, even the compensation couldn't compare with a morning like last Saturday.

Last week he had been named dux of the school and as a reward his father had given him a free weekend; no shop duties at all. Actually, it had been his mother's doing, he was sure, but in any case he made the most of it.

By 8.30 they were on the river and by nine the wind had kicked up and darkies were ruffling the water before beating into the sails. They tacked more than five miles to the University bend before turning and running before the breeze back towards the boathouse. The thrill of racing the small skiff through hard, bumping, choppy water was almost incomparable.

Then quite abruptly the wind died. But even that was almost as good. Before, they were too busy even to talk. Now they had the chance to relax in the bottom of the boat, to yarn and occasionally wave at the girls sunbathing on their back terraces by the river bank.

Amazingly, one of them waved back. That very seldom happened but when it did it set off a chain reaction which was practically a ritual. The three boys were instantly alert.

"She does it," Barney Millen declared.

"What? What does she do?" Pal set it up.

"She fucks."

"G'wan, how can you tell?"

"She waved at us didn't she?"

"Yeah . . ."

"Well." It was self-evident.

Joe Swanneth, consulting sociologist, delivered the second opinion: "Course she fucks. I think that's Glenda someone. My brother's taken her out."

It was Swanny's brother and Swanny's boat. There was no room left for argument.

9

By Pal's rough reckoning, Swanny's brother had fucked more girls in one Queensland town than Casanova had in the whole of Europe; and Swanny's brother wasn't even nineteen yet. Pal had just finished reading Casanova's memoirs, which Barney had taken from his father's study and brought to school, so he was in a good position to compare. But it wasn't the sort of thing you brought up. Swanny was bloody touchy about his brother. There'd be an argument and the whole morning would be spoiled. Besides, he was supposed to give the book back when he'd finished it and he wanted to read it again. He kept it under the shop in an old onion sack and read it while weighing up potatoes into 4lb and 7lb bags. Pal knew his father was suspicious about his recent enthusiasm for the job but he was equally confident that as long as the old bugger got his spuds weighed and packaged in abundance he'd let sleeping dogs lie.

So, for a few reasons instantly computed, Pal stayed silent about Casanova and relished the rest of the ritual.

Barney waved like a shipwrecked sailor but this time elicited no response. "She's probably had more fucks than feeds."

"I wouldn't be surprised," Swanny said. From a hundred yards through a Brisbane heat haze he had definitely decided it was Glenda. "My brother went up her like a rat up a drainpipe. She's a nympho."

"Swanny," Barney said, "if we went over there now and asked her, do you reckon she'd let us?"

"Let us what?"

"Fuck her, of course."

Pal joined in again: "Do you mean all three at once or one at a time?"

"I don't care, as long as I can put it in."

"I wouldn't be surprised." Swanny considered the matter. "Nymphos want it all the time. If they can't get it, they go berserkers."

"Well, what are we going to do about it?" said Pal. "Do you want to take the boat over and ask her?" Swanny's excuse would be one of the usual ones whenever something like this happened: There wasn't enough time; he didn't feel like it just now (which was always a lie); or his brother might find out and give him a hiding. That happened a lot. Brotherly affection seemed to be a one-way street.

"Nah, not Glenda," he said finally. "You never know what you might catch from her."

That was a new twist. It was one of Casanova's abiding problems; but the logic of the consequences to Swanny's brother seemed to be lost on his companions.

"Jees, I wouldn't worry about that," said Barney. "They can cure

10

that kind of thing with a couple of injections these days. My sister told me about it." Barney's sister was a much better conversation piece than Swanny's brother. She was seventeen, nearly four years older than Barney and Pal. Swanny was senior by a year to his companions.

Pal wanted to turn the conversation to the beautiful Helen Millen, especially as the current object of their lust—whether it was really Glenda someone or not—had just left the back terrace and gone indoors. The tension of decision went with her.

"Anyway, she's gone now," Pal said. "What did your sister actually say?"

Pal recalled the subsequent conversation with half his mind while he packed three grocery orders into the little wagon for the afternoon delivery. Barney was the envy of all the kids because of his sister and he knew how to make the most of it. If you didn't interrupt he'd get down to the most intimate details. Apparently, Helen walked around the house practically nude through the summer and she couldn't care less, Barney said, if he went into the bathroom while she was taking a shower. Pal suspected it didn't mean all that much to Barney either, but to an only child it meant a hell of a lot. Pal felt he knew every contour, every hair, every beautiful bulge of the lovely Helen's body. In fact, when she came into the shop as a customer he found it hard to concentrate on serving her and kept her waiting as long as he could without his mother or father noticing.

But, as he laid in more newspaper to separate the second and third orders in the wagon, thoughts of the river and of Helen Millen faded. The job at hand, for all its drawbacks, had that one great compensation. If you wanted to put a name to it, you could call it sex. He had never put it quite that bluntly before, but it was true. It was probably the sexiest job in the world.

The thrill was always the same, yet better each time it happened, each time he knocked or called from the back door. There would be a sound of footsteps from the shadows within and in a few moments he would be welcomed by one of his women. And they were *his* women; from old Mrs Skinner who always seemed to have a cup of tea in the pot for him with little cakes or biscuits and who chatted about school or the weather while he unloaded the groceries on to the kitchen table; to the Special, the Prize, the one who made cricket and footy seem like games for kids, and somehow beneath him. They were his women and he was alone with them in an otherwise empty house and it was as sexy as hell.

Mrs Skinner too was an exception. With her, he always unloaded the groceries himself. But with the others he had developed a technique where he started the unloading and then fumbled with the check list so that they would take over. Invariably, they chose to bend

11

down and take the groceries out of the wagon and let him check them off on the list. In the beginning it surprised him. One would expect that they would rather be waited on and have him do the bending while they checked but it never happened that way. He thought about it and decided the reason was simple: They were women so they wanted things, especially new brightly-wrapped things, even groceries. They were new possessions and the women couldn't wait to get their hands on them.

That made it all so easy. It wasn't his fault if every time they bent down over the little wagon their dresses fell open at the top and sometimes they were wearing hardly anything underneath. Summer was best. Even though they were almost always wearing brassieres, they were often loose and as they bent down practically all their tits would be showing.

It was hard to concentrate on the list but he forced himself to, even when he was damn sure his excitement was showing and he had an almost overpowering urge to touch it, or to touch them, those soft white breasts only a couple of feet from his eyes and hands.

Only once had he made a mistake with the list and the woman had looked up sharply and caught him looking. He shuddered as he thought of it again. It had been terrible, but delicious. If it hadn't been her, the Special, there might have been hell to pay. But with her, Mrs Elizabeth Hendry, it was different. For a moment she looked startled and he felt himself blushing so hard his ears were tingling. But then she looked at him in a different way and actually smiled.

" How old are you now, Palmer?" she asked.

"Thirteen, nearly fourteen, Mrs Hendry," he said and thanked Christ it came out evenly.

"I see," she said. "I thought you were older. You look older."

He couldn't think of anything to say.

"Well," she said finally, "would you mind finishing here? I have to go and get changed. Mr Hendry is coming home today and I have to put on my glad rags for him."

Pal knew Mr Hendry was a salesman for King Tea whose territory covered the North Coast. Last year when they had been at Mooloolaba during the school holidays he had seen his father talking to him outside a shop there.

As she walked away to another room Pal watched her. The sunlight was coming through a verandah window behind her and her legs were outlined through her translucent skirt. She was not a big woman, about an inch or so taller than Pal who was nearly five feet three. But her legs were nice and her breasts jutted out invitingly. She had dark, curly hair and a small straight nose. But when you looked at her your eyes seemed to fix naturally upon her mouth which was always

12

moving, to smile or to pout or to purse together as though she was constantly thinking of something new and expressing it through her mouth. Her teeth were white but a little stained at the edges from nicotine. And no matter what time of the day he came, Pal always noticed that she smelled of perfume. He had no idea what brand it was but it was the type that arrested you, made you think of it for a moment. It was an exciting smell. This day, the day she had caught him looking and walked away, it had seemed particularly strong.

He was grateful and relieved and excited all at once by her actions. And when she left the room she kept talking to him from the bedroom as he hurriedly unpacked the remaining parcels.

"Palmer . . . is that what your friends call you?"

Pal hesitated. He had always liked his nickname but in this situation it seemed childish and inappropriate.

"Some of them do," he compromised. "Others, the younger ones, call me Pal."

"Pal . . ."from her it sounded throaty and interesting. "I like it. It's a good name for a young man."

There was a silence.

"Is that what your girlfriends call you?"

Pal noticed that his fingers were unsteady and he was breathing quickly. By now she must have taken off her dress and was probably getting out of her other clothes. Maybe she would have a shower before she changed into clean things. He thought the bathroom was off the verandah and she would have to pass by the open door from the kitchen to get to it. He waited before taking the next parcel from the wagon. If he delayed long enough she'd have to pass by the door and he would be waiting. He could hear her moving about on the thinly carpeted floor of the bedroom.

He racked his brains for the appropriate response to her question, one that would keep her interest and put him into her league as an adult. She must be about thirty-five and while that was old it wasn't really old, not as old as his mother for example.

If he said he had no girlfriends she might think him young and inexperienced. But if he said he already had a girlfriend—which he didn't really, unless you counted Ellen Cooper whom he had taken to a tennis party at Swanny's place and on whom he had scored an eight (downstairs, outside)—she might think he was already taken and lose interest.

"Actually," he said, "I don't really have any girlfriends in Brisbane. No one steady." That was good. It gave him the sophistication of a man who's travelled round a bit, at least beyond the city limits.

"I see," she said. "Does that mean you have girls in other cities?"

Good. She was quick on the uptake and definitely sounded interested.

"Just one, actually," he said. "I mean just one city, not just one girl. I was in Adelaide a couple of months ago with the Queensland Aussie Rules team and we met quite a few girls there."

There was a long silence from the bedroom. By now she would definitely be undressed if she was going to change completely or if she was going to take a shower. But unfortunately the groceries were all unpacked and there was nothing legitimate to keep him there. He walked a few paces towards the open door to the verandah. Perhaps she hadn't heard him. Anyway, he couldn't leave without saying goodbye.

Just as he stopped she appeared at the doorway.

"I didn't know you were a footballer, Palmer," she said, but the words were lost on him. She was wearing just a brunch coat of the same kind of almost transparent material as her dress had been. But this time she was definitely wearing nothing underneath. He could see the points of her nipples pressing against the inside of the coat as she stood there. They were beautiful. He could almost see their pinkish coloration. He didn't know whether he could see it or just imagined he could. With a tremendous effort he dragged his eyes up to her face. She was smiling slightly, her mouth arching in a tiny gesture which told him she knew the effect she was having on him.

"Oh yes," he said finally, "I was in the state team. We went to the carnival in South Australia. We won the pennant in our league." The words came out in a rush.

"But you still had time to collect a few girlfriends," she smiled.

He was blushing again. It was almost better when he could talk to a voice from the bedroom. He was certain that if he tried to carry on the conversation something infantile would spring unbidden to break the spell so he just grinned, he hoped, modestly.

The house was quite silent now and her teasing chuckle seemed to echo from the weatherboard walls.

"Well, I mustn't keep you, Palmer," she said. "I see you have another order to deliver and I must have my shower."

He wanted to say something adult and flippant like "Would you like me to scrub your back?" but that would be going too far. If she politely refused it would destroy him, destroy everything.

"Yes, I must go," he said deliberately, taking the initiative for a good exit. "Dad will be wondering where I am." Christ, why did he have to say that? His father knew exactly where he was and he could easily make up time by rushing the delivery to Mrs Vawdrey who was always buttoned up to the neck anyway. Though she did have a terrific set and it was a pleasure just to look at the fantastic shape of them.

14

Mrs Hendry walked with him to the back door. "Goodbye then," she said. "I'll see you next week." She paused. "I'll look forward to it."

It was a fabulous, beautiful jolt. I'll look forward to it. There could be only one interpretation to it. She wanted to see him again.

"Yes indeed," he grinned. That was the only possible interpretation. It was as though she had reached out and gently touched him. Jesus Christ, she wasn't the only one who'd be looking forward to it. And next time, for Christ's sake, he would make sure that her order was the last on the list. That way he could stay as long as he liked (and as long as she wanted him to) without some old biddy ringing up his father or mother complaining that he was late.

As he turned at the bottom of the back stairs he had one last glimpse of her as she turned to go inside. As she moved, the brunch coat opened a little at the bottom and for an instant there was a flash of white skin high up to the inside of her thigh. Then he was running, pulling the wagon behind him, heading for the front gate. He ran the whole half-mile to Mrs Vawdrey's house. She was out and he didn't give a damn, just left the groceries on the front steps then day-dreamed his way home.

That had been two weeks ago. Last Friday had been similar but subtly different.

When he arrived with the order (the last on the list, the first two having been completed in record time) she was wearing tiny shorts and high-heeled sandals that made her legs even nicer and more shapely than he remembered. They seemed quite free of the short coarse hairs that most dark-haired women seemed to have and he wondered if she had shaved them specially. Her red T-shirt was cut low to the tops of her breasts and when she moved he could see where the straps of her brassiere joined to the cups.

Her face seemed to be newly made up, the bright red greasy lipstick accentuating her mobile Ava Gardner mouth. And as he entered the kitchen the smell of her perfume seemed to envelop him. The whole effect was devastating and, if he could possibly believe it, was even partly for his benefit, incredibly flattering.

But it made him uneasy. He was suddenly aware of his bare feet. No one (except Graeme Nurse who was a pansy and, of course, the girls) ever wore shoes to school. But now he felt conscious of his feet and his old cotton shorts and his rather faded blue shirt which was getting too small for him and had a button off.

Her outfit made her seem younger and that too wasn't right. It jarred with the image of her which he had carried in the quiet moments of the day and dwelt lustfully upon at night. It wasn't right,

15

yet it had its own excitement. It made her in a way more accessible and while that thought terrified him and turned his legs to soft plastic, it immediately had the opposite effect on another part of his anatomy. He prayed quickly and silently that it didn't show. But the bloody thing had a mind of its own and even as he concentrated on controlling it he felt it press with increasing urgency on his Chesty Bonds. And when he set the wagon by the lino-covered kitchen table, she actually volunteered to do the unloading.

"You check the list and the prices, Palmer," she smiled, looking directly at him. "After all, you're the young genius."

He could do without the "young" part but he liked being called a genius.

"I've never been called that before," he said.

"Oh, but haven't you just been made dux of the school?"

"Oh that," he said. "How did you know about that?"

"A little bird told me." She grinned mischievously at him as she bent down to reach the parcels. Having her last on the list had another advantage besides giving him plenty of time to be with her. The groceries were right at the bottom of the wagon and she had to bend right over to get them. As she did so the front of the loose T-shirt fell away and the whole of her brassiere-clad breasts could be seen. In fact he could see right down the groove between the two as the tight brassiere held them apart. He knew this time that she was aware he was looking but he didn't give a damn. Even when she looked up and saw him he didn't turn his eyes too quickly back to the list. She smiled again and continued the unpacking, calling the brand names as she went, interrupting herself only to continue their conversation.

"One packet of Rinso; one cake of Solvol; two pounds of sugar; one bottle of Mynor cordial; this little bird also said you were captain of the school . . ."

"One Mynor G.I., check. This little bird" (his mother for sure; she had been talking to his mother about him) "seems to know a lot about me." Actually he was delighted she knew about his accomplishments. He had been thinking of ways to let her know without appearing to be skiting, especially about being school captain. He was proud of that. Being dux was certainly an honour but it was also a hell of a responsibility. Everyone expected him to win state honours in the Scholarship next month but he had other things on his mind distracting him from his studies.

"One tin of Darling Downs ham; a jar of Vegemite; a small packet of Weet-Bix; she doesn't know as much about you as I do . . ."

Christ, what did that mean? "One Weet-Bix, check; really?"

"I'm sure she doesn't know about those girls in Adelaide." Again the smile before she dipped back into the wagon ". . . four pounds of potatoes; and a piece of pumpkin and that's the lot."

16

She straightened up and looked at him: "She doesn't know, Palmer, does she?" It was a statement rather than a question.

His tumescence, which had started to subside aided by the litany of grocery brands, now sprang to life again, threatening to break clear through the jockey shorts and probably the cotton trousers.

"No, she doesn't," he said.

"Well, there's no need to worry; I won't tell anyone. It will be our secret, okay?"

"Okay." They were conspirators now, sharing their first secret, a lie. There had been one girl in a South Australian country town somewhere in the Barossa Valley who had sat on his lap in the bus going from the school to the football ground. She had sent him a letter but he'd thrown it away as soon as he had read it and now he couldn't even remember her name . . . Joan someone.

"Do you write to them, these girls of yours?"

"Sometimes."

"All of them?"

"Actually, there's only one who writes" (the lie was more manageable that way) "but I'm not really that keen." Maybe now she'd drop the subject.

But she was persisting. "How aften does she write? Every day?"

"No, no. Not every day."

"Every week then." Jesus, why couldn't she leave it alone? The girls he knew, all of them, were children compared with her. If only he could say that without seeming like a child himself.

"Actually," he said, "they aren't the kind of letters I bother to reply to. In some ways, girls are very young."

Her mouth moved to smile then her lips came together and she looked serious, to his eternal relief.

"Yes, I can understand that. You seem very mature for your age, Palmer. And you're getting quite tall too. Here, let's see." Quickly she bent down and removed her sandals then walked behind him. "No, don't turn around."

She put her back against his and lifted her arm over her head moving her hand back parallel to the ground so that it came just into sight above him. Then it fell to touch his hair to compare their heights. He could feel her bottom pressing and moving against his and as she gestured their legs came together from the knees down.

"Jesus." He hadn't meant to say it aloud, it just whispered out between his teeth as the warmth of her legs caressed his.

"Pardon?" she said. He turned as he felt her move and in doing so brushed against her breast which was itself halfway through a turn in his direction. He sprang back as though he'd run into the fence at Stalag 17.

"Just as I thought," she said, apparently ignoring his shocked leap

17

backwards and the reason for it, the touch which sent the blood rampaging through his system so hard that it actually began to hurt. "You're almost as tall as I am."

His nerve cracked. It was as simple as that. It was all happening too fast. He had to get out quickly before he did something stupid like grab hold of her or bust through his bloody fly buttons or something. He wiped the sweat from his forehead with the back of his hand.

"I'd better get going," he said. "I think Dad wants me to do another delivery this afternoon."

"Oh." She looked genuinely disappointed. "I thought mine was the last for the day. I wouldn't want to hold you up." Was there a double meaning in that? God, the whole world was a double meaning.

"I thought so too." His voice sounded strange, as though he'd been hit in the neck by a bumper. "But just before I left Dad said there might be another one."

"I see." She saw all right. She couldn't bloody help seeing. If he turned around he'd probably hit the wall with it. "You wouldn't like a cup of tea or something?"

"No I'd better go. Next time though that would be very nice." Next time he'd be ready for it. And he wasn't thinking about tea.

"All right then, Palmer. I'll see you next Friday."

He started towards the door then remembered the wagon and went back for it.

"I'd better take this."

"Yes," she smiled. "See you again."

"PALMER!" His father's voice cut through his thoughts. "Haven't you packed those orders yet. It's nearly four o'clock." "Coming, Dad."

The packing was finished. He tucked the three orders into the back pocket of his shorts and went into the big living section at the rear of the store. He stopped first at the bathroom, wet his hair thoroughly, debated using his father's Californian Poppy and decided against it. It stank and it was greasy. If he was going to smell anything this afternoon it was going to be her perfume and, by golly, if she was going to be running her fingers through his hair he didn't want her hand ploughing through that glue.

He had thought about their next meeting so much in the past week that he felt almost cold blooded about it now. He had lived through it a hundred times in anticipation and there was no way it could turn out as fabulous as his imagination had painted it. Anyway, it was probably all in his mind. She was a married woman after all. She didn't have any kids of her own and she was probably just lonely being in the house all day with no one to talk to.

Maybe. And then again, maybe not.

The part wouldn't go straight. It was always the same. When you didn't give a damn how your hair turned out the parting was straight as a die the first time you combed it. But when it was important the parting finished up like a cow pad and the bit at the back near the crowns—he had two crowns which his mother said was a sign of aristocratic breeding—stuck up like paspalum in a field of couch.

Maybe she really was interested in him as a . . . well, that's right, as a man. A young man certainly, but a man with a cock and balls and a face to be smothered in sexy kisses. Maybe right now as he walked from the bathroom to his bedroom to look for his sandals (there would be no embarrassment over bare feet today) at this moment she might be putting on her make-up or getting on her glad rags, preparing herself like a harem girl for his visit.

The sandals were in the lowboy along with the rest of his shoes. He should have looked there first; but if he had they would have been under the bed or somewhere else and it would have taken just as long to find them. That was the way with clothes.

Socks? No, only the Graeme Nurses of the world wore socks with

19

sandals. Maybe he should have washed his feet but they would only get dirty again on the way.

"Palmer!" His father sounded angry. "Those orders should have been delivered hours ago."

To hell with him. "I'm just leaving now." If he waited a moment or two his father would be called back into the shop and he wouldn't have to face him on the way out.

No such luck. The heavy footsteps came towards the bedroom.

"Well, get a move on." His father was at the bedroom door.

"I'm going."

"What are you dressed up for?"

"I'm not dressed up."

"You're wearing shoes for the first time in recorded history."

"I often wear shoes. Anyway, these are sandals."

"Well, make sure you go straight there and no stopping off on the way."

If only he knew, the old bastard. "I said I'm going."

He called goodbye to his mother as he went through the shop and on to the footpath. She was serving Harry Constantine, the sports writer for the *Telegraph* and called goodbye without looking up. Thank God she didn't notice his sandals.

Harry Constantine waved to him from inside as he passed by the front display window. He liked Harry. He had written a story about him in his column after he had been picked for the Queensland side. It had gone into the scrapbook with the others. What with cricket and football and the annual city sportsday, he was starting to get a pretty fair collection.

The first two deliveries were close by and there was no real need to hurry through the sticky Brisbane heat. Despite his father's panicking he was only a few minutes later than usual. But he hurried anyway.

The road beneath his sandals was hot and he could feel the warmth coming through. The clouds were gathering over One Tree Hill, the nearest spur of the Taylor Ranges, and there could be a storm around sunset. But that was hours away.

Meanwhile, the crickets were drumming in the long grass by the road, a dog was barking, the occasional car passed him as he either pushed or pulled the little wagon down Lambert Road. He glanced automatically at their number plates as they passed. Alan Whiting had seen Q850-349 but his latest was 850-130. Barney reckoned he had seen 855-something but no one believed him.

At the bottom of Lambert Road, where it joined Seven Oaks Street, two giant jacarandas stood like great mauve beach umbrellas shading the entrance to the street. There was a saying that when the jacarandas bloomed, there was panic in the streets. And it was true. Their flowering heralded the examination season and his stomach always tightened when he saw them.

In only a month he would be sitting for the Scholarship, the first great scholastic hurdle of his life. Those who passed the Scholarship went on to secondary school and free tuition in the state schools. Those who failed either repeated a year or, he thought, their parents had to pay to get them in. He wasn't sure about the paying part. The question of failing had never really been a possibility.

But as dux his sights had to be set on the Lilley Medal awarded annually for the highest pass in the state. Only one student at Ironsides had ever won the medal in the nearly fifty years since the school was established. It was an impossible task but he had to try.

In class they had recently completed the test papers of former years and he had passed well, in fact he had topped the class again. But they weren't prize-winning passes and while this fired him each time with a new determination to get down and study, when he left the school grounds the enthusiasm seemed to stay behind. When he should have been studying in the evenings after he finished his homework he preferred instead to read other books, to explore new worlds rather than return to the boring blandness of the textbooks. His mother had borrowed From Here to Eternity from the library and that had taken him two weeks to read while she searched in vain for it. When the choice was between *From Here to Eternity* and one of the set books like *Quentin Durward* it was really no contest.

But he really would have to button his mind down tonight when he got home and do some hard, slogging work. The thought itself made him feel virtuous already. Why, he might even cut short his visit with Mrs Elizabeth Hendry, explain firmly to her that he would like to stay for a cup of tea, or even a fuck if she was so inclined, but it really would have to be some other time. Right now, he had a medal to win.

The thought sustained him through the first two deliveries but by the time he rounded the corner of Bertram Street where she lived he was starting to waver. If she really wanted it so badly, if she absolutely insisted that he stick his cock into her then hell, he would be less than a gentleman if he refused. He grinned. Less than a gentleman.

The back door was open. He tried to smooth down the paspalum before he announced himself but it was useless. Anthony Steele would never have had such problems with his bloody hair. No wonder Anita Ekberg went for him, the smooth pommy bastard.

"Mrs Hendry, it's Palmer Lingard," he called. But the house was silent. "Hello, anyone home?" Still nothing.

She was out.

21

As the tension fell away from him he suddenly realised how excited he had been. For three weeks the thought of her had been constantly with him, growing in clarity and intensity each day and each night as he lay holding himself, re-living the time he had spent with her, letting his imagination take the scenes further until she took him by the hand into her bedroom, peeled back the bedclothes, kissed him and pulled him down on top of her.

A dozen times he had been with her, undressed her, felt her nipples and stroked her beautiful hairy cunt then put it into her while she squeezed him so hard the breath went out of him and he spurted inside her.

And now, nothing. He brought the wagon inside. There wasn't even a note for him on the kitchen table; not a word of explanation. And after all she'd said about looking forward to seeing him again . . . she was a bitch. She'd been stringing him along like a kid. That was the only possible explanation. A bitch.

"Is that you, Palmer?" The words bolted into his head like skyrockets. Oh Jesus. She was home. You're not a bitch, you're a fantastic bloody woman.

"Yes, it's me." It is I, for Christsake.

"I'm in the bathroom, Palmer. Come closer, I can't hear you properly."

Oh Jesus Lord Christ Almighty, she's in the bath. She's waiting for me in the bloody bath. He could hear the sound of splashing water quite clearly now.

The bathroom was next to the kitchen, but to get to it he had to go on to the verandah and as he passed through the doorway he stumbled slightly as his sandal struck the scuffed linoleum. It did nothing for his composure.

"I've brought the groceries," he said as he bent to adjust the sandal strap. Ridiculous thing to say. What did she think he'd brought, the *Collected Works of Walter Scott*?

"You're earlier than I expected," she said. "I thought I'd be out of here by the time you arrived."

As he rose from his squat he suddenly realised that the bathroom door was slightly ajar. From where he stood he was looking straight into the mirror on the front of a medicine chest. There was just the opposite wall reflected in it now, but when she stood up . . .!

"I started out a bit late but I made up some time with the other deliveries."

She was splashing up a storm now. He could hear the water running over her lovely pointed breasts and down her white belly.

"I see. Does that mean I'm the last on your list?"

Of course it does, of course it does. "That's right."

22

She stood up. He heard the rush of water then caught a glimpse of her shoulder in the mirror. For an instant her face flashed across the little screen. He was looking straight at her but she didn't seem to notice. If only he were a few inches taller. He stood on tiptoes but the image was gone.

"So you don't have to rush away then."

Rush away! God, he'd stay until, well, from here to eternity. "That's right." Jesus, sparkling repartee.

He was only three or four feet from the door now. He heard her footsteps as she stepped out of the tub.

"Oh dear."

"Anything wrong?"

"I'm afraid so. Palmer, I've come in without a towel. Would you be a dear and get one for me?" She didn't sound too worried about it. In fact, even through his static-filled mind there seemed to be a smile in her voice.

"Certainly, where . . ."

"In the linen cabinet . . ." her face appeared round the door then her hand pointing ". . . over there."

He stared at her, then turned abruptly. Where, Jesus, where? The door of the linen cabinet stood open and he grabbed the nearest towel. When he turned again her face had disappeared and he walked right up to the door, now half open, holding the towel in front of him.

"I have it."

The door swung further open and she reached out to take it. She was smiling and as her hand moved towards it the top of her body followed slightly, just enough so that the whole of one beautiful glistening white breast appeared. Pal sucked in an involuntary breath and felt the perspiration break out around his eyes. Then she had taken it ("Thank you, Palmer") and was gone.

But the image of that gorgeous, fantastic breast stayed before his eyes. His shorts, he realised, were standing out as though he was carrying a portable diving board inside them. And now the door was almost fully open.

He knew he only had to move a couple of feet to his left and he would be able to see right into the bathroom. Just a couple of feet. But he was rooted to the spot. What if she was looking at the door? What if he moved and she closed it on him? What if she didn't realise what she had just shown him, what he had just seen with his own bloody eyes?

But what if he never had another chance? What if he was hit by a truck on the way home? He moved, and the floorboards screamed in protest. But she didn't look up.

She was there, half turned away from him, one leg on the bath tub

23

as she dried it with short vigorous strokes, looking intently down at her toes which were painted with crimson nail polish. Obviously she hadn't heard the banshee yell of the floorboards. As she moved, one breast was exposed to him in profile and with each stroke it jiggled and touched the top of her knee. The nipple was pointed and pinkish-red, or was it reddish-pink, or was this happening at all for Godsake. If she turned just slightly she would have to see him. He had to move, get out of her line of vision, back behind the door.

The floorboards shrieked again but he was safe now, out of sight, his hand in his pocket squeezing his erection and at the same time desperately willing it away. But even from his new position he could still see her through the space between the door and the jamb. If she came out and he was like this he would have to turn away. Or maybe she wanted to see it, even hold it herself. No, no. He had to stop thinking about it, say something that would take his mind off it for a moment.

"I'd better unpack the order."

She turned towards the voice. The towel was in front of her, moving slowly over her groin, her legs slightly apart.

"Oh yes, that's a good idea. You do that while I get dressed."

He wanted to yell and cry and go back and walk inside the bathroom and grab her and touch her all over and run away and laugh and stroke himself till he blew it all out and take her in his arms and put his tongue in her ear and unpack the order and squeeze her tits till she cried for it and get the hell out, all at once. He did not want her to get dressed, not now or ever.

"I suppose Mr Hendry is coming home tonight," he said as he moved reluctantly back into the kitchen. At least he could keep her talking.

"No, as a matter of fact he's not. He's going to be away for another week."

He could hear her moving around in the bathroom. His fingers were trembling as he removed the first parcels.

An inspiration. "Would you like to check the order?" She would have to come into the kitchen now.

"Would you like me to?" Jesus, what a question.

"I think it would be best." Maybe she'd just walk in naked and start checking off the list, just standing there in front of him, completely naked.

He was staring at the doorway as she entered. She wasn't exactly naked. She had thrown on the brunch coat she had worn the other time he had been there and as she came in she was still doing up the buttons. She left the top and bottom buttons undone and smiled as she entered:

24

"I'll do the hard work and you can check the list if you like." It was almost too much to ask for.

She had combed her short hair and freshened her lipstick in the bathroom. Pal thought she looked beautiful.

"All right." He took the list out of his pocket but barely glanced at it as she bent to extract the groceries. He moved to one side of the wagon so that it no longer impeded his view. As she moved, the coat parted at the top and swayed back so that practically her whole body was exposed. He was completely excited now but he no longer bothered to conceal it. It would have been a hopeless task anyway.

He noticed with pleasure that she glanced at it several times as she rose with the parcels. There was a smile playing about her lips but he was sure she was breathing harder than the unloading warranted. She was excited too, he was sure of it. She hardly bothered to call out the groceries for him to check.

As she finished, she looked him full in the face. She was no longer smiling. "Well, that was hard work. I think I deserve a bit of a rest."

He nodded. No reply formed in his mind and at the moment he doubted his capacity to speak.

"Come in and talk to me for a moment." She turned to the door which led in the direction of the bedroom.

"Okay." Pal followed her through the lounge room and into the bedroom. There could be no doubt now. She definitely wanted him. No doubt at all. But still he doubted.

The bedroom was darker than the kitchen. A thin patternless carpet covered the floor and their footsteps were soft compared with the clatter on lino in the other parts of the house. Her perfume filled the room and he felt a little light-headed as he breathed it deeply. The big double bed in the centre of the room was covered with a chenille bedspread the same colour, he noticed irrelevantly, as the jacarandas he had seen on the way. A thought of the exams flashed through his mind but was instantly banished as she sank on to the bed bottom first then drew her lovely long white legs after her, the thin coat tucking itself under her and exposing her almost to the waist. With an effort of will he looked her in the face, but there was still nothing he could think of to say.

She patted the bed beside her. "Here, Palmer. Sit down here and talk to me."

"All right." More sparkling repartee from the dashing womaniser, Palmer Lingard, St Lucia's answer to Casanova.

"You must be tired too, pulling that wagon up and down the hill around here."

"Yes, I am a bit." Tired was the last thing in the world he was.

"Well, you lie down too."

25

He took a deep breath then leant back towards the pillow but before his head reached it she had her arm out and his head came down on it. The arm moved slightly so that the back of his neck was resting on it. He swung his feet up but in doing so struck her ankle. Those bloody sandals.

"Ouch, what's that you're wearing?"

"My sandals. Just a minute, I'll take them off. Won't take a minute." He tore the sandals off without undoing them and returned to her arm, his own arm coming over naturally to rest on her stomach. From his soft headrest he was looking directly across to her left breast which was completely exposed, the nipple standing up straight against the housecoat, and as he moved his arm the coat moved even further from it.

"Mmm, that's better," she said. "You know, Palmer, a woman gets very lonely in a house by herself all day with no one to talk to." She paused. "Even an old woman like me."

It was obviously a cue. "You're not old," he said indignantly. "Not old at all."

He felt her smile as her cheek moved against his forehead. "It's nice of you to say so, but I'm afraid it's true."

"No." He wouldn't hear of it.

"Of course, I do have some visitors. Mr Fenwick, the Rawleighs man, comes once a week; and then there's Jimmy Burns, the baker, but I don't like him very much. He's not a very nice type. He comes Mondays, Wednesdays and Fridays. He was here this morning."

Where, here on the bed? Not bloody likely.

"Then there's the butcher, Donny McApline . . . he's nice. I like Donny, don't you, Palmer?"

He hated McAlpine. He was a big loudmouthed prick. He was listening now with only one ear as she continued her list of visitors. He had another problem. His crotch was starting to hurt. He wanted to move his left arm which was starting to go to sleep under him down inside his pants to adjust himself. But he didn't want to move. It might break the spell and she would tell him it was time for him to go, time for her to rest.

But it was unbearable. He had to move it. He squirmed a little and in doing so his other hand moved up involuntarily and cupped itself under her breast. She stopped mid-sentence.

"Mmmm." He could feel the vibration of her neck. She moved so that his hand completely covered her breast now. But his problem was becoming worse and he squirmed again.

"What's wrong, Palmer, aren't you comfortable?"

"No, it's just that . . ."

She half sat up, looking down at him. He shut his eyes.

26

"Oh." She was smiling again. He could hear it in her voice. "You can't be comfortable. Let me loosen them for you."

Oh God. He lay back on the pillow as she extracted her arm from under him and sat up completely. She was staring at it now. She had to be. He felt her hands unclasp his belt and then move down, unbuttoning his fly. One button, two, three, then she stopped. It must have jumped out at her, white Chesty Bonds and all. The relief was immense, but still he couldn't open his eyes.

She lay back again, taking up the same position as before.

"My goodness," she said and he could hear her smile again, "you are growing up, aren't you?" Silence. Then she spoke again. "This is nice, isn't it?"

He moved one leg over hers and it came completely out of his underpants now and rested on her thigh. She must feel it, she couldn't help it. "Yes, it is." Emboldened, his hand moved back to her bosom, underneath the housecoat this time.

"Palmer."

"Yes." He squeezed the breast a little and she moved against him.

"Have you ever done this before?"

God, what a question. No, no, no, nothing like this. Nothing, never like this. "Not really."

"Not even with your girl in Adelaide?"

"No."

She was quiet for a long moment. He squeezed her breast again, more positively this time. She sighed. At least it started out as a sigh but ended as a kind of groan.

There was another silence. He moved his leg further over hers until his knee rested on the bedspread just below her crotch. From there, there was only one place to go. But he couldn't do it; he couldn't go any further.

His groin was tingling as she moved against him. This time the groan was his. She pulled her head back, moving away and focusing on him. "Palmer . . ."

"Yes?" He looked back at her.

"Do you like me?"

Jesus Christ. What did he say to that? I like you, I love you, I think you're the most fantastic woman who ever lived. I'd like to stay here with you and fuck you until I died.

"Yes, of course I do."

"Really?"

God, she was starting to sound like a bloody girl.

"Yes, really."

"That's good because I like you too." She was playful. "In fact, to prove it, I'm going to give you a big kiss."

27

As she spoke she moved under him until the whole of his body was between her legs. He was looking down at her mouth as she lifted her head to him. Then her lips were on his and he felt her tongue pushing against his teeth. What did that mean? He opened his teeth a little and it pushed inside his mouth, filling it. It was fantastic and terrible at once. If she pushed any harder he would be sick. He threw up every time he went to the dentist. He had a sensitive throat. But then it withdrew to the front of his mouth and he could think again.

One thought grabbed his mind and held it. He was doing it. He was about to fuck a woman. She was moving under him and he felt the head of his cock moving slowly into her. He was doing it. She pushed again and he was inside, completely inside. But even as she moved he could feel himself beginning to come. It was a moment of blind panic. He couldn't, he shouldn't, not so soon. It was supposed to last much longer than this. If he came it would be over, but there was nothing he could do about it. He had to. He pushed back, once, twice and it was there, shooting out, releasing him, relieving him. It was fantastic, but it was wrong; it was too soon.

"Oh my God."

She groaned again. "No, not yet, not yet." She pushed against him again and again, draining him. But now it was hurting and he wanted to be out of it, had to be. After all, it was over. He had fucked her; what more did she want? He was resentful but for some reason he felt guilty as well. She hadn't liked him shooting so soon. He had done it wrong.

Her hair was sticking to the side of her face with perspiration, her body felt greasy on her stomach and she was panting now, harder even than he was. He was shrinking inside her, coming out.

Her hand came up and wiped her forehead and she opened her eyes as he rolled off her. He didn't know whether to thank her or to apologise. It was suddenly very quiet in the room. He could hear a clock ticking. He hadn't noticed that before. It was very loud. Why didn't she say something?

"Oh dear."

What did that mean? Was she happy, sad, angry, what? She turned towards him. She was smiling. Thank God.

"You really do like me, don't you, Palmer?" It was a statement rather than a question.

She looked older than he had thought her. He considered the statement-question. "Yes, I do."

"Then give me a little kiss and you must be going."

He wanted to go; but the thought of kissing her was not attractive. Her perfume smelt raw and a bit unpleasant.

"Yes, it's getting late. I think there's a storm coming."

28

He sat up and buttoned his fly expertly, one-handed. He had practised that in case he lost a hand in an accident. But she didn't notice. She was looking at his face. She still hadn't said anything about the fucking. Was it all right? Did he do the right thing? Was it good?

"Well . . ." he said.

"Come on, give me my little kiss." She adjusted the housecoat so that it covered her again. He leaned awkwardly over and kissed her firmly on the lips. She returned it in what seemed a motherly fashion and released him.

"Thank you."

What was that for—the kiss or the fuck? The kiss, obviously.

"That's all right." Now that really did sound stupid. But what the hell, it didn't matter now. He got up from the bed and walked to the door. In fact, nothing mattered now. Nothing in the whole wide bloody world. She smiled and waved to him.

"Bye."

"See you next week."

He almost ran to the kitchen. The wagon clattered down the back stairs in front of him. He had done it, actually done it, actually fucked a woman. Not just a girl, but a real, live adult bloody woman with hair and tits. And she'd loved it. 'Course she had, otherwise she would have told him so. She'd wanted it and he'd given it to her, right in the cunt. In fact, if he wanted to, he could probably go back right now and give her another one. It was fantastic, the greatest thing that had ever happened and was ever likely to.

Until next week.

Fat, heavy drops of rain were starting to fall, making inkspots on the bitumen roadway. He smelt the rain. It had a beautiful fresh smell clearing the lingering scent of her perfume. Soon it would come down in buckets. He felt the grass of the footpath becoming wetter under his feet.

"Jesus, my sandals." They were still at her place. He couldn't go back now. She was probably having a sleep or something.

It was strange that, the way she had stayed on the bed when he left. She might at least have come to the door with him. It must have tired her.

But when she awoke she would see the sandals and put them away. He would pick them up next week before her husband came home. But there was something else. His father had seen him wearing them when he left. What if he caught him coming home without them? Never mind, he'd think of something. Anyway, it didn't matter a damn what his father thought now. The deed was done and there wasn't a damn thing he could do about it.

29

It was raining heavily now. He threw his head back and laughed as the rain splashed on his face.

"Send her down, Hughie."

She had loved it.

'Course she had.

And next week Jesus, just wait till next week.

THAT NIGHT in bed he re-lived the afternoon minutely, remembering things that he couldn't recall registering at the time but which now returned with total clarity: the two or three long black hairs around her nipples; the scarlet polish on her fingernails; the way she gathered her housecoat at her crotch when she said goodbye to him; the little beads of perspiration on her forehead at the place where her dark hair began. These formed part of the whole picture as he reconstructed it behind closed eyes, his pillow taking the place of her body as he came to climax and, shortly afterwards, repeated the whole process with the same result.

Then, though his mind was still racing, he was physically replete.

His first fuck. The greatest feeling he had ever known. He sought some of the really high spots of his experience to compare it with.

The century he had scored three weekends ago was a big feeling. He had opened the batting and was the last man out, scoring nearly two-thirds of the team's total and virtually winning the match. The blokes had clapped him from the field, even the opposing side.

The football match Probables versus Possibles at Perry Park when the selectors chose the state side. In the second quarter he had won the ball in a scuffle in his own goal square, raced 20 yards and passed it to Kenny Smith in the centre. Smithy returned it to him further downfield. He played on from the chest mark and belted a long torpedo right into the arms of his own full forward. Six points.

Even before the flags went up he knew he had been chosen for the state side.

Both experiences still gave him a tingling of pleasure at the back of the neck.

But they were not really comparable with the afternoon with Mrs Hendry (he would have to start thinking of her as Elizabeth). When he was with her, even when he was inside her, he was completely on his own. There was no one else remotely involved, no team, no spectators. Becoming school captain and then dux were individual efforts too but completely incomparable. This afternoon stood on its own, in more ways than one.

He smiled to himself. Fucking was so different and so good that it was strange that more people didn't do it more often. In fact, it was pretty odd that everybody didn't do it all the time, instead of working,

31

or eating, or playing cricket. Perhaps instead of a sports afternoon every Friday they should have a sex afternoon where everyone took their clothes off, teachers and all, and had fucking practice.

There were two women teachers who would be terrific, Miss Oliver and Mrs Holloway. Miss Oliver had the biggest tits he had ever seen.

Mrs Holloway was always talking with the boys. Once she asked him if her stocking seams were straight. It was in a corridor of the new building and she was just about to go into her classroom when he passed by.

"Pal," she said (everyone in the school called him Pal except Mr Alfred the head teacher who called all the boys by their surnames) "can you see if my stockings are straight?"

Then she turned away from him and looked over her shoulder as she lifted the skirt to the back of her knees.

"Yes, they seem okay," he said and cursed himself for the rest of the day. He should have said, "No, they're terribly crooked" and taken hold of them and run his hands right up the inside of her legs. But you only thought of these things afterwards and even if he had thought of it at the time he wouldn't have had the guts to go through with it. Anyway, he consoled himself, it was hardly the way school captains set an example.

Tomorrow was Saturday. He would have to help in the shop in the morning, then in the afternoon he would study as the team had a bye in the cricket tournament this week. It was probably just as well. He hadn't done much tonight apart from his homework which took a couple of hours. He should have read some of the history book again. He had tried to but it was so damn dull that remembrances of the afternoon kept intruding, exciting him. He had put the textbook aside and tried H.G.Wells's *Short History of the World*. It was an absorbing book and he had spent many hours on it at other times but tonight it couldn't hold his interest.

He heard the radio going in the lounge room and for half an hour he joined his mother listening to a Jack Davey Show as she darned his father's socks using a kind of wooden rock to hold the threadbare section in shape. Davey was quick as a whip and very funny. Some of his jokes were a bit off-colour and his mother laughed then looked over at him to see his reaction. Usually he pretended he hadn't understood and laughed to himself but tonight he had made a point of laughing aloud even when the cracks weren't so funny. It had been a childish thing to do but he wanted to let her know that he had changed, something had happened to change him. She had looked at him a bit strangely, he thought, but had said nothing. It was just as well his father was still in the shop. He would have made some deprecating remark and there would have been *words*.

32

They were always having *words* these days. For some reason his father was always at him. In his eyes he could do nothing right. Even the things he did do well, things the whole world applauded, were belittled by his father. Football was a typical example. His father had never come to a match to watch him play. Not even when the team came back from Adelaide with the pennant and had played against sixteen-year-olds in the curtain-raiser before the Grand Final. Half his class had been there, some of them with their parents, but his father said he was too busy in the shop to get away. Bullshit. One of the girls would have been glad to come in for the afternoon and earn some overtime.

He had played a burster of a game too and the next day his picture was in an action shot in the *Sunday Mail*. You couldn't see his face, and he wasn't in the centre of the picture, but at least he was there. That was the closest his father had ever come to seeing him on the football field.

It had made him angry for a while but that passed, and then it just hurt and that stayed. It took half the thrill away. He wanted his father to be proud. Hell, other fathers wouldn't have missed it for the world. In fact, when he was a father he'd go and watch his son play tiddlywinks if he was any good at it. Still, that was a long way off.

But Jesus, was it? He turned over on his back and stared into the darkness. What if he got Mrs Hendry pregnant? What if it had happened this afternoon? It could have, quite easily.

He knew the system well. They had shown a Father and Son film at the church (his father hadn't come to that either and he wasn't sure whether they'd let him in on his own) and these little tadpoles in the spermatozoa had swum up the passage looking like something out of an old black and white Mickey Mouse cartoon until they found a fat, round egg and one lucky little bugger popped inside. Once he was in, the egg somehow sealed itself off and when others tried to get in they bumped their heads on the hardened shell and faded away to die.

There wasn't much about how the tadpoles got there, just a short sequence intimating that a male organ was pressed against—not in but against—a female organ and then they mysteriously entered and started swimming like hell. That was the only sexy part because no matter how they put it someone was actually fucking someone else at the time just like he had fucked Mrs Hendry (Elizabeth).

God, that would be something. Pregnant. He hadn't used a frenchy either. He had seen plenty of used ones down at Kayes Rocks where the lovers went and Barney carried one around which he said he'd got from his sister. But he would never have the guts to go into Miss Chapman's chemist shop and actually ask for one. She probably wouldn't sell it to him anyway. There was probably an age limit; and if there wasn't the old bag would almost certainly call his mother and tell her her son was in trying to buy frenchies.

But Mrs . . . Elizabeth didn't have any children so it was possible she was barren. Of course if she wasn't barren and it was Mr Hendry who was sterile then the shit would really hit the fan.

She hadn't seemed worried. She had just lain there waving goodbye to him while the tadpoles took off, careering up the passage like live torpedoes homing in on the egg, if there was any egg to be found. The film didn't say much about that either but obviously they wouldn't keep travelling up and down her system looking for a non-existent egg. He had an instant vision of a couple of runaway tadpoles popping up in her eyeballs, staring about madly for a missing egg then tearing off to some other extremity in an endless race to see who got there first.

But the film really was a phoney. It hadn't said anything about the fantastic feeling it gave people to do it. The Rev. Strachan had given a talk afterwards and that was almost as bad. He'd said nothing about the way just looking at a woman could give you a horn and how your heart started pounding and you were getting incredible sensations in your loins, and after you did it you puffed as though you'd just played forty minutes of football though you'd really done nothing more strenuous than jump about a bit on a bed. All he said was that it was an expression of love and it was performed by people who were married.

An expression of love. Of course, he didn't love Elizabeth Hendry, at least not in the way Rev. Strachan meant. He loved the time he was with her and talking to and fucking her and even just looking at her. But you couldn't call that love. And even though she let him, she probably didn't love him either. She certainly hadn't said so and really it was hardly to be expected. She was so much older.

Then there was the other stipulation, marriage. He couldn't imagine being married to her and anyway, the fact was that when they did it they weren't married. Their union had not been blessed by God or the Church. Rev. Strachan would definitely call it a sin. Two sins: lust and promiscuity. He, Pal Lingard, was lustful and promiscuous. It was possible that promiscuity applied only to females. For a moment he was tempted to switch on the light and look it up in his *Shorter Oxford* but the impulse passed. The simple and sobering fact was that he had sinned.

And of course he had been observed: God, or Jesus, or perhaps the Holy Ghost, had quite literally seen him. No. It was Jesus of course. For as long as he could remember, the presence of Jesus had been nearby.

And by now the sin was noted down in the mystical ledger of sins in the one column and good deeds in the other. If, when you died, there was a favourable balance of good deeds you went directly to heaven, but if the balance was unfavourable you went to hell.

Though he constantly blasphemed and used His name in vain, he felt closer to Jesus than to God the Father and certainly closer to Him than to the Holy Spirit, who seemed to be a kind of pimp who occasionally interfered in human affairs off his own bat. Apart from causing a ruckus at Babel which seemed spiteful rather than logical, there didn't seem to be too much He had done or which was known about Him. In fact, the whole business of there being a Holy Ghost in a world where God the Father was all powerful, all knowing and all seeing, and where Jesus was at once God and the Son of God seemed illogical.

The concept of the Trinity was difficult to grasp. He had tried after church one morning to talk to Rev. Strachan about it but the conversation had been unsatisfactory. Rev Strachan wouldn't follow a point to its logical conclusion and in the end he had said that simple human logic was not enough. Pal had to have faith.

Well, he had faith. But this one point was hard to hold. Jesus seemed a reasonable, wise, logical person. It would not have been in Him to demand an illogical faith.

It was probably this feeling for Jesus, this respect for His good sense and (he was sure) His sense of humour which was behind his knowledge that Jesus had been with him today.

It gave him a strange feeling to think of Jesus actually watching him fucking Elizabeth Hendry. He wished again that he had lasted longer; it gave him no pride to have finished so quickly. But at least Jesus would have known that it was his first. If he had lasted for half an hour or even longer like Casanova, Jesus would know he had done it before and that would make it much more serious.

But, Pal chuckled, it did conjure up a strange picture: Jesus looking down from the ceiling of the Hendrys' bedroom with a look of faint surprise and a little smile on His face, saying: "Hullo, there's Palmer Albert Lingard committing the sins of lust and promiscuity with Mrs Elizabeth Hendry. Thou art making a pretty poor fist of it, Palmer Albert. In fact, it's only by the skin of thy teeth that thou managed to commit it at all. It is obviously thy first in this category of sin so I'll charge it all to Mrs Elizabeth Hendry's ledger. But for My sake don't do it again or by Father it will have to be reported."

He sobered immediately. It wasn't funny. It wasn't. He had sinned against God and against His laws. He had broken at least one Commandment (Though shalt not covet thy neighbour's wife) and had been a partner in the breaking of another (Thou shalt not commit adultery). It was stupid and childish to think of Jesus actually seeing

35

the sin. He was aware of it because He knew his thoughts, his emotions. These were registered every second of his waking hours and they, rather than the actual deeds, formed the ledger upon which he would be judged when he died. If he died tomorrow then today would weigh heavily against him. But, he felt sure, it would not be enough to tip the scales against the good he had done already. In comparison with some people he knew and some he had read about, he was well in credit still.

Of course, you could never be certain. Sometimes sinful thoughts slipped out before you had the chance to check them. Mrs Holloway, for example. He had thought how fantastic it would be to run his hands up inside her legs. But he didn't actually do it, though he might just as well have if he was being judged on the thought rather than the deed.

It seemed that either way you were in trouble. To do it without thinking about it was just as bad as thinking about it and not doing it. No, that couldn't be so. There was no wisdom in that. There had to be a balance, a judgment. There were times when he had wished his father dead, but later had bitterly regretted his thought and had wished him health and happiness for the rest of his days. The one should have balanced the other, or if not completely balanced, then the love he had for his mother should more than make up the difference.

As often happened, Pal's cogitations stimulated rather than soothed and he felt himself becoming increasingly awake and alert. Perhaps he should turn on the light and read for a while. That often helped. Or he might actually get up and study for an hour.

He debated it and decided in favour of study. He slept only in pyjama shorts and in the summer covered himself only with a sheet to ward off the slight chill of early morning. He sat up in bed and looked through the open louvres to the street lights in the little valley which was part of Taringa, his part.

Out there in the darkness between the lights his women slept, one of them with his semen inside her. The sperm would be dead now. But they were his. He had made his mark, planted his seed. He wondered if by chance she was looking out her windows toward the Gailey Road hill, thinking of him and what had happened this afternoon.

A sudden thought struck him. He would have to decide whether to tell the blokes about it. He hadn't given them a thought, but of course he'd have to tell them. He couldn't telephone; this was something that had to be done face to face or they wouldn't believe him.

He had never mentioned his women to the others. They knew he had to deliver the orders but he had let them think it was just a chore. He had often been tempted when they were talking about

36

their sisters or brothers or the things they had seen and done, but had resisted because even with them he was vaguely ashamed about looking down women's fronts. But that wasn't the only reason. He felt that if he talked about it, it would lose some of its attraction, some of its excitement. As it was, it was just between himself and his women, no one else.

Now of course it was different. Having actually done the deed they had all been aching for and talking about for so long he would have to share it with them. They would be green with envy. They would hang on every word.

He wouldn't be seeing Swanny or Barney until Monday at school. Tomorrow afternoon was for study and on Sunday there was church in the morning and in the afternoon he would earn some money caddying at Indooroopilly golf course. But he couldn't wait until Monday to break the news.

A couple of the blokes might be at church. Alan Whiting would be and he was a good listener, and a good talker. He liked Alan. He would appreciate it; and if he told the others they would be halfway to believing him even before he opened his mouth on Monday. They'd be all over him, pestering him for the gory details. He grinned. A problem solved.

A soft breeze from across the valley touched his face and chest, carrying the scent of frangipani from the trees in the big yard outside his window. It was a gentle smell, not harsh and provocative like hers. The frogs and crickets were self-contentedly clacking and chirruping their static into the clear night after rain. He pushed Elizabeth Hendry firmly from his mind and climbed out of bed to turn on the light above his desk.

Sir Walter Scott in a blue cover lay to one side, a well thumbed copy of *The Cruel Sea* behind it. He was tempted only for a second. The medal was a hopeless task but so much was expected. He had to be up there somewhere or everyone would be disappointed—his mother, his teachers, his friends, but especially himself. He would have to live with it. How fantastic it would be to win.

PAL tucked the green scout tags back under his elastic sock garters one final time before mounting the steps to the church. Every Sunday he made a mental note to cut the damn things off when he got home and every time it seemed unimportant when he arrived. Not unimportant exactly, just less important than the other things on his mind.

He had been in the scouts for only two months before he left. It had taken him that long to realise that in that troop anyway the so-called code of discipline of the older scouts was just a stupid excuse for bullying. The only good part of the whole experience had been going with his mother to the Scout Shop in town to buy the uniform and all the other paraphernalia. The shop had a terrific atmosphere of camping and surviving in the wilds using nature and strong white ropes, building matchless fires and cooking bacon and eggs by a forest lake on a clear morning. The reality, of opposing cliques, of fights, of sucking up to the scoutmaster for promotion, was so far removed from the expectation that the whole thing seemed a fraud.

But, he supposed, you couldn't blame scouting as such just because the scouts themselves were bits of bodgies. In fact, that was a lesson he had learned at church. Just because some Christians were sinners that didn't mean that Christianity was sinful. On the contrary Christianity was the Way, the Path out of sin, the way back to God. And, like the Scout Shop, the House of God had atmosphere too, though of course it was a completely different type of atmosphere.

He felt it as he took the hymn book from Mr Etheridge and stepped around the stained wooden screen which kept out the bright glare of the street. It was a solemn, peaceful atmosphere and he wondered momentarily why he always felt that same tightening of the stomach as when he saw the jacaranda blooming. The carpet was thick and soft under his shoes and as he walked a little way down the aisle each step made a hushing sound. He was early and the long pews were mostly empty. He looked around for Whitey but he hadn't arrived. He usually came with his parents but sat with the blokes near the back. His own mother and father came to church only at Christmas and Easter.

He felt a hand gripping his elbow tightly. A little startled, he swung around as Mr Etheridge leaned close to him, pushing him towards an empty row.

"Here's a seat, Palmer Lingard." The grip was tightening sharply.

"All right. Thank you, Mr Etheridge." You had to humour him even though he was half mad.

"That's all right." Etheridge waited until his charge was settled on the pew before returning to the entrance.

Pal knelt on the polished board at the back of the seat in front and bent his head. Then he glanced back at the usher as he walked away. From his angle Pal could see a shadow and a distinct space between Etheridge's completely bald head and the lustrous black wig he wore.

If the wig was designed as a cosmetic then it must have been designed for someone else. The sharp edges emphasised rather than concealed Etheridge's baldness. It was more like a badly fitting skull-cap than a wig and, as the usher grew older and his neck shrank and wrinkled, it became progressively looser. If Etheridge moved his head quickly the wig stayed where it had been like a compass needle pointing north and the effect got to be pretty comical, particularly in the sanctified atmosphere of the church. He always sat in the back row and, after all his active ushering before the service, usually wound up with the wig aiming somewhere over his left ear.

It was impossible not to notice him and bloody difficult not to giggle, especially if Whitey or someone started first. One time Rev. Strachan had stopped in the middle of his sermon and just stared at the blokes in the back row until they stopped. That was embarrassing.

But the really amusing part was that Etheridge didn't seem to realise that they were laughing at him. Of course they shouldn't laugh. The poor old bugger couldn't help it. You should show compassion for those more unfortunate than yourself. No. Less fortunate than yourself. Everyone was fortunate; but old Etheridge wasn't as fortunate as some.

Actually, his was a strange, sad story. In England before the war he had been very handsome, with a beautiful head of hair, and married to a woman who was on the stage in London. But something happened in the war, some accident or wound or burn and Etheridge had returned home completely bald. He lasted about five minutes with his glamorous wife and, broken hearted, he bought a wig and migrated to Australia. Everyone had heard the story. Etheridge made no secret of his tragedy.

Pal remembered the genuine grief he had felt when he heard it first. But after a while as it was repeated and repeated over the years, it lost its poignancy and finally its credibility. If it had been that way Etheridge must have been the oldest soldier ever to serve in the British Army.

39

But that wasn't the vital point; the experience might have aged him before his time. The really unbelieveable part was that a mean, pinched-up old pommy like him could ever have been married to a glamorous actress (whose name, incidentally, he would never reveal). It didn't gell. There was nothing about him that could ever have been attractive. He had no lips; his ears hung out like limp washing; and his eyes sagged at the bottom.

For a short time two years ago he had been Pal's Sunday School teacher but he hadn't lasted long. He refused to stick to the set lessons and instead told stories about the other parishioners. They made great examples of the sinfulness abounding in the world. They were fascinating stories and Pal was sorry when Etheridge was elevated to usher after all the kids had told their parents the beaut story of how Mrs Jeffries the organist got her black eye.

Old Etheridge hadn't been too happy about it and Pal knew he was suspected of tattling to Rev. Strachan. Etheridge hadn't actually accused him but he was definitely carrying some kind of grudge.

Pal's knees were beginning to hurt and he still hadn't said his opening prayer. No one ever told him what was expected of this first ritual. People didn't talk about it. He suspected they used the occasion simply to announce their presence at church, rather like tuning in the radio before an important programme. You had to be sure the signals were getting through loud and clear.

There was a movement in the seat beside him and he opened his eyes.

"G'day, Pal. Anyone sitting here?"

"No. I've been waiting for you, Whitey." Alan Whiting had bright carroty hair and freckles. Barney, who was an authority on such matters, said his nickname should be "Bluey" because of his hair and had started using it hoping it would catch on. It never did and Whitey couldn't have cared less one way or the other.

"Why, what's been happening?"

"Oh nothing." Pal still hadn't decided how best to break the news. It had to be done carefully so that Whitey would be absolutely convinced he wasn't bullshitting. He had to be subtle.

"Well why did you say you'd been waiting for me then?"

The church was filling up and the congregation was murmuring softly. Pal noticed a streak of sunlight shining through a stained glass window further down on his side of the church. Tiny glowing particles of dust were moving slowly in it and it was touching the hair of some girls sitting in the front row. It looked like the sunbeams he had seen in pictures at Sunday School, on which angels slid down to earth.

"We usually sit together, don't we?"

The Rev. Strachan swept in from the vestry, softly closing the door behind him. The murmuring stopped suddenly like in a school classroom when the Head entered. Actually, with his looks Rev. Strachan could almost have been a headmaster. He dressed the part with his starched white collar beneath a college grey suit and academic gown. But he had a long, narrow, pointed nose which detracted a little from his rather severe air. It reminded Pal of Pinocchio after he had told a couple of lies.

"Yes but the way you said it," Whitey was whispering now, "I thought something had happened."

"Well as a matter of fact it has."

"I thought so. Why didn't you say so in the first place?"

They went down on to their knees with the rest of the congregation as the Rev. Strachan bowed his head and rubbed the side of his nose. It was a habit. Pal suspected he had read about Pinocchio too and was checking to see if any new lies had been recorded.

"Well go on, what is it?"

"Shut up, Whitey." Out of the corner of his eye Pal spotted Etheridge staring at them out of a face which was strangely angled to the hair above it. He looked like a flounder with two eyes on the one side of his head.

". . . Lord, we ask Thy blessing upon this, Thy congregation. We ask for Thy forgiveness for we have sinned mightily. We come, Lord, to sing Thy praises in Thy House . . ."

"What's wrong?"

"People are staring at us. Do you want to get tossed out?"

"Who's staring?"

"Etheridge for one." This wasn't going at all well. It was hard to be subtle when you had to whisper. Maybe it would be better to wait till the service was over and they were outside.

"Who cares about that old looney?"

"I do. Now shut up."

"All right. See if I care."

". . . that You are always with us, through our hours of trial, no less than our moments of triumph . . ."

"All right. I'll tell you then."

"I couldn't care less."

". . . that You gave Your only Begotten Son, our Master, the Lord Jesus Christ, who died for our sins and Who now sitteth . . ."

"I've had a fuck."

"What!"

Half a dozen heads around them jerked backwards at the sound, swivelling to its source, baleful eyes beneath furrowed brows.

"Jesus, there's no need to shout."

41

". . . for the Lord Jesus Christ is with us, the living Christ, and as we try to live out our lives in the way He taught . . ."

"It just slipped out."

"Well for Christ sake control yourself."

". . . following the Way, His Way, accepting His discipline . . ."

Pal didn't dare look round at Etheridge or the others. He could feel their eyes spearing into his back. But it was done. The words were out. It was a relief.

"Tell us about it."

"Later."

"Jesus."

". . . Jesus Christ, our Lord, Amen."

For the next forty-five minutes, Pal concentrated on the service. For a while, Whitey nudged him and tried to re-open the conversation but Pal repulsed him. Let him wait for it. By the time the service was over he'd believe anything. He was tempted for a moment to embellish the story and have Elizabeth (she was Elizabeth quite naturally now) telephoning him every day pleading with him to come around to her place and do it again. But there were dangers in that. Besides, the truth was enough.

Rev. Strachan relished his sermons and Pal liked listening to them, not so much for their content, which was usually obscure and repetitive, but for the beautiful fluency of their delivery. With his light baritone voice rising and rolling in fine cadences, Rev. Strachan strung together seemingly endless phrases and clauses hardly ever losing track of the subject or the verb. Sometimes as an exercise Pal parsed them as he went. There were plenty of pregnant pauses between sentences.

Today the lesson was about the House of God on Earth, the Church and the churches. It was an interesting subject, one on which Pal had some thoughts. He had decided that unless it could be shown that there was a God-like concentration in the actual atmosphere inside the churches, the buildings themselves were pretty pointless. If you believed that God was everywhere, overseeing everything—and that seemed reasonable enough—what was the point of spending money on buildings in which to pray. You could do that anywhere.

Not that he prayed much any more. The things he really wanted, like winning the cricket premiership or the Lilley Medal, were not supposed to be the proper subjects for prayer. That was fair enough. If the prayers were granted someone else would miss out through no fault of his own. In any case, those prayers were never granted. He had found that out a long time ago.

There were only two other types he knew about. One was the

42

Forgiveness Prayer. When you did something wrong you had to ask forgiveness. But if Jesus knew that you really regretted it—and He would know that easily enough by reading your thoughts—an actual prayer about it seemed unnecessary. The other type was the last he had used. Possibly, just possibly, it had worked.

Last year his father was desperately sick with his asthma. The doctor was coming three times a day. They had erected a portable oxygen tent over his bed and on one occasion Pal had watched as the doctor injected an enormously long needle into his back. That was a terrible day. His mother had cried and said it was possible he would die. Pal suggested they pray.

They knelt down on the lino in the kitchen and said the Lord's Prayer. At the time they were too upset to be embarrassed but afterwards they never spoke of it, never once.

His father's condition continued to worsen and the following day he was taken to the hospital. But he pulled through and it was possible that if they hadn't prayed he would have died. There was no way of knowing but Pal was tempted to believe it. He wanted it to be true.

Many times when they were arguing he wanted to shout it in his face: "If it weren't for me, you wouldn't even be here. You'd be dead now." It would have flattened him. But he suppressed the urge. Once it was out he would probably never be quite able to believe it again.

The House of God sermon was almost over. Rev. Strachan was off bricks and mortar now and on to the temple of the soul. That made a little more sense and it signalled the beginning of the peroration, the wind-up, the climax.

It was fascinating the number of sexy words in the language, words people used every day without thinking about it. Say he was a radio announcer giving a commentary on the Rev. Strachan's sermon:

". . . and now ladies and gentlemen we are about to witness the Rev. Strachan reaching his climax . . ."

Sometimes in a bus he would tune in to other people's conversations. Two women: ". . . so I took hold of it with both hands."

"Did it wriggle?"

"Not with the grip I had on it."

Two men: ". . . we rolled her over on the beach and started scraping."

"How many of you?"

"Just m'self and a couple of mates. But we were really thorough. We were at it all day."

The Rev. Strachan interrupted: "For this is what we must all become. We must become children again. We must be prepared to be

43

born again, born again in the eyes of the Lord, ready to lay down our pride and our vanity and come humbly, beseechingly, to Him, our Master, and say to Him: 'Lord, forgive me for I have sinned; I am a sinner'."

The echoes faded. The pause seemed endless. When at last he resumed the quiet in the congregation was complete.

"And then, and only then, will the Lord raise us up to Him; enter our hearts and our minds and be with us always." Just an instant's pause this time. "Let us pray."

Outside, the bright light gave everything a dark green border until Pal's eyes adjusted. Whitey couldn't wait until they reached the bottom of the steps.

"Who?"

"You wouldn't guess in a million years."

"Elsie Greening?"

"Nope."

"Glenys Emmett?"

"Give it a break; she's only a kid."

"Yeah, but I've heard she went down the creek with Barney Millen the other arvo."

"Don't make me laugh. Who told you that?"

"Barney."

"Well, that explains it then."

"All right, then who was it?"

"Well it wasn't a kid. I can tell you that."

"Really?"

Whitey was completely with him now, He could have said Gladys Moncrieff and Whitey would have believed him.

"As a matter of fact, you don't know her."

"Well why did you make me guess if I didn't?"

"I didn't make you do anything."

"Ah, c'mon Pal, who was it?"

"A woman. A married woman."

"Holy bloody hell. Who?"

"I'm not saying her name but she lives in Bertram Street."

"Gawd. How did it happen?"

"Oh, in the usual way." That was a mistake. He'd gone a little too far.

"What usual way? Don't give me that stuff. What's the bloody usual way?"

"Well she went and laid on the bed. Then I did. Then it happened."

"What happened?"

44

"What do you mean 'what happened'? I fucked her, that's what happened."

"Just like that? You mean you didn't even ask her first?"

"Not exactly."

"Well did you or didn't you?"

"No I didn't."

"Stone the bloody crows. You mean she just lay down on the bed and you went over to her and put it in without even saying . . . without even asking?"

"There wasn't any need to ask. You don't have to ask these things. If they want you to, you know right away. You don't have to ask."

"Did you say anything?"

"Not much."

"You must have said something. You must have said 'Open your crack' or something."

"Jesus, what does it matter what I said? The important thing is that I did it."

"Well it's hard to believe you did it without saying a bloody thing to her."

"Jesus, Whitey, I didn't say that I didn't say anything."

"Yeah, well it sounds to me like you're making the whole thing up."

That did it.

"It does eh? Well, you just listen to this."

IT WAS not until the following Wednesday that Pal realised he was in love with Elizabeth Hendry. It happened very simply. Looking back, it had probably been happening all week and the ice cream incident was just the last straw. He didn't know for sure, but probably.

That Wednesday afternoon she came into the shop and his father jumped to serve her. Pal began to blush the instant she walked through the door. He could feel it all over his face. He was completely aware of her and he could tell as he caught her looking at him with the hint of a smile that she could feel it too. The shop was suddenly filled with all the static electricity of a summer storm.

It was the first time Pal had seen her since it happened and she looked completely different from all the other times he had been with her. She was wearing a light yellow dress with a V-neck and little lines of blue flowers at the hem and around the short sleeves. Her short dark hair was glowing with flecks of red and amber in the late afternoon light which flooded through the big display window.

She was still sexy, but that wasn't the main impression she gave. She was pretty. Pretty and sweet and young and nice, even ladylike. Obviously his father thought so too because he was playing up to her like hell: "Good afternoon, Mrs Hendry. You're looking very charming this afternoon."

Christ, if his mother had been in the shop the old bugger wouldn't have dared.

"Good afternoon, Mr Lingard," she said. "Hello, Palmer." Terrific. That put him in his place.

Pal choked something out, then buried himself in a hole in the freezer, scooping out a fourpenny ice cream for the brat he was stuck with.

It was the quiet part of the afternoon in the shop. Most of the children were home from school and the women were starting dinner for their families. Soon the men would be calling in on their way home from work. Usually Pal looked after the shop on his own in this period while his mother prepared the meal and his father took a shower. It was sheer chance, plain rotten luck, that his father was there at all. Still, it would have been worse if his father had been serving the kid and Elizabeth had come in. He would have been struck dumb. As it was, he wasn't exactly Bob Dyer.

46

"I really just came to put my order in," her voice echoed around down in the ice cream well. "Will Palmer be able to bring it on Friday?"

She was looking directly at him as he reared out of the arctic depths.

"Yes, that should be no problem," his father said. "Provided the boy gets home from school on time."

Jesus, the dirty, stinking, old . . . Pal crushed the scoop down on to the ice cream cone, splitting it to the bottom of the stem. Hastily he tossed the broken cone into a rubbish tin and grabbed another. Fortunately the ice cream (chocolate brickle) stayed in the scoop.

"I've always found him very prompt and efficient." There was just a touch of firmness in her voice.

Beautiful. She was practically telling the old bastard off.

"We aim to please," his father said.

Trust him to grab a share of the credit if there was any going.

Pal's customer, Francie Bell, a freckle-faced eight-year-old horror with tawny plaits, mumbled something through her fist, distracting him. She should have been home hours ago. But the Bells didn't seem to give a damn about their kids. They were out on the streets till all hours.

"What did you say?"

Again something unintelligible muffled its way through the grubby fingers.

"Here," he said. "Here's your ice cream. Now, what did you say? Do you want something else?"

The hand came away. "I said I don't want chocolate brickle. I asked for strawberry. I hate chocolate brickle."

"But you asked for chocolate brickle."

"I didn't. I asked for strawberry. I hate chocolate brickle."

Jesus.

"If she wants strawberry, give her strawberry," his father cut in. "The first rule, you know, is to listen to your customer." He turned away. "Now, was there something else, Mrs Hendry?"

Pal was speechless. The reprimand was not only uncalled for but completely unexpected. It was something his father never did, never in front of a customer, no matter what he had done. No one wanted bickering behind the counter, least of all the customers. And what's more the bloody kid had asked for chocolate brickle, even before Elizabeth Hendry walked through the door. There was no possibility of a mistake.

Pal stood stupidly holding the quickly melting ice cream. He was caught between a terrible rush of fury at his father, a wild desire to plaster the ice cream all over the brat's face and a rising awareness of

47

total embarrassment and humiliation in front of Elizabeth.

For a long moment there was no movement at all in the shop. He could feel the others staring at him, waiting for him to act. But there was nothing he could do except put the ice cream back, squeeze the thing out of the cone back into the well. And if he did that he admitted his stupidity, tamely accepted the unjust rebuke and grovelled in front of her. In front of her! It was the one thing he couldn't do. But to argue with his father or with an eight-year-old kid over an ice cream was unthinkable.

And now the moment had passed when he could get out of it gracefully. Christ, he felt a bloody lump in his throat. Don't say he was going to blubber. Please, God, not that.

It was just at that moment that Elizabeth Hendry moved. She did it so quickly that he hardly noticed her coming toward him until he felt the soggy ice cream leave his hand.

"Mmmmm, that looks good. Did you say chocolate brickle? That's my favourite." She threw a sidelong glance at the child and a quick wink in Pal's direction as she lifted the ice cream to her lips.

"Hey!" The child reached up. "That's mine. That's my ice cream."

"Oh really. I thought you said you wanted strawberry."

"It's mine."

"Well, if you're sure . . ." Her show of reluctance was pure Hollywood. The child grabbed the cone with one hand and deposited four pennies on the counter with the other.

"It's my ice cream."

As the child marched defiantly out, biting greedily into the ice cream, Elizabeth Hendry smiled confidentially at Pal.

"Children," she said. And the way she said it left no room for doubt. She was speaking as one adult to another. The tone of her voice, the look on her face, the friendly, easy smile all confirmed it. Children are a trial, they said. But, as adults, we just have to put up with them.

It was then, at that moment, that Palmer Albert Lingard fell in love with Elizabeth Hendry.

His father interrupted them. "Was there something else, Mrs Hendry?"

"No thank you, Mr Lingard." She started to walk out then turned in Pal's direction. "I'll see you Friday then, Palmer." Her tone gave nothing away.

"Yes, I'll be there about 4.30." His voice seemed to echo in his head on the way through.

She smiled a reply and left.

Pal walked straight out of the back of the shop, through the living area and into the spacious backyard. He could feel his heart

48

thumping erratically. His mouth was dry and pins and needles were running up and down his back. From the yard he could see her as she passed by the butcher's shop on the other side of the intersection. He was grinning all over his face as he watched her. There was too much energy inside him. If he didn't do something he would blow a valve. He wanted to wave and shout at her, run after her and take her arm the way Cary Grant would and escort her home past all the houses, all the eye-filled windows, all the passing cars, proclaiming their togetherness.

He felt a terrible surge of jealousy as she waved to someone inside the butcher's shop. That bloody loudmouth, smartaleck bastard, Donny McAlpine, no doubt. He was a pig who never tired of sneering at Pal and his accomplishments. A bloated, fat-faced pig. She should have cut him dead.

Still, what did he matter! Hah! A song jumped into his mind and he sang a few bars the way Bing Crosby did: "They try to tell us we're too young/Ba-ba-ba-boo/Too young to really be in love . . ." Ha, ha. Christ, how could it be?

He picked up a tennis ball and hurled it against the stone retaining wall in the garden. It came off the wall at odd angles and was terrific practice for wicket-keeping.

He was still at it half an hour later when his mother called him for dinner. But by then everything had changed. His euphoria was dead. Instead, he was filled with shame and loathing. For the first time in his life he was disgusted with himself. And he had made a decision.

Dinner was a quiet meal. Surprisingly his father made no reference to the incident, at least while he was there. There were two interruptions when customers rang the counter bell and Pal volunteered each time while his mother put his dinner back in the oven. His father might have said something when he was out but he didn't think so. It would have shown.

When the meal was over Pal offered to look after the shop till they closed.

"Are you sure, dear? Don't you have some study?" his mother said.

"I finished my homework as soon as I got home. I'll take a book and study between customers."

"Well, if you're sure . . . the Scholarship's only a month away you know . . ."

"If the boy wants to do a bit of work about the place, leave well enough alone," his father said.

"Now Bernie, you know that's not fair."

He didn't catch his father's reply. By then he had escaped to the quiet of the empty store. It had a good smell, a mixture of vegetables, spices, people, cheese and dust; a comfortable, easy smell.

49

Pal took up his usual position on a stool at one end of the counter and opened the Social Studies book he had grabbed from his schoolbag in the storeroom on the way through. But the print quickly blurred. His mind was on his decision: he was not going to wait until Friday to see Elizabeth.

He couldn't wait: he had to explain. He had to tell her what a rotten, childish fool he had been. He had to wipe the shame away, tell her and hope to God she would forgive him. Then, if she did, there was a hope for something else. He hated to put a name to it. It was one thing to sing about it; something else altogether to actually say it or even think it. Especially when he thought of the way he had defiled her, not only in the school grounds but at church, in the House of God.

He felt sick as he recalled the way he had bandied their experience about in front of his so-called mates, how he had used it to impress them and make a big man of himself. He remembered the reception they had given him on Monday morning. They were waiting for him at the Big Gate—Swanny, Barney and Dick Westerman. Whitey was there too but he stayed in the background until Pal acknowledged him. That was the signal that he didn't mind Whitey passing on the news.

Mind! God, it was part of the plan, it was the whole plan and it had worked perfectly. They were all convinced. He was first among them to have done it, to have actually had a fuck (God, what a crude, filthy word) and all they wanted were the details, all the intimate details so that they could be part of it, could imagine themselves doing it too. And he hadn't let them down. Oh no. He had revelled in it.

"C'mon, Pal. Tell us about it."

"What, Barney?" He played it for all it was worth.

"You know, what you did on Friday."

"Friday, now let's see. That was the day we had a scratch match at home and I retired at 35 not out . . ."

"Yeah, we know all that. What we want to know is what you did after you retired."

It was unconscious humour, but the others didn't seem to see the joke. He controlled himself.

"Oh, you mean my deliveries."

"You know what we mean. Is it true? Did you really have one? Did she really let you?"

"Well, it wasn't quite as easy as that."

"No? Whitey said she was just waiting for you. You didn't even have to ask."

Jesus, not that again. "Well I didn't exactly ask her with words. It was more the way I said ordinary things, you know, it's your attitude.

50

You don't have to ask. She knew what she wanted and so did I."

"And . . .?"

"And so it happened."

Dick Westerman, the fastest runner in the school and the smallest kid in their class, took over the cross-examination.

"Who was it?"

"I'm not saying. Just a woman I know."

"Is she old? Is she tall? Is she pretty?"

"She's not old and she's not very tall. But she's not young and she's not short either."

Impatiently, Barney interrupted: "Are you going to tell us about it or not?"

"Depends what you want to know."

"Well, was it good?"

"It was fantastic, bloody fantastic."

"Really?" Their attention riveted him. "In what way?"

"Every way."

"Jesus, did you undress her or did she do that herself?"

"Actually, I didn't have to. She was undressed when I got there. She was in the bath."

"In the bath?"

"Is that where it happened? Did you fuck her in the bath?"

"No, we went into the bedroom."

"On her bed?"

"Yep."

Swanny wanted more details: "Did you suck her tits?"

He hadn't thought of that. "Not exactly. I'm not a bloody baby, you know."

"You don't have to be a baby. They love that. My brother says it drives them crazy."

"Really?" He might try that next time.

"Yeah, he says that's all you've got to do. If you get as far as sucking their tits, they'll let you do anything at all. He says . . ."

"Ah c'mon, Swanny," Barney interrupted again, "we don't want to hear about your brother. We want to hear about Pal and his sheila."

But before they could continue the first bell rang forcing the group to scatter. As school captain, Pal was responsible for the morning parade. It was a highly prestigious job. Theoretically, it was his duty to have all ten classes of children and the fife band—more than five hundred pupils all told—in line and at attention by the second bell at nine o'clock. But in reality there was little for him to do. The teachers supervised their own classes and it was only when one of the teachers was off sick that he took over. Even then, it was a small task.

51

When the parade was ready, he mounted the twenty-one steps to the vestibule, turned for one last look, then entered the cool passageway at the centre of the main school building. The head teacher's office ran off the vestibule and he knocked firmly on the door which, as usual, flew open at his first touch. Behind it, the Head, Mr Arthur James Alfred, stood coiled ready to spring upon the new day.

"Cakey" Alfred. The nickname was inevitable, but inappropriate. A. J. Alfred was far too efficient to have made the historic mistake of his royal namesake. What's more, Pal thought, no upstart baron would have dared challenge this man's rule. Though he hadn't felt them himself, "Cakey's" six-of-the-best were legendary.

"Parade ready?" The same words were crisply enunciated every day since Pal had taken up the duty in the middle of the year. A girl was school captain for the first half of the year.

"Yes, sir."

"Very good, Lingard. Come on."

Pal followed the Head out to the top of the steps overlooking the parade. As they emerged into the bright sunlight the Australian flag unfurled at the top of the high flagpole and the band played "God Save the Queen". Every morning it gave Pal an immense feeling of pride to stand with the Head at the top of the steps. He was singled out. When they looked at him, they all looked up. He enjoyed it, especially on Monday. The blokes were grinning at him and whispering among themselves while the Head made the day's announcements. But they were down there in a different world. Occasionally the Head gave Pal an announcement to make if it concerned sporting activities. That was good too. But there were none today.

The formal part of the parade completed, the Head gave the order to "Quick march" and the band began a rousing "Cock o' the North" as the pupils filed into their classrooms.

At eleven o'clock and again at lunchtime Pal remained the centre of attention as they dragged every last detail of his Friday afternoon out of him. By the time they broke up at 3.15 he had told every part of the story at least twice and some parts three and four times. Only one fact had been held back—her name. They didn't really press him for it until the three of them were walking home. But then Swanny was insistent.

"Come on, Pal. What harm can it do? You've told us what street she lives in. Why not tell us her name?"

"What we could do," Barney said, "is go to every house in the street and ask."

"Yes, I'd like to see you do that." Pal was getting sick of it. He was starting to feel uncomfortable. Enough was enough.

"Course we could. We could knock on the door and say, 'Mrs Lady, has Pal Lingard been fucking you lately?'" That brought a laugh.

"Very funny."

"Better still," Swanny said, "we could follow you on your deliveries. We could come in with you and tell 'em we just came to watch."

"Now cut it out, Swanny." It was just the kind of thing he would do.

"Well why don't you tell us then?"

"Because."

"Because what?"

"Because I don't bloodywell want to. Because I know just what you buggers would do. You'd go there and hang around outside the fence or throw stones on the roof or something and she'd know I told you."

"No we wouldn't, Pal." Swanny was trying to sound sincere. "Really. We wouldn't do a thing about it."

"Well, if you wouldn't do anything about it, why do you want to know then?"

"Just in case."

"Just in case what?"

"Just in case one day, say, we were in your shop and she was leaving with some parcels, we could offer to carry them home for her and if she invited us in we'd know we were on to a good thing. You know. We'd be prepared."

"Yeah," Barney agreed, "like boy scouts." Another burst of laughter in which Pal joined this time.

It would never happen, of course. Even if he told them, they wouldn't have the guts to do anything about it on their own. It probably wouldn't do any harm to tell them. They were his best friends after all. And they would probably keep at him till he did anyway.

"Come on, Pal," Swanny persisted. "We wouldn't tell anyone. Cross our hearts and spit."

"Yes you would."

"No we wouldn't, would we Barney? Fair dinkum, Pal."

"That's right, Pal. We wouldn't mention it to a soul."

"That's a promise?"

"Promise."

"Well, I don't know."

"Look, there's lots of things we've told each other that no one else knows about. If I was the one I'd definitely tell you."

There was no doubt of that. "I suppose so."

"I sure would. And remember the time you broke Geddes's window playing cricket. We never told then, did we?"

"Yeah."

"And the time we bored a hole in the girls' dressing room at Toowong baths. Remember?"

"You did that."

"Yeah, but you looked too and no one said anything, did they?"

"All right, I'll tell you. But remember, you promised."

"Okay, okay."

"Well, her name is Elizabeth Hend . . ."

"What!" Swanny looked stricken. "Not Elizabeth Hendry, the one with the curly hair and the big mouth . . ."

"It's not a big mouth, it just looks big . . . what do you mean, do you think you know her?"

"Yes, I do. Jesus. I do. I know her."

Pal was shocked and disappointed and angry all at once.

"How could you know her?" It wasn't right. She was his woman. No one, least of all Swanny, had the right to know her.

"I do know her. She worked in my mother's place for a while. I know her."

Swanny's mother owned a dressmaking shop in Taringa which she ran in her spare time.

"I don't think she ever worked for your mother." Pal was grasping at straws. "She's always home during the day. She told me."

"No this was about six months ago. I saw her at the shop. Her husband works for King Tea, right?"

That was it. Pal was devastated. "Yes, I think so."

"I knew it." Swanny was triumphant. "He came to pick her up at the shop one day in his van."

Pal said nothing.

"I thought it might have been her when you said Bertram Street. Hey, do you know what?" Swanny grinned.

Barney was anxious to join the conversation again. "What?"

"I think my brother's taken her out."

"Don't lie," Pal said.

"It's not a lie. I think he has. I think he took her home from the shop one time and they went out."

"Be careful, Swanny."

"I only said I think so. I'm not sure."

"You're bloodywell making it up. Now take it back."

"All right, I take it back. I said I wasn't sure."

"Okay."

"I'll ask him tonight."

"You will not. Remember you promised. And so did you, Barney."

"Don't look at me. I didn't say anything."

"I know I promised," said Swanny, "but that was before. I knew her all the time. That's different."

"A promise is a promise. Now you swear you won't even mention it to your brother."

"Ah, I'm sick of this. You're always lording it over us."

"No, I'm not."

"Ah, jump in the bloody lake. Come on, Barney, let's go down to Bertram Street now and ask her. You probably made it all up anyway."

Barney was more than happy to join the action.

Pal took off his schoolbag. "Swanny, if you take another step towards Bertram Street, you'll be sorry."

"Yeah, what'll you do?"

"Just try it and see."

"Okay." Swanny had a start of only four to five feet. It wasn't enough. Pal caught him in five yards, grabbed the top of his schoolbag which he carried on his back and jerked it backwards with all his strength. The older boy came down on it with a loud bang, the top exploding open and books and pencils scattering across the footpath. He writhed on the ground completely winded, making hard rasping noises in his throat.

Pal turned as Barney bore down on him. Barney carried a port which he swung at Pal's head. It grazed his shoulder and knocked him off balance but not off his feet. The bag flashed around again but this time he ducked away and as it passed him he jumped in on Barney's back, throwing his arm around the other boy's neck. Now Barney was off balance and they toppled backwards together. At the last moment, Pal threw himself away from under his opponent and Barney hit the footpath on his back, his head striking the cement like a hammer.

When he looked down there was blood coming from Barney's scalp and his face had turned white as a sheet. Pal was scared.

"Barney, are you all right?"

"Get away from him, you bastard." Swanny was getting his wind back but he stayed seated on the ground arching his back in pain.

"Yeah, well it's your fault. You promised."

"So what. You're just a smartaleck bastard. You're a shit."

Barney was shaking his head and looking dazedly at the blood on his hand where he had touched it.

"Jesus, I'm bleeding."

"I'm sorry, Barney. It wasn't my fault."

"It was so," Swanny shouted. "You think just because you're the

55

bloody school captain and the bloody dux you can do anything you like. You think you're just great but really you're a swell-headed shit."

"That's got nothing to do with it," Pal said. But his words carried no conviction. He was vulnerable. His accomplishments made him guilty. He never mentioned them when he was with the blokes. He knew instinctively that they resented him and it would have been better if he had made friends with the smarter kids in the class. But he didn't want to. He had more fun with Swanny and Barney. Yet he knew deep down that it was true. He *was* better than they and, much as he tried to conceal it, it probably showed.

"It's got everything to do with it." Swanny was relentless now. "Why don't you just piss off."

"I wouldn't have broken a promise." It was true but it only added fuel to the fire.

"Ah piss off. Are you okay, Barney?"

"I think so."

They had completely excluded him now. There was nothing to lose.

"Well, just don't go to Bertram Street or you'll be sorry."

"Don't worry. We wouldn't piss on her if she was on fire."

"Ah, get fucked." For the first time in a long time Pal was choking back tears. He left them sitting on the footpath, Swanny collecting his books and putting them back in his bag.

The next day they gave him the silent treatment. He had expected it and was prepared but it hurt just the same. And, if anything, today—Wednesday—was worse. The silent treatment was still on and it was amazing the way the others who knew nothing about what had happened were only too eager to join in. It was like a disease the way it spread. Either you were a hero or you were the worst in the world. There was nothing in between.

It was unnerving. It made you feel like someone you weren't, someone you didn't particularly admire. And when you felt that way you acted more like the person they made you than the one you really were.

That was the only possible explanation for an incident at lunchtime. He had found some little kids fighting behind the old building after the first bell and had reported them to their teacher. He had never done that before. One of them was little Joey Custance and he could still see the surprised, hurt look on his face when he turned him in. Joey sometimes walked home with him after practice on the afternoons he wasn't delivering orders. He hung around at the nets until practice was over.

Pal gave a mighty sigh and climbed off his stool for the last time to close the door for the night. The whole thing was a mess. But he did have one consolation. When he woke up it would be Thursday and he would be seeing Elizabeth. At this stage, apart from his mother (and he couldn't mention a word to her), it seemed that Elizabeth was the only friend he had left. But that was hardly an adequate description. You didn't talk about your woman as a friend.

He would tell her everything, everything that had happened since the last time they were together, really together; all the thoughts he had had about her and about them; the way he truly felt about her; and the wonderful feeling she gave him, the greatest feeling he had ever known. And then it would be her turn. God, that was something to look forward to.

He pulled in the bristle mat and slammed the door, switched off the lights and headed for bed.

IT WASN'T just any other morning. Everything had to be exactly right. Pal peered anxiously through the louvres at the overcast sky and switched on the mantel radio beside his bed. The seven o'clock news said there was a cyclone building up at sea east of Bundaberg. Brisbane could expect some rain and gusty winds later in the day. Damn. It was not good news, not the way he had wanted the day to start. Thursday afternoons his father played bowls at Toowong Bowling Club and it was bloody important that nothing should prevent him from going today.

Still, it wouldn't be a disaster if he stayed home. It would just make his plan more complicated. With his father around it would be that much more difficult and risky getting the suit out of the house.

He had decided about the suit last night while planning the day ahead. His sandals were already at her place so he had to wear his shoes (bare feet were unthinkable). They were fairly new and if he polished them they'd look okay. But what about the rest—pants, shirt and so on? He was trying to decide between a pair of heavy college grey shorts his mother had bought him at McDonald and East's just before the football trip and the tailored summer shorts he wore to church when the idea had sprung full-blown into his mind. Of course! His father's green suit.

His father was a conservative dresser but lately Pal thought he had started to show a bit of imigination. A month ago he had come home with a new green suit that was really quite stylish. There weren't many opportunities for him to wear it apart from his Liberal Party meetings and a few socials at the Bowling Club but he took every chance to have it on. Pal admired it. He liked the tapered trousers, the heavy, padded shoulders, the narrow, single-breasted lapels and the dark emerald colouring.

It was just what he needed. It would give him the mature, sophisticated look of a young adult. It would allow him to say all those things he had to say to Elizabeth without feeling awkward and childish. Clothes were important that way. While they didn't actually make the man, they added to your confidence. They helped make the right impression. Last night he had become more and more convinced that the suit was the solution.

But now, in the cold light of day, he wasn't so sure. It just might

58

look as though he was bunging on an act, trying to be someone he wasn't. Also, his father was much bigger around the shoulders and the waist and he was still three or four inches taller. But what the hell. Hadn't he already tried the coat on and seen himself for a second or two in the mirror? The coat had looked terrific.

Pal deliberately pushed the doubts out of his mind and climbed out of bed. It would all work out just the way he wanted it to. Today was his day. There were no orders to deliver. When he came home from school he would just tell his mother he was going out to play cricket or something, sneak the suit out of his father's lowboy, change in the spare room at the back and slip out the back door. When he returned he would simply retrace his steps through the back door, hang up the suit and no one would be any the wiser. Perfect. He could smell bacon and eggs cooking in the kitchen. He grabbed his towel and ran for the bathroom.

The morning passed with agonising slowness. He couldn't concentrate on schoolwork as Mr Perkins droned through a history lesson then a series of "trick" questions set in earlier Scholarship arithmetic papers. There were more important things to think of.

Fortunately his attention was taken for granted and "Polly" kept his questioning to the slower members of the class. Pal was able to devote himself completely to the plan for the afternoon. He would rehearse every word, every gesture he would use in his meeting with Elizabeth. Everything had to be exactly right.

He thought of ignoring his betrayal, of pretending he hadn't said a word to anyone about last Friday. That would be the easy way. But it wouldn't be right. He would still feel guilty. He would still be guilty. He cringed inside once again when he thought of how he must have sounded when he told Whitey and then the others. Like a crude, disgusting kid. And it had happened only three or four days ago. He marvelled at the way he had changed and matured in such a short time, probably a year for every day. No, that wasn't the way. He couldn't ignore it.

Another way was to just blurt it out, tell her everything in a rush and pray that she would forgive him. That was what he had wanted to do after she came into the store and the Bell kid had put on such an act over the ice cream. But that had dangers. He might sound completely immature and she might want nothing more to do with him. It was a risk he couldn't afford to take. If she rejected him and threw him out, he didn't know what he might do. It would be the end of everything.

The third alternative was the one he decided upon. He would be calm and reasonable. He would confess his childish stupidity but first he would explain how quickly and how much he had changed since then. That was the key to it. When he showed her how much he had changed it would be as though they were talking about someone else, someone they both knew from the past, some young boy who had disappeared forever. In a little while they might even be able to laugh at him, this childish figure from the past.

It all depended on the way he put it, the words, the tone of voice, the appearance, the sympathetic look, the rueful smile. Everything had to be right.

He assumed the blokes were still giving him the treatment so at lunchtime he stayed away from the oval and ate his sandwiches alone on the grass overlooking the basketball court where the girls played with their skirts tucked up under their panties. (Some of them had nice legs, but nothing like hers, nothing like Elizabeth's.) The treatment didn't worry him too much any more. It didn't really matter what Swanny and Barney did. The treatment was just the sort of thing you'd expect from kids like them.

He finished his lunch and took his papers to the bin then wandered over to the top of the embankment overlooking the oval. There were three or four separate cricket games in progress overlapping each other on the gravel-surfaced sports ground. Every year the P. and C. Committee grassed it during the Christmas holidays but by May or June the grass was dead again and they were back to the gravel with the big concrete pitch in the middle. If you learned to play football on this oval, Pal thought, you were ready for anything. His knees and elbows were permanently scarred.

Still, it was a good oval, a lucky ground for him. It would not be long, he thought, before he would be playing his last match on it. After Scholarship he would be going to Grammar where all the grounds were covered with lush green grass. It wouldn't be the same.

Actually, he recalled, his father had helped build the oval. During the depression it was one of the projects the Government had organised for the men on relief. His father would have been very young then, nineteen or twenty at the most. But it was another link with the school, one of many. His father was an Old Boy for a start. That made him practically unique. So was his godfather, Uncle Brian Chalmers and Uncle Brian's father had been the first head teacher in 1915 when there were only twenty or thirty children at the school. And now his own contribution: school captain and dux, the only student in the history of the school to have his name on the Honour Board twice. He was proud of it. Why shouldn't he be?

"You're not playing cricket today?" Barney's voice cut through his thoughts.

Pal looked around. Swanny was nowhere near so apparently

60

Barney had come to make peace on his own. If he accepted, that would put Swanny at a disadvantage. He would be on the outer then. But not for long. The three of them would soon be back together as usual. All he had to do was give the signal. It would be enough if he just asked about the cut on Barney's head. That was as good as an apology. But what was the point? What did he owe them? Nothing, that's what. Not a bloody thing. They started it. He had nothing to apologise for. And even if he did, how long would it last this time? If they could only grow up a bit, it might be all right but as it was . . .

"I said, you're not playing cricket."

"That was very clever of you, Barney. Did you work that out all by yourself or did Swanny help you?"

"Jesus, I was just saying . . ."

"I heard you the first time."

"Well, what's wrong with you?"

"Barney, you wouldn't have the faintest idea." Pal turned his back and started towards the taps under the school. The hell with them. What did they know?

Barney stayed where he was.

A spatter of raindrops fell as he reached the new building. Pal looked up at the dark grey sky. Soon it was going to rain like hell. His father wouldn't be able to go to bowls so his mother would be in the house when he got home. That would make it doubly difficult to get the suit out and back again without being seen.

His only hope was that his father had left early. If the game was washed out after they started he would stay at the clubhouse drinking beer with his mates instead of wasting time playing bowls first. That had happened before; especially in the last few months.

The afternoon, unlike the morning, was racing by. But without knowing exactly why, Pal was becoming anxious. The rain was one thing, of course. Soon after classes resumed there was a heavy storm, then it steadied off and now looked to have settled in for the day. There was very little wind as yet, just steady driving rain. He was starting to feel that the whole thing might be a mistake. Maybe it would be better to wait until the regular visit tomorrow. If he went today she wouldn't be prepared. She might be out. She might have some women there for afternoon tea. Mr Hendry might have come home. He was really taking an awful risk.

But no, that wasn't all of it, either. She had told him Mr Hendry wasn't due home till tomorrow. She said she never had visitors and anyway she wasn't likely to go out in the rain. No, the fact was he admitted, he was getting scared. The thought of going to see her had seemed so reasonable last night. Even this morning he was looking forward to it. But now he wasn't sure.

No, he was being stupid and childish again. Of course she wanted to see him. Of course she would understand. He had to see her and talk to her. He wanted to.

Finally he decided to let Fate make the final choice. If, when he arrived home his father had returned from bowls, he would put off his visit until tomorrow. But if he was still out that would be a sign that it was right for him to go today. An omen. After that he relaxed. It was out of his hands now. God, who controlled the rain, would decide.

The final bell was like a starter's gun to him. He was out of the classroom and running even before its last echoes died.

The car was gone. The garage was empty and his heart bounded against his chest. He was completely out of breath from the run home. He paused for a moment before going inside.

The shop was crowded and he found his mother in the storeroom on the way into the living area.

"Hello, dear. Do you know where that new carton of Leggo's pickles is?"

"Hello, Mum. Here." He went straight to the carton and extracted a bottle of pickles.

"Thank you. Now you get out of those wet clothes and get yourself a cup of Milo."

"Okay." He kept his voice very casual. "Is Dad still at bowls?"

"Yes." His mother took a jar of Vegemite from a shelf and consulted a list in her other hand. "I hope he's not too late." It was her only reference to the Thursday afternoon beer drinking. She made it every Thursday.

"Mum, can I go over to Swanny's place this afternoon? He wants me to help him with some maths."

"All right. But don't you be late either."

It was another sign. She could have said no. She could have asked him to stay and help in the shop. Everything was going to work out perfectly. He went straight to his parents' bedroom and pulled out the new green suit. He found his shoes under the bed and took them with the rest of his clothes into the spare room. He had to be quick. The longer he was here, the less time he would have with Elizabeth.

He changed everything: underpants, singlet, shirt, then trousers, some socks, the shoes (it was pointless to clean them if he was going to walk in the rain) and then his maroon Queensland tie, the one they had given him when he made the state team. Finally, the coat. He stood up from the side of the bed and immediately his doubts returned.

The pants were far too long and they looked baggy around his legs.

The belt didn't have enough holes to keep them tight around him. Never mind, he would get one of his own belts. This he did and when it was threaded through the loops it made a big difference. They were still too long but he could roll up the ends. He had to do that anyway to keep them dry. The coat felt too big and too long but there was no full-length mirror in the spare room and he didn't dare go into his parents' room. But in the tiny wall mirror it looked okay. If he hunched his shoulders over a little it didn't look as though it was going to fall off him and when he moved his arms almost all of his hands were out of the sleeves.

But it wasn't individual pieces of clothing that were important, it was the overall effect. He felt that was satisfactory. Not brilliant, but satisfactory. It felt good. He chuckled. It made him feel good. Confident, man of the world. Casanova rides again. Luckily there was a comb in the spare room and wonder of wonders, the parting went right the first time. Now that definitely was a sign.

Carefully, so as not to disturb the parting, he fitted his sou'wester on to his head. Then his black raincoat. Actually, now he thought of it, it was just as well it was raining. If people had seen him in the green suit they might have been suspicious. As it was, he could roll the legs of the pants up under the raincoat and apart from feeling a bit bulky around the shoulders no one would know the difference. After one last grin in the mirror he went out the back door and closed it softly after him. All he had to do now was get there without running into someone he didn't want to meet. Swanny, for example.

He went out the side gate and crossed the intersection. His route took him past the butcher's shop and he glanced sideways to see if McAlpine was there. He wasn't. That smartaleck would have found something clever to shout at him that would have made him feel lousy. He was like that. He never had a good word to say, always a sneer. But not this afternoon. Not *this* afternoon.

The wind was starting to kick up and small twigs and branches were spinning off the lantana and the blue gums on one side of the road. The rain was still strong but now it came in bursts as though someone were throwing giant bucketfuls from One Tree Hill down across the valley. He stepped around the puddles but his shoes filled up with water anyway. It seemed to run straight down his raincoat and into his shoes at the back. But it was unimportant. Underneath the raincoat the rest of him was dry.

He loved the rain. He liked the feel of it splashing against his face. He liked to watch it as it swept against the houses and the trees. He liked the fresh clean smell of it. But he loved the sound of it when he was inside and it was beating down, drumming and humming on the galvanised iron roof. The sound made you feel safe and cosy. It gave

63

you other feelings too. You wanted to lie down on a bed with a woman. The rain made the light soft and dim and romantic. You looked at the woman as she walked across the room towards the bed. She was watching you too and you could see by the little smile on her face that she knew what you were thinking. She knew it and she wanted it too. As she reached the bed, her clothes fell away and she was smiling down at you. Her face was Elizabeth's face and her body, her beautiful woman's body was Elizabeth's too. She bent over towards you . . .

Pal took the corner from Seven Oaks Street into Bertram Street at a trot. Her house was eight down the hill on the right. There were three or four cars parked in the street and if he went out to the edge of the footpath he could see her white gate over the top of the butcher's delivery van.

He stopped dead.

Was it possible? He couldn't think. He racked his brains to remember what she had said. When were the butcher's deliveries? They were lying on her bed and she was telling him how lonely she got. But did she say what day, what time McAlpine came? Tuesday. He was sure it was Tuesday. He felt numb.

He started to walk again slowly down the hill towards the house but as he drew closer the angle changed. The truck wasn't outside her place at all. It was two houses this side of it. His spirits jumped again. He was right. It was Tuesday. He was absolutely sure of it now. McAlpine was at Mrs Bellamy's house or maybe even the one further up the hill. God, what a relief.

Nevertheless, Pal continued his slow walk towards the Hendry house, keeping close to the poinciana bushes which lined the footpath. If McAlpine came out of one of the houses he could step behind a bush until he drove away.

When he reached the Bellamy house he decided to make a dash for it. His wet shoes skidded on the grass and he fumbled with the gate catch but then he was inside the yard and around the back out of sight from the road. He was safe.

He felt breathless, as though he couldn't possibly get enough air into his lungs. As he climbed the back stairs he tried deep breathing exercises but they didn't help. Then he remembered and ran back down the stairs to check under the house. It was empty. Mr Hendry was still away. It was okay.

He was still puffing when he reached the landing at the top of the stairs and started to undo the buttons of his raincoat. But one very important problem, he realised, had been solved. He now had an excellent way to start their conversation.

He would tell her the way he felt when he saw the delivery van. How concerned he was that McAlpine shouldn't see him coming in. He might even make a joke of it. Yes, that was good.

He dropped the raincoat in a corner of the small landing and removed the hat carefully so that he wouldn't muck up his hair. The back door was closed but opened noiselessly when he turned the handle. He adjusted the coat and pulled up the trouser belt one last time then leaned inside with one hand on the doorknob.

The light was dim and soft, getting darker further back into the house. It was like entering a cave. The rain was making a heavy sighing noise on the roof. He stepped inside.

"Hello," he said. "Is anybody home?"

Silence.

He walked a few steps into the kitchen. There was a teapot and a cup and saucer on the table. Perhaps she was lying down having her afternoon sleep. He walked towards the lounge which led to her bedroom.

"Hello, Mrs Hendry, are you home?" Damn. He had planned to say Elizabeth but the other came unbidden. Think, boy, think.

"Ah, Eliz . . ."

"Who's there? Who is that?" It was her voice. She was home. Thank God.

He walked towards the bedroom then stopped. He stood stock still. He heard whispers, but louder than whispers, then a movement, a sound, as though someone had dropped something on the floor.

"It's me, Palmer," he heard himself say. God, no. There was someone else in there too. The whispers came again. Then:

"Palmer, stay there. What do you want?" Her voice was hard and panicky. It grated on his ears. It was true. There was someone. They were in there together. In bed. He stepped back as though his face had been struck.

"Palmer, are you there? Just wait."

It was the only possible explanation. But it couldn't be. It wouldn't be allowed to happen. Not after all the planning, not after the signs, not after everything that had happened to him. It wouldn't be allowed.

Then the second blow struck. The man inside was McAlpine. Parking his truck up the hill had been a trick so that people wouldn't know where he was. No, that was too much. Not that swine, that bloated pig. Not with her. Suddenly he wanted to run, to get away, to be out of it, but he was held there. He tried to turn but he couldn't. He stared at the bedroom door. He was only a few feet from it and on the other side there was more movement, more whispering. He couldn't stand it. He had to know.

"Please God," he whispered and the words of the prayer fell over each other in his mind, "Don't let it be him. For the rest of my life I will never ask You for anything else. I will never lie or sin. I will love and honour You and Your only begotten Son. Please, please don't let it be him."

The door opened a crack.

"What do you want?"

"I came to see you . . . who is it? Who's in there with you? Is it him?"

"There's no one with me. It's none of your business. Now be a good boy and . . ."

"No!" The word came out in a ragged cry. Not that. Not ever that. He was no longer in control of himself. He leapt at the door with all his strength. She was knocked sideways as it flew open.

Across the rumpled bed, the man jerked his head up, his hands holding the half-buttoned fly of his cream bowls trousers, his face strange and ugly and frightened, his hair stupidly unkempt.

"Look, Palmer . . . Pal . . . son, I, never before in my life . . ."

Pal didn't realise he was vomiting until his stomach muscles dragged him off balance and he staggered a pace forward. Then the man was coming towards him.

"Son, I swear to you . . . you're going to have to understand what it would do . . ."

A hand came out toward him. He wheeled away from it, stumbling backwards through the doorway. The spasm was past and he straightened, knocking into a chair and his father kept coming at him.

"Noo-oo!" He was running. His feet slipped on the wet stairs and he crashed to the ground. The mud was on his hands, his knees, his elbows but he was up again, running again, running through the rain to the open gate and up the hill, running past the houses and the cars, running as the wind whipped the wet suit against his legs and caught in the wide coat which billowed around him, running past startled faces and small cries of surprise, running till he heard a sound which frightened him and brought him back to himself, the low keening of someone in pain.

And then he stopped and looked around. There was no one but himself and he was under the great jacaranda tree at the entrance to Seven Oaks Street. He stopped the sound and his breath came in shudders. He looked down as the rain beat into him. The suit was like a clown's outfit, a clown he had seen a long time ago at a circus. He had gone with his father and his mother.

He couldn't go on. He had to wait here. He had to wait and think until it was all clear. There was something he had to decide. He had to sit down and think.

After a long time he stood up, took off the coat and wrapped it into a bundle and walked the rest of the way home. He entered the side gate and walked to the back of the house where the concrete incinerator was belching brownish smoke defiantly into the rain. He dragged the heavy iron lid aside and pushed the coat in. Then he took off the trousers and they hissed as the flames met them.

Inside, he changed back into his dry clothes and went to his bedroom. The bed was soft and warm and he was very tired but the sound of the rain troubled him. In a little while his mother came in:

"Pal, what is it? Why are you in bed? Are you all right?"

"Yes," he said quietly, "but I think I caught a chill in the rain."

"Oh dear. Well you just stay there and I'll bring in your dinner. Do you want something to eat?"

"No, nothing thanks. Is Dad home yet?"

"No. I think it's going to be one of those nights." But there was no sadness in her voice, just the tiredness of a long day. "But it is his one day off. One of the girls will stay on and help out in the shop. Now you get some rest. Get into your pyjamas."

"All right."

The rain stopped and he slept.

A long while later he woke. He had been dreaming that he could hear a man crying. His bed moved and he thought he heard heavy footsteps, but when he opened his eyes there was no one else in the room.

Brolie's Story
II

I'M SURE he never knew how much they both loved him, his father as well as his mother. If he had known, and if he had realised what his leaving would mean to them, he would never have gone. At least, not when he was sixteen and not in the circumstances they would soon find themselves. I believe he would have stayed despite his desperation to be away from everything and everyone he knew.

But equally I have no doubt that he didn't know how much his father cared for him. He never truly believed that anyone, apart from his mother, ever truly loved him; anyone at all. He had a great power to give of himself, to give totally and utterly, but so little power to accept.

I could never understand whether it was that he felt himself unworthy of anyone's affection or whether he simply assumed that everyone felt the same way towards him, that all people to whom he gave of himself naturally reciprocated and there was no need for the fact to be demonstrated. I know that whenever it occurred, an act or a word of deep affection, he was genuinely surprised to receive it. It must have been either immense modesty or absolute selfishness, but whatever its source it represented a gap in his make-up, a flaw that blinded him to much that was happening around him and to him. As his wife, I was never able to come to terms with it. But I always felt that the fault, somehow, was mine.

As for his mother, I don't believe she questioned any of his qualities. If he did wrong it was a circumstance forced upon him and if he did good the thought was his own.

She was not a big person but I found her imposing and even a little frightening. I don't know why I should have found her that way. Certainly there was nothing in her appearance to instil any sense of fear.

Mrs Lingard was very small and dainty, almost thin, even before she became ill. In the shop, which was the only place I saw her, she was always on the move. But though apparently intent on the customer she was serving, she seemed to have an awareness of those around her that made you feel she knew that you in particular were waiting and she was doing her level best to get to you. She talked to you in a crowded shop and everyone felt included in the conversation and able to respond. And the conversation was always about pleasant

71

things, things you felt pleased to be involved in.

Now what is there in that to be frightened of? Yet it was there:—an intensity, even in the laugh and the widely set green eyes—the same colour as her son's—that belied her daintiness. There is one simple explanation, I know. It could have been that I feared her because of my feelings, whatever they were then, for Pal. Perhaps, subconsciously, I saw her as the lioness guarding the den to outsiders. But I think that, at best, was only part of the explanation.

Mr Lingard was quite different. Where she was extroverted, he had a quietness, a reserve. Across his forehead and around his eyes there were deep, deep furrows. He spoke softly and instead of a laugh there would be a smile, instead of a retort an acceptance, a nod. This was the only way I saw him but my father told me of one occasion, apparently after he had been drinking, when his personality changed completely. He was talkative, even garrulous and was making embarrassing and unappreciated compliments to a woman customer, offering to buy the men a drink and insisting on it whatever excuses they offered. But that was later, long after Pal had gone and by then they were under a terrible strain.

I did not know them well. If they were not busy in the shop they would chat with me and tell me any news of him. I pretended that I was interested in a casual, conversational way but it didn't deceive them. You see, they knew there was nothing casual or conversational about anything connected with him. They knew there was a quality in him that precluded the easy, friendly relationships possible with others. They had seen it so often. They were part of it.

I think that they liked me, but I can't be sure. I had the feeling that when they talked to me about him they were doing so less for my benefit than to hear the story again themselves.

But this was all after he left for the west and I fear I am telling it badly. There were two years after his Scholarship and before he went away and they were important years, luminous years when the smallest slights were shattering and the most minor flirtations the stuff of dreams.

But before I tell of that time there is one more thing about his parents which has stuck in my memory and which seems important. They would never talk about him together. If his wife came into the store, Mr Lingard would close up instantly, even if his story was incomplete. He would refuse to finish it and ignore any questions about it. And since in all other things he was so easy and obliging this seemed completely out of character.

If Mrs Lingard was the story teller and he entered the room he never stayed long. No word ever passed between them, not even, so far as I could see, a meaningful look. But there was suddenly a tension

72

which stayed until the intruder left. Later, when I saw *Who's Afraid of Virginia Woolf* on stage I was struck by the similarity. But the situations were not really similar since Pal actually existed and the characters could not have been more dissimilar. Only the quality of the tension was the same. One night after we were married I tried to tell him about it but he wouldn't listen and I became confused and made a mess of it.

In those days before he went away I would see him two or three times a week on the bus to town. We both travelled to Roma Street station and then he took the trolley bus up to Grammar on the Terrace while I went by tram to St Mary's in the Valley.

At first, we just nodded and he smiled. Then one day he sat next to me. It should have been perfectly natural, an ordinary meeting between teenagers who had spoken quite often in the store and who knew each other reasonably well. But at that age and in that time nothing was ordinary about a public meeting between a schoolgirl and a boy. You felt the whole bus was staring at you, that everyone had their ears pricked seeking a double meaning in your words, ever ready to denounce you to Sister Benedict for flirting or "unseemly behaviour".

Besides, he was a Grammar boy and I was a St Mary's girl, a Catholic. Our different uniforms set us apart and erected a barrier to the naturalness of the meeting.

He was a year younger. With anyone else that would have been an insuperable barrier to any kind of conversation. At that age a year was an endless gulf. But somehow he simply stepped across it as though it barely existed.

I remember that first meeting so clearly. When he sat down I was consumed with fear. People were looking, I could feel it. I had nothing to say to him in the new environment. He might touch me with his leg or his arm and I would jerk away and embarrass him and myself. He might laugh loudly and then every eye in the bus would be on us. Should I wait until he spoke or should I try to start the conversation? If I spoke at all I might say something that offended him or made me seem stupid or superior, I didn't know which.

I stared blindly at the textbook in my lap and the seat hissed with his weight and his shoulder touched mine. I jumped inside but I don't think he felt it.

"Do you like St Mary's?" He said it as though we were simply continuing a conversation which had been started a little earlier and momentarily interrupted.

"Yes, it's okay." I fitted my tone to his without even thinking about it.

"What are you taking?"

"Physics, Chemistry, Maths I, Maths II, English, History, Scripture . . ."

"Scripture."

"Yes, and Latin, French and Music."

"Tell me about Scripture. What do you learn? Who teaches you?"

"Father O'Hanlon. He's very nice."

"Is he a teacher at the school?"

"No, he's a priest. But he spends a lot of time at school. He takes our form and the third formers too."

"What does he talk about?"

"About the Bible, about the life of Jesus, the saints, the Church."

"What saints?"

"There are so many. What do you want to know for?"

"We don't have that. I was just interested to know what it was all about. It sounds like a kind of advanced Sunday School."

"It's more than that."

He was silent for a moment. Then: "Do you believe in it?"

"What?"

"All this stuff about God, and the Holy Ghost and the miracles of Jesus."

"Of course I do. Don't you?"

"I don't know. Sometimes I do, other times it seems like a whole lot of garbage. What about the Immaculate Conception, do you believe in that?"

I blushed. I felt my whole face glowing and prickling. I was suddenly aware again of all the people around us. They must have heard him. They must be staring at us.

"Yes," I whispered finally.

"I beg your pardon?"

"I said, yes, I do. Please keep your voice down."

"Why?" he said.

"Because . . . I don't know. Let's talk about something else."

"Why?" he said.

"Because people might be listening."

"So what. Is there some rule about not talking about it. If there is, it just proves what I think. The whole thing doesn't make any sense at all."

"It's in the Bible."

"So are a lot of other things. What about Isaiah 36 verse 12. That's in the Bible too, isn't it?"

"What's that about?"

"You look it up and see. It's horrible. But it's in the Bible."

"Is it about the Immaculate Conception?"

"'Course not. But that's not the point. The point is that if you think

74

about it—the Holy Ghost and the angel and Mary—it just sounds like a story someone made up after it happened, after Jesus became famous."

Two stops passed without another word between us. Then I said: "Where do you get these ideas? Is that what they teach you at Grammar?"

I remember his laughter and people staring again and then we were at the Roma Street terminus where we parted.

After that, when we travelled on the same bus we usually sat or stood together. But this happened only in the mornings. In the afternoons he always had some kind of practice to go to—cricket or swimming in the summer, football in the winter months and tennis in between. There were many other times when the conversation took wild turns which left me equally confused and breathless. If there was ever any "small talk" from him—the things about which adolescents are supposed to talk, whatever they might be—I have forgotten the occasion.

I caught the bus three stops before him and I devised all sorts of tricks to keep the seat beside me vacant until he came on board. Some days I would put my suitcase on the inside seat and bury my head in a textbook, deaf to the grunts and murmurs of other passengers searching for a seat. Other times, when a passenger bore down determinedly towards me I would develop a fit of sneezing and loud nose-blowing which invariably turned him away. Once, on a busy Friday morning, I actually limped on board stiff-legged and stretched myself across the seat until just before he entered when the paralysis miraculously disappeared.

Of course, I never told him any of this. In fact, I don't really think I fully admitted to myself just how important our meetings were to me. But they were. They were so unlike the rest of my existence which was, I suppose, no more or less exciting than that of my friends but which by today's standards seems painfully closeted and circumscribed.

Our uniform was a shapeless, sexless, beige smock worn over equally unattractive fawn stockings with brown lace-up shoes and a brown felt hat. I shudder to think of it now but at the time we simply accepted it. Our lives revolved around the school, the family and the Church. Boys, in whatever form, simply had no place, at least until Junior year. Then there were very occasional mixed parties and two school dances a year.

The dances were very formal and humourless affairs held in our big gymnasium which we decorated with paper streamers, and were attended by all the Sisters, many of the girls' parents and some of the priests who taught at the school and said Mass for the boarders. There were always more people standing around supervising than

75

there were dancing. But for all that, they were the social pinnacles of the year and we talked about them for weeks before and afterwards.

It was expected—no, demanded—that our partners come from either St Joseph's or Nudgee, our brother Catholic schools. A Grammar boy would be completely out of place. Even if my parents allowed me to invite him—and that was only just possible—Sister Benedict would not be pleased. Nothing would be said, directly anyway, but I would be marked down as "difficult" and in small ways their displeasure would be made very clear to me. I had seen it happen to another girl. I have no doubt that she was passed over as a prefect simply because she brought a Churchie boy to the year-end dance.

I knew all of this when I made my decision to ask Pal to take me to the second term junior dance. I knew all the problems it involved but I didn't care. It became almost an article of faith with me. If I couldn't go with him I wouldn't go at all.

Not that I was overwhelmed with suitors. I was a quiet girl, not outstanding at any sport, not blessed with ravishing good looks, not, I suppose, over bright though I always seemed to do well in examinations. But I lacked the personality and vivacity that set others apart and brought them the "popularity" we all yearned for.

Pal, on the other hand, was all the things I wasn't and wanted desperately to be. He had, I thought, a complete lack of inhibition. Crowds didn't bother him. If the spotlight fell on him he was ready for it. There was a confidence in him, a recklessness almost, that I envied above all other qualities. In our bus seat conversations he challenged all the rules, all the conventions, all the axioms, not in any deeply intellectual way but with feeling and with reason.

He was insatiably curious about the Catholic religion and this spurred a response in me. But the effect was not to weaken my faith. On the contrary, the more I studied and questioned the more convinced I became of the essential rightness and strength of my religion. And the more I argued with him the more desperately I wanted to change his mind, to persuade him. In all other things I deferred to him, but my religion was my own. It was precious.

That might have been a small part of my motive in wanting him to take me to the dance. Perhaps I wanted to show him the school and the Sisters and the other girls to let him see how ordinary and unexceptional it all was. I don't know. Certainly that was not a conscious part of my reasoning. I didn't try to analyse it. I just wanted him to take me and nothing would stand in my way.

I began to mention his name at home and discovered to my surprise that my father liked him. "A good stamp of a boy."

My mother thought the Lingards very nice people and of course Connie thought he was "fabulous". "He looks like James Dean," she

76

said in one of her wilder flights.

None of this was decisive, but it was a good start. Much more important was finding a way to ask Pal himself. I didn't know how to begin, or where. I could hardly go to the shop and ask him as he dashed from customer to customer. I didn't want to telephone him from home because Connie would be hanging on every word and I would have to get my father's permission first. That wasn't part of the plan. If, when I asked permission, Pal had already accepted, it would be that much harder for my father to refuse.

The bus seemed the wrong place too. There was nothing flirtatious about our talks on the bus. There was an intimacy in his directness which I found exciting and good but there seemed to be no element of sexuality in it. There was no artifice in his words, no hidden meanings. He seemed to hold nothing back.

For example, when he talked about sport, as he often did, he talked of the thrill and the power it gave him. In his first year at Grammar he had been selected in the first eleven. This was very rare and he was proud of it. But his pride in his achievement was nothing compared to his love of the game itself.

"When you are out there in the middle," he said once, "you are completely and absolutely on your own. There are eleven other blokes with no other job, no other thought but to get you out. So for a start the odds are eleven to one against you. But really they're much more than that because they can make any number of mistakes and still have another chance the very next ball to get you out. The batsman has only one chance. One mistake and it's all over.

"And even then there's more to it. On top of that you have to make runs; you have to dominate the bowling; you have to break the bowlers' hearts. You have to cut through the field placing. You have to co-ordinate your running with the other bat. You have to out-think the opposing captain. And you have to put it all together without a single mistake." He paused and looked at me.

"But when you do it, when you find your touch and you're cutting them to shreds and they're doing your bidding and you're totally in charge, there's just no feeling like it in the entire world." He grinned, as much to himself as to me. "And that's the time you have to be careful. That's when they'll slip one through."

But for all his openness, or perhaps because of it, it wasn't an ordinary boy-girl relationship. There were other reasons too—the difference in religion, familiarity, my tacky shapeless uniform. And I suspect too that he had locked away that truly vulnerable part of himself which had somehow been so badly injured.

So, with all the obvious avenues closed to me, I decided upon a plan which I felt met all the necessary criteria. We would meet in yet another environment; I would be wearing a real dress; there would be music and dancing.

In Brisbane then there were two big dancing studios which catered for the school crowd on Wednesday afternoons and Saturday mornings—Sandy Robertson's and Moss's.

Sandy's was in the Valley and was patronised overwhelmingly by the Catholic schools. Moss's was on the top floor of an old rowing club boatshed between the Grey Street and Victoria bridges overlooking the river from Circular Quay. And that was where the Protestants gathered, boys from Brisbane Boys' College and Churchie and Grammar and girls from the better Protestant schools—Somerville House, Clayfield College and St Margaret's.

St Mary's girls were not encouraged to go to either. We had dancing lessons once a fortnight at school in our junior year, half of us taking the boy's part then changing places the next dance. But if we went anywhere at all on Saturday mornings it was to Sandy's. I went occasionally but I never enjoyed it and always vowed I would never go again. The idea of sitting, pretending to talk to the girl next to me while the boys looked us over, terrified and repelled me. I didn't want them to ask me but I was terrified they wouldn't and I would have to sit there alone while everyone stared. That never happened. There were always many more boys than girls. But that didn't stop the fear of it.

Pal, I knew, went to Moss's on those mornings he wasn't playing sport or helping in the shop. With the August holidays only four weeks away, and just before them the end of term dance, I knew I had to make my move. And Moss's was the obvious place.

I was lucky. A seemingly innocent question about his football schedule told me that the following Saturday would be free and thus, if his father let him leave the store, almost certainly a dancing morning. It was sure enough for the risk to be worth the taking.

Next, I had to find someone who would go with me.

I couldn't go alone. I had never been to Moss's before and there would be no one else I knew there. But there was only one girl in my class I felt would be willing to take the risk and go with me and she was no special friend: Natalia Androvski. In fact, she had no real friends at school. Girls didn't interest her, either then or later. She had a reputation for being "experienced". Once, one of the girls swore she saw her at the opening of *H.M.S.Pinafore* at His Majesty's with a man. "He must have been at least thirty," she said. Natalia wouldn't confirm or deny it. Some even said she smoked cigarettes at home in front of her father but, since no one had ever been asked to her home, there was no way of knowing. Still, with her it was possible and we liked to think it was true. She was the only girl in the school on whom the uniform seemed to have a touch of style.

When I finally asked her if she would come to Moss's she gave a surprised smile. Not, I suspect, at the thought of going but that I should have been the one to ask her. But she agreed quite readily. Almost too readily. I wanted her to ask me why so that I could tell her about my plan and perhaps talk it over with her. But she just agreed and we decided to meet outside and go in together.

In the days that followed I saw Pal only once. That was on Friday morning but the bus was crowded and we couldn't even stand together.

Then suddenly it was Saturday morning and I was on another bus and heading for Circular Quay. Twice on the way along Coronation Drive I almost changed my mind and went home. But when the bus stopped I couldn't find the impulse to take me off my seat. Besides, I thought, I could hardly leave Natalia waiting endlessly outside the dance hall. I would never be able to face her again.

Perhaps he wouldn't be there. The thought was almost a relief.

Then we were alongside the boatshed and I was getting off. Natalia was waiting under one of the big Moreton Bay figs which lined the Quay and she looked, well, not pretty, but interesting. She had long blond hair, very white and wispy beside her face. Her sleeveless frock was plain white with a straight skirt, very simple and understated. I had taken such pains over my outfit before choosing a floral dress with a full skirt and a rope petticoat underneath in case Moss's allowed jiving which was just becoming the rage. I wanted to be prepared for anything. Also, I had taken an old discarded lipstick of my mother's and applied it at the bus stop. She had no make-up on at all.

I could see that the effect was to make me look overdone and even a little cheap. My heart sank again. But then she saw me and smiled and I felt better. I knew my figure was as good as hers and I was a good dancer. Everyone said so, even my father.

"Hi," she said.

"Hello, Natalia. I hope you haven't been waiting long."

"No, I just arrived. Let's go in."

"How much is it?"

"I don't know. Four shillings, I think."

"It looks very crowded."

It was. We paid at the door and pushed inside through a big group gathered around the entrance to the dance floor. Outside it had been pleasantly cool with a nice breeze from the river but in here it was hot and sticky and, until my eyes became used to the light, very dim and shadowy.

As we entered a record was playing an old Glenn Miller tune and

79

the dance was a Gypsy Tap. The dance floor was packed and in the open doorways leading out on to the wide verandah on the river side groups of boys stood watching and waiting either for new partners or perhaps the courage to walk across and ask those who remained sitting in the long row of chairs which lined the opposite wall.

The music was at full volume and over that there was the bumping and sliding of unskilled feet in sensible shoes; then the talking and laughing and shouting of the spectators. The whole mixture of sound echoed back on itself from the walls and the ceiling.

It should have made me more nervous but curiously it had the opposite effect. It was an eiderdown of sound, warming and soothing at once. Inside it, I felt surrounded and part of it and anonymous all at once. I felt I would fit in. If Pal were here it would be easy to ask him, even if I had to shout the words.

We made our way through the perspiring circle of dancers to some seats in the corner. But just as we sat a B.B.C. boy in his green uniform touched Natalia's arm. His lips moved and she nodded. They moved into the stream of dancers.

My eyes never left the dancers. Apart from the few in school uniform, most of the boys wore white shirts and ties. The girls were wearing twinsets or skirts and blouses or light dresses like my own. I didn't even notice that no one had yet asked me to dance, I was so intent on the crowd.

Then I saw him and I found myself getting up off my seat instinctively going to him to let him know I was here. I caught myself and sat back on the hard wooden seat wondering if anyone had seen me but still without taking my eyes from his face. He was coming around the end of the hall towards me, dancing with a small dark-haired girl who was talking very fast and holding his attention. They passed within six feet of me but he didn't notice. I was still staring at them as they slid away from me when an upturned hand touched my knees.

"Would you like to dance?"

I looked up into a pimple-pitted face topped by greasy blond hair. I nodded and moved into his grip.

"You looking for someone?" He shouted it in my ear.

I shook my head.

"Where are you from?"

"St Margaret's," I said immediately. I hadn't planned it. In fact, I hadn't thought about it at all. But suddenly I was lying about my school. Not from shame. Just, I suppose, that I wanted to belong to this new group.

"St Mag's, eh?" said the face. It grinned. "You must know Peta Simpson then."

I didn't know any Peter Simpson and I didn't see any reason why a St Margaret's girl should, unless he had somehow been smuggled into the school posing as a girl or something. I suppose my blank expression told him something.

"Don't you remember last year's Head of the River?"

The St Margaret's dance had been held on the night of the school rowing championships, I knew, but no more. I remained blank.

"Peta was the one that got up on the table with all the B.C.C. blokes and sang 'Hairy Mary'. Don't you remember? She got expelled."

A Sister Mary was head teacher of St Margaret's. Another part of the picture fell into place. I nodded, but inconclusively.

"Don't you remember? 'Hairy Mary/Had a little Indian/Hairy Mary/Had a little Indian/Hairy Mary/Had a little Indian/One little Indian boy . . .' remember?"

I completely lost the thread of the conversation then and just nodded or shook my head as I thought appropriate. The face kept singing the "Hairy Mary" tune and it clashed with the rhythm of the Gypsy Tap we were supposed to be dancing, confusing us both. I pretended to be annoyed when he lost step and kicked my shoe and after that he just hummed occasionally.

I was straining, trying to see Pal and catching occasional glimpses of him. When the dance finished, the face led me halfway back to my chair and departed, still humming the monotonous tune.

I found Natalia. Her partner had taken her all the way back and was standing near her chair talking very fast while she looked up at him, a half smile on her face. When I approached she simply turned her attention to me, leaving him stranded in mid-sentence.

"Enjoying it?" she said.

Her partner moved away. "See you later."

She didn't appear to hear him.

"Yes," I said. "I like it. Better than Sandy's, but everyone here seems to want to talk to you all the time."

She smiled.

"Natalia," I said, "what do you tell them when they ask what school you go to? Do you say St Mary's?"

"No."

I was sure she didn't. Otherwise I wouldn't have had the courage to ask.

"What do you say then?"

"I don't tell them any school. I make up a different story each time. I told that one I was a factory girl supporting my invalid mother. He was very nice about it. Next time . . . I don't know. I'll just have to wait and see."

It was no real help to me. I couldn't make anything like that sound plausible. Still, if I found Pal in time I wouldn't have any more worries.

Another record started—a Boston two-step—and the boys came in from the river side. There he was, right at the front of a group and heading across the floor on our right. He was ten feet away when he recognised me. He looked more surprised than pleased but he changed direction. One of his friends was closer to us and in Pal's sideways movement he was pushed towards me. I could see from the corner of my eye that he had made up his mind to ask me but I kept my face firmly towards Pal. If only he would speak first I would be safe. I could ignore the other boy without being bad mannered. Even if they spoke together it would be all right.

Pal's voice was very clear when it came.

"What are you doing here?" he said.

He said it not unpleasantly. He may even have been smiling a little as he spoke. But the accusation was unmistakable. I had no right to be there. I was an intruder in this part of his life. My place was on the bus or in the shop. My place was to listen as he talked, not to push myself into other parts of his existence. My place was to be a Catholic at Sandy's. I opened my mouth to reply but there was nothing to say.

Then the other boy touched me and spoke and I was on my feet looking at Pal as he asked Natalia to dance. It didn't seem to worry him in the slightest that his friend had asked me first. On the contrary, I think he was relieved.

"What are you doing here?" . . . I thought them the five cruellest words in the language . . . "What are you doing here?"

I don't remember the dance. But when it was over the boy led me back to my seat and I waited for Natalia. I waited through the next dance, a slow, interminable foxtrot, refusing offers to participate, not even glancing at my prospective partners as they stumbled their requests.

I caught sight of them several times, dancing close and talking but I really didn't care. I felt exhausted. I didn't want to dance and I didn't want to leave. I didn't feel I had the energy left even to stand up, much less go through the motions of dancing. So I sat and waited.

After the second dance he brought her back to our place, smiled at us both and quickly walked away.

"Well!" she said.

"What's up?"

"That boy. You know him, don't you?"

"Yes," I said. "We sometimes go to town on the same bus."

"Yes, he said so."

"What else did he say?"

"About you?"

I nodded.

"Not much. He just said you travelled on the same bus sometimes."

"Is that all?"

"I think so. But my God he can talk. You wouldn't believe what he was talking about."

"What?"

"*Crime and Punishment*."

"What kind of crime?"

"*Crime and Punishment*. The book. Dostoevsky. He's just read it. He spent two whole dances talking about it."

I had heard of the book only vaguely. Pal had never mentioned it in any of our bus talks. "Dostoevsky . . . he's Russian, isn't he?"

"He's the greatest writer who ever lived. Haven't you read it? Haven't you read *The Brothers Karamazov*?"

"I don't think so."

"If you had, Brolie, you'd remember."

I was silent.

"He has. He's read *The Idiot*, *The Brothers Karamazov*, all of them. But his favourite is *Crime and Punishment*. That's what he told me. His favourite is *Crime and Punishment*."

"Have you read all those books?"

"No, but I've read *Crime and Punishment*, thank God. But what a thing to be talking about . . . at this place."

I had never seen her so animated, but I wasn't sure I grasped the reason for it.

"He's only in sub-junior, you know."

"Of course I know."

I felt her looking at me.

"Brolie," she said, "is that why you came here this morning? Because of him?"

"No," I lied. "Of course not. I didn't even know he'd be here."

"Because if it is, you can dance with him. I'll find someone else."

"No, no. I told you. I didn't even know he'd be here."

"It doesn't matter to me."

The music had started again but we ignored it.

"When he comes back," she said, "you can dance with him."

"Is he coming back?"

"I suppose so. He said he was. You do like him, don't you?"

"No, honestly." It suddenly became very important to me to convince her. "I just see him on the bus sometimes. I really couldn't care less. Really."

"All right," she said.

83

We sat out the rest of the dance in silence.

The next dance, a quickstep, and the one after, a Pride of Erin, we danced with other partners. Pal was nowhere to be seen. Then, on the final dance, he came towards us. I thought for a moment he was going to ask Natalia again but he turned to me.

"Would you like to?"

"Thank you," I said.

We went through the motions. I tried to feel lively and pleased and gay but it was no use. All I felt was a kind of lassitude. And when he asked me about Natalia—what was she like; where was she from—I felt no resentment at all.

"She thought you were coming back to ask her for another dance," I said.

"Really? Well, perhaps I will."

"This is the last dance."

"Oh well, maybe next week."

"She was expecting you. Did you tell her you were going to ask her again?"

"No, I don't think so."

We danced in silence for a while, then I said: "Are you going straight home after the dance?" If we caught the same bus it was just possible that I would find the willpower or the desire to ask him. But he shook his head.

"No, some of us are going down to Albert Street to get a Griffo burger. Do you know the place? It's next to the St James."

"No."

"You should try one. I have one every time I come here. They're terrific. The greatest." But there was no invitation to be read into his words.

The next thing I remember I was on the bus in a seat by myself.

Dostoevsky and Griffo burgers. Even today I can't think of one without the other. The mixture was so absurd, so incongruous, so maddening that it stuck in my mind. Dostoevsky and Griffo burgers.

Of course, I stayed away from the second term dance. But I am not sure now whether it was the drama of the gesture which appealed to me—the lovelorn virgin locking herself in her tower—or whether it was just the easiest way out. At least there was no need to go through the awful business of finding another boy to ask. But at the time, especially when I was with him, it gave me a fine sense of principle. And the fact that he was unaware of the sacrifice I was making only made it the more tragic and dramatic.

Yet such feelings, though I laugh at them now, were shatteringly important at the time. And later, when he was away, they formed an important part of my memory file when his name was mentioned or a thought of him came to me. Even now I suppose it is not really possible to separate the adolescent feelings from the whole picture. It all merges with the pain of loss, of the hurt he so viciously delivered, and the good, good times.

When we met again on the bus it was (for him at least) as though the whole episode had never taken place. We talked. He shared his thoughts with me and many of his experiences. Occasionally in the second year he mentioned something that had happened at a dance or a party but I never learned whom he had taken and of course I couldn't ask.

Then, in the last two or three months of his junior year, he changed. He seemed to close up. He would start a sentence then fall silent or change its direction to something unconnected with the original thought. He wouldn't look around when he came on board as he always had, checking to see where I was sitting.

At first, of course, I thought the only possible explanation was that he had found a girl. No, I can put it better than that. He had fallen for another girl. I was still proud enough then to assert my own femininity, if only to myself. But I was wrong. It wasn't another girl (at least no one special), it was something that had happened at home, something that absorbed and distracted and punished him.

But if he was indifferent and disinterested I was not. In fact, it was probably his indifference which dragged me in further. I have sometimes thought of all human relationships as being like a kind of mutual investment trust with a fixed investment required, so that if one partner fell short the other had to make up the difference to bring it back to the required level. It has seemed to me that, once the relationship begins, the investments and withdrawals of emotional commitment follow involuntarily. One is forced, almost in spite of oneself, to come forward with ever greater deposits as the other moves away taking ever greater lumps from the mutual fund.

And that was the way with us, at least at that time. No matter what I said or did, within my own very prescribed limits, I couldn't break through to him. Then, soon after the end of the school year, he was gone.

I was not aware of it at first, but one day I overheard Mrs Lingard talking about it at the shop. He had gone to a relative's property about three hundred miles west of Brisbane just beyond the Darling Downs. He was a jackeroo.

It took a long while for the news to sink in, for me to accept the fact that he had gone away. And it was just as hard to see him as a jackeroo fitting in to what I imagined to be the rough, mindless life of the bush. He was a city boy. A Brisbanite. It was hard to adjust my mental picture of him to fit those high-heeled, broad-brimmed drawlers who descended upon Brisbane in their herds at Show time. But when he returned after a year for a couple of weeks' holiday—a fact that the Lingards had separately announced to the whole district several times over—I was expecting the complete transformation.

I was wrong again. He was changed, greatly so in appearance. He was sunburned a deep brown. He had grown much taller and stronger looking. You could see his jaw muscles move when he spoke and he had a quietness and a reticence as though he didn't quite belong in the confines of the store any more. But it was far from a transformation.

He stayed such a short while but at least we had one or two opportunities to talk and he seemed interested in my life. I wasn't sure whether he was happy in the west; and it seemed to me that he wasn't either. But it was new and different and when he talked about the good things—the satisfaction of hard work, the independence, stories of his great uncle who owned "The Place" as they called it—he was enthusiastic and he made it seem good. A good and happy place. Uncomplicated.

Suddenly he was gone again and I had to rely on stray bits of news from his parents. We, the customer/audience, learned from his mother of the search for the man lost, the snake bite, the cattle rush and other Adventures of Pal that, I suspect, lost nothing in the telling. But there was nothing in the stories that told me how he was feeling, what it all meant to him, what his plans were. I had to piece that together in my mind and it was something that I enjoyed doing.

I was away with my family at Mooloolaba surfing the next time he came down so I didn't see him. But when we got back from the holiday Mrs Lingard said he had been asking after me. And in the same conversation she told me about his new project.

He had left The Place and gone to the far west in a shearing team. He would spend the whole season—nearly seven months—in the real outback: Julia Creek, Cloncurry, Winton, Charleville, Dajarra, Duchess, Carrandotta.

During that year he wrote very infrequently and he could not have chosen a worse time to neglect them. By then the B.C.C., the Brisbane Cash and Carry which was the forerunner of the supermarket, had established a branch only a hundred yards from the Lingards. Business was falling off. The shop was no longer the packed house of good-natured crowds bantering with Mrs Lingard and the two girl assistants. First one of them left, then the other (to become a cashier at the B.C.C.) and still it seemed his parents had time on their hands.

My father told me that the B.C.C. had offered them a good price for the store and Mr Lingard the managership of the new "facility" but that he had refused. I don't know why. I can't imagine that he ever expected Pal would want to take over the business some day.

Perhaps he held on to it just because it was his—his own store.

It was then too, I think, that Mrs Lingard became ill. Or perhaps that was the following year when Pal was back on The Place and studying at night for his Senior or even later when he had begun to write his stories and miniature plays. I'm not sure. It's hard to remember.

Suddenly, just now, I said to myself, "I'll go and ask him. I'll go and ask Pal." And as I said it, right on top of the thought, chasing it like a smile then a slap, came the realisation once again that I cannot do so. In the next moment I can feel all the energy draining out of me. I can listen to my own breathing and hear it becoming faster and shallower and know that there is nothing I can do to stop the crying that will come soon.

It is not as bad as it was. Now it is soft and there are inside me only echoes of the jolting panic I used to feel in the early days. But I have a long way to go before the echoes fade completely. I wonder if that day will ever come. Yes, it must. These days I can sometimes sail along for many hours without even a thought of him and even at night I can most often think his name and think of a time we had without sadness.

I think the writing helps even though sometimes, like now, it all comes back in waves that push me against my will and loosen my grip.

And then I think: there is so much more to be said, so much more to write, not for him but for me. And that sustains me.

Pal's Story
II

PALMER LINGARD sat easily in the heavy, old-fashioned saddle, his back straight but relaxed, the lower half of his body rocking forward and back at the pelvis, the movement absorbing the steady undulation of the horse beneath him. He held the reins loosely in his left hand just below chest height. The other hand dangled from the thumb pushed habitually into the off-side pocket of his thick denim trousers and it slapped gently against his leg with the horse's rhythm. His feet, like his shoulders, stayed firmly parallel to the flat ground.

It was a stockman's seat and it served him well enough in the long days of mustering sheep and cattle on the 30,000-acre property. It was firm enough to maintain authority over the horse and that was particularly important with a young gelding like Solomon, the horse he had chosen for the long ride today. But at the same time it was loose and supple so that he could absorb the shock if the horse stumbled or shied. It allowed him, at a good slow canter, to scan deep into the box and sandalwood scrub on his right as they made their way along the fence line to the back of the big paddock.

But most importantly it gave him the freedom to let his mind stray from the mechanics of the job. And in the long, long days on the Mitchell grass plains and in the ironbark ridges, that freedom was his blessing and his curse.

At first, the day soothed him. In the early morning when the sun was rising and the white frost in the gullies was melting slowly into the red earth and the silver-eyes and magpies and whipbirds were calling their beautiful and incomprehensible messages, it gave him a strong and satisfying pleasure. He breathed it in and felt complete. He held the soft bark of the mottled grey box trees momentarily with a cupped hand as he passed them and felt the warmth just under the surface. He broke off switches of sandalwood and smelled the exotic perfume of the sap. He bit into the twigs, tasted the sharpness and spat out the black bark while his mouth tingled and felt clean.

The horses were always lively in the mornings too and with some of the young ones like Solomon he had to lean right back as he went down the gullies. If he lost his balance and his head swung forward over the withers Solomon would kick up his heels and he would be over the neck and into the damp, icy grass. He had been caught a few times in the early days, but no longer. After four years he moved on reflex.

But even after so long the mornings retained their beauty for him. On the tracks and in the open country the dust stayed moist on the ground and the sun warmed his face. It was a good time.

But after ten o'clock there was a change. The dust was dry now and rising with any breeze. His old windbreaker was long since stuffed into the spare saddle bag and the sweat was starting to run down between the hair on his chest. His back was a black mat of flies which stuck to his shirt and left it only to raid the moisture at his eyes and on his face. The wild belly-laugh of the kookaburra, so pleasure-filled two hours ago, was beginning to sound humourless and ironic. The magpies and the silver-eyes were quiet and the harsh grating squark of crows was starting to make the time measurable. The horses' heads were lowering and their eyes glazing with monotony. It was the time when the bush was becoming still, its colours flattening with the dust, and the snakes were starting to move dreamily through the tall grass to the rocks and clearings where they would curl in the sun and sleep until the heat of the high noon woke them and sent them back to the shade.

After ten o'clock the day had to be endured. The dogs walked under the horses' bellies for shade, not bothering even to chase the half-blind rabbits struggling in bewilderment and confusion as the myxomatosis grew in their bodies and killed them.

For Palmer, the mid-morning change brought an end to his mental peace for the day. After that there would be no careless pleasure in all the long hours till dusk. The anger would start, as it was starting now, with a sudden realisation that his stomach muscles were bunched together and his teeth were clamped down hard on his jaw which was aching with the strain.

When he recognised the symptoms he took a long, deep breath and willed his muscles to relax. The toes of his high-heeled riding boots danced a little in the stirrups as his calf muscles went suddenly limp. But even as he breathed out he knew that parts of his body were tensing again, the way they did in a dentist's chair when he suddenly found himself hardly breathing and his shoulders were straining out of the high-backed seat.

Soon he would kick Solomon into a fast canter for a quarter-mile down the fence line. That would knock the tension out of his body and for a while it would stay loose. It would take time before the images and words in his mind and the hard, relentless knot of frustration and anger in his stomach found their way back.

Again he pulled his teeth apart. It was coming hard today, probably because he was alone. With Boss and young Ritchie along there was talk when he wanted it to distract him. Young Ritchie talked whether he wanted him to or not but most of the time Palmer barely listened. He tuned in often enough to keep the thread of the conversation and the kid was amiable enough. He didn't object when he was told to shut up.

Boss was entirely different. He talked when he knew Palmer was in the mood for it and when he needed it. He had a sixth sense about such times. Palmer sometimes felt that only a small part of Boss lived in the great old sun-creased frame. The rest of him was outside in a wide aura settling on those around him, probing deeply into them and finding their strengths and their hollows. The wide-set brown eyes were gentle as a woman's but their pupils were so wide even in the bright sun that they seemed able to encompass more than other eyes were designed to. Palmer saw only kindness and wisdom and a rough humour in them but he had watched and was constantly surprised as other men flinched away and refused to meet them directly. Even the voice, which was low and gravelly and seemed to Palmer to carry with it the threat of a chuckle in every new thought, worried other men. They became defensive and angry with themselves and all around them when he talked.

A picture flashed into his mind and held. He was sitting on the top rail of the high stockyard fence; in front of him and just below the level of his knees was Boss. He was taking off his old sweat-stained brown hat so that the blue-white hair, dark at the edges with sweat, reflected the light into Palmer's eyes. Boss wiped his forehead with the crook of his elbow then swept the hat back on again. But all through the ritual gesture his eyes never left the face of the horse dealer.

"I don't think so," he said and his voice came from deep in his chest. "I'll give you thirty."

"Thirty quid!" The dealer broke from the old eyes and turned to the five stock horses standing quietly in the yard.

"I paid forty each for 'em. I've been on the track for a week and you offer me thirty."

"Thirty. I don't think you'll lose."

"What do you mean, I won't lose? O' course I'll lose." The dealer was shouting. He was a hard, wiry man. A bushman. He prided himself that nothing riled him. He worked at ringing, droving, horsebreaking, the jobs of a steady, taciturn man. The only time he shouted was at a dog or a stray beast breaking from a mob or maybe once in a long while at a woman who got under his skin.

"You think I stole 'em, don't you?" He was still shouting. "I tell you sixty quid and you offer me thirty. You think I stole the fucking things."

"No, I don't think so. I need them but you can take them down to the next place if you like."

93

"You do. Don't tell me. I can see what you're thinking. You think I stole 'em."

"Thirty's a fair price."

"Look, if I stole them I'd want the best price, wouldn't I? Right? If I stole them I'd want to get all I could out of you and then piss off into Roma or somewhere as fast as I could."

Boss said nothing.

"I'm right, aren't I?"

There was another silence.

"Well, I'll tell you what I'm going to do then. I'm going to give 'em to you for thirty. I'm gonna take a bloody loss, see. And I'm gonna turn right around and go back to Morgandale. I'm gonna stay in the Morg. for a week and if you hear anything about any stolen horses all you have to do is ring up the bloody constable and he can come and get me. I'll be in the pub." He stopped, out of breath. Palmer suspected it was the longest speech he had made in his life.

"Do you want cash?" Boss asked.

"Nope. Don't give me cash. Give me a bloody cheque and you can cancel the bloody thing if you think they're stolen. You can ring up the constable any time you like."

Boss made out the cheque while the dealer walked among the horses stirring them around the yard.

"Look at them," he shouted to Palmer. "There's not one here over ten years old."

Boss handed over the cheque and the dealer stuffed it into a back pocket. Then he climbed the fence and walked across the gravel road to his horse. His blue kelpie trotted out of the shade of a fence post towards him. The dealer kicked the animal just under the chest and sent it somersaulting into the dust with a squeal of fright.

His horse shied as be grabbed the reins and swung himself aboard but the dealer stuck easily to the saddle.

"Ring him any bloody time you like," he shouted at Boss and kicked his mare into a hard canter. The dust swirled up from the horse's hooves.

Palmer looked down into Boss's face which was wrinkling into a grin.

"Do you really think he stole them?"

"I don't know," Boss said. "But he seemed to think so."

Palmer smiled at the memory. You either loved him or hated him. There was no in-between. Palmer loved him and respected him and it still astonished him when the old man deferred to him. But this had happened constantly since he had returned from the sheds. He had begun to suspect, against every instinct he possessed, that it was a ploy to keep him on The Place. He knew the old man wanted that but he knew just as surely that he wouldn't resort to a deception to keep him there. He had only to ask and Palmer would agree.

But perhaps that was the reason he didn't ask. If the offer wasn't articulated there would be no obligation. This way the understanding was just there and with it was his guarantee of freedom. He could leave when he wanted to, when the time was right. If he stayed, Wilderwood—The Place—would be his when Boss died. But it would probably be his whether he stayed or went away. Apart from his mother, there was no one else.

He would have to decide soon. He knew it and the decision was pressing on him. It was that which was tightening the muscles in his belly. But it was only one of the things, one more piece in the pattern of his life which spread itself out in his mind and gnawed at him.

Chasing scrubbers was really only an excuse. Mostly it was just being alone on a Sunday with the silence and the rhythmic movement of the horse beneath him.

But there was, he admitted, a bonus. It was the chase. When he came on the scrubbers—stray long-horned Herefords which had been missed in a muster of the paddock years ago and had bred wild—there would probably be eight or ten in the mob. The young cattle had never been worked. The others knew man as an enemy, something to be feared, something to run from. When they heard him they would stand up in the shade watching the direction of the sound until they saw him. Then they would snuffle and snort among themselves until the young bulls broke and ran wildly for the scrub. The mob would scatter and he would have to pick his marks early and stick with them.

He would go for the strong ones. The young bulls. The others might run themselves into the ground and not be able to make the long walk home once he had them steadied down. The young bulls had spirit. But in the first quarter-mile they also had speed.

He would try to round them early then guide their charge to the fence line he was walking now. Once they were out on the rough track all he had to do was drive them the seven miles home. The two dogs at Solomon's heels would keep them from breaking back into the timber and his stockwhip would keep them moving along.

But both dogs and whip were useless in the chase. Worse than useless, they impeded him. With a dozen beasts breaking in different directions the dogs wore themselves out changing their minds. And in the hard, thrilling gallop through the bush the whip would tangle in the leaves and branches and unseat him if he tried to use it. Some stockmen kept it swinging over their shoulder but Palmer had made a rough wire holder on the leather flap of his saddle. During the chase he wanted nothing loose, nothing protruding where it could bump a tree and throw him off balance. Balance was everything in the chase, balance and co-ordination between horse and rider. He was able to guide Solomon through light timber at a gallop with barely a touch on the reins. The sway of his body brought the horse left or right and his knees clamped hard on the old saddle.

He decided against the hard ride down the fence line and wheeled Solomon into the high grass toward the big patch of native wattle which covered this part of the paddock. There was an old dam a couple of miles on the other side of the wattle and he might pick them up there. In a paddock the size of Moonlight which spread in a rough rectangle over nearly 7000 acres the dam was as good a place as any to start.

A hundred yards into the wattle he changed his mind again and turned back toward the fence. The scrub was too thick. The thin black stems kept whipping into his face and the cobwebs between the trees stuck to him and he had to brush the spiders out of his clothes. There was no opportunity to think.

The wide gate at the back of the paddock was only a quarter of a mile away now. He would turn right at the gate and a mile or so further along he would leave the cross fence and head west into the paddock. That way he would be facing the home paddocks when he reached the dam.

His jaws were clenched again. He pulled his teeth apart and reached an arm down by Solomon's shoulder to pull out a long stem of grass. He bit off about six inches and shoved it into his mouth. The chewing would relax his jaw muscles and keep the tension out of him.

Suddenly annoyed at himself he kicked the horse into a canter and instantly realised that that too was an escape. The whole plan of chasing the scrubbers was an escape, a deliberate distraction. The chase, the danger of the gallop through the timber, the constant alertness he would need to hold the bulls if he caught them, it was all designed to distract him, to hold his mind at bay.

"Jesus, damn!" he yelled. His horse quivered under him and he reefed back on the bit as they reached the gate.

The sudden sound of a shot startled him. It was a long way off but it came so hard on his own shout that it was almost an answer. Automatically, he looked down at the powdered earth by the gate and saw the explanation. A party of kangaroo shooters had driven through into Sticks, the long narrow paddock which formed the back boundary. The shooters had been on The Place for nearly a week now.

Boss had allowed them a month. It would cut down the numbers. The roos were a pest. They broke fences and ate as much grass as the

96

5000 sheep on the property. If they weren't shot, the sheep would go hungry in the dry spells when feed was low while the kangaroos could just move on and ravage some other property.

In the old days, when Palmer first arrived at The Place, Boss wouldn't allow a shooter anywhere near the station. He said they shot as many sheep in the dark as they did Roos. They lit fires in the bushfire season and were dangerous to have around.

But that was when Aunt Caroline was still alive and instead of two hands there were twice as many and Boss spent every day on a horse or in the Land-Rover. It was all different then. They organised their own shooting parties.

They would leave just before dusk on the weekends, Palmer and Tim, the other jackeroo, standing on the back of the battered half-ton flat top and Rankin the overseer in front with old John Harrigan at the wheel. They shot until dark, taking only the legs as feed for the dogs, then rigged the spotlight to a twelve-volt battery and shot again until midnight. Towards the end they didn't even bother with the legs.

At first it was like a carnival to Palmer, the kangaroos passing like little ducks on a miniature shooting range. But it was serious too. If you could shoot straight you were that much more of a man. You could handle a gun. You could make a head shot through brigalow at sixty yards with an old bolt-action .22 and when the animal toppled you felt proud.

"Good shot!" they said and you had to admit it: some people had it and some didn't. A steady hand, nerves of steel, a straight eye. They were the ingredients of manhood.

It grew on him too. After six months he was going out on his own most evenings and shooting two or three before dark. But by then it was more than machismo. By then he had learned the pleasure of killing, of choosing one animal from a leaping pack, of holding it in his sights as they fled for the deep shadows of the bush and at the last possible second of gently squeezing the trigger.

Rankin the overseer had been the one who had encouraged him; Rankin with the foxy face and the perpetual sneer. And it had been Rankin who had told him to kill the sheep on his second day at The Place when he had watched a killing only once before.

He shook his head to dispel the memory and sought a new topic to take its place. Nothing came. He listened for more shots but there were none, just the low murmur of an engine a long way off. He turned Solomon's head south along the cross fence and pushed him into a steady walk.

So many things had changed since the early days. Now Boss spent most of his time at the house while Palmer and young Ritchie tried to keep The Place running. It was too much for two. Boss helped with the mustering occasionally and the yard work and he kept the books, but he was getting old.

No, it wasn't that. He had been old for a long time but now it was almost the only thing you noticed about him. And more painful than that, it didn't seem to bother him.

Again Palmer forced his mind away from a thought. If he pursued this he would come back to the question that haunted him, the decision, the plan he would have to make if he chose to leave Wilderwood, the strength it would need to start a new life, especially the life he knew he wanted and must have.

He wanted to be involved, to be doing something that absorbed him completely, that brought him new knowledge and forced him to extend himself. But what was available? Where could he find a job in Brisbane, or anywhere, that satisfied him? And even if he found it, who would have him? What was he qualified for? His Senior pass was something, but not much. In a sense, it had only made matters worse.

He had enjoyed the study. He looked forward to the end of the day when he came back to his hut over the road from the homestead and opened the books—Breasted's *Ancient History, The Principles of Economics, An Introduction to Logic, Macbeth*—he devoured them all and his hunger remained.

He enjoyed the trips to Roma too. Every weekend closeted with Sam Jacobson in his big old house on the outskirts of town; stuffing himself with knowledge every evening of the week then pouring it all out at the weekend, picking it over with Sam, dissecting, analysing, arguing, learning.

The arguments with Sam were the high points of the week. But arguments was too strong a word. Sam's gentle blue eyes would twinkle and shine as he led him on with socratic questions, led him on until he'd so boxed himself in that the only defence was attack. And that was parried so easily, so deftly, so kindly that he found himself nodding in agreement.

And at the end of the evenings Sam would shake his head and call a halt. "You have to pace yourself, Palmer. Pace yourself. You've got a whole lifetime ahead of you. Don't try to do it all at once. Go to bed and we'll continue in the morning."

When Sam had retired as headmaster of Roma High School he had simply moved from the state-owned house by the school to the big old home at the other end of town and continued to do the only thing he knew and the only thing he cared about. Now, instead of the formality of a classroom, there was the quietness and intimacy of the carpeted lounge and the book-filled study. He had been a master, a headmaster, and now he was called a tutor. But only the title had changed. He was a teacher.

He had never married but he was an integral part of many families in the district. Where others more ambitious had used Roma as just another stepping stone, Sam had stayed. This was his town. Its children were his pupils and his pleasure, his work and his recreation.

In winter there would be a fire in the big open grate and as they talked Anna, a tall, open-faced country girl who looked after Sam, would bring them hot cocoa and from behind Sam's back find an opportunity to smile an invitation at Palmer. He would nod his head slowly in reply, pretending he was answering Sam's quiet words of instruction.

His relationship with Anna had started the second night he stayed over at Sam's house. They had spoken together the previous morning at breakfast and she had seemed dull but not unpleasant. He knew she had been in some kind of trouble with the courts and that Sam's intervention had kept her from going to a state home but he knew none of the details.

Then, in the evening after he had climbed into bed with a book he heard a timid knock at the door and it was pushed open gently.

"Can I come in?" she said.

"Yes, of course."

She was wearing a pair of men's pyjamas under what looked like one of Sam's old overcoats. She walked across and sat on the side of the bed. Her face was made up but the lipstick was crooked and it gave her a lopsided appearance.

"Are you going to be coming here every weekend?"

He nodded. "For the rest of the year anyway. Whenever I can get away."

"That's good. You don't know what it's like being stuck here. It's like being back at school all the time."

"But Mr Jacobson's a nice bloke . . ."

"He's all right, I suppose. But I'm glad you're coming back."

"Except at shearing and crutching time."

There was a silence. She hugged herself and shivered elaborately.

"It's cold here. Can I get in with you?"

"Christ, what would Sam . . . Mr Jacobson say?"

"He's fast asleep. Anyway, his room's miles away. He'll never know." She smiled at him and he returned it. As she pulled off the overcoat her wide pendulous breasts swayed out of the open pyjama shirt. He moved aside to give her room.

They were very quiet and afterwards she said: "That was nice. You're very gentle."

"It was good."

She reached for the overcoat and put it on. "Don't forget to come back next weekend."

At first he felt a stab of guilt, as though he was abusing Sam's hospitality. But the feeling passed. The memory of that nine months of study and work and argumentation and simple lovemaking was unmarred.

But now it was passed it left a gap, a frustration, an anger. It had all worked out so differently. Nothing had gone the way he had planned it. But at the time he had decided to leave home there was no real, detailed plan. There was only a motivation and an absurd belief that it would all come to him and fall in his lap. He had been so sure of himself then, so insufferably sure. They were sitting in the big lounge room behind the store when he made his announcement that he was leaving. A Sunday night. The shop closed early.

His father brushed it aside: "Don't be stupid. You have two more years at school before you get your Senior then three years at teachers' college or university."

"I'm not going back to school."

"Palmer, you're sixteen years old. You'll do what I tell you."

"I'm not going back to school."

"Why? Give me one good reason."

"I'm sick of it. There's nothing there for me."

His mother put her teacup back into the saucer. "How can you say that? You know you're going to have a first class Junior pass; you're in the first team . . ."

"The first eleven."

". . . at cricket. You have friends there . . ."

"Children."

"Your reports speak highly . . ."

"The masters are fools."

"Stop interrupting your mother."

"I'm not interrupting. I'm correcting mistaken impressions."

"Well don't correct her then. You're only sixteen remember."

"I could hardly forget since you've reminded me of the fact twice in the last thirty seconds."

"And don't get smart with me. You're going to stay at school and that's all there is to it." His father left and in the next room a chair squeaked and the evening paper was rustled and smacked.

"You shouldn't answer your father like that, Palmer. You know how upset he gets."

"Yes, I know. I'm sorry, Mum. But I'm serious. I'm leaving school after Junior. In fact, I'm leaving Brisbane."

"Leaving home? But why? What's wrong with your home? What gets into you, Pal, that gives you these sudden notions?"

It had been a while since she had used the affectionate diminutive and it made him feel all of his sixteen years.

"There's nothing wrong with home, Mum. You know that."

"You have to make an effort to get on with your father. The way you two fight, I sometimes feel like leaving home myself."

He grinned. It was unthinkable. But then he looked away. It was true. They never seemed to stop fighting and she was always in the middle, always the peacemaker. Sometimes she really must want to get out of the place. She was always over-tired from the long hours in the shop and just when she tried to rest and relax there was another argument to adjudicate. But damn it, it wasn't his fault.

"I know, Mum, and I'm sorry. But he's impossible to talk to. He either makes pronouncements or just walks away."

"He's not the only one to blame. There has to be give and take on both sides. You have to learn how to approach him. It's not so much what you say but the way you say it that upsets your father. And after all, he does have a point. You are only sixteen."

"There, you see. Now you're saying it."

"But it's true, Pal. You can't deny it, not even with your celebrated mental powers."

"The sarcasm doesn't become you."

"Really?" She had a trick of lifting just one eyebrow. It was disconcerting. He had practised before a mirror but couldn't master it.

"Please, Mum . . . In his eyes," he looked towards the open doorway, "I'm not really even sixteen. I'm still a child of twelve and always will be. Even in your eyes I'm still a child."

"I didn't say that."

"You don't have to say it. It's in your attitude. The thought of my leaving home, of going out and looking after myself in the world is completely horrifying to you, simply because you still see me as a child."

"Palmer, I know you . . . better than you think I do. You're never going to be satisfied with the kind of job you could get with only the Junior as your qualification."

"I'm probably not going to be satisfied with any kind of job, no matter what my qualifications are. That's beside the point. I'm not talking about some job I might or might not take ten or twenty years from now. I'm talking about life, about the world, about living and experiencing all there is. Can't you see that? I'm talking about meeting and knowing new types of people, about seeing things, about going places where no one I know has ever been, where no one knows me, where I'm not just the son of . . . where I'm someone in my own right. I want to learn the real things about life, the important things, not the dates of some ridiculous European battle. India, for example.

I want to go to India."

His father appeared at the doorway. "India, for God's sake, what will you do when you get there?"

"Do?"

"Yes, do. What will you do to earn money?"

"Work, I suppose, the same as everyone else. Work and observe and learn something more important than the price of bloody Kellogg's cornflakes."

"Don't swear."

"Jesus . . ."

"Don't swear, I said."

"I wasn't swearing. I was blaspheming."

"Well don't blaspheme. Good God . . . ."

"Oh, that's beautiful. Did you hear that, Mum? That's beautiful."

"There's nothing to laugh at, damn it. Stop it. Try to show some commonsense for once in your life."

"Commonsense is a good name for it."

"And don't get smart again. Just think for a moment. How the devil are you going to get to India in the first place? Do you expect me to pay your fare?"

"From you I expect nothing."

"Well that's good because it's exactly what you'll get."

"Please." His mother looked from one to the other. "We aren't getting anywhere like this. Pal seems to have his heart set on leaving . . ."

"Are you siding with him again?"

"No, dear. I'm just trying to understand . . ."

"How can you hope to understand a sixteen-year-old boy who suddenly, out of the blue, decides he's going to India? God!"

"I'm not only going to India. I said that was just one of the places I want to see before I'm through. India, Japan, China, the Argentine . . ."

"Japan. You'll get on very well with the bloody Japs. You can ask them what became of your Uncle Bill. What happened to him in Changi. They'll be delighted about that. They'll welcome you with open arms . . ."

Palmer jumped to his feet. "Jesus Christ, Changi! Do you hear that? Changi. What's that got to do with anything? Can't you talk sense? Can't you extend yourself just for once and try to talk a little sense?"

He saw the blow coming almost in slow motion. There was all the time in the world to duck, to ward it off, to move backwards and let him blunder by. But he didn't move. He couldn't quite believe that the fist was going to reach him or, if it did, that it would make an

102

impression. It would bounce off him and he would stand immobile, steady as a rock while the old man wrung his fingers in pain.

But when it struck it blasted into his face and suddenly he was slipping sideways on to the lounge, thrusting his arms out to break his fall and staring into his mother's face which looked back at him in astonishment. A moment later the pain in his cheek bone was tearing at him as he sprawled on to the couch.

There was a long moment of total silence, then the slamming of a door. He heard the car start and his mother's face was coursing with tears she scarcely bothered to wipe away.

Palmer was in bed with his light off when his father returned. He heard the heavy footsteps coming down the hallway then through the spare room towards his bedroom. The door opened and almost immediately he smelt the beer. The liquor fumes surrounded him and made him feel queasy in the throat. Then he heard the familiar laboured breathing of an asthma attack. He kept still, his eyes tightly shut. Perhaps if he said nothing his father would go away.

But the sound of the breathing remained and in spite of himself he felt a sympathetic constriction in his own chest.

"Palmer . . . Pal, are you awake?" The voice was soft, just above a whisper and punctuated involuntarily by the effort of breathing. He stayed motionless, suddenly afraid of what might follow.

The legs of his chair beside the desk scraped across the floor. A hard, sickly exhalation of breath told him his father had sat only three or four feet away. Still he willed his eyes shut.

"Son, I don't know whether you're awake or not. But I think you are. I think you can hear me." He had expected the words to be slurred with beer but they were not. Now he knew what was coming and the realisation made him tense involuntarily beneath the covers.

"Pal, I just wanted to say I'm sorry. I'm sorry I hit you." There was a pause. "I'm sorry for a few things in my life and some of them you know. You know what I mean, don't you? There was that one thing . . . I'll never forget it, that bloody slut . . . no, no I can't blame her, I know that. It was my fault and I have to live with it and, do you know, sometimes I don't think I can. Sometimes I think . . .

"You are awake, Pal, aren't you? Because I want to tell you something and I want you to remember it. It's hard for me to say. It's not something a father says to his son and if I wasn't half shot I probably wouldn't be saying it now. But I'll tell you anyway." The breathing laboured a long moment.

"I admire you. I admire what you did—the way you said nothing to your mother, the way you acted as though nothing had happened. I didn't expect it. I didn't know what to expect but the way you handled it bowled me over. Not a word about it. Nothing. And I admired you for it. But I know it's there inside you all the time and, even though you never let on, I know that it's in your mind and when you look at me you can still see me the way I was that afternoon.

"And I'm afraid, son, that it's finally got you down, that that's the reason you want to get away from us, from me, that you can't stand the sight of me any more." The voice was breaking and faltering. "If I thought that I had driven you away from home and that all this stuff about India . . . Don't you see what that would do . . .?" There was a long silence, then a hard, deep, rasping breath. "God. I don't know . . . maybe it's best. Maybe you should go. Maybe in a few years you'll be able to come back and we can start fresh. You'll be able to see me differently. I just don't know."

When it started again, the voice was calmer. "Maybe you know best. But tonight I could see that something had happened. You'd made up your mind and I couldn't reach you, I couldn't talk to you the way I should have. It's always been like that. Always, ever since you were a baby. Not even then really. I never even saw you as a baby. For the first four years of your life I hardly saw you at all. I was fighting a bloody war while you and your mother . . . while you and your mother . . ." The voice was slurring now and the awful wheezing made the sound hard to catch.

"So, I don't know. I don't know anything any more. Except I do know that I'm sorry. I came to tell you that I'm sorry I hit you and I'm sorry for everything else. Everything. It has all been my fault and I accept it. I accept the blame. I just hope that one day you'll forgive me. Not now, but one day when you're a little older and you've learned a bit more about life and about people.

"Now I'm going to bed. But for the first time in a very long time I'm going to kiss you goodnight. I don't care whether you're asleep or awake. I suppose it doesn't really matter."

Palmer heard the chair move, then the smell of the beer became strong and sweet and curdly in his face.

With time to think and to calculate and to understand the importance of his act, he turned his face then his body away to the wall. The smell and the breathing receded quickly. After a long, long silence, the footsteps retreated and the door closed quietly.

Palmer shuddered and came alive to his surroundings again. Solomon's walk had slowed until one unshod hoof just passed the other and no more. The horse shook its head as Pal pulled lightly on the reins, resenting the interruption to its dozing. As it did, half a dozen flies broke from the long fringe of hair between the ears and returned again just as the movement ceased. Palmer took off his brown felt hat, shook out the tiny twigs and leaves from around the crown, and wiped the sweat from his eyes with the sleeve of his shirt.

Then he dismounted and bent under the horse to tighten the girth which was hanging loose beneath its belly. For the chase the saddle had to be firmly secure. There was nothing quite like the stark terror of a rider whose saddle was slipping over the withers of a galloping horse. The harder you pulled on the reins the further forward on to the neck the saddle rode. Then, in panic, the horse put its head down and bolted while you inched forward inexorably, all balance gone and the hard ground with broken logs like jagged rocks waiting to tear into you.

As he grabbed for the strap, the sharp pungent odour of the sweating horse met his face and the warmth of its hide touched his cheek. It was a living thing. After a while, working in the paddocks day after day, you tended to forget. He had never found any of the animals—horses or dogs—to be the idealised "mates" of the old bush. He never thought of them as being company in the long hot days in the paddocks. They were just there. They had a job to do and they did it only passing well. It might have been different in the old days, but he doubted it. The legendary dogs by tucker boxes and the faithful hounds who waited outside the pub doors to lead a drunken master home belonged with the Black Beauty set. The stories were about on a par.

The presence of the animals had, if anything, the opposite effect upon him. They gave him a sense of aloneness, of loneliness that came sharp and chilling in the insect-ridden heat of the bush day. It was harder then, more forceful than at dusk when he walked alone in the horse paddock or climbed the windmill by the house dam and watched the bats flit erratically through the dusky red light. That was a melancholy time when the earth itself and all the things upon it stood separate and alone, neither revealed nor concealed but insubstantial and disconnected. He felt a kinship then even with the lonely milker boxed in the rough stall away from her calf or the small herd of "killers"—worn-toothed wethers—that drifted ceaselessly around the horse paddock somehow aware that yet again one of their number was gone and the odds were closing in on each of them. In the twilight, as the red deepened and died, such crazy personifications were believable and comforting and infinitely sad.

But in the glare of noon the aloneness, the loneliness was somehow more bare, more naked, more vivid and inescapable. And the presence of the animals made it worse.

Strange the way such a small thing as the smell of a horse's hide could trigger a whole chamber of emotions and memories. Or perhaps it was the memory of his parents and the irrational flush of guilt he felt whenever he thought of them that had brought the loneliness in its trail. But with the sense of aloneness there was now another sense which followed so close as to be almost a part of it, an antidote taken even as the poison passed down the throat and into his system. Perhaps he had induced the one only to enjoy the other more.

Adele. No, not just Adele but Adele and the little play. Even more: Adele and the little play and Marcia, her daughter.

Palmer swung into the saddle, his off-side boot dropping automatically and precisely into the stirrup. He turned Solomon off the rough track by the fence and into the paddock. The dam was only a quarter of a mile away now. Until he reached it he would treat himself to a fine consolation. The loneliness would whip away on the darting swirl of a willy-willy. He chuckled to himself. It was gone already.

When he had arrived last night the huge lounge room of the Baggett homestead was already crowded. Usually he hated to arrive late and enter a full room but this was different. Tonight he was a celebrity and as he came in there were one or two good natured shouts from the men and smiles from all the women. Humphrey Baggett came over to him his hand extended and a wide happy grin pushing his cheeks up to meet the bushy white eyebrows.

"Hello, young Lingard. Come in, come in. We've been waiting for you."

He took the hand firmly. It was the fleshiest part of Baggett's cordlike frame; fleshy, and surprisingly soft, moist with the warmth of the evening and the crowded room.

"Where's Boss? Isn't he coming to hear your work of art?" Baggett threw his bony chest out and laughed to the room. Boss had never been back to the monthly play readings since Aunt Caroline had died but each time Baggett forced a reference to it, finding some obscure consolation in his own cultural magnanimity, his concession to the arts, to the finer things. It raised him, quite literally, above the herd.

"No, not tonight. Sorry I'm late. We were dipping sheep and Boss wanted to get it finished." Though untrue, it was an effective rejoinder. In the district, long hours and hard work were at the summit of social values and were the subject of as much boasting and as many lies as sexual prowess in other circles. Baggett dropped the subject.

"Anyway, you're here now. Don't suppose you'll break loose and have a drink, will you?"

Palmer smiled and turned away. His abstinence was common knowledge and in that community a source of mystery and distrust. It set him apart and inhibited the easy camaraderie available to others.

106

Mrs Baggett poured him a soft drink from a small table loaded with every kind of drink imaginable, from cherry brandy to vodka to schnapps and even a magnum of warm champagne. The only drinks he had ever seen served were scotch, rum and beer.

Palmer looked around the room. He had been aware of them from the moment he entered—Adele sitting on a long divan with the junior Tom Reed, whose father's place was probably the best in the district, and the new jackeroo from Stoney Creek, Parkinson's place, and, on the other side of the room as far away from her mother as she could get, Marcia Champion deep in a lounge chair with Roy Conybeare sitting on the arm peering down her ample cleavage over the top of his whisky glass.

Adele's eyes were on him and he smiled. She had been in the act of disengaging herself from the young men as his glance touched her and their eyes held as she walked the few steps across the room towards him. She was a finely built woman, unusually so for a grazier's wife, and tonight she was in black, which set her even further apart from the others. Over her shoulder he could see Mrs Wardle in a garish floral which billowed around her wide hips and seemed to be creeping like a live thing over the spindly legs of little Harry Simpson, Baggett's manager who was squeezed into a corner of the sofa. The picture made a fine contrast.

"Hello, Palmer. How do you feel? Nervous?"

He grinned. "Nope."

"Really? I'm surprised. I know I would be if my first play were being produced." She smiled.

"You can hardly call a play reading a production. And it's not even a play anyway, just a dialogue. In fact I wish you hadn't talked me into it. I don't feel nervous: I feel like a bit of a bloody idiot."

"Now don't be silly. It's just nerves, opening night nerves. You wait; they'll love it. Do you know your words?"

"I ought to."

"Well, you've got nothing to worry about, have you? Where's Humphrey? I think we ought to begin."

"I don't know. Maybe he went out the back to get some ice or something. Anyway, there's no need to rush. Let them have another couple of drinks. It'll loosen them up."

"See, you are nervous. Don't be. There's absolutely nothing to be nervous about. You wait. They'll love it."

"So you said." He was now thoroughly nervous. "Where's Mr Champion . . . I mean, John? Didn't he come tonight?"

"That's better. I've told you, he prefers you to call him John. He doesn't like to feel like an ancient either." He smiled over her shoulder at Marcia who had started towards them from the other side of the room. Tom Reed, who was probably his best friend in the district, was also headed their way.

". . . No, I don't know what's wrong with him these days. He said he had some book work to do but really, book work! He can do that any time. Do you think he could be jealous?"

Before he could answer, Marcia joined them, then Tom came into the circle.

"Who's jealous?" Marcia said.

"Hello, Marcia. G'day. Tom." They shook hands. "Richard Brinsley Sheridan, Bernard Shaw and Arthur Miller, that's who. The first two are turning in their graves and the other one . . . well, I hate to think what he's doing. Marilyn's probably trying to take his mind off it."

"As only she knows how," Tom chimed in.

"Now, now, you two," said Adele, suddenly the mother of an eighteen-year-old daughter again. She glanced sideways.

Marcia caught the look. "Really, mother . . ."

"Marcia . . ."

". . . all right, Adele. But you carry on as though I'm a child . . ."

"All right, all right dear. But with these two young rogues you can't be too careful. Now," she turned away and Palmer took the opportunity to touch Marcia's hand, half consolingly, half flirtatiously; he wasn't sure which he felt the more deeply ". . . where's Humphrey Baggett? We must get started . . . get the show on the road, eh?" She smiled confidentially at Palmer and walked away through the crowd.

"Do you know your part, Tom?"

"No, I'm sorry, old son. I hardly had a chance to look at it. We've been working cattle all week and I've been so buggered—s'cuse me Marcia—that I haven't been able to keep my eyes open."

"Not to worry."

"But I've read it though. I think it's really first rate. I don't know much about these things but I think it's bloody good—s'cuse me Marcia."

"Tom, for God's sake will you stop excusing yourself. You sound like my mother."

"Steady on."

"Well you do, doesn't he, Pal?"

"Well . . ."

"Anyway I've read it too, even though I haven't got a part, and I think it's wonderful. Truly. And I'm not just saying that because it's you."

"Well, I don't think it's exactly wonderful."

"'Course you do," said Tom. "Where did you get the idea?"

108

"Yes, I've been wondering that too. It must have been when you were with that shearing team. Did anything like that actually happen?"

"Something exactly like that."

"You mean," Tom said, "that you actually heard of these blokes bribing abos with kangaroo meat? A black gin each for a leg and a tail?"

"Actually they wanted two each but the old gin wouldn't be in it. They settled for one a piece."

"Ah bullshit—s'cuse, I mean, I don't believe it. Hell, Palmer this is 1960. Those things don't happen any more."

"I was there, Tom."

"Where?"

"I was there." He looked his friend in the face. "I was there. I was the first. I won the bet."

There was a movement at the end of the room. "Okay, all right, ladies and gentlemen. Could I have your attention please." Baggett paused for silence, then for effect. "From the company that brought you *School for Scandal, The Importance of Being Ernest* and *Master Dudley, the Maiden's Delight*—the Morgandale Players—we are now proud to present the World Premiere," a few chuckles filled the pause, "of a hitherto unknown play by a hitherto unknown playwright . . ."

Palmer smiled at the memory and pushed aside a sandalwood branch with his forearm. The play reading had been atrocious. Adele's black gin had the accent of a nigger minstrel playing Scarlett O'Hara and Tom had recited his lines with all the animation of a fence post. Then, when he and Tom had dragged off the McIntyre twins to the kitchen to rape and beat them, the two girls had giggled so much he had actually felt tempted.

But at the end, when there were just he and Tom left in the centre of the room which they were using as the stage, trying to pretend it had all been a game but unable to look at each other, unable to throw off the sickening truth of their actions, the audience had been quiet and totally attentive. He didn't want that feeling to end. They were caught up in it and he had felt their emotions changing and swaying and following his words in time with the rhythm of his voice and the strength of his own feelings. It was a fine, good moment. And when he stopped they stopped too, knowing it was the end but prepared to let it go on if he chose.

Then they had clapped and laughed at themselves and shaken it off. Humphrey Baggett had clapped him on the back and hidden his embarrassment in extravagant praise.

Palmer pulled gently on the reins and Solomon stood still. Through

109

the trees the horsehoe-shaped earthen dam was visible directly in front of him. The area around the dam was lightly timbered—a patch of belah and sandalwood breaking on to a stretch of open country for a hundred yards, then more sandalwood getting thicker until it merged into a heavy growth of brigalow. The branches of the brigalow were stiff and the black trunks hard as iron. If they were around the dam he had to head them before they reached the brigalow. Once in there he couldn't get above a trot. The trees were packed together three and four yards apart, becoming denser the further you went in and, while it would slow a horse and rider, the cattle could keep up a fair pace.

He had to head them on the left and push them through the belt of belah which ran nearly to the fence line he had ridden earlier in the morning. Once they were out on the fence line the dogs would keep them moving towards the home paddocks and the big stockyards by the homestead gate.

There were no cattle on the red earthen mounds of the dam or by the water and his eyes searched the shade of the surrounding trees. By noon they would be resting, perhaps even sleeping in the shade. He called the dogs behind softly and they obeyed reluctantly. They could smell the water.

Still there was no sign of them. He urged the horse gently forward and its ears pricked up in anticipation. Its head lifted and he could feel a new mettle in its walk. But still nothing.

He pushed the whip handle further into its wire holder then swung around quickly to check that his saddle bags and quart pot were not twisted around and sticking out. The crickets had fallen momentarily silent. His head moved steadily from left to right. They had to be there. But if they were, he was damned if he could see them and by now he was only thirty or forty yards from the dam.

He stopped the horse again. Bugger it. There was nothing there, not even a stray sheep. That was all there was to it. He'd build a fire and make some tea and eat his bloody sandwiches and fuckingwell ride home again.

The dogs too had stopped and were lifting their heads then dropping them, panting in the heat but apparently alert to the silence and the tension of their master.

Suddenly, about sixty yards to his right in the line of sandalwoods there was a harsh crackling sound as an old scrubber bull reared to his feet and lumbered against the tree beside him. In the next moment other shapes appeared, moving jerkily up and forward, gathering towards the old bull, then, as he moved away, scattering in small groups—two cows and their calves, a heifer and three young bulls, another cow in calf.

Pal swung the reins over and kicked both heels into Solomon's

110

flanks. The horse leapt forward into a hard canter then a gallop in four strides. The two dogs broke to left and right, racing to flank the mob then dashing back to scissor across each other's tracks, barking with a mad excitement and frightening the cattle even more.

In thirty yards Pal had picked his marks—the young heifer and one of the bulls that had run with her. They had cleared the sandalwood and a small stand of belah and were galloping across fairly open ground heading for the brigalow. If he could keep up his pace he would round them just before the heavy scrub.

Pal took one hand off the reins and yanked his hat down harder. He stood in the stirrups with his seat not touching the saddle. As he bent over the horse's neck, Solomon spurted forward in response.

There was a hard thrill at the base of his throat as he set a new course every ten yards to meet a new combination of hazards. They leapt a fallen log and the small branches of a sandalwood tree slashed across his face, blinding him momentarily. He ducked an overhanging branch then leaned hard left, his knees pressed tightly to the saddle flaps urging the horse to go with him. He was welded to the animal and they flashed between the trees, moving and counter-moving, calculating distance and angle, each anticipating the other as the space between them and the cattle shortened. Forty yards, thirty-five, thirty. The scrub was thickening but they were almost there.

The brigalow loomed up on his left quarter but there was no slackening of pace. He kicked again and as he did so the horse swerved slightly and unexpectedly. His knee struck a tree trunk and the force of it righted him in the saddle. He kicked again, pushing the horse forward between two saplings. The cattle were aware of him now and they seemed to increase their speed. In twenty yards, in three or four seconds, they would hit the brigalow. He had to turn them first. Above the wind in his face he could hear their breath burst out of their guts as their forelegs pummelled into the ground.

He was on them. The heifer shied away at the first line of brigalow and Solomon, still at full gallop, followed the beast, suddenly unaware of his rider, suddenly caught in the training that had become instinctive, to spin the beast around, to turn it.

Pal saw the blackiron trunk of the brigalow rushing at him for just an instant. . .

His first thought was that it was sheep's blood. The blood, the gushing of blood from its throat as he sawed with the knife, trying desperately to cut through the wool and slice the exposed windpipe. His hands were slippery from the sweat and blood and his arms, his whole body, was shaking with the strain and hatred and terror of that first killing. The warm body of the sheep struggled under him and he stabbed at the throat, missing by inches then piercing the animal's

111

jaw. The knife stuck and he could hear himself sobbing as the sheep bucked and kicked out of his slipping grasp, trying to stand, its legs flaying back and forth across the cement slab at the base of the gallows, scratching the cement in a panicked search for some crack or groove, some leverage.

Then it rolled and found a foothold, sliding out of his grasp as he crawled then ran after it on trembling legs, falling on it as it reached the homestead dam, his hand scrabbling over the earth and finding a rock and smashing it down, smashing again and again on the sheep's head until the blocd spread all over him and all over the earth.

Slowly and dimly he became aware that the blood was his own. It covered his face and his hands and when he rolled on his side the stain seemed to follow him so that wherever he looked, whatever part of himself he could see, suddenly became covered in it. It was in his eyes, blacking out part of his vision when he turned his head.

He lifted a hand to wipe it away but stopped as the thought reached him: there was no feeling in his head. There was no point of reference. There was nothing to touch there, a strange frightening space in his awareness. His hand would pass straight through the place where his head had been and that would confirm the horror that jolted into his consciousness.

But he knew it and if he knew it he was thinking and if he was thinking it was with a brain. I think; therefore I am. It struck him as ironic and amusing. He must remember that. I think; therefore I am. Fred the frog. The cartload of frogs.

Wherever he was, he was there. He was alive. Alive and kicking like the kangaroo.

The kangaroo swam in the waterhole and kangaroos can't swim. He was sitting on his horse just back in the bush from the waterhole and he could see Rankin the overseer with the branch of a tree pushing and frightening the kangaroo back into the deep part of the little billabong. Pushing it back and laughing with his broken teeth and his idiot's eyes and his beak like a crow's beak. Pushing it back and laughing at the sick coughing sound from the animal's throat as the water lapped around its straining neck and seeped into its nose and throat. Laughing, as its small paws broke the surface of the water and beat it into little ripples. Laughing, as a fine red haze covered Pal's eyes and he spurred his horse out of the bush and at the overseer; then falling quiet for the fight that lasted for as long as Rankin could stand, lasted until his hard, wiry frame went slack and the blood around his mouth ran down his cheek. Lasted until his guts came up and he spewed into the waterhole and the sun beat down and dried the laughter out of him and dried the kangaroo.

A dog was beside him making a whining noise, a gentle sound,

112

gentle and painful at once, the sound an animal makes when it is confused and unsure and apprehensive. It licked his hand then sneezed and shook itself, clouding its aura with auburn dust.

The dog's face was above him so he must be lying on the ground. The sun was glaring into his eyes and his hat was missing. He couldn't feel his hat. But then he could see it by moving his head sideways and when he did, his cheek and his ear became sticky and warm. He jerked away from it, thrusting an elbow back to support himself and pulling his leg up towards his chest in one half-movement before the pain slashed into his leg just above the ankle and he screamed.

The pain snapped him instantly to full consciousness. The sun was burning his face and as he squinted the dried blood on his cheeks pulled at the skin. Fresh blood traced new courses down his forehead and he felt it gathering in his eyebrows. Cautiously now, he lifted a hand to his face to wipe it aside and some flies, disturbed by the movement, left his hand and his face and whirred around his eyes, landing again almost as soon as the movement ceased.

He remembered the chase, galloping between the trees. That meant his horse was somewhere around but he couldn't see it. He was in Moonlight. He had been chasing scrubbers. It was Sunday. He was somewhere in Moonlight. He had ploughed into a tree head first and when he fell his leg must have caught in the stirrup. He didn't know how far he had been dragged or even if he had been dragged at all. Probably not. If he had, his clothes would probably have been torn off him and he would have scraped away more skin.

His leg was beginning to throb and the pain shot the full distance from his ankle to his groin and made him gasp. But still there was no pain in his head, no feeling at all.

He seemed to be existing simultaneously on two different planes. He could see his body and feel the agony of the leg which was obviously broken. He could see the blood caked all over the front of his shirt and feel more of it trickling down the side of his neck. He could feel the sun and the earth and the flies and know that he was half-sitting, half-lying somewhere in a 7000-acre paddock with no horse and no way to get home. He could see it and feel it and know it, but another part of him refused to accept it. It was almost as though the whole phenomenon was presented for his observance, not to be acted upon but merely observed from a small but impersonal distance.

He stayed quiet and still, trying to mesh the two planes, forcing himself to an awareness of all the elements, knitting the physical back into the mental and the emotional, watching half-mesmerised as a dog—which one was it: Charley?—trotted back and forth on an arc within his vision barking at him, single barks which demanded

113

attention, emotionless barks neither angry nor threatening. Barks.

There was a dark cloud just above his vision, a solid dark cloud fringed at the top with bright gold and only by force of will could he keep it from descending.

The pain was more vicious now and was spreading up the right side of his body. He had to move. It was imperative that he move. He pushed the ground behind him with his hands and sat upright. For a moment the cloud threatened to envelop him but he forced it away and leaned back panting against the tree trunk. Now he must think.

Boss and Ritchie knew he was going out today, but did he tell them where? No, he didn't. They knew his habits and they knew he liked to ride in Moonlight. But it would be hours before they missed him and came looking. Perhaps all night.

He turned his head and saw the dam then, just over the earthen wall, the pommel of his saddle. His horse, Solomon, was there drinking in the dam. Christ. All he had to do was catch the horse and somehow get himself into the saddle. The horse would find its way home. But first he had to stop the bleeding from his head. That was imperative. Imperative. A good word. Think of it. Concentrate on it.

But how? How would he stop the bleeding. He needed a bandage. He should wash it in the dam then bandage it. His shirt, obviously. He would pull his shirt off, tear it into strips, then bandage his head with it. Then he would catch the horse and ride home. Perhaps he should save part of his shirt and make a splint for his leg.

He looked around among the gnarled brigalow roots for a straight stick. There was none. But there was a thick branch about five feet long which had apparently been broken off as he smashed into the tree. If he could crawl over to it and strip away the leaves and twigs it would make a serviceable crutch. Yes. That would be the beginning. The first imperative.

He waited a little longer, gathering his strength, then moved away from the tree, dragging himself backwards towards the branch. One leg was free of pain but he discovered that when he tried to move it and push himself back with his heel it twisted the bones of the other leg, multiplying the pain a hundred times and tearing the breath out of him.

Instead, he relied on his arm and shoulder muscles and he made progress. The branch was only five yards away but the ground was rough and each movement brought another stab of agony. Also the bleeding from his head, which seemed to be coming from high on the forehead near the hairline, came faster and flowed down into his eyes and he had to wipe it away with every new movement.

The dog, he noticed, had stopped its barking and was crouched forward, its front paws extended, its eyes following each move. He

114

could no longer see the saddle over the dam but he would have noticed if Solomon had left. Having some plan, some aim, had also brought him the concentration he needed and he was conscious that his thinking was becoming clearer.

Then his hand touched the branch. Solid brigalow. It should take his weight.

After another short rest he stripped away the twigs and smaller branches. As he worked he became aware of a high-pitched noise in his head, like the sound of the buzz saw behind the shearing shed when they were cutting firewood; as the teeth bit through and they pulled the block away, it often broke unevenly and just touched the tempered blade creating a very high note, the ping of a silver bell, still audible when the next length of timber hit the rasping steel teeth. But now the sound stayed at its peak, a deathless high chime, a tone. If he ignored it, it would go away.

The branch was clean now and it would do. He positioned the thick end under his right armpit and swung his left arm around behind the tree trunk gripping it. He took a deep breath. If he pushed himself backwards with his good leg, the tree behind him and the makeshift crutch would force him upwards. Gingerly he bent his left leg until his boot had found a partly exposed root which would act as an anchor against the inside of his high riding heel to give him leverage.

Then he pushed. His broken leg twisted in the movement and the black cloud was again fringing his eyes. The pain was like a blow in his stomach but he fought it off. He was clear of the ground. One more solid push would do it. He strained again and this time he was ready for the pain and he held on grimly to the tree behind him, the crutch under his right shoulder providing an additional balance. He felt light-headed and sick but at least he was upright. Now all he had to do was cross the sixty or seventy yards to the dam. Just seventy yards. It might just as well have been seventy miles. There was no way he could do it.

But what was the alternative? If he stayed where he was he would probably bleed to death.

There was just one other chance. The dog's eyes were still fixed on him.

"Charley," he said. His voice was like the scraping of iron sheets. The dog came forward. It looked eager, pleased to be spoken to. He looked over to the dam. Solomon was still standing by the water but his head was up and he was staring back at him. If he did it quietly he might just get the dog to round the horse and drive him back closer to the brigalow. If it came within ten or fifteen yards he would be able to catch it.

"Charley," he said again but softly this time. He lifted his arm, pointing towards the dam and the horse: "Get-a-way-back." Again his voice was quiet, just above a whisper. The command registered but the dog hesitated.

More firmly, "Get-a-waaay-back." The dog whirled and at the same time spied the horse. It raced towards the animal, charged at it, yelping wildly, bounding over itself and momentarily losing its footing in its eagerness to obey.

Solomon retreated a few steps then turned in fright and cantered away. The dog pursued it, the mad yapping echoing back to Palmer as they disappeared into the bush.

"Oh Christ," he said. "You dumb, fucking bastard. You fucking, dumb bastard." The curses interchanged and became a litany before the anger passed.

He saw them once more. The dog had turned the horse and it came galloping back past the dam but now it was headed west towards the centre of the paddock, the dog still barking and occasionally jumping to snap at its shoulder.

Now there was no choice left. He had to reach the dam. Sooner or later someone would check the dam. And he was thirsty. Suddenly his mouth was parched. The high-pitched sound was back again, louder now and insistent. He was aware too of another sensation. There was an ache at the base of his skull that was spreading forward and driving into him. He tried to relax, to let the pain beat at him from a distance, but it was no use. It grabbed him and squeezed.

He had to move or he would fall over. He squeezed his eyes shut then took a step. His balance was precarious but he remained upright. He stepped again, the end of the crutch thrusting into his armpit. Another step, then another. He wouldn't look up. No use discovering how far it was. With his left hand he clung to the trees to steady himself and to rest. He covered five yards, then ten, then fifteen. But the hobbling steps were becoming shorter, the rests longer. The blood was flowing rapidly again and he seemed unable to fill his lungs. Twenty yards; twenty-five. He was out of the trees now and though the ground was not so rough there were fewer supports.

Involuntarily, he glanced up at the dam. About forty yards to go. The crutch had broken the skin under his arm and it stung. The leg seemed to be going numb again but the sound of the saw was so loud he was becoming confused. Forty yards.

I think I can, said the little engine. I think I can; I think I can. It was his mother's voice. I think I can; I think I can.

Over the sound of the saw he heard a snap. It sounded more than anything like the crack of a breaking branch. Then on top of it there was a cry and it was cloudy and dark.

It was night and he and Tim were outside their hut having a good

116

long piss before going to bed. It was a cold night and steam followed the streams of water to the hard ground. He liked talking to Tim. He was a good listener and he spoke his mind. He was a Victorian farm boy with big meaty hands and a slow grin.

"Ah, that's good," he was saying. "Nothing quite like it."

"Tim, will you look at those bloody stars. Look at them. Christ, they're everywhere."

"Yeah."

"Really makes you wonder, doesn't it?"

"Yeah, I s'pose so."

"No, really."

"You mean that astrology stuff you were talking about?"

"Not exactly. Well, that too, I suppose."

"I can't buy it."

"Astrology?"

"Yeah. I mean, I know there's a lot of people who swear by it but it just doesn't seem possible that something so far away, some star, is going to have any effect down here. Not to me anyway."

Pal laughed. "Well, when you're standing out in an open paddock pissing on the ground it doesn't sound like much of a theory."

"Right."

"But there are so many beliefs. The Hindus and the Buddhists believe they come back to the world as insects and animals and Christ knows what."

"You never know, maybe they do."

"Come on, Tim, you don't believe that, do you? What are you going to come back as? I think you'd make a good camel."

"Ah, get stuffed. I didn't say anything about us coming back as animals and lizards. You said . . ."

"Oh I see. That's a thought. It's getting cold; let's go inside. I see what you mean though. The Hindus and the Buddhists have their reincarnation and keep going back and forth while the Christians—you Christians—have your heaven and hell; the Moslems have whatever Moslems have. A multi-faceted God."

"A what?"

"A multi-faceted God. Something for everyone. Made to measure."

"I didn't say exactly . . ."

"No, but think about it."

"Jesus, Pal, you're not going to get started on that again."

"Why not? What else is there, Tim? And it's possible, you know. It's possible that they're all right, all the religions. It's possible that this great Intelligence can accommodate them all. Do you see what I mean? For the western world Christianity might be the right, ah, prescription, the right formula, the best religion for their way of life. And for the others, with their different backgrounds and different circumstances, Hinduism or Taoism might fill the bill. Do you see what I'm getting at?"

"I s'pose so."

"I'm not talking about a personal, individual God. But something bigger, some great Intelligence . . ."

"Yeah. Well you could be right. But if we don't go inside in a minute my balls'll freeze and nothing'll help me then."

"Okay." Pal grinned. "Anyway, Queenslanders are okay."

"What's that got to do with it?"

"God's own country, my boy, God's own country."

"Ah, get out . . ."

But it is. Tim has gone away but it's important to tell him. Hector Bannerman knew. Hector Bannerman asked him to stay behind when the shed cut out; the last shed of the season. Hector wanted him to help him shear the dead ones and he agreed. How could the others refuse him? What did the man who made up the union rules know about eight years of drought? What did he know about a fellow human being, a man in his prime, no more than forty years old, who had watched while the Mitchell grass plains his father bequeathed him dried up and burned out, browned and blackened until not a blade, not a single blade, remained on 40,000 acres? What did he know about a proud man sending his wife to the city to get a job and support his kids while he paid off his stockmen, rounded up his sheep and walked them slowly down an endless track looking for feed to keep them alive until shearing. Walking them with dust in his face all day and the cursed bright stars at night.

Of course he stayed behind. And when they could, they plucked the wool out of the carcasses and stuffed it in the bales. As for the others, those that had died more recently, they sheared them with hand shears by the mudholes and in the wide paddocks and prayed, not for rain, but for a wind to take the stench away; the stench that was in his belly now, that would stay in his belly until he died.

Tim should know. Tim should have been there when the last one was done and the rolling black clouds from the northeast barrelled over the land and the rain tore into the dirt and washed the good soil into the river beds. He should have seen Hector Bannerman lying face down on the earth with the rain beating down on his back. He should have been there in God's own country then.

And now it's too late. He's gone with the fading stars and the fading sound of a high-pitched bell, the sound the old saw makes behind the shearing shed . . .

He opened his eyes. Marcia's face stared back at him. She was sitting on a chair only three or four feet from the bed. Then she and the chair seemed to drift backwards away from him, further and further, as though someone had put the wrong end of a giant telescope to his eyes. She appeared to rise from the tiny chair and her mouth was moving. She was coming back towards him, coming out of the tunnel of the telescope.

". . . get the doctor," she said and now she was moving away again out of his vision. The doctor. He must be in hospital. It was the bite; the snake bite. He remembered it very clearly.

They had made a pact. Whenever they saw a snake they would get off their horses and kill it. No matter where they were, what they were doing, alone or together. It was a pact; a question of honour.

And he hadn't let them down. When he saw the big brown he barely hesitated. It was his own fault that he had forgotten his piece of wire that flattened to the ground and broke the snakes' backs. He would use a stick the way he had many times before. There were plenty around in this part of the paddock.

The snake was aware of him and he ran around in front of it. You had to take them from the front. If you came at them from behind they could whip around and strike the full length of their bodies; throw themselves at you and bury their fangs into you from six feet away.

It stared at him, the blue forked tongue darting and quivering between its jaws. A big one. A vicious, disgusting, evil thing. His heart was drumming in his chest. The snake's head was six or seven inches from the ground swaying slightly, the eyes never leaving his, unblinking eyes. It was waiting; waiting for him to make a move; waiting for an opening, to strike or to escape, whichever presented itself first.

Then it began to move slowly towards him. He must be between it and its nest. He took a step backwards and crouched, his hand brushing the ground behind him for a solid stick, his eyes never leaving the snake's eyes.

There was a movement behind him. He glanced backwards just in time to see the strike. Another brown just like the first. Its mate. It struck for the wrist but he pulled back so quickly its fangs caught only his finger, his right index finger, and as he lifted the hand the snake came with it, attached to it. He couldn't shake it off. He screamed and screamed but it wouldn't let go. Then it dropped away and in a frenzy he trampled it, trampled its head with his heavy boot, twisted and mashed its head into the dirt.

The other was gone and he was coming to his senses. He had to get back to the house but first he had to cut the finger and let the poisoned blood run out of him. He pulled out his pocket knife from the leather holder on his belt and sawed into his finger. It bled. But he had wasted time killing the snake. The poison was in his system and he had to get back. He leapt on his horse and galloped for home. Jericho, the paddock they were mustering, was only a mile from the house and there were only two gates between. But by the time he reached it his arm was becoming heavy and aching and there were pins and needles in his neck.

Boss made a tourniquet just above his bicep and bundled him into the car. He drove one-handed. The other reached across to shake then to slap Palmer's face. "Stay awake," he shouted. "Do you hear me, boy, stay awake." The slaps were hard and they squeezed tears out of his eyes which stung. And then they were at Morgandale's tiny hospital and Boss was half-pushing, half-carrying him up the steps.

Doctor Barrett was standing over him, Marcia was beside him looking over his shoulder. "Palmer," the doctor was saying, "can you hear me?"

"It was a brown. I killed it . . . What's that sound? It sounds like the dinner bell. Is it dinner time?"

"Palmer, listen to me," the doctor said. "You've had an accident. You've broken your leg and we think you might have fractured your skull. Don't try to move. Stay quite still and just relax." The doctor bent over him and he could smell the man's breath.

"Accident?"

Marcia came closer. "Yes, Pal, don't you remember? The kangaroo shooters found you. They said you were dying. We thought we'd lost you. Don't you remember . . ."

Lost? The sound was becoming louder and they were retreating again down the tunnel. But he had to tell them. It wasn't he who was lost it was old John Harrigan, the cowboy. Didn't they know? Everyone knew. John Harrigan was the one. He was out there somewhere in Sticks and they were riding all through the night up and down the paddock calling his name and cooeeing and hearing the echoes rolling back from the ironbark ridges. And it was all his fault.

John Harrigan. A good man. A nice old man. Palmer met him at the gate the first day he arrived in his battered old truck. He liked him immediately. He had the kindly face of a part-Aboriginal and when he climbed out of the truck his head barely came up to Palmer's shoulder.

"Boss in?" he said.

"Yes, he's over at the house."

"What about Mrs Cunningham. She there too?" he spoke very rapidly.

"No, she's gone to town for the day."

"Okay, thanks. I'll go over and see him."

"I'll get a lift with you."

"Okay, jump in." He started the truck by touching two loose wires together. "You a Cunningham too?"

"My mother was. My name's Lingard, Palmer Lingard."

He nodded vigorously. "Thought you were. You've got the Cunningham look about you." It sounded like a compliment.

Palmer left him at the house gate and went around to the shed to paint neat's-foot oil on to some old saddlery. "See you later."

"Yeah, okay."

As he rounded the corner of the house he saw Boss walk down the path to the gate and shake the old man warmly by the hand. A little later the old truck started up and the two of them drove up past the house dam to the deserted shearers' quarters. Later Boss walked back alone.

Palmer intercepted him. "Who was that?"

"John Harrigan. Tell you about it later."

It was after dinner and he was sitting with Boss and Aunt Caroline out on the gauzed-in verandah looking out across the horse paddock. On their far left, beyond the dam, they could see a light burning in the shearers' quarters.

"He's had a lot of bad luck," Boss was saying.

"Most of it he brought on himself," Aunt Caroline said quietly.

"Well, that may be so. But he was a good man and a hell of a worker when he was young. He built that place up from practically nothing."

"Yes, and drank and gambled it away."

"Well it wasn't easy for him you know." He turned to Palmer. "You see, son, John Harrigan married one of your aunt's best friends, one of the Taylor girls . . ."

"Bess Taylor."

". . . Yes, and she's never quite forgiven him. His father was one of the early settlers down on the Moonie and, well, he married a half-caste and the Harrigans were a pretty wild bunch in those days."

"They would steal the horse out from under you, Clem."

"You couldn't say that about John though, could you? He was a cut above the rest. He worked like the devil on that piece of land. And he got no help at all from the Taylors. Not one of them ever went to see them or offered to help them out. Not one. And they lived through some pretty hard times. It's very hard to blame John Harrigan for what happened."

"What was that?" Palmer said.

"Well, during the wool boom things improved for everyone. Wool

121

was two hundred pence a pound and more. The Harrigans, I think for the first time in their lives—their married lives anyway—had money to spend. I think the trouble started when John bought a horse, a racehorse. He got mixed up with that bloody racing crowd and he started to hit the bottle a bit."

"More than a bit."

"All right, dear. And then he started punting and the outcome of it all was that he lost the property."

"It killed Bessie."

"I know that's what you think, dear, but you're not being quite fair. She had her share of it too, you know."

"Clem, she never touched a drop in her life."

"Well, if that's what you want to believe, all right, I won't argue with you. But anyway the point is that she did die—they said it was a heart attack—and John got all twisted up inside. He's spent a couple of years in mental homes but he's all right now. He's over it now."

"How long is he going to stay here?" Aunt Caroline asked.

"As long as he does his job. We're lucky to have him. He can stay up in the shearers' quarters. He can work as the cowboy, do the milking, clean up the garden a bit and he'll be able to help us in the paddocks at shearing time. He's a good man. He'll fit in."

Aunt Caroline looked unconvinced but she knew when she had said enough.

Palmer was glad. No one liked rounding up the milkers at the end of a long day in the paddocks or the yards, then rising half an hour before the others in the mornings to do the milking.

And Boss was right. Harrigan was a good man and he did fit in. He was quiet and he minded his own business but he was always the same—calm and unhurried and easygoing; and at the end of the day his work was always done. He was pleasant to everyone, even Rankin who obviously disliked him and called him "the Abo", but never to his face and never within Boss's hearing. In a month, he was spending most of his days in the garden with a smiling Aunt Caroline.

Then it was shearing time. He and Rankin and Pal were mustering Sticks while Boss and Tim worked another paddock.

They started early and at the entrance to the paddock, Rankin sent Palmer down one flank about two hundred yards from the fence line while he took the other side. He sent John Harrigan up the centre. They would meet with the sheep they had gathered at the back dam then one would drive them back down Palmer's fence line while the other two zig-zagged through the paddock looking for stragglers.

It was January and the heat burned into their backs. The dogs were tongueing even before they left the home paddocks.

When Palmer reached the back dam Rankin was waiting. He had

made a fire and they ate their lunch.

"Where is the old Abo bastard?" Rankin said again and again.

"Will you lay off," Palmer said finally. "Just lay off."

"Well, where is he?"

"He'll be along."

Harrigan arrived with a very small mob just as they finished. His eyes were glazed and he didn't answer for a long time. Finally he said, "I got a bit slewed."

"Well you can just turn around and go right back again. And this time try to keep your eyes open for some sheep."

"For Christsake, Rankin, he hasn't had any lunch."

"He can eat it as he goes along."

"Look, I'll go down the centre. Let him push these down the fence."

"He goes back down the centre and until you're the fucking overseer keep your fucking opinions to yourself. Now let's get moving. You take the sheep down the line."

He should have persisted. He should have found some way . . . If only the old man had said something. But he didn't. He just turned his horse around and started back into the paddock.

It was late afternoon before Palmer reached the entrance gate and Rankin was already there with a good sized mob. He seemed able to find sheep in the thickest scrub. Rankin took the mob home to get them yarded before sundown while Palmer waited at the gate.

After an hour he began to make forays into the paddock, returning to check the gate every ten minutes or so. Then he went deep into the scrub calling and cooeeing. The sun set and through the darkness lights appeared along the fence line. He rode towards them. Boss and the others were in the Land-Rover.

"Any sign?"

"Nothing."

"Do you want a spell?"

"No."

"Well take this. Your aunt's made you some sandwiches."

He went back into the thick scrub and called some more. A dozen times, a hundred, there was a movement in the bush ahead of him and he trotted towards it but as he reached it shadows played on the grey moonlit ground and the bush around him fell quiet.

He could hear the sound of more vehicles as the Parkinsons, the Baggetts, the Champions and the McIntyres joined the search. Many times during the night he was lost himself. The Southern Cross seemed to be darting all over the sky. But the lights and the sound of the Land-Rovers set the perimeters of the paddock for him and he kept moving. By dawn he was back at the entrance gate.

"Go home," Boss said. "Get some sleep and a fresh horse."

Other neighbours were at the house asking for instructions and offering help. He pointed them in the direction of Sticks and went inside to eat. He couldn't sleep. It was another day like yesterday, blistering hot with no wind and no moisture in the air. He rounded up all the horses in case they were needed and picked one for himself.

Boss was deploying a team of a dozen searchers.

"Is he still in the paddock?" Palmer asked.

"We don't know. There's so many bloody tracks around the gates that he could be anywhere. The dingo fence is down and he might have gone through into Parkinson's place.

"What do you want me to do?"

"You go into Moonlight. You know it as well as anyone. Take Tom Reed with you."

In Moonlight they crossed and counter-crossed, zig-zagging as best they could, up and down the paddock. Nothing. They met at the centre dam at lunchtime and fell asleep for an hour in the shade. Then they went back again, back and across, from ridge to plain, from belah to wattle where they had to dismount and lead their horses.

"If we don't find him today," Tom said, "I don't think we'll find him at all. Not alive anyway."

They saw nothing.

At night they joined the Land-Rovers. The search was extended across the whole property then into Parkinson's, another 30,000 acres of scrub and timber. Then, at dawn, they drove back to the house. But when they reached the main gravel road a quarter-mile from the homestead Tom trod on the brakes.

"Christ, look at that," he said.

"Look at it," Palmer breathed.

There, passing at a slow easy canter were thirty or forty riders, a small army, strung out in bunches down a hundred yards of road.

"I know some of them," Tom said. "The O'Tooles from Flinton, the Allensons, the MacDonalds. They're all from the Moonie. Word must have spread down there. God, look at them."

The rising sun lit the sheen of the horses' hides and flashed on the metal buckling and the silver spurs. The lead rider opened the wide homestead gate and they cantered through. Aunt Caroline had made a mutton stew in the outside washing copper and she fed them almost as soon as they dismounted.

"Yeah, we got word last night," one of the O'Tooles said. He had ridden forty miles.

Boss sent the Wilderwood team out mustering on the far side of the property away from Sticks. His eyes were sunk back in his head and

124

his big, gravelly voice was down to a whisper.

"Shearing's only a week away and we've got to get those sheep in," he said. "And he could just as easily be there as anywhere else."

When they returned that night they were sure he would be found. But though there were a dozen reports of lone riders seen and lost he was still away.

Boss went to bed. They were searching for a body.

Palmer stayed with the search. If he were dead, Palmer had killed him. The suspicion had grown to a certainty. If only he had persisted. If only he had told Rankin he was taking the centre line and they would fight it out in front of Boss at the end of the day. If, if, if.

His eyes burned into the dark shadows and the grey box trees rustled their leaves in the cool night and hid their secret places. The endless cooees answered each other and the wallabies ran dazzled towards the truck lights and veered into the barbed wire fences. Wild pigs grunted out of the high grass around the dams and ran squealing into the darkness. Palmer came back to his hut for a quick shower and when he opened his eyes it was midday and he was lying full length on his bedroom floor.

That day—the fifth day—they found him. He had spent every minute of the last five days in Sticks. He thought they were Rankin's men searching for him to berate and humiliate him, to take away his job. When they found him he was hiding behind a tree and they had to coax him to join them, to get into the Land-Rover and come home.

He could barely walk. He stared at them with glassy eyes. He showed no emotion when they unsaddled his horse and its hide came off with the saddle cloth. It had not been unsaddled for five days. He just stared at them.

But he was alive. He was found.

MORGANDALE District Hospital was at that time the best kept and, after the Grand Hotel, the best patronised establishment in the town. It was built during the boom years of the Korean War and it had become a symbol for the graziers and the townspeople, a link to that fine, heady time when money was no object, when homes at the Gold Coast and annual world tours were almost obligatory, when Mercedes Benz cars were as common as Land-Rovers (and occasionally used for the same work on the properties), when every property had a tennis court and every grazier's child went to school in Sydney or Melbourne.

Then, the hospital had seemed a necessity, a rightful convenience. Roma was seventy miles away from many of the properties and Morgandale only half that distance. The difference could save a life, the people said, and the state government—their state government—had reluctantly acquiesced.

Now, the world tours and the Mercedes and the finishing schools were gone but the hospital remained. And the people of Morgandale and district cherished it and cared for it with an intensity and a devotion far out of proportion to its intrinsic worth. Support for the hospital was the object of every street jumble sale, every tennis day at the remaining Morgandale courts and every picnic race meeting at the Tom Reeds' property. And when a local grazier won a major prize at the Brisbane Show for one of his sheep or cattle, his neighbours made it clear that a donation to the hospital was in order.

They rarely met the slightest resistance. On the contrary, there was an informal and unacknowledged competition among the property owners to surpass the donations of previous years. When Rolly Parkinson had won Grand Champion Shorthorn Bull in 1958, his donation of a full-sized X-ray machine had put everyone else to shame. It was immediately rumoured that Humphrey Baggett was planning to donate an electrocardiograph but nothing came of it except that everyone then believed the hospital was incomplete without the machine and Baggett's financial position was suddenly suspect.

And while the graziers made their donations, the townspeople contributed in their own way. Working bees were organised annually to give the building a new coat of paint. A roster was drawn up among

126

the men and women to keep the garden tended and the lawn outside watered. Several young girls of the town were pressed into service as nursing aides to the matron and two sisters who worked at the hospital permanently and lived together in a neat little house behind the small white building.

The hospital had ten beds—eight in an airy public ward, which was divided by white movable screens as the distribution of sexes demanded, and two private rooms. Next to the main ward was the operating theatre and beyond that the doctor's office and surgery.

In the beginning a doctor was stationed at Morgandale full-time but he was absurdly under-employed and the government insisted that, instead, one of the Roma doctors be asked to drive over for surgery three times a week and make himself available for any emergencies. The Morgandale hospital board agreed, not because the government had made its case but because they had quickly learned it was almost impossible to get a doctor to stay.

However, the new arrangement suited everyone. Roma hospital agreed that whenever possible the same doctor would handle all Morgandale's work and for the last two years the job had fallen to Dr Peter Barrett, a young man not long out of his residency at Brisbane General who had come west, he said, for the experience and independence, the autonomy a small community would provide.

The people of Morgandale and district liked him and he seemed to reciprocate the feeling. He was good looking, but not so good looking that the men distrusted him with their wives or daughters. He was pleasant and affable and he didn't act as though he was the sole repository of all medical knowledge the way other, older doctors had. He talked to them in down-to-earth terms and they understood and respected him for it. Perhaps more importantly, he was extremely competent. He very quickly became part of the community.

Matron Glassop and the sisters were respected too but in a different way. Unlike the doctor, who seemed to have more in common with the grazing community, they mixed mostly with the townspeople. They took a part, at Adele Champion's insistence, in the skits and songs and one act plays that made up the annual Morgandale concert in the Country Women's Association Hall. But usually they kept to themselves.

The Morgandale hospital was home for Palmer for four months after the accident. Looking back, he thought of them as good months, a creative and absorbing time, a watershed, somehow abstracted from the rest of his experience, cut off from the routines of living and decision making. At least until the end.

At first he was only half aware of the activity around him. Faces—Peter Barrett's, Marcia's, Adele's, Boss's—loomed into his vision, spoke a few words, then retreated. The sisters and the aides fussed around him, sitting him up, washing him, feeding him and every day changing the bandage on his head.

But as the days passed he was able to take notice, to understand and then to participate. When Dr Barrett arrived on the tenth day, he was sitting up staring out of the window of his private room looking down the main street of Morgandale, a gravel street so wide that people drove across it.

"You look a lot better today," Barrett said.

"Yes, I feel better. It's just that there's this bloody ringing in my head all the time. Makes it hard to sleep."

"I'll get sister to give you something at night. I wouldn't worry too much about it. It will probably pass."

"You know, doctor . . ."

"Peter."

"Peter, I thought a fractured skull meant they rang down the curtain."

"It depends on the type of fracture. In your case the skull had a hairline crack but, as far as we can see, there's no permanent bone damage. But you'll be here for quite a while. Unless, of course, you want to move to a bigger hospital in Roma or Toowoomba."

"No, no. Not unless you insist."

"I've thought about it. In the beginning I didn't want to move you. You never know what these roads might shake loose." Barrett tapped his head and grinned. "But now you've been progressing very well. As long as you don't fall out of bed, you should be all right."

"That's not really likely, is it?" Palmer indicated the arrangement of ropes and pulleys that held his leg clear of the bed.

"No, I guess not. Is the leg giving you much pain?"

"Not now."

"It was a nasty break. The bone came through the skin and I've put a window in the cast so that we can keep an eye on the wound, change the dressing and so on. You won't be riding any more horses for a while."

"That's no hardship."

Barrett looked surprised. "Really?"

"Well, I'm worried about The Place, of course. But I'm not sure I want to go back. Don't mention this to anyone, but I'm thinking seriously of going back to Brisbane."

"I see. Well, you'll have plenty of time to think it over."

"Yes. Peter, what about this noise? It never really stops. It's just that sometimes I'm more conscious of it than others."

"All I can say is: rest and relax. Try not to worry about it. I'll come and see you in a couple of days. In the meantime, I don't think you'll be bored." He grinned. "There's been no shortage of visitors."

"You mean Marcia?"

"Yes, and her mother. For a while they were both here. I couldn't get rid of them."

"I vaguely remember Marcia being beside the bed at one stage . . ."

"Yes," Barrett said. "Well, half your luck. I'll see you on Wednesday."

He was glad when Barrett left. The effort of talking had taken more out of him than he expected and he felt slightly dizzy.

Visiting hours at the hospital were as informal as the staff who administered them. But his three most frequent visitors—Marcia, Adele and Boss—knew the hospital routine and timed their visits accordingly. After some confusion in the first few days they fell into a regular pattern, each coming every third day, usually in the late afternoons.

Marcia was beside his bed five days after the accident when he first became fully conscious. She was there again the following day and the day after. And each time she had cried.

On the day after the doctor's visit, she pulled the high-backed visitor's chair over to the bed and laid her head on his chest.

"You're going to be all right," she said.

"Of course I am." His hand went down to stroke her light brown hair.

"God it's been terrible. No one's been able to sleep. Mother's been bitchy with me, and with Dad. We haven't done anything right since it happened. Why is she like this, Pal? Is she in love with you or something?"

He smiled. "No. I think she thought she might be losing a protégé and gaining a daughter."

"What do you mean?"

"I don't know. It was a stupid thing to say. I'm still a bit mixed up."

"No, you're not. What did you mean?"

"I suppose I meant that your mother seems to see me as good raw clay and she wants to have a hand in shaping it. And as for you, well, you don't know her very well, do you?"

"No . . . Yes . . . I don't know."

"You should."

"What?"

"Get to know her better. I think you'd make a great team."

"The Champion sisters?"

"Yes, it would have to be that." He grinned. "Perhaps you know her better than I thought."

"Perhaps. Anyway, let's not talk about her." She pulled her head back from his chest but her hand stayed on his stomach making gentle patterns on the skin. "Do you know what I thought about most when we thought you might be going to die?"

"No, what?" He was consicious of the hand. It was having two opposing effects on him. He could feel the blood gathering at his loins and at the same time the ringing in his ears was distracting him and beginning to hurt a little.

"I thought about that night at the Hannaford Beach Ball."

The Hannaford Beach Ball. He had taken her to the annual blowout at Hannaford's School of Arts dressed, like everyone else, in what they imagined to be the season's casual wear on the Gold Coast some three hundred miles away. He had driven the old flat-top truck and on the way back, ten miles from home, they had broken down. It was the kind of situation he had dreamed about and he had made the most of the opportunity. But at the last moment she had repulsed him and they had straightened their clothes and begun the long walk home. He still remembered Adele's frosty greeting when they arrived at the Champion homestead after dawn.

"What about it?" he said.

"I was thinking that if only I'd known what was going to happen to you, I wouldn't have acted like some Victorian schoolgirl on her first date with a man."

The buzzing in his ears was painful now.

". . . if you had died," she was saying, "just imagine how I would have felt."

"I wouldn't have felt too good myself."

"No." She paused. "What do you mean?"

"Well if I was dead . . . Marcia, I really don't know what I mean." The room was starting to spin. "If you don't mind, I think I'll have to have a bit of a sleep."

"Pal, I'm sorry." She withdrew the hand. "You look white. Shall I get the doctor or the matron?"

"No, no. I'm sorry. I'm still a bit wonky. Are you coming tomorrow?"

"No. Tomorrow's Adele's turn. I'll see you Sunday." She smiled from the doorway. "Don't die before Sunday, will you."

"I promise," he said. "I mean it."

By Sunday he was much improved. The buzzing was almost inaudible. But shortly after she arrived and just as he was working the conversation to the Hannaford Beach Ball again, one of the sisters opened the door and looked in. After that she was distracted and he was unable to re-establish the atmosphere.

He didn't try to push it. He knew it was paramount in both their minds and at the moment, with his leg trussed up to the ceiling, real progress was impossible anyway. There was plenty of time.

He was still smiling when Boss arrived. He was surprised. He wasn't expecting him until the following Tuesday. The smile faded instantly. Boss walked slowly into the room, his broad, bony shoulders slightly stooped, and sank into the chair.

"How's the leg?"

"Not bad. I think I'm on the mend. How are things on The Place?"

"We'll get by. I've taken on Jimmy Renneberg."

Palmer looked at him questioningly. Renneberg was a notorious drunk. He had worked as a stockman on many of the properties in the district but had left each job either when he had a big enough stake for a bender or when he had been sacked for drinking on the job. Palmer remembered the big cattle sale the previous year when he had driven a mob from Wilderwood and stayed over for the sale. He had found Renneberg on the third morning when he went to the stockyards to catch his horse for the ride home. He was lying flat on his back in the mud. Ants were crawling into his nose and mouth and the stench of vomit had attracted a horde of flies. Palmer had run to a tap, filled a bucket of water and hurled it over the man. Renneberg's lips moved. Palmer bent over to catch the words. "Rum," he heard. "Give me a rum."

Boss was defensive. "He's a good worker when he's off the grog," he said. "He'll do until you get back."

"That's going to be a while, Boss. The doctor says I'll be here for at least another three months. And even then I don't know whether he'll let me on a horse with this leg."

"Don't worry. We'll work something out."

"How about young Ritchie. How's he going?"

"The same. He still gets lost in the horse paddock." Boss tried to smile but it died in the making. "Son, there's something else."

"Yes?"

"You know I sent a telegram to your mother and father when this happened. We didn't know whether you'd pull through or not and I thought they should know."

"Yes."

"I expected your mother to be here practically the same day . . ."

"There was no need . . ."

"Maybe not, but at the time we thought it was pretty serious. Anyway, I got a letter from your father today that explains it. Apparently she's not too good."

Palmer was surprised. There had been no mention of any illness in her letters. He hadn't been home for nearly a year but at that time she had been as lively as ever. A bit thinner perhaps but she had never been a big woman.

131

"I got a letter from her a week ago," Palmer said. "She said they were stuck at the shop. Business was picking up."

"Yes, well it's nothing to worry about. As a matter of fact they aren't sure what it is. Probably one of those wogs women get."

"Why did Dad write to you? Why not me?"

"I think he didn't want to worry you. As I say, it's nothing to worry about. I just thought you ought to know. But don't mention it in any of your letters."

"All right, if you say so."

"When you get old like me, you can't keep secrets any more."

"Boss, don't give me that 'old' stuff again."

"You can't get away from it, son. I was just thinking the other day, they're talking about sending someone to the moon and when I was a youngster they were just inventing motor cars. Motor cars.

"I remember one time in Brisbane, it must have been about 1925, my brother Albert—your grandfather—made some money on one of his business deals. He always had some kind of deal in the wind. This one, I think, was in whaling . . ."

"Whaling?"

"Yes, he and some of his friends financed a whaling expedition—God knows how they did it—but it was a great success. When your grandfather got his share of the profits he went straight out and bought two cars."

"Two?" Palmer was caught up in the story, but at the same time a fear nagged at him. Boss was rambling. It wasn't his way. The old voice droned on . . .

"Yes, two cars. Two T-Model Fords; and he had them painted bright yellow. I was there and I remember following him from Queen Street down to Fortitude Valley with him and Dulcie, your grandmother, in the front and me with all the kids, your mother included, in the back."

"What happened to them?"

"What?"

"The cars."

"Oh, they went the way of all Bert's possessions. They just went. I wouldn't be surprised if he gave them away. Cars and houses were just like toys to him. He never grew up. But he had more fun, he got more out of life than anyone I ever knew."

Boss stopped, almost, it seemed, waiting for a cue to continue.

"He died before I was born," Palmer said.

"Yes, the Depression killed him. They were very hard times. He had to take the kids out of school, the two boys and your mother, and send them to work. I offered to help him out but there wasn't much I could do. We were struggling ourselves." He looked up again.

132

"It must have been a terrible time. My father's never spoken about it."

"Yes, it was bad. Not as bad as it's painted sometimes, but bad enough. Your grandfather lived through the worst of it and then one day he just keeled over, just as things were getting better.

"There was only one consolation. He didn't live to see his own sons killed in the war. Dulcie had to take that on her own. It must have been like the end of the world. I know it was for me when your Aunt Caroline passed away."

Boss's eyes were rimmed with tears. Palmer didn't know how to break the silence. He had never seen the old man like this.

Then Boss heaved a great breath and brushed the back of his hand across his face.

"I'm a bloody great hospital visitor, aren't I?" He smiled. "You see what I mean. I'm getting old."

"Never."

"Hah. It'll be no fault of yours if I'm not, busting yourself up and scaring the living daylights out of me. Now you just get yourself well and come back to The Place. It'll be crutching time soon and you'll have to get yourself some extra men."

"I will?"

"Yes. It's time you learned how to hire and fire. If you can drag yourself out of this hospital there'll be a manager's job waiting for you. I'm going to take a bit of a rest and let you earn your keep for a change."

"But Boss . . ."

"That's enough now. We'll talk about it next time." He picked up his hat from the end of the bed and waved it as he went out.

Palmer wanted desperately to call him back, to talk it out. He felt his stomach muscles starting to bunch and a sudden flash of pain in his head. But the tension passed almost immediately and the pillows were warm around him.

It was better this way. He would have time to digest it, to adjust to it, to decide once and for all whether he wanted to stay in the bush or return. There was no real hurry.

The news of his mother was disturbing, but with Boss in such a mood it was hard to know how seriously to take it. Her letters had been cheerful enough though they were not as easy to read as they had been. And it was strange that his father had written to Boss rather than himself.

No, it wasn't. Of course it wasn't. His father had hardly ever written to him. Palmer pushed the thoughts away. It would do no good to lie there worrying about it. He would start worrying when there was a good reason and not just some maudlin fear of Boss's.

But thoughts of his mother returned and plagued him into the night. Always in the past when he had thought of her it had brought with it a good feeling, a sense of belonging, a knowledge that no matter where he was or what he was doing she was never far away. It had been that way for a long time, but especially since he had left home. He knew instinctively what her reaction would be to any new situation. And he knew that whatever decisions he had to make, this knowledge was a sure guide, a benchmark.

In all the time he had been away, the images of her—serving in the shop, bending over the sink, smiling, saying goodbye—could be recalled at will. And whenever they came, the feeling of safety and security came with them.

Her letters had helped. The fortnightly letters and the packages of books which had followed him even during his months in the shearing sheds—classics, American potboilers, plays, detective stories, family sagas—they helped but they were only a small part of it. The images and the good feeling were there beneath the surface all the time.

But now there was something else: a disquiet that persisted. Finally he switched on his light and wrote a letter home.

Then he sank back into the pillows. Tomorrow Adele would come and he looked forward to her visits as much as Marcia's. It was hard to believe sometimes that they were mother and daughter. They were a study in contrasts. Where Marcia was soft and accommodating, Adele was sharp and challenging; where Marcia stroked and purred, Adele struck sparks. They had only one characteristic in common, an instinctive sexuality, intense and provocative and demanding a reaction.

In Palmer the reactions were almost equally strong but entirely different in character. Adele had a glamour, a worldliness that her daughter lacked and, because of her age and her marriage, an illicitness and the promise of experience. With Marcia there was a sentimentality, a taste of honey; but with Adele th rousal was as much intellectual as emotional.

From the beginning of his time in the hospital Adele had brought him books from the Champions' library. He read indiscriminately as he had always done. But now he found himself trying to understand the writers' techniques—how they built tension; how they made time pass without actually saying "two years later"; how they described things and people. But there seemed to be no set pattern, no universal measure. Each had his own method, his own style.

Adele's insistence on his writing the "play" for the performance at the Baggetts' had come, despite his protestations, from his own suggestion. He had encouraged her to encourage him. He now saw his deception and understood it; he had needed the protection of a pretence that it was all her doing, just in case it failed, in case they laughed at him.

But they hadn't laughed. They had been genuinely affected and that knowledge brought him more pleasure than he had known before. And, as his health improved, he felt building in him the desire, the need, to do it again. But it was a formless thing, a great impulse which lacked a vehicle for its execution. It wasn't only the memory of the play reading. Since the accident he had slowly become aware of something else, something more urgent and demanding yet more difficult to define or to understand.

It lay there underneath his thoughts and words. He was aware of its presence as one is aware of another person in a dark room. There was the same half-fear, the same uncertainty, the same power to threaten and alarm. It seemed not to be guiding him towards any specific goal but rather to be moving him unwillingly from the place he now held. Not unkindly, not forcefully, but with the seductive whisper of promise and the intimation of great strength. It was a spiritual feeling, yet it carried no sense of the religious, no mystical plateau of cool breezes and gentle rain calming the tortured soul. Rather, the opposite: the flurry and swirl of unleashed passion, the spearing pain of great loss, the magnificence of personal pride.

His knowledge of its existence he kept deeply to himself. Yet paradoxically it demanded to be shared without discrimination. It demanded an outlet. It demanded to be put on show, to be flaunted before an audience. It demanded that he express it and, through it, himself. The only means of expression he knew was to write. It demanded that he begin to write.

But that was the extent of it. No classic plots or powerful, visible characters burst upon his brain demanding to be captured and transcribed. No fine-sounding phrases, no sense of background and atmosphere, no sound of conflict. Just a Presence, a demanding thing, demanding with the promise of great reward.

"The problem," he told Adele the following day," is that I don't have anything to say that hasn't been said better by a hundred men before me. What do I know that the rest of the world doesn't know already?"

"It's not a matter of 'saying' something," she said. "You don't set out to lecture people. You just tell a story."

"What story?"

"Palmer, you're always telling stories about your time in the outback. That play . . ."

"It wasn't really a play."

"Well, whatever it was. They loved it. I told you they would. Think

135

of all the other things that happened to you out there. Call them what you like: plays, stories, anything. The important thing is to write it down."

"I don't know, Adele. Even if I could, that Old-Bush, Henry-Lawson, Banjo-Paterson thing is all right here—we understand about drovers' and shearers' wives and min-min lights, or at least we think we do, but that sort of thing means nothing to people in the city. Even if I did write them, who would buy the stories? And anyway, I think that Old-Bush business went out with lace-up boots. It's just not like that any more. Civilisation is upon us."

"Palmer, you just write the stories and leave the rest to me."

"You?"

"I'm not completely unlettered you know. I did have a passable education. I have seen a little of the world. I do know one or two people who aren't complete savages."

"Yes, of course Adele, I wasn't suggesting . . ."

"And no more argument. This is a heaven-sent opportunity . . ."

"Heaven-sent?"

"Yes, and you should grab it with both hands."

"But why me? Why me?"

"And now, Palmer, you're fishing for compliments that you don't need and you're not going to get. The plaintive cry from the young genius—why me, he gurgled, why me."

Palmer laughed. It was true.

"And now I'm leaving." She stood up. "I was planning a motherly peck on the forehead but since the forehead is swathed, you'll have to settle for this." Her lips brushed his cheek and her perfume filled his nostrils. She turned at the foot of the bed.

"The sister told me they're letting your leg down all day tomorrow so you'll be able to sit up in bed. When I come back I want to see this filled." She fished a foolscap writing pad out of her outsized shopping bag, placed it on his meal tray and blew a kiss.

An hour later he opened the pad at the first page. He stared at it. It was plain white paper with ruled blue lines. And it was empty.

He continued to stare and it continued empty, untouched. Unlettered, she had said: "I'm not completely unlettered." What did that mean? Unlettered, like the blank page. It had a nice delicate sound but did it mean anything? If the two negatives cancelled each other that meant she was lettered. Perhaps she was filled with letters the way pillows are filled with feathers. Of course it could mean that she had some letters after her name: M.A. perhaps. Adele Champion, Master of Arts. No better: Adele Champion, Mistress of the Arts. Much better.

Still the page remained empty. Now it mocked him, challenged and mocked him at once, dared him to touch it, to put himself upon it and give it life.

It sounded so simple. Just tell a story; a story of the bush, the outback, the shearing sheds. But what story; what sort of a story?

Well, he could always tell the story of Alan Brogan, the presser who wrote poetry. That was something . . .

The presser, the man who lifted great armloads of greasy wool from the bins into the bales, trampled the wool down into the corners of the coarse jute sack, then stacked and piled more on, trampled some more, piled some more, and finally engaged the heavy press lever and with the rhythm of abundant strength pounded and pounded the lever, forcing down the strong timber press-top and packing the wool into the bale. The presser, the strongest man in the shearing team, the middleweight champion of Julia Creek, the hardest drinker in the northwest when the mood was upon him, stacked his last bale for the day then strode back to his bare, temporary, impersonal room in the quarters to write long, lyrical poems about the flight of birds and the sound of clear water bubbling over smooth rocks. There must be a story in Brogan . . .

The empty page stared back at him.

But if there was to be a story there had to be some action. There had to be a beginning, some action, then an ending. Now that was a profound thought. A few more like that and he'd be right back where he started, which was exactly where he was. Christ.

But there *was* some action. There was that time in the Great Western Hotel in Hughenden when he and Brogan had been sitting on the high bar stools playing chess. They were between sheds. They had been in Hughenden for nearly a week and most of that had been spent in the Great Western bar. The chess helped to pass the time and he always won because Brogan drank beer.

Brogan never knew when he was licked. He always came back for more. But on this occasion he was in a good position. He was a knight and two pawns up and Palmer's queen was threatened. Brogan rubbed his hands together and chortled to himself. Palmer had made some stupid mistakes. He had to concentrate more. The bar was full and the noise was distracting.

Noisiest of all were the McWhirter brothers, two New Zealanders who both sheared left-handed and talked with loud, high-pitched voices becoming louder and higher pitched with each drink. They never listened, just talked.

Palmer made his move. The queen was out of danger now and there was a way he could win. Brogan frowned and stared at the board. Palmer watched his face and saw the change of expression as Brogan recognised the trap. His chin went down on to his hand.

137

"Hullo," said Dougie McWhirter, "what's this? The intellectuals at it again? Locked in combat, eh? Now let's see, why don't you jump him here, here and here." Some beer from his glass slopped on to the board. "Then you'd crown a king and you'd be able to come back again."

"Piss off, McWhirter," Brogan growled. McWhirter appeared not to hear.

"Or isn't it draughts. No, it can't be draughts, they aren't the right shape. Hey Ernie, what's this intellectual game these intellectuals are playing?" His brother joined the circle.

"I don't know," he said. "What's an intellectual?"

Palmer couldn't tell whether the movement was deliberate or whether McWhirter was pushed forward by the gathering crowd. Alan Brogan wasn't interested. As the chess board and pieces hit the floor he spun out of his stool and slammed a fist into Doug McWhirter's throat. McWhirter staggered back to the white tiled wall.

The bar erupted. Tough, active men bottled up in a town for a week suddenly found an excuse, a release. Old and new grudges were suddenly being worked off. The violence fed on itself. Palmer found himself in the thick of it and, at least partly because of his sobriety, well able to take care of himself. He jabbed and hooked lefts and rights at Ernie McWhirter who was starting to fold. He aimed a punch at a tall rouseabout called Pop-eye on account of his bulging thyroidal eyes and was in the act of delivering it when his wrist was clamped from behind.

Brogan swung him around. "Help me with these fuckin' pieces," he said. They crouched at the footrail, picked up all the pieces they could see among the feet and legs then pushed their way between the fighters out on to the street.

"We'll finish it at the Royal." The bar of the Royal was deserted. Word of the fight at the Great Western had reached there first.

For almost an hour they tried to reconstruct the game, but it was useless. Two bishops and three pawns were missing and they couldn't agree on the placement of many of the rest. Brogan picked up the board, tore it down the middle and tossed the two halves on to the floor.

"Fuck it," he said. "Elsie, give me a bloody beer . . ."

Palmer stared at the paper. It was inside him. That was a story, surely to God. If he just turned the "fucks" into "damns" or something and wrote it all down he'd have it.

He rolled the pencil around in his hand. He needed a beginning. All he could think of was "It was the best of times; it was the worst of times". Perfect, except that it had been used before. What was

138

another? He couldn't think. The quotation rattled round and around in his head: "It was the best of times; it was the worst of times." What was the rest of it? He couldn't remember.

Perhaps if he lay back and closed his eyes it would come to him, the perfect beginning to a story. "Once upon a time", he thought stupidly. "One time". That was more like it. Pithy. Very bloody pithy. "Once". Even pithier. It was impossible to concentrate . . .

The sister shook him awake. "You've got all night to sleep," she said. "First, have your dinner."

The page remained empty. It was still empty the next day when Marcia arrived.

She looked very pretty. She had obviously come directly from Mrs Moffatt's, Morgandale's combination seamstress, milliner and hairdresser. Her hair was teased out and combed high to give her several extra inches and to fine her rather plump lines. Marcia, Palmer thought, would be one of those women who spent much of their lives watching their weight. But at the moment there was no doubt it was extraordinarily well distributed. He had no difficulty in shutting out the story and concentrating on his visitor.

She was wearing a low-cut green frock which revealed the rounded tops of her large breasts and flared out from the hips, emphasising her comparatively small waist.

When she entered she pulled the chair over closer to the bed and smiled. "How's the patient today?"

"Surviving. How's his most beautiful visitor?"

Marcia dipped her head and her smile broadened. "No need to ask any more about the patient. He's obviously back to form."

Palmer answered her smile. "It's the effect you have on me. Why don't you come and sit here." He patted the bed beside him.

"What if matron comes in, or one of the sisters?"

"They won't. They're as regular as clockwork. They won't be here for at least an hour."

Marcia crossed to the bed and stood beside it. "What about your leg. I don't want to hurt your leg."

"My leg is terrific."

"Yes, I'll bet."

"No, come on." He patted the bed again.

"All right. Just for a minute. I suppose we have to humour you."

"Right. Humour me."

She sat on the bed and he took her hand.

"Now," she said. "What have you been doing with yourself since last time?"

"Nothing. Absolutely nothing."

"What's the writing pad for? Have you written home?"

"Not for a while. As a matter of fact I've been trying to write a story. Instructions from Adele."

"Really. How far have you got?"

"Nowhere."

"What's wrong?"

"Oh, I just can't seem to get started." He released her hand and let his own rest on her leg.

"Why don't you write a poem, the way you did that time, you know?"

He remembered the poem. Like all his poems, it embarrassed him to think of it. He had written it to Marcia in her last term at school. They had met two years previously but it was only in those term holidays that they had begun to go out together. When she had returned to school he had been overcome with longing and had written the poem, a long syrupy ode. The memory set his teeth on edge.

"Well, I might do that too," he said. "But at the moment I've been commissioned to write a story."

"I've still got it," she said. "I've never shown it to anyone."

His hand touched her knee under her dress. Her hand slipped unremarked beneath the sheet and played gently across his stomach. But this time there was no adverse reaction. His head stayed clear, his mind sharp.

"That's good," he said. "It was written just for you."

"What about all the other poems?" she said. "The ones you showed me. Are you going to have them published?"

"No," he said. "Some were published, you know, in *The Worker*, the union newspaper, when I was in the sheds. But not the others."

"You should."

His hand crept higher, inside her thigh now. She pretended not to notice.

"They were trash. 'The simple shearer walks to his stand'," he quoted, "'Takes his handpiece in a hard-knuckled hand, Removes the comb; brushes the sand. Is that what you see when you look down the line?' . . . It was doggerel, the kind of thing they lapped up out there. The only reason I wrote them was . . . as a matter of fact . . .'"

"No, I didn't mean those. I meant the other ones."

"Oh," he quoted again:

" 'In the warm stillness of evening,
When toil is but a memory,
I hear a distant melody,
A softly throbbing rhapsody,
And then from out the mists of thought,
You come to me, Natasha...' "

140

"Yes," she said. Her eyes were soft. "Who was she?"

"Oh, a girl I used to know."

Through the blinds which covered the window to the main street, slivers of fading sunlight edged into the room. Her full, ripe lips were slightly parted and she was breathing between them. His hand touched the outside of her panties and he felt her reaction.

"It's strange," he said. "I wrote that a long time ago. Since then I've hardly done anything. Except that shearing stuff and the one to you."

He was now totally aroused and as her hand brushed across his stomach it touched him. But instead of drawing away, the hand stayed in light contact.

"It was beautiful," she said again. He was hardly aware of her words. He pushed his penis upwards across the back of her hand and he felt her fingers pull back then curl warmly around the length of it. His own hand crept beneath the elastic leg band of the panties and moved forward into the moistness.

Slowly her head moved down towards his. His other hand went around her shoulders and drew her down to him. Her lips were soft and warm. His tongue went between her lips and he felt her hand tightening then beginning to move slowly up and down his hardness. One of his fingers was inside her and she opened her legs to accommodate a second.

Their kiss ended and she pulled her head back a little.

"Oh, Pal. We shouldn't. Something might happen to you."

"Don't be silly," he said softly. He felt her shudder as his fingers penetrated further, then push back towards him, back and then away and back again. The rhythm of her own stroking was increasing and he could feel himself beginning to lose control.

Suddenly the high-pitched sound was back inside his head, driving into his brain like a needle. But instead of distracting him, the pain became part of the experience, neither heightening nor lessening it, but staying as part of it. He pushed his pelvis upward again and another shaft of pain, from his leg this time, registered in his consciousness. His fingers fondled and pushed, withdrew and pushed again.

"Oh, Pal," she said. "Oh Pal, oh Pal, oh Pal."

"Christ."

He spurted on to his belly. He felt one moment of ecstasy then blackness, a close, suffocating blackness. Nothing.

He opened his eyes. It was just an instant later. She had fallen forward on the bed beside him, her face buried in the pillow. Her hand had released him and they were both panting in unison. He drew his own hand away and she shuddered again as he did so.

141

She pulled her head back from the pillow. Her new hairset was mussed across her forehead and there were beads of perspiration on the bridge of her nose.

"God, Pal. You look terrible. Are you all right?"

"I'm fine," he said. "Just fine." The pain in his head was gone but his leg was aching like the devil.

"We shouldn't have," she said.

"Don't be silly," he repeated. He kissed her again, a long sweet, satisfied, pleasure-filled kiss. Then they smiled.

"How long have I been here?" she said.

"Stay as long as you like."

"No, I must go."

The door opened and Matron Glassop entered. She had a sharp, lined face and thin lips. But her appearance belied a dry sense of humour. "I hope you're looking after my star patient," she said. "Not getting him too excited."

Marcia quickly stood up and stepped away from the bed. Palmer could see the glow of her ears from behind.

"No, no," she said. "I mean, yes, I have been looking after him but I haven't . . ."

"Yes, dear," the nurse interrupted, her eyes twinkling. "I know what you mean. Off with you now. It's time for the professionals to take over."

Marcia was almost through the doorway when she turned to say goodbye.

After dinner Palmer went immediately to sleep. The ache was gone from his leg and he was exhausted. Then suddenly he was awake again. His room was pitch dark. It must be the middle of the night still. He fumbled at the light switch. It was only 2.30 yet he was totally awake. The door opened and a face appeared.

"Anything wrong?" It was one of the sisters.

"No, nothing," he said.

He reached for the pad. Now, in the cover of night, it was perfectly clear. The story laid itself out in his mind. There was no need for a beginning, at least not the kind of formal, pedantic beginning that had been rattling around inside him for the past two days. No need for histrionics at all. Just tell the story.

"The presser was a poet," he wrote. Then scribbled it out. "Alan Brogan, the presser, wrote poetry. His mates hated him for it." Better. But if they were his mates, how could they hate him? Of course they could. Anyway, what the hell. It was true. If there were things that had to be corrected he could come back to them later. But first, get it down.

As he wrote, he felt it again—the Presence. It was as though

142

something had entered the room, had come to sit beside him, to watch over his shoulder and then to enter him, to go all the way inside, to direct his hand, to take him back to that time, to show him that bar and let him hear the sound of laughter, raucous, beer-stained laughter, to replay for him the words, to put lights on the high points and shadow on the dross.

He wrote as fast as his hand could travel over the page. But still he couldn't keep up with his thoughts. His mind was going too fast. He had to drag it back, to crank the inner mind, the Presence, in slow motion to give him time to finish the sentences. The pencil snapped and in a panic he scraped the light pine away from the lead with his thumbnail.

He covered two pages, then five, then he no longer bothered to count. He could smell the dust on the street between the Great Western and the Royal. He could feel the cool night air. He could see the cheap cardboard chessboard tearing unevenly and its separate halves floating to the floor, spinning and floating to the floor.

Even before he finished the writing, the story was ended in his mind which was racing on to other incidents, other stories. Images and words leapt at him. Conversations, part real, part fictional, jumped into his mind. He drew a line under the first and began a second. The title came first: "Christmas Dinner".

After the fight he had become friends with Ernie McWhirter. Perhaps because of it. They had travelled together in his Volkswagen from Cloncurry the two hundred miles to Urandangie on the Northern Territory border. But the day before they left, a Saturday, they had lost all their money in a pontoon game at the 'Curry's billiard saloon. Every penny. Thank God the car was full of petrol and they had some jerricans under the hood. That night they slept on the river bank with an old kangaroo skin fur for warmth. At dawn the next day they went to the local baker and asked if he had any stale bread he was planning to throw away. He gave them half a loaf.

Then on the way back to the river and the car they saw an old rattle-trap fruit cart, a Chinaman at the wheel. They hailed him and Pal tried to keep his attention as McWhirter sneaked around the back of the cart. But the Chinaman was suspicious and McWhirter had about two seconds to make his theft.

"I just grabbed the nearest thing," he apologised as the Chinaman's cart disappeared around the corner. He pulled out of his left pocket a beautiful red tomato and from his right an enormous onion. It was the best Christmas dinner, or if not the best the most hilarious, Pal could remember.

As he wrote, the taste of that tomato and the feel of the juice running down his chin was with him.

143

His pencil raced on over the white pages. The mockery had turned to servitude. He felt the power inside him, unlimited power thrusting him onward, pushing him along ahead of it, riveting his attention, all his senses and all his experience focused on the one bright, white page with the blue lines tending to his needs.

A shaft of sunlight suddenly caught and reflected on the page and he realised the day had begun. Sounds from the ward outside intruded and he heard the noise of a vacuum cleaner. But there was no vacuum cleaner in the hospital. They swept the floors. The hum was coming from inside him and it was becoming louder and flying up the scales until it was ringing, ringing like the sound the old saw makes, ringing and ringing and ringing.

He closed his eyes and dropped the pencil. It was fading again, but slowly, so slowly, like another sound of long, long ago . . . the air raid sirens over Brisbane were signalling the All Clear and he and his mother were climbing out of the bomb shelter in the backyard and he was running upstairs to turn off the bathwater. That was his job. He tried to reach the bath before the sound died and he never did. It was just too far away.

One of the girls came in with a little tub, some towels and a washer. "You or me?" she said. He couldn't remember her name. She said it every morning.

"I'll do it myself today," he said.

"Spoilsport." She giggled every morning too.

He slept. Then he took up his pencil and wrote again.

Boss came. Every visit was the same now. He would talk, first about The Place and the way they were making do until he returned. And then about the old days, the difficult times, the bad years when the rains stayed away or the floods ravaged the paddocks and smashed the fences on the creek crossings, or when bushfires had blazed on ten-mile fronts through thousands of acres of grassland.

He remembered sitting enthralled on the front verandah of the old homestead as Boss had told his stories in the past. But then there had always been a rough humour in them, a chuckle at the misfortune and some homely moral crudely drawn

Now the stories were overlaid with an awful melancholy. Boss seemed to tramp through them on heavy boots and even, Palmer began to suspect, to enjoy their sadness and their sense of unrelieved hardship. He seemed to be pawing over his life like an old bear with a piece of meat and finding only the maggots, the distasteful things.

Palmer no longer looked forward to his visits. Partly because of

144

the old man's mood but as much because he could feel himself drawing away from The Place. He no longer identified with it and spread his vision across it as though it were almost a part of him, the way he had ever since he had come back from the sheds. It was beginning to belong to his past. And much as he tried to drag himself into Boss's opening conversation, to fire his words with reassurance and enthusiasm, he was able to listen to his voice with a dispassionate ear and to hear the counterfeit in it. The realisation made him impatient with himself and with Boss for making him that way.

Adele came. She blew into the little room and filled it. When he had given her the writing pad, she handed it back to him.

"I can't read it," she said. "You read it to me."

"No. I'll write it out again when I have the time."

"And when will that be?"

"Today. This afternoon. Just as soon . . ."

"You mean just as soon as I get out of your hair."

He grinned.

"Say no more. Who are we poor mortals to interrupt the flow of genius?"

"Christ, Adele, cut it out. I haven't read it myself yet. It's probably terrible." It was a lie. He had read it and read it again. He thought the first story was magnificent; incomparable. He had wanted to have it rewritten but there were other things that seemed more pressing. His time in the sheds was crystallising itself into a series of incidents and major events that seemed to be following a pattern of their own. He had to take time out to transcribe his rough lettering.

On her next visit it was ready. He had spent the best part of two days in the rewriting and transcribing. He found that though it might have read well at first, there were a multitude of changes to be made. Small things: passive to active tense, indirect to direct speech. They were important. They added life and immediacy.

"I'll read it when I get home," she said when he handed it over.

"No. Read it here. I want to know what you think."

She took an interminable time.

He was staring at her when she finished.

"I don't know what to say," she said.

"Well for God's sake say something. Do you like it or not?"

"I don't know. I don't know what I think."

"I see." She must have hated it. It was amateurish, gauche.

"The next one might be better," he said.

"No, Palmer." Her voice was urgent. "I didn't mean it was no good. God no. It's just that I've never read anything like it before. It jumps out of the page at me. It's real. It's disconcerting. I was

145

expecting something else . . . I don't know, something else."

His stomach bounded into his chest and quivered there. He said nothing.

"I'm going to take it home and type it out. Then I'll send it to a man I know. You see, I don't know how much I'm influenced . . ."

"Who?"

"Arthur Morely. You've probably heard of him. He used to have a column in the *Courier-Mail*. I knew him a long time ago. I haven't seen him for ages but he'll remember me." She smiled. "He'd better."

Palmer had heard only vaguely of the man. He had read some of his columns in the paper which arrived at Wilderwood three days late and he had always enjoyed them. They had a gentle touch of humour, a kindliness that was missing in the slickness of the other columnists.

"Do you think he'd mind?"

"No," she smiled. "I don't think so. In the meantime, you get on and do some more." She leaned over him. The smile was gone. "I think it's just wonderful," she said. She kissed him quickly on the lips. "At least I think I do. Write some more. Here's another pad in case you run out."

"Pencils?"

She dived back into the bag. "Three. When they're worn out just let me know."

When she had gone, he lay back in the bed running his tongue around his lips. The taste of lipstick remained. It reminded him of a woman he had met in Winton, the wife of the publican, the first mail-order bride he had ever met. He had heard of them, people who advertise their availability in the newspapers, view matrimony, but she was the first he had ever met. She had told him about it as they made love in his room while her husband was in his nightly stupor. Her name was Ramona and she was looking for a man to help her kill her husband. Palmer had listened, horrified but entranced, as she had spelled out the plan. He had lain awake for the rest of the night after she had gone, too shocked to sleep. Next morning he learned that at different times she had asked nearly every member of the team. Every one of them had reported back to the husband in oblique ways, leaving out the sex but warning him as subtly as they could. He had just nodded and poured them another beer.

He reached for the writing pad.

The next morning Peter Barrett came in to see him again.

"A big day," he said.

"How's that?"

"Time to get you out of this bed." One of the sisters entered pushing a wheelchair. Palmer was pleased. The physical inaction was beginning to pall. The room seemed to be getting smaller every day.

They helped him out of bed and into the chair.

"Stay on the verandah until it gets too warm for you, then one of the nurses will help you back into bed," Barrett said. "It will give you a chance to meet some of your fellow patients."

"Okay."

Palmer sat in the sun and felt the wind on his face. But after an hour his leg began to ache and he took himself back into the room. The other patients on the verandah—Mrs Armstrong, who had burned herself badly when the toolshed caught fire, and Jimmy Donohue, who had sprained his back in a fall from a rough horse—had talked and distracted him. He was glad to be back in the peace of his room.

He had lost track of the days. Tom Reed had visited two days ago and that meant it was a Thursday today. Tom's had been a duty visit. Palmer could see he hated the atmosphere of the hospital and had found it difficult to talk to him. Despite their friendship, Tom, like his father and probably all the men of the district, found illness and disability a sign of inherent weakness in the patient and it made them uncomfortable. He wouldn't be back.

Palmer didn't mind. His days were suddenly full and his nights overcrowded. He felt himself gaining strength and, while the writing was exhausting, each time he returned to it he felt more confident, more able to handle the effort. It was like the beginning of a physical training programme. At first, every muscle in the body ached but then the system adjusted and found a new capacity within itself.

Today it was Marcia's turn. She had been back three times since their first passionate scene on the bed and on each occasion they had repeated the mutual gratification. The last time they had thrown the small bolt locking the door and he had stripped her to the waist. She had very large, soft, shapely breasts. Too large, she said. She wore a tight brassiere to reduce their size. He found them luscious and provocative but her own vague sense of discomfort about their size transmitted itself to him and detracted from his enjoyment. Also the act itself, while exciting and momentarily ecstatic, was, finally, unsatisfying and incomplete.

In the past his leg had hampered him. But now he could move it without pain provided he put no weight on it. His head was clearer too and only in his moments of highest excitement or late at night when he had been concentrating on the writing pad for a long stretch did the pain and the sound return to distress him.

He was sitting in his chair beside the bed intent on his fourth story—more a portrait than a story—of Jimmy Jam-Tin, an old drunken bum whose only mission in life was to create new and

147

elaborate schemes for cadging drinks. He was a master of practical psychology with the ability to size up a new mark instantly and devise the perfect method of appealing to his special weakness. Palmer had bought him drinks in Richmond all one afternoon while Jimmy told hair-raising stories of the old far west.

He was about to exchange the blunt stub of a pencil for a new one when he heard the door close and the bolt pushed into the latch. Then two soft, warm hands closed around his eyes.

"Guess who?"

He grinned. "None other than Morgandale's answer to Marilyn Monroe."

She slapped him lightly on the side of the face.

"Pal, stop that."

When he saw the hurt look on her face he was sorry for the crack.

"I just meant you were beautiful and glamorous and sexy as hell. Is that so bad?"

"Well I don't mind being beautiful and glamorous. What are you doing?"

"More of the same," he said.

"More writing? Pal, you must let me read it. Adele just refuses. She's been typing away in her room for days, not going out, except to come here and see you. I'm doing all the cooking and Daddy's getting sick of it. In fact, he's getting pretty sick of you if the truth be known."

"Me?"

"Yes, he says whenever he sees his womenfolk they're either just going to visit you, just returned or, with a glare at Adele, too busy with your work to do anything else about the place."

"Hell. What are we going to do about it? What do you suggest?"

"You tell Adele to stay away." Her seriousness was only half feigned.

"I suppose that's one possible solution," he said.

"Now you stop that."

He laughed. "Help me back to the cot."

He leaned heavily on her as he hopped the three steps across the room. When they reached the bed he pulled her down on it with him.

"Your leg," she said. But she made no attempt to move away.

He turned on to his back and looked into her face which was close to his. Her brown eyes, he noticed, were flecked with tiny gold spots.

"The leg's just fine." His arms went round to her back and they kissed.

"Mmmm," she said, then: "You know what?"

"What?"

"You're at my mercy."

"I'm afraid so. What are you going to do about it?"

148

"I haven't decided."

His hand touched the zipper at the back of her neck. She was wearing the same style of dress she had worn the first time they had been on the bed together, but this one was a light brown, almost fawn.

"Well you'd better tell me soon," he said. "Let me know my fate."

"All right. But first I have a question."

"Fire away." The top of the zipper began to move under his hand.

"Pal," she said, the earlier bantering gone from her voice, "do you love me?"

Christ. His hand stopped dead. How should he answer? Not with the truth, of course. He didn't know what the truth was. He didn't know what love was. He knew what she thought it was but to him it was something else, something all-consuming, total, irrevocable, fired with limitless passion. And that was not what he felt for Marcia or anyone else. He loved her sweetness and her kindness and her generosity and her beautiful, soft body. But what was that called?

"Darling," he said. He had never used the word before. It sounded strange and stilted. "I don't know the answer. Maybe I do. I'm not sure."

There was a long silence. His hand stayed poised on the zipper.

Then she smiled. "I'm glad you said that. If you had just said, 'Yes, Marcia, I love you; I love you', I think I would have known. You wouldn't have been telling the truth, would you?"

"I don't know."

"I do." She was still smiling. "Now I'll tell you a secret."

The zipper continued its downward course. "What?"

"Promise you won't tell anyone."

"I promise. I promise."

She giggled. "I'm not wearing any panties."

Now it was his turn to be serious. His hand left the zipper and ran down under her dress. It was true.

He kissed her and with his left hand wrestled the pyjama cord undone. She moved over on top of him. He dragged his leg across into a more comfortable position and she lifted the front of her dress out of their way. Then he pulled the sheet over the top of them.

"Wait," she said. "Just a moment."

"What's wrong?"

"Quickly, hand me my purse." She took out a white tablet and reached beneath the sheet.

"God, yes," he said. "I didn't give it a thought. Where did you get it?"

"Shhh." She kissed him and he penetrated her. She fitted snugly and warmly around him and his instant thought was that she was not a virgin. He was momentarily surprised. He had thought she was.

149

Their kiss ended and she nestled her lips against his ear.

"Oh Pal, that's good. That's so good."

They moved slowly in unison, then faster, more urgently. "It's good," she said. "It's good; it's good; it's good; it's good . . . oh!" The cry came from her throat but he was heedless of it. He plunged again and again and crushed her down on him as he climaxed inside her. Then she lay beside him. After a while she said, "I wonder what she'd say if she could see us now."

"Who?"

"Adele."

"I hate to think."

"Yes. You don't have to worry. I'd never tell her. Never. She'd make life hell for me . . . and you."

They were quiet.

"Marcia?"

"Yes."

"I wasn't the first, was I?"

"No." she paused. "Once, when I was at school . . ."

"It doesn't matter."

"There was one big difference."

"What's that?"

"I love you."

He looked across at her. Tears were flowing unchecked down her face.

"Why are you crying? Darling, please, don't cry."

"It's nothing. I'll be all right in a minute."

The next afternoon he was dozing when Matron Glassop shook him.

"You're wanted on the phone. It sounded like a young lady. Can't imagine who it would be."

He struggled out of bed and into his wheelchair. The phone was in the doctor's surgery.

He recognised her voice immediately. "Yes, Marcia, what's wrong?"

"Nothing's wrong, Pal. I just wanted to talk to you."

"Why don't you come in and say hello properly?" He grinned into the phone. "Are you coming in today?"

"No, I'm driving to Roma."

"What's on there?"

"Nothing. I have to get something. Some tablets."

"Oh, I see."

"But you won't be lonely. That was the other reason I called."

"I'm expecting Boss a little later."

"Well, the mail came at lunchtime and she's very excited about a

150

letter from a Mr Morely. Do you know him?"

"I know of him. Look, I'll have to go."

"Yes, she's probably there already."

"Right. Bye."

"Pal, did I tell you today that I love you?"

He pretended not to hear and cradled the receiver.

A letter from Arthur Morely! He spun the wheels back towards his room. When Adele arrived half an hour later it seemed as though he had waited half a day. "There," she said, handing him the letter. She looked triumphant.

"What's this?"

"You just read it. The first page. The rest wouldn't interest you."

He scanned the first lines quickly:

"Dear Adele,

"First let me thank you for sending the Palmer Lingard stories which I am returning under separate cover . . ."

Palmer looked up. The excitement which had been building since Marcia's call was threatening to leave him.

"He's rejecting them."

"Just read on."

He turned back to the page:

". . . As you know, fiction is not really my line of territory, but I must say that I agree entirely with your assessment of this young man's potential. The stories overflow with a life and a vibrancy which are quite overpowering. As first efforts they are quite outstanding . . ."

"First efforts!"

"Yes. Now finish it."

". . . We have taken a copy of *Christmas Dinner* and the editor of the *Sunday Mail* magazine would be willing to run it with only minor changes in our Christmas issue . . ."

"Jesus." The page blurred. Palmer wiped his eyes.

". . . However, I am afraid we cannot use the others. They are just not suited to our publications and frankly I think they need a good deal more work. Which is not to say they are of a lower standard than the one we have accepted. On the contrary, they are potentially much better. But I think you would agree that they lack discipline. There is far too much straying from the central theme. Minor incidents are inflated beyond their intrinsic value to the story. Palmer Lingard should buy himself a blue pencil (since he is stuck in hospital, perhaps you could do it for him) and he should not be afraid to use it. I could make some suggestions as to where the stories might be cut and edited but I think that on re-reading them the 'offending' sections will be clear enough to him. I hope so.

151

"Once that is done, you might wish to let the following publications take a look at them . . ."

There followed a short list of magazine titles which meant nothing to Palmer.

". . . I am delighted to see, Adele, that you haven't changed . . ."

"You haven't changed?"

"That's enough."

His mind was whirling. A story accepted. A story of his was going to be published. His name would be splashed across the page. His story would be read by thousands; tens of thousands; perhaps hundreds of thousands.

Adele's eyes were shining. "Well," she said. "What do you think?"

He shook his head. "I'm lost." He paused. "Adele, I really don't know how to thank you."

She walked across from the chair and sat on the side of the bed. She smiled and looked into his eyes. "No thanks needed. I think I'm as happy as you are."

"God, isn't it fantastic? I never dreamed . . . I mean I really didn't think there was a chance in the world. Deep down I think I knew they were good, but this isn't the way it's supposed to be. I should have starved in a garret somewhere first." He felt slightly hysterical.

She took his hand. An image of Marcia and a rush of guilt intruded and was instantly banished.

"But," he said "it's not all good, is it?"

"What do you mean?" Marcia's face returned. Now she was sounding like her.

"I mean, they have rejected the better stories . . ."

"Potentially, dear, potentially." In her animation, she clasped his hand to her breast. He could feel the hardness of it through the back of his hand. Then she released it and dragged her big shopping bag over to her feet.

"Here." She handed it to him—a fat blue pencil.

He laughed. "Adele, you're a wonder."

There was a soft tapping on the door and Boss's head appeared around the corner. Christ. Palmer had said nothing to him about his writing. It had seemed out of place in their conversations and in a way even disloyal. He should probably have spent all his waking hours thinking of The Place and the improvements he would make if he returned to it—increasing the stock numbers, fixing the sheepyards, branding the new calves. It was ridiculous and illogical but the feeling of disloyalty persisted.

Adele had no such inhibition. "Clement Cunningham," she said, "you ought to be mighty proud." Palmer cringed at the words. The use of Boss's given name jarred. Adele was the only woman in the district who used it. The old man managed a half smile.

"What, of this young fella?"

"Yes indeed. This young fella," she mimicked, "has just had his first story accepted for publication."

Boss looked over at Palmer. "Story?"

"Yes, Boss." It sounded like an admission of guilt. "I've been scribbling a few things. It helps pass the time."

"Now Palmer Lingard, you stop that. He's been working very hard and he's sold practically the first story he's written and it will be the first of many, many more." She turned to Palmer. "I won't have you tossing it off like that." Then back to Boss. "He's a very talented young man."

"Now cut it out, Adele," Palmer said defensively.

"No," she replied, "I will not."

There was a silence in the room. Boss walked over and sat heavily in the visitor's chair. Adele remained sitting on the bed.

"Well," Boss said with another attempt at a smile. "This is a turn up for the books. Congratulations on selling the story, son. How much did they give you for it?"

How much? He hadn't even bothered to ask. He had seen no mention in the letter. He looked at Adele.

"Ten pounds," she said promptly.

Boss lifted his eyebrows. "Ten pounds. What are you going to do with it, buy some more books?"

"I suppose so."

"That's good. It'll be good pin money for you. I wish I could pay you more on The Place. But of course, you do get a raise with the new job."

"What new job?" Adele looked at Palmer.

"Boss wants me to manage The Place when I get out of here."

"Manage Wilderwood? But you can't, Palmer. You'd be working twelve hours a day and doing the book-keeping at night. There'd be no time . . ."

"You mean for his writing?"

"Yes, his writing. And you shouldn't say it like that, Clem. As though it's some kind of childish pastime. It's important."

"He'd always have the weekends. Sundays anyway."

"Sundays! It's not enough. There's a talent here and I won't have it wasted away; I won't have it . . ." She stopped. Another word and her voice would have cracked.

In the embarrassed silence, Boss said quietly, "Any word from home, son?"

It was a stab, a lunge at the heart with a fine blade. And it was directed as much at Adele as Palmer. It excluded her from the

153

conversation. Boss knew as well as Palmer that she had met his parents only a few times. It enclosed the two men in a family bond and made her the intruder, the upstart.

Palmer took a deep breath. "No, Boss. But I've been wanting to talk to you about it. When I get out I think I will go home for a while. If Mum's not well I'd like to spend some time with her. Anyway, I want to find out the score for myself." Adele blew her nose noisily on a tiny white handkerchief.

"Yes, yes. Of course," Boss said. "But you will be coming back?"

"I'll have to see."

Boss nodded his head slowly. "Well, boy, it's up to you. I won't try to force you into something you don't want."

"Boss, I'm not sure what I want."

"I understand." He picked his hat up from the arm of the chair and walked slowly to the door. "Goodbye, Adele. Come around and visit me sometime and brighten an old man's life up."

"All right, Boss," she said.

When the door closed, she turned to Palmer. "Now, look . . ."

"Please Adele, not now."

"All right. I'll leave you alone too." She kissed him lightly on the lips. The shine was back in her eyes.

"There's just one thing," he said. "I didn't see anything in the letter about ten pounds for the story."

"There wasn't." She smiled. "Arthur Morely doesn't know it yet but that's what he's going to pay you. I'll write to him tonight."

When she had gone, he reached for the new set of crutches Peter Barrett had left in the room. He couldn't stay in the room. He had to get out into the open. He felt like an advertisement he had seen in a magazine where Don Athaldo fought against the strength of two draught horses pulling in opposite directions. He had to be away from it.

Alone on the verandah, it was cool and the dust had settled. The sun was bursting red flames defiantly into a wide, cloudless, twilight sky. A dog ran in grey silhouette across the Morgandale street, its head pushed forward, heedless of the world around it.

How was it possible to feel so elated and so sad at once? Why was it that every triumph had to paid for with pain? How did other men cope? What did they do when to do anything was to cause pain and to do nothing only intensified it? What was It up there among the new stars that decreed such dilemmas? The road was never clear. There was no perfect time, no perfect choice. Only a balancing of uncertain factors. A judgment. All that was sure was the pain.

He shook the mood away. He reached for the crutches. He would think of Marcia, and then he would sleep.

NOW the days and the weeks fell into a new pattern, a routine much more ordered and controlled.

Boss came less frequently and when he did their talk was desultory, inconsequential. They were marking time. Every time he came he seemed a little more stooped, more tired. It seemed to Palmer that Boss had almost accepted the fact that he would be going away. Almost, but not quite. The door was still open and he still waited on the other side. But it was the other side now.

There remained a tacit understanding that even if he did return to Brisbane permanently he would not do so until another man had been trained to take his place. There would be a time after he had been home—perhaps three or four months—when he would come back to see the new man settled in. If, indeed, he decided finally that his future lay elsewhere.

Palmer told himself he was still uncertain. From a purely selfish viewpoint, there were obvious disadvantages to his leaving. The most obvious was that there was no job for him in Brisbane, no way to earn a living. The possibility of his working in the shop was not even considered. In any case, he could not live at home again. He had to be on his own, independent, unfettered.

But, while a second story, then a third were accepted, his total income from his writing reached a not-so-grand £35 and there seemed little chance that he would ever earn enough to live on that alone.

·But with each day he was mentally and emotionally drawn further away from The Place. Now, when he thought of "home" it was the streets of Brisbane and the little corner store that came to mind.

Adele suggested that he write to Arthur Morely for advice, telling him the kind of work he wanted and asking for suggestions. But Palmer had put it off. He didn't know the man. It seemed wrong to involve him in it. He should work it out for himself.

In the meantime, his writing hours were fully occupied. The frenetic pace of the first stories had slowed and he was working to a routine of his own. He felt his work was improving. Always, as he wrote and caught himself up in the time and the place and the mood of his story, he felt the Presence returning and driving him on. But now he was better able to hold it in check, to control it, to accept its force without losing his own perspective. Already his first stories seemed amateurish and overwrought.

His health was greatly improved and now he found himself looking forward impatiently to his release, to the reunion with his mother. His father had written briefly and reassuringly. She was going to be all right. But to add to her troubles she had cut her hand in a kitchen accident so he was writing for her.

He was now an expert with the crutches and Peter Barrett had promised that the cast would be taken off in a couple of days. His head bothered him only occasionally. The bandages were off and the hair had grown back over the widow's peak where they had shaved it to clean the wound. There was a deep red scar high on his forehead which disappeared into the hairline.

But there was another aspect to his decision which troubled him. If he left he would be leaving Adele and Marcia behind. Of course, Adele made frequent trips to Brisbane and with her the break would never be complete. There would always be occasions when they would meet and be together. He had no doubt that their relationship would endure, that she would see his departure not as a leave-taking but as just another step, a change in locale.

Marcia was different. She had no real interests outside the property and the social life of Morgandale and Roma. Since she had returned from school she had cooked for the men and often the family as well when Adele was otherwise occupied. She had cleaned house, done much of the shopping and attended all the tennis days, play readings, polo matches, parties and balls that the district had to offer. She gave no indication that she wanted anything more from life. Morgandale was enough. She was part of it.

But that was a Morgandale of which he too was a part. And in the past few weeks the parties and tennis days had been neglected. The whole of her existence seemed more and more to be focusing on him alone. She was at the hospital each day she knew Adele would not be there. She now came in the mornings, afternoons and occasionally even at night. She seemed to have an endless variety of excuses to explain her sudden trips.

At first he had found the attention flattering and he had matched her passion and her pleasure in love-making. But after nearly three months it was becoming oppressive and disconcerting.

She interrupted his writing. Almost, it seemed, deliberately, as though his writing was the embodiment of her mother's link with him which she wanted to blot out with her presence and her affection.

But her attitude towards him and even herself had changed. Where once she had been modest and even a little embarrassed by her figure, now she flaunted it and displayed herself to him at every opportunity. Three or four times they had almost been caught in bed by the sisters

156

or the doctor coming unexpectedly to visit. He began to suspect that she wished to be caught, to have their liaison witnessed and certified by someone else.

But if that was her intention, the small hospital community needed no visual proof. Her numerous visits were enough and the locked door took care of any remaining doubts. The nurses seemed to extract a special delight from it and the opportunity it gave them to joke with him. Matron Glassop took to knocking elaborately on his door even when it was wide open.

However, he was deeply grateful that they restrained themselves when Adele was there. Marcia herself took great care to monitor her mother's movements and never to risk a confrontation. It was the only concession she made. When Adele was with him he found himself watching for signs, a clue that she had heard the gossip. But if she was aware of their relationship she gave no sign.

Barrett's attitude was different from the rest of the hospital staff. Not hostile, but not approving either.

"Marcia not here?" he said when he looked in one morning.

"Hardly. It's only eight o'clock."

"From what I hear time doesn't seem to matter much with you two."

"Well, perhaps you shouldn't listen to rumours."

"I have pretty good sources."

"Yes, of course. She has been here a lot," Palmer said. "I hope we haven't been breaking any rules."

"I really couldn't say, could I?" The implication was obvious and Barrett's tone was more than half serious.

"No."

"Pal, I won't say any more than this but I want you to know that I have a lot of respect for Marcia, and for her mother. I wouldn't like to see either of them hurt."

"Well for Christsake neither would I. When can I go home?"

Barrett resumed his professional manner. "I'm taking the cast off tomorrow. We'll put a bandage on it for a week and then you should be right to go. I would have sent you off a couple of weeks ago but there's no one at Wilderwood to look after you and you'll still have to take it easy for a while."

"Will I be able to walk on it? It can take a fair bit of weight now."

"That's partly because of the cast. It will be very tender but we'll give you a walking stick and you'll be able to get around all right."

"What about travelling? I want to go to Brisbane for a while to see my parents."

"If you go in the train it should be okay. But you might find driving a bit difficult."

"No, the train's all right."

One week. The thought consumed him after Barrett had left. One more week after nearly four months. God, it would be good.

Adele came that afternoon. "One week," he said as she walked through the door. "One more week and I'll be out."

"And you're going straight to Brisbane?"

"Yes."

"Then please go and see Arthur while you're there. It can't do any harm and it might do you a world of good."

"If you say so."

"I do. He's expecting you."

"What?"

"I said he's expecting you. I've written to him and he's said he would like to meet you very much."

"What for?"

"Oh, just to talk. It's not every day he gets to meet a budding young author."

He laughed. "You never give up, do you?"

"No I don't. I'm glad you've finally learned that." She paused. "Palmer," her tone was serious "have you ever thought of becoming a newspaperman, a reporter?"

The suggestion was not really a surprise. She had thrown out hints in this direction previously and he had thought about it. The idea appealed to him, but he was nervous about it. It was so different from any of his experience so far. Another world.

". . . I don't mean forever," Adele said. "But I think it would be good for you. Good for your writing."

"I can see that. It's an exciting idea. But God, Adele, I know nothing about newspapers."

"Palmer, they're not going to ask you to become editor on the day you arrive."

"No, but there must be so many people ahead of me."

"Perhaps. But at least they will have seen that you can write. That must be a help. Anyway, talk with Arthur and see what you think then."

He nodded. A newspaperman, a reporter, a journalist. He wondered what the difference was. But they were exciting words. He had a vision of himself in a trench coat with a hat pulled down over his eyes and a little card stuck in the band. "Press" the card said. "Press."

When the cast came off, the foot felt suddenly as though it belonged to someone else. It rose in the air almost without his assistance. But when he put it down the pain shot into the bone.

"Steady," Barrett said. "Just take it easy."

158

"Okay." The walking stick was much more manageable than the crutches had been.

Marcia arrived soon afterwards and he was able to walk to the door to meet her. He threw the latch himself.

For once he was genuinely pleased to see her. In contrast with her costumes of recent weeks, she was wearing a highnecked blouse and skirt and her make-up was less flamboyant. He liked her much better like this. She seemed subdued but when he kissed her she responded as passionately as ever.

He broke away. "Did you hear the news?" he said.

"Yes, Adele told us last night. You'll be leaving in a week."

"About a week. But there's something else." He was serious now. Since his talk with Adele he had been rehearsing the way he would break it to her. She seemed to sense what was coming. She sat quietly beside him on the bed as he spoke.

"Darling," he said, "you know I'm going to Brisbane for a while to see my parents."

"Yes."

"Well, it's just possible that I won't be coming back. No, I don't mean that. I will be coming back for a little while to help Boss get another man settled in. But it won't be permanent; just a couple of months."

"I see."

"But I'll be able to get back here for holidays and you'll be down in Brisbane from time to time. It's only three hundred miles. It's not the other end of the world."

"No."

"And when you come down you can come and meet my mother. You'd love her and she'd like you too."

"That would be very nice, Pal."

"We can write. And though Boss still doesn't believe it, there is such a thing as a telephone."

"What are you going to do there?"

"I'm not sure yet. There's a chance I might be able to work on a newspaper."

"Is that Adele's doing?"

"In a way. She's written to a man who works on the *Courier-Mail*. A Mr Morely. Do you remember the letter he sent?"

"Yes, I thought it might be something like that."

"It won't be the same without you, you know."

"No. Or you either." She turned to him. "I really will miss you."

He kissed her hand and they lay back on the bed. He moved on top of her, fondling her breasts then moving his hands down and working her underclothes off. He looked at her questioningly and she nodded.

159

Sometimes recently she had inserted the white tablets before she came into the room.

"Oh God, Pal," she said as he entered her, "I love you." And again, "I love you; I love you." Her voice cracked and as he drew back he could see tears running down her cheeks and falling into the white linen. "No, don't stop, don't stop. Oh."

"Jesus," he said. "Jesus, Jesus."

And afterwards, when she cried some more, he put his arm around her shoulders. "There, there. Come on, now . . ."

"Pal, don't go away."

"Darling I have to. I have no choice."

"You do. If you wanted to, you could stay."

He was silent.

"Pal, if I asked you, would you?"

"Stay?"

"Yes."

"I don't think you would ask."

"I might if I was pregnant."

A shaft of cold air blew down from above him and settled in his stomach.

"Don't joke about it."

"Pal, I'm not joking." She buried her face in his chest.

"No!" It came out more loudly than he intended. "No. Jesus Christ, you can't be. How do you know? Are you sure?"

"I've missed two periods."

"How could you. I've only been here . . ."

"Four months less one week."

"But you still can't be sure. Have you seen a doctor?"

"No, Pal. I don't have to. I've been sick every morning. I've known for nearly a month."

He was angry; fighting against it. It couldn't be true. It was wrong. It smashed into everything he had planned and sent the whole thing scattering. It grabbed him and held him back.

"Why didn't you tell me? Why didn't you say something?"

"I was hoping . . . I don't know. Pal, please don't be angry. I couldn't stand it. My second period was due two days ago. I thought something might happen."

There was a knock at the door. He walked the few paces and opened it. Matron Glassop said, "Anything wrong?"

"What? No. Nothing." God, if only she knew. But she would know. She'd have to know some time.

"All right," she said. "Don't overdo it." His walking stick still lay by the bed. He hadn't noticed.

They would all have to know. Everyone. The nurses, Barrett, Boss,

160

John Champion, and worst of all, Adele. Christ, what would she say? Maybe she knew already.

"Have you told your mother?"

"No, of course not. I haven't told anyone. I didn't know what to do." She was crying again, louder now. If he didn't calm her the matron would be back. He sat beside her again and she moved against him.

"Shhh. We're going to have to think. God, what's to be done?"

But from the first, the two possible alternatives had been utterly clear: marriage or an abortion. There was just no other possibility.

But it was more than that. She would never be happy away from the country, away from Morgandale. She could never share that other part of him which had grown to absorb and delight him. She could have no part in it and that would destroy her and destroy their marriage.

If they married he would have to stay here, take Boss's offer and resign himself to the mindless aridity of it, to the frustration of an Adele Champion living vicariously through protégés and dreams.

But the alternative was just as bad. It would cripple Marcia for the rest of her life. He would have to take her to Brisbane, to a place where she could be operated on. Adele and the whole district would know and it would stay with her for the rest of her life. Every day of her life. Every time she saw her mother's face or the face of a friend.

And with him too. Not just the pain and anguish to Marcia but the knowledge that he had decided. He had given the signal to put an end to the thing inside her. His own thing, a boy or a girl, a son or a daughter. Or was it really that? Was it some kind of protoplasm; something without mind or feelings, without hopes, without impulse, without real life? Would she not learn to live with it? Hadn't it happened before to others in the district? Hadn't they too learned to accept and finally to overcome it? Perhaps. But was that relevant? Was anything relevant? Christ. The words were spinning back on themselves and a familiar ache was beginning at the base of his skull.

"What do you want, Pal?" she said.

"Marcia, I don't know."

She was clear-eyed now. The tears were gone and the black mascara smudges wiped away.

"You don't want to marry me, do you?"

"Marcia, I don't know. You'll have to give me time to think it through. I don't think we'd be happy together. Not like this."

"I won't try to force you, Pal."

"There's only one alternative," he said.

"Yes. I thought about going away to one of those homes and having it and then letting it be adopted. I couldn't do that."

"I didn't mean that."

"I know you didn't. You probably didn't think of it. You meant an abortion, didn't you?"

"Yes."

"Where?"

"In Brisbane, I suppose."

She took a deep breath. "All right," she said.

"What?"

"I'll have one. I'll have an abortion."

"Just wait and let me think. There must be another way."

She looked at her watch. "Pal, I'll have to get home. It's three o'clock and they'll be wondering . . ."

"All right. That will give us both a chance to think about it. Come in tomorrow."

He kissed her on the cheek. He could hardly bear to touch her.

". . . and don't worry."

But it would not be any different in the morning, he knew that deep inside him. In the morning it would be the same. He flopped back on the bed. His thoughts went nowhere. The same alternatives careered back and forth. The same instincts jarred him away from each of them.

He had to talk it out with someone. Suddenly he had an overwhelming urge to be with his mother. She would know what to do. But she was so far away and there was no time. His next thought went naturally to Adele but that was absurd. But who else was there? Boss perhaps. Yes, there would be no censure there. Boss would understand. Even if he just sat while Palmer listened to himself talking it would help. He would know himself better. He would see it clearer.

He would call Boss tomorrow. He would talk to Marcia in the morning and in the afternoon he would call Boss and ask him to come in. They would talk. And there was just a chance that something would happen in the night, that by morning Marcia would tell him it was all a false alarm.

The evening and the night were endless. He watched the sun come up through the trees and just after dawn the wind began to blow from the west, a hot, dusty wind from the desert.

Marcia came and he saw before she spoke that nothing had changed.

The day dragged like the night.

At three o'clock he hobbled to the doctor's surgery and gave the Wilderwood ring on the party line—two shorts and a long. There was no answer. Boss must be in the paddocks or the yards. He would call later.

162

He tried again at four. Then at five. There was still no answer. Finally at 5.30 young Ritchie was on the other end.

"Boss there?"

"No, isn't he with you?"

"No, I didn't expect him today."

"He left about half an hour ago."

"Okay, I'll wait for him."

"Pal, I'm very sorry." The young jackeroo's voice sounded genuinely sad. Christ, what was that all about. Surely he wasn't going to miss him that much on The Place.

"Yeah, well I'll see you later."

"Okay."

Back in his room he tried to imagine how Boss would take the news. But his thoughts wouldn't stay in line and suddenly the room and everything in it was repugnant to him. Marcia and the images of their love-making remained on the bed. He had to get out.

He reached into the small locker beneath the bedside table and took out his denim trousers, the ones he had been wearing when they had brought him in. The nurses had cleaned and pressed them but the shirt was beyond repair. Still, it was good to have trousers on again. He was that much less an invalid. He could talk on more equal terms with the old man. Then he hobbled out of the room to wait on the verandah.

The wind was stronger now and when he stepped outside the force of it pushed him slightly off balance. He grabbed a chair and steadied himself. The wind was swirling the dust up from the streets and turning it, spinning it into the air which was already thick with dry leaves and small twigs and branches. The trees around the tennis court and the hotel swayed and seemed to push back against the wind, whining their complaints with the murmur of their leaves.

He sat in the chair and watched the road until the big blue Ford rounded the far corner of the street and pushed its way through the flying dust.

Boss slammed the car door and held his wide hat with one hand. In the other was a piece of paper.

Palmer stood up to meet him. The old man took the three steps quickly and came directly to Palmer. His face was creased and tightened against the wind and the dust, but there was something else too. He put a big hand on Palmer's shoulder.

God, what was it? Had Marcia told him? Had she told Adele and had Adele called him and sent him in? No. It wasn't that. It had nothing to do with that. He knew before Boss spoke that it was his mother. He had the same look as the day when the letter from his father had come.

"Son," he said. "I'm very sorry. I could have telephoned but I thought it better to come myself."

"What? What is it?"

Boss handed him the paper. It flapped and quivered in the wind making it hard to read. Then he turned his back to the wind and held it still. It was addressed to him.

"Bert Miles must have thought you'd gone home already so he brought it out," Boss shouted against the wind.

It was a yellow piece of paper, the words written roughly in black ink. "Mother seriously ill," he read. "Come home immediately if possible. Dad."

He looked blankly up at Boss's face. He had expected it, but the words refused to register. He looked at the big eyes with the wide pupils. So wide, he thought. Then the words slapped him like the wind and he crumpled back into the chair.

Boss leaned over him and even in the hard wind he could smell the sweat from the old man's shirt.

"Son, there's no train tonight. If you want, I can drive you."

"No," he said. He was utterly calm. He was an island of calm in the wind. It couldn't reach him. He was still and calm and the wind avoided him. "No," he repeated. "You can't leave The Place. It's all right. I can drive myself."

"Are you sure? What does the doctor say?"

"It's all right, Boss. I can do it."

"I brought some clothes just in case."

"Just give me a shirt and some boots. They had to cut my boot off."

"They're in the back of the car."

He leaned against the wind as they walked to the car. It supported him. He threw the walking stick into the front seat. He handed Boss the pyjama top and pushed his arms into the khaki work shirt. He pulled on one boot. The other would not fit over the bandage.

"How will you get home?" he asked Boss.

"Someone will give me a lift."

Boss handed him some money. "Petrol."

He eased himself behind the wheel. There was nothing more to say.

"Son, I'm very sorry," Boss said and his deep voice echoed in the closed car. "Telephone me . . . let me know if anything happens."

Palmer nodded. He was wasting time. The car started and he turned it out of the grounds towards the main street. Boss stood in the swirling dust by the neat, white hospital building. He was still holding his hat by his side. Palmer turned away and concentrated on the road. It would be gravel roads for the first sixty miles and then the smooth black highway. He pushed the accelerator down and the pain ripped into his leg. He held it down and for an instant he savoured the pain.

164

Then he eased back and the pain receded with the speed. Three hundred miles.

For an hour he drove without thought, his concentration fixed upon the rough, potholed and corrugated road. He was aware of an ache in his leg but he held it in check. Then he was on the long straight highway. He was away from it. The thought reached him and held on to him. He was away. He was running away. He was not running to see his mother. He was running away from Marcia, from himself. No matter what the excuse, he was running away. She was left behind with his thing in her belly and he was free. There was a rush of pleasure to his chest. Free.

He shook his head. What kind of an animal was he? Was there nothing that could reach him any more, nothing real or genuine? It was wrong. The feeling of freedom was wrong. How could he think it? What was wrong with him?

He pressed down hard on the accelerator but drew back immediately. The ache was becoming unbearable. He slowed the car and looked around. The walking stick. Of course. As he drove, he transferred it to his right hand then pushed the rubber tip on to the accelerator. He wedged the curved end under the seat by his leg. The car careered forward and he fought for control. He tried again and this time it held at a steady seventy miles an hour. With one hand on the wheel and the other keeping the heavy stick in place he could rest his leg. The relief was enormous.

He drove that way until he reached Dalby. His leg was stiffer now and more painful but as soon as he was out of the town he readjusted the stick and rested again.

His mind stayed free and clear. When he thought of his mother he held just one image, just one. She was putting her teacup back into a saucer and she lifted an eyebrow, just one eyebrow. Whenever he thought of her he forced his mind to that one image and held it there.

At Oakey he repeated the manoeuvre with the stick and drove on towards Toowoomba. He increased his speed. No cars overtook him. Headlights flashed towards and passed him in bright double blurs like foxes' eyes in a spotlight.

Down the range past Toowoomba he changed into second and let the gears hold him at a steady speed. On tight curves he braked with his left foot and wrestled the wheel. He stopped for petrol at the bottom of the range. The garage was brightly lit.

"You okay?" the attendant asked when he brought the change. He nodded and stuffed the money into his pocket.

Now the traffic was thicker and the stick no longer useful. Eighty miles to go. He clamped his jaws shut and held the pain at bay. But now the lights and the traffic were disrupting his mental control.

Other images of his mother intruded and he fought in vain to keep them away. He felt his defences beginning to wash away and an anger replaced his calm.

Why hadn't his father warned him? Why only now? Why hadn't he let him know earlier? Even a few more days would have helped. He could have travelled a week ago, a month ago. He could have transferred to the same hospital. Or was she in hospital? Yes, of course she was. Why had his father deceived him with that letter? And what the bloody hell was wrong with her anyway? What was it? One of those wogs women get, Boss had said. What the Christ was that, for Christsake?

He pushed the accelerator to the floor.

On the outskirts of Brisbane the traffic thinned again. He looked at his watch. One fifteen. The anger had passed as suddenly as it came. They had wanted to spare him. He could see his mother's hand in it. There was nothing he could do. And in fact his father had warned him. He had known Boss would talk and would break it gently to him. It was better that way than with a letter. But then why the letter telling him that everything was all right, an accident in the kitchen?

He paid toll at the Indooroopilly Bridge. Nearly there. He was on familiar roads now, the streets of his childhood, and at each corner there was a memory, a nostalgia. The pain was strong in his leg and his thigh was trembling with the effort after so much inactivity. But he would make it.

A light was burning in the shop window when he pulled into the garage. They always kept the light on.

His father was waiting at the side door. They shook hands. His father's grip was firm.

"I'm glad you came, son."

Palmer swivelled around and pushed himself out of the car. The walking stick slipped on the gravel surface and he fell into his father's arms. He opened his mouth to say something but nothing came. It was dark; dark and quiet.

He was in his old bed and bright sunlight was pouring through the louvres. He was instantly awake, instantly aware of the situation. He pushed himself out of bed and pulled on his trousers. His father was in the kitchen.

"I thought I'd let you sleep. You looked about done."

"Yes. What's the score, Dad? Is she . . ."

"Yes, there's been no word from the hospital. I've closed the shop. We can go there now."

"Right."

His father gave him a clean shirt and they drove to the hospital.

"Tell me about it," Pal said. "What is it and why did you write that letter?"

"Son, I don't think they know what it is. There's something wrong with her blood and there's just nothing they can do. For the last twenty-four hours she's been in a kind of coma. There's no pain. We can be thankful for that."

"But the letter, Dad. Why did you tell me there was nothing to worry about?"

His father shook his head. "When she couldn't write any more I had to do it. I had to sit on the bed where she could see what I was writing. She had one of the nurses post it."

"But you could have written yourself."

"Son, there was nothing you could do. I didn't think you could travel and there was nothing . . ."

"It's all right, Dad. I understand."

They stood on each side of the bed looking down at her. She seemed to be just breathing; light shallow breaths that barely moved her chest. She was so thin there was almost nothing left of her.

Palmer took her hand and her eyelids flickered. He looked down at the soft, thin hand and something splashed on it. Her eyes opened. She looked at him and he saw them focus then turn to his father, her husband, and back to him.

There was a faint smile and her lips moved. They both bent to hear.

"My boys," she whispered.

Then the eyes were closed and he moved backwards away from her, away from the soft hand and the small figure. He couldn't stop the

167

sob that came out of him or the one that followed or the one after. His father was beside him again and they were going down the steps, slowly down the steps towards the car.

They went the following day but this time she didn't wake. On the third day the doctor stopped them at the door. "It's all over," he said.

They were sitting in the kitchen. Some people had called and his father had shaken hands with them at the door and sent them away. Pal stayed at the table. He couldn't move. The thought had been rolling round in his mind since they had left the hospital. He had kept it away but now it returned with an insistence that would not be denied.

It was all clear to him now. It was the story of creation, of life and death, of birth and rebirth. A sacred thing. For every death there is a new birth and the world moves forward. The new replace the old and the world moves forward. It was the great plan his old minister, the Reverend Strachan, had spoken of and taught him so long ago. And he was a part of it. A link in a great unbroken chain.

His father came into the room. His face was ashen. The deep furrows across his brow and around his eyes seemed burned into him.

"They try to be kind," he said. "But it doesn't help. It only makes it worse."

Palmer barely heard him. There was something he must do. He must call Marcia. He must tell her he was coming back, tell her the plan, tell her the way it would be. They would be happy. They would have their child and he would work the land, graze his sheep and his cattle and raise a dozen kids. And when there was time, he would write. He would write it all down and his children would read it and learn.

It was right and proper. He wanted to tell his father. He had wanted to tell him, to talk to him almost from the first. But he couldn't find the words. He had grown out of the habit. And at such a time to add another burden would be wrong. No. This would be his own doing; his own responsibility.

"Son, I'm going to have a drink," his father said. "Do you want anything?"

"No. No, I want to use the phone."

"Go ahead. You know where it is."

He went into the storeroom behind the shop and placed the call. Person to Person. Miss Marcia Champion. As he waited he visualised her face, the look on her face when she came to the phone, her full, red lips and her white teeth and her brown eyes—her face listening to him and changing with his words. The phone rang and he grabbed the receiver.

168

It was a woman customer sending her condolences. He thanked her and rang off.

Again it rang, but this time he could hear the crackle and buzzing of the Morgandale party line.

"Pal?"

"Marcia?"

"Yes, how is your mother?"

He took a deep breath. "She died this afternoon."

"Oh, Pal, I'm so sorry." Her voice sounded strange, as though she were talking in a tunnel.

"Marcia, I wanted to let you know straight away."

"Yes, thank you. I'll tell Adele and Daddy."

"No, I . . . thank you. But there's something else, Marcia. Marcia?"

"Yes, I'm still here."

"Darling, that other matter. I wanted to let you know. I'm coming back. Just as soon as I can get away, I'm coming back. Do you understand?"

There was an interminable silence. It grew almost to have a sound of its own.

"Marcia?"

"Pal, you didn't call. It's too late."

"What?"

"I said it's too late. There was no word. For two days there was no word. I went to see Peter Barrett and . . . Pal, I can't talk about it on the phone."

He was staring straight ahead at a shelf of canned fruit. The luscious orange-coloured peach halves were painted on the can's wrapper, its label. He stared at them. They looked so fresh and alive.

"Pal . . . Pal, I thought that was what you wanted. Pal . . ."

He placed the receiver carefully back in its cradle.

In the kitchen, his father was sitting quietly at the linoleum-covered table, his hand cupping a crystal glass. He looked up as Pal limped towards him. There was some colour back in his cheeks. Pal was pleased.

"I'll have that drink now," he said.

His father rose and turned towards the refrigerator.

"A beer?"

"Do you have some rum?"

"Yes."

Much later he found himself standing out in the spacious backyard. He had been standing motionless for as long as he could remember. He was looking up at the limitless space and the stars and they were blinking back at him through the fine powder of the sky.

169

"Fuck you," he said.

Then he shouted it. "Fuck you! Fuck you!" He hurled his walking stick down towards the road and he heard the echoes of his voice back across the little valley where the street lights shone and the people slept.

The frangipani tree rustled its leaves and blew its sweet, soft perfume in his face.

Brolie's Story
III

BY THE TIME I heard of his mother's death, heard he was back and went to the shop to see him, he was gone.

I went to her funeral with my mother. I had just started working in my father's accounting firm and he gave me the morning off to go. My mother and I waited outside the Methodist Church and shook hands with Mr Lingard when they came out. Pal wasn't there.

"Do you know where he is?" I asked.

Mr Lingard shook his head.

At first we all thought he had returned to the west and there was some talk about his thoughtlessness; about the way he had walked out on his father at such a time; how he hadn't even bothered to go to his mother's funeral. I don't think my mother ever understood. It was beyond her comprehension.

A few days after the funeral Mr Lingard opened the shop again and I talked to him.

"No," he said. "He hasn't gone back to Morgandale."

"Has he been in touch with you at all?"

"No. He said he was leaving but he didn't say where he was going. I'm not worried about him. He can look after himself."

There was a calmness about the man which seemed unnatural to me. He should have been more concerned. But from the way he spoke they might have been strangers. And that part of it I will never understand. In all the four months he was missing, Mr Lingard's attitude never changed. Every day or so I found an excuse to go to the shop and check with him and every time the answer was the same—the same resigned, matter-of-fact response, the same silly, unreasoning conviction that he was all right, that he would come back when he was ready, when the wound had healed. What he would have done if he had known the truth I do not know.

In my own way, I looked for him. In the mornings, I stopped riding to work with my father and took the bus to George Street. Then I walked all the way down Adelaide Street to Creek Street, across to Queen Street then up past His Majesty's and the Regent Theatre to Albert Street before I turned left into Elizabeth Street. At lunchtime I would wander up and down Queen and Adelaide Streets and in the evenings I would repeat the morning's pattern in reverse until I reached the George Street bus stop.

172

I lost count of the number of times I thought I recognised him, usually from behind. I would see the back of a head of light auburn hair just above medium height and set on broad shoulders moving purposefully through the footpath crowd. Each time there would be a bounding in my chest and a bloodless feeling in my wrists and I would increase my pace until I was close enough to see that it was not him but some stranger who must have wondered at the hostile stare.

I can't really explain, even now, the reason for my terrible anxiety at the time. It had been nearly two years since I had seen him and spoken to him. Certainly, I had kept abreast of his news but after so long I had no clear picture of him in my mind any more.

I had been involved in other things. After matriculating from St Mary's I went straight to the university. My father wanted me to study Commerce with the idea of joining his firm after I graduated and, since I showed no special adaptability to anything else, I agreed. It was less complicated that way, though I admit that sometimes I had a hankering to emulate other girls like Natalia who went into the Arts faculty and seemed to lead much more glamorous and uninhibited lives.

But I was not unhappy with my choice. I had plenty of free lecture time and the work was not especially difficult. On the whole, I enjoyed university life. I joined the Newman Society which at the time was one of the most active clubs on the campus and in my third and final year I helped to organise some of our programmes and meetings. We had a very wide range of guest speakers—visiting theologians and lay scholars as well as priests from the diocese—and the discussions that followed their talks were always stimulating and good.

My father encouraged me to join the Debating Society too but I went to only a few meetings. I found that though I could see the weaknesses in opposing arguments from the safety of my chair, once I tried to explain them from the lectern, or worse, just standing on a stage without even the protection of a lectern, I became tongue-tied and I couldn't find the words to fit my thoughts. Then the thoughts themselves became confused and I lost the thread. After one such experience I stayed away. Once was enough.

Also, in my second year I joined the choir at St Stephen's Cathedral in the city. The cathedral was in Elizabeth Street not far from my father's office and he would wait for me on the week nights there was practice and bring me home with him in the car. Father O'Hanlon, the priest who had taught me Scripture at school, was now attached to the cathedral and it was strange for me at first to find him in this new setting. At school he had seemed so old to me but now I could see that he was really quite a young man, no more than forty, and his work with the choir seemed to give him much more pleasure than the

173

lessons he had taught to raggedy schoolgirls at St Mary's

Soon I was going to church there every Sunday and on Saturday evenings Monsignor Guy or one of the other priests would hear my confession. Occasionally it was Father O'Hanlon's voice on the other side of the curtain and though the first time I found it a little strange, the feeling passed quickly.

I came to love the cathedral and to know its workings quite well. I talked with the priests and they seemed to like me. Apart from Father O'Hanlon, I think Monsignor Guy was my favourite. He was a tall, severe, dark-complexioned man with bright, dark eyes, almost black, and a heavy growth of beard. There was an air of strictness, of harsh sanctity in his appearance and one felt sure that when he preached a sermon it would be filled with fearful imprecations and slashing attacks upon sin and sinners. But amazingly, the moment he began to speak his face and his bearing seemed to relax and his sermons, delivered in a soft tenor voice, were of hope and pleasant expectation. The change was so remarkable that once I made the mistake, or so it seemed then, of mentioning it to him.

"I take it as a compliment," he smiled. "You know, you're in good company. When I went to Rome with the Archbishop he told me one of his colleagues—I won't say who—told him I looked far too much like Savonarola for my own good."

I smiled. He was anything but that.

"But since you liked the sermon so much, Brolie, I wonder if you'd do me a favour."

"Certainly, Father."

"Every week we have to take a copy to the newspaper. Father Bracken used to do it but he's left us now. If it's not too far out of your way, would you mind dropping it in? There's a Mr Cranborne there who will take it from you."

"I'd be glad to," I said.

Soon it became a regular duty for me and though it did take me a little out of my way I quite enjoyed being involved; even when Bishop Halsey gave the sermon I was the one who stayed behind and took it the few blocks to the *Courier-Mail*.

So there were many activities to keep me occupied and to push out his memory while he was away—my study, my time at the cathedral. And of course there were boys and young men who were good companions and some not so good. Perhaps if there had been someone special, the memory of Pal Lingard might have faded altogether. But, as it happened, the result was just the opposite. Instead, I found myself comparing them with him and always there was an element in their characters which he lacked or which he possessed in greater measure. Either way, they failed by

174

comparison.

Often when I returned home from some dance or party with one of them I would have an unreasoning urge to sit down at my study table, a beautiful, smooth table my father had made for me, and write him a letter. I told myself it wasn't a letter really, more of a diary and he was just a face, a memory, a focal point, a substitute for the rather stupid practice of writing to oneself. If I addressed my thoughts to him they would become clearer in my mind. They would flow better when a reaction could be imagined. That was my rationale and it was necessary to my pride. I kept the letters and I have them still. I have not read them for a long time but they are almost committed to memory. He never saw them.

Also, the shop was a public place and the lives of its owners were played out in public. We had all seen with each passing week the change that was taking place in Mrs Lingard. We were spectators as the leukaemia robbed her first of her animation then of her life. It was partly that which drove the customers away. They could admire her courage, and Mr Lingard's, with their words and their minds but something deep in their hearts, some primal fear, some horror of association with the taint and the atmosphere of impending death, drove them away in spite of themselves. I felt it too. But I overcame it. It was important to me and I sought strength in prayer. I prayed to the Holy Mother and, as always, She answered me.

I prayed for Pal too when the news of his accident reached us. And after that there was no question in my mind, no doubt at all that he would be spared. And when, so soon afterwards it seemed, I opened the Sunday paper to see his name and to read his story as we sat around our big living room after church, there was a sense in me suddenly that was marvellously uplifting and calming at once; as though I were both a spectator and a participant in his life.

So I searched for him. In the streets and on the buses and in the crowded traffic of the city. Sometimes I would rise early to hear Father O'Hanlon or Monsignor Guy say early Mass at the cathedral on my way to the office. On those occasions I remember thinking that the first person I would see when I walked out on to the footpath would be him. And he would walk up to me and say, "Brolie, you've changed", and he would smile and I would see that he was really thinking, "would you believe it? The ugly duckling has turned into the swan."

But I did not find him. He was gone for four months and I learned later just a part of what had happened to him. I didn't learn it in a single conversation or even in a series of related talks. I had to piece it together from single references, from allusions to other things. We might be passing a storehouse or a factory and he would say, "I worked there once", and I would know that it was useless to question him further. If I asked when, he would say, "That time". It was always "That time". The time when he stayed in a filthy old boarding house near Boggo Road jail; when he drank beer and rum in the public bars of the Spring Hill hotels; when he forgot his way home and slept in parks hiding from police cars or in dark corners of the city streets; when he worked as a storeman and packer, a garage attendant, a factory hand, no single job lasting more than a week or two.

And there were other things too. Terrible things. He never even hinted at them. He hid them. But I knew they were there and they frightened me.

I did not find him. If I had . . . well, there are so many ifs. I did not know it but I was not the only one looking for him. She found him. Adele Champion. She came down from the country and with a greater practicality than I—no doubt due to a greater experience of life—she simply went to the police and reported him missing. The police found him almost immediately. By then he was known to them.

Adele Champion. It is as hard now for me to write her name or to think it as it has always been. I know that I'm unfair to her. I know that all the choking hatred I poured out on her name and her image was, in a sense, a symptom of my own frustration and jealousy. My own inadequacy. She was able to give him something which was quite beyond my power. I couldn't compete. But even if I had tried, it would have made no difference. He would still have turned to her. I know that I'm being unfair to her but I can't help it. I hate her.

I met her only three or four times. After the first occasion I never wanted to see her again. I never wanted him to see her again either but that was too much to ask for. She was charming and attractive, with an oval face, a pointed chin and a very pale complexion which was made even more pale by her shining dark hair. When I first saw her, she must have been nearly forty. That means that on the last occasion she would have been forty-seven or forty-eight. But I have no impression of her ageing and changing over the years. She had one of those small, trim figures that remain unaffected by advancing years.

She found him. She took him to Mr Morely and got him a job on the newspaper. Then she went back to her family.

Mr Lingard told me the news and in his quiet way there was a hint of triumph in his manner, as though I had been the alarmist. Perhaps it was justified but I think not. Looking back, I believe much of what followed can be traced to that terrible, desolate, lonely time.

Of course, the Sunday immediately after I heard the news I could barely contain myself through the service and when Monsignor Guy, whose turn it was that week, handed me the notes I skimmed over the footpath towards the newspaper building.

By then I had been going to the *Courier-Mail* with the cathedral sermons for more than a year and it had become a pleasant routine. I would arrive at the office in Queen Street opposite the G.P.O. at about one o'clock and the doorman, whom everyone called Joe and who looked like a retired railway clerk, would see me coming and pull open the big swing door into the lobby. He had a wide, endearing grin and it fascinated me because he had no top teeth. Or if he had, he left them out and gave them a rest on the Sabbath.

"Afternoon, miss," he would say. "I think you know the way, don't you?" On my first visit he had shown me the way and after that he repeated the same sentence every week as though he were giving me credit for being a fast learner.

The way was not difficult. You walked straight into the lift, pressed the third floor button and when the doors opened there you were. First door on your right and you had made it to the reporters' room. They called it the General Room and at that time on a Sunday it was almost deserted. The rows of old, marked and grooved timber desks, some with typewriters and all with big black telephones, always reminded me of a classroom in a condemned secretarial school.

Usually there were two or three reporters at their desks and when I entered they smiled at me as I made my way down the aisle to the back of the room where the churches' editor, Douglas Cranborne, established his little domain. Mr Cranborne—I never did feel I could call him Douglas—was a pleasant enough man, I suppose, though I found him the least attractive of the Sunday afternoon regulars. He was large and soft looking with pale hair and a habit of looking down his nose at you through non-existent spectacles perched on the end. He had no sense of humour and though he was Church of England himself he always found something to say about Bishop Halsey which made it appear they were on intimate terms. I found him a little daunting.

Another of the regulars was John Lavelle, the police roundsman. He had shiny dark hair and sleepy eyes. "Like George Raft in his dancing days", Pal once said and it sounded just right. Whenever he wasn't busy, John would make a point of chatting with me for a few minutes on my way out. At first, I think he had in mind to ask if he could drive me home. But when he saw I wasn't interested we just talked.

Then there was Remus McCabe, a fat, ginger-haired man who was acting chief of staff and who sat in a glassed-in office at one end of the General Room, preparing assignments for the reporters who began work later in the afternoon. I liked him but I never knew when to take him seriously. He took great delight in saying the most extraordinary

177

things in strange American accents. He had been stationed in New York for a couple of years and the accents seemed to be a habit with him when he was with people he didn't know very well. Naturally, all the reporters called him "Uncle" and, when he wasn't being a New York cab driver or a southern plantation owner, he did have a rather overbearing avuncular quality as well.

I reached the big swing door of the building and Joe gave me his ritual greeting. But suddenly I didn't want to go on. I was afraid. There were too many thoughts, too many feelings crowding in on me.

What if he had completely forgotten me? And after all, why shouldn't he? He had been in a completely different existence. So much had happened to him out there, things that were completely outside my experience. We would have nothing in common any more. There was nothing for us to say to each other. I was just a ghost from his past and probably not a very welcome ghost at that.

I was terribly tempted just to give the sermon to Joe and ask him to take it up. But I knew that wouldn't solve anything. Next week would be the same and I couldn't go on avoiding him indefinitely. And what's more I didn't want to avoid him. I wanted to see him and talk to him. But not now. Not just at this minute.

The lift door slammed behind me. I pushed open the door to the reporters' room. He wasn't there. I breathed again. Mr Cranborne took the notes and asked after the bishop's health and I had to admit that I didn't know he'd been unwell.

As I turned, I saw John Lavelle talking to another reporter whose name I didn't know. A tall, eagle-faced young man. It might have been James Wilson Jenner who was later killed in Vietnam. But in any case, John broke away and intercepted me. I was hoping he would.

"And how's Our Lady of the Cathedral today?" he asked.

"Well, thank you. What dreadful crimes am I going to read about in tomorrow's paper?"

"Will you settle for a hit and run. A little girl on a bike . . ."

"No. How horrible. Is she going to be all right?"

"No. She was D.O.A."

"Oh dear."

"They'll get him, though. They've got the number and the car's easily recognised. The windscreen was smashed when the girl . . ."

"Please. I don't want to hear about it."

"Sorry, but you did ask."

"I should have learned better by now." There was a silence. For a moment the image of the little girl put everything else out of my mind. Then I remembered.

"John, do you know Palmer Lingard? No, that's silly. Of course you know him."

"You mean the new cadet?"

Just then Remus McCabe joined us. "Hey, Lavelle," he said. "What's with the broad?" I'm not sure what he was being. Perhaps a Lower East Side Italian. "What's de idea bringin' broads inta da office, huh? What can we do for yuh, babe, huh? Huh? And what's with the white drag, lady? Hey, Lavelle, you moonlighting as altar boy again?"

John grinned and I giggled in spite of myself.

"Come off it, Uncle," he said. "Brolie's just been asking about Pal Lingard . . ."

"Lingard, huh? She knows da kid, huh?" He turned to me. "Lay off da kid, lady. He's goin' ta be all right, see."

"What's wrong with him?" I said.

He dropped the accent and his expression was serious. "Nothing," he said. "He'll be okay. Have you known him long?"

"Yes. About ten years. But I haven't seen him for a long while."

He turned back to Lavelle. "Did you tell her what he did?"

"No, she just mentioned him when you interrupted."

"Don't get smart, Lavelle. No one's indispensable, yah know." Then: "Are you a friend of his?"

"Yes, I think so. As I said, it's been a long while . . ."

"Yeah. Brolie, come inside with me for a minute, will you. And wipe that grin off your face, Lavelle. Da broad's a lady, see."

Inside the glass walls, all his playfulness was gone. He lit a cigarette and leaned back in his chair which squeaked with his weight.

"Maybe you can help me," he said.

"I don't see how."

"Well, you know him, which is more than anyone else does around here. Me included."

"I still don't see . . ."

"Brolie, what sort of a kid is he?"

"I don't know what you mean. He was always very bright. Very active."

"Moody? Temperamental?"

"No. Not temperamental."

"I see. Well, let me tell you the story. Maybe you can fill in some of the gaps."

I nodded.

"You don't mind, do you?"

I had half a mind to tell him I didn't want to hear. It seemed a little like eavesdropping and it made me uncomfortable. But before I could say anything, he took a puff of his cigarette and started again.

"For my sins," he said, "which are legion, I'm the paper's cadet counsellor. It doesn't mean much, but among other things I look after the new cadets and see that they shape up or ship out." He paused.

"Lingard's an exceptional case in the first place because he's so much older than the rest so we've started him off as a Second Year. But because he knows nothing about newspapers he's going through the same early training as the others."

He sucked his cigarette again. "Well, the first day he reported for work I sat him down with the rest and tried to explain the mechanics, you know, the simple mechanics of writing a newspaper story. They all listened like good schoolkids and then I gave them a hypothetical story and told them to go away and write it.

"The story was just something I made up on the spur of the moment. A man is taken by a shark while he's swimming on one of the south coast beaches; the lifesavers try to get to him on their surfboards but can't; a bystander rushes into the water but that's no good either. He's too late to save the unfortunate soul in the water but he'll probably get the George Cross in the New Year's Honours list. Okay? A simple, straightforward story. The page one lead, certainly, but not a complicated story."

"It's a horrible story," I said. "Why would you think of a terrible thing like that?"

"I don't know, it just occurred to me. It was just an exercise, for Godsake. So, I gave them an hour to finish it and by then the other three had handed in their copy. But not friend Pal. He settled himself in a corner with a pencil and a writing pad—the others had picked theirs out on typewriters—and wrote like a bat out of hell. I gave him a little longer, then I went over and told him he'd done enough and to give me what he'd finished. And to put it politely—a damn sight more politely than he put it—he declined. I gave him another half hour and this time I didn't muck around. I told him I wanted it right now, pronto. I won't repeat what he said and I think if anyone else had said it I would have thumped him. Maybe I should have."

"Why?"

"Brolie, it's been a mighty long time since I've taken that kind of abuse and it'll be a bloody long time before it happens again."

"So what happened?"

"Nothing happened. I left him to finish his story which he did about six hours later and when I came in next day it was waiting on my desk, all neatly typed, all twenty quarto pages of it."

"Twenty pages," I said. "That seems long."

"For a newspaper story? Of course it is. It's impossibly long. But any resemblance to a newspaper story was, as they say, purely coincidental. It was a short story; fiction. At least I think it was. In a way, it read as though he'd been there and seen it happen. Is that possible, do you know? Did I, by some fantastic chance, just happen

180

to pick a situation that he'd been involved in? Was there anyone in his family or any friend taken by a shark at some stage? If there was, I could understand it."

I shook my head. "No, I'm certain of that. I would have heard about it. There was no one."

He ground out the cigarette in an ashtray. A spark stayed alive and the smoke curled slowly towards me.

"So, you think he made it up as he went along?"

"I don't know. There might have been a time when he was very young . . . no, I would have heard about it. I'm sure I would."

"Well," he said. "There you are then."

"Do you still have the story?"

"Yep," he said. "Do you want to read it?"

"Yes, if I could. I could bring it back to you next Sunday."

"Okay." He leaned down and pulled the pages out of an open briefcase by his desk. "I think it'll surprise you," he said. "He can certainly write, the so-and-so."

"It's nicely typed," I said.

"By Mavis Calloway," he said. "Miss Mavis Calloway. The dragon lady herself. Secretary and faithful retainer these forty years to our noble assistant editor, Arthur Morely."

"I see."

"If you do," he said, "then you're a jump ahead of me. Old Mavis hasn't done a tap for anyone but Arthur since Adam was in short pants."

"Perhaps Mr Morely asked her to."

"Nope. Friend Palmer told me that himself. He just left it on her desk with a little note when he went home that night and when he came in next morning, presto, there it was in his box. I even checked with Arthur. He knew nothing about it. Not that he minded. Arthur got him the job, you know. Some old flame—sorry, some old friend—brought him in off the streets a couple of weeks ago. Do you know her, by the way?"

"Who?"

"The woman. Is it his mother?"

"No, his mother died a little while ago."

He nodded. "Well, there it is. A mystery at every turn."

I rose to leave. I still had the feeling that I was not being fair to him, that I was somehow prying into his affairs behind his back. But now that I had the story I wanted to be on my own so that I could read it. Remus McCabe came out from behind his desk. I folded the pages of the story.

"I'll give it back to you next week," I said.

"That's all right. In fact, you can give it back to the man himself if you like. I've just been making up the roster. He'll be on the early shift next Sunday."

"Oh. All right." I hurried out of the room.

I didn't read the story until that night. I was conscious of it all the way home and all through the afternoon, and the temptation to take it out and read it was almost overwhelming. But I resisted it. I savoured the expectation. Until I was in bed I didn't even peek at the first page. But then, comfortable and snug, I switched on my reading light and took it out.

It was fascinating. It started, I thought, just like a newspaper article: "A man was fatally attacked by a shark while swimming with hundreds of holiday-makers at Palm Beach yesterday." And for the next few sentences it continued in that rather heartless, journalistic vein. But then suddenly it changed. The whole character and style of the writing changed. The sentences became longer and the descriptions of the people and the scene became more clear and more evocative. More exact. More intimate. It was as though a painter had begun sketching in pencil and then had suddenly seized his brushes and palette and brought his canvas to life. Suddenly you were no longer outside the scene. You were involved in it. You were part of it. You felt the man's terror. When he screamed, you felt the same sound rising in your own throat. When you looked helplessly on from the shallows, you felt the same horror and pain that the onlookers felt. The same emptiness in the stomach, the same trembling at the knees.

In no time at all I had finished it. I was back safe in my bed. I found that my hands were shaking.

I read it again and then a third time and each time the effect was the same. When I reached the end I had to shake myself mentally, to force the images away, to remind myself that it was only a story. I was a very long time getting to sleep. Each time I closed my eyes the images returned. Finally I got up and drank some warm milk and after that it was better.

The week dragged for the first four days then hurried by for the next three. Then once again it was Sunday and I was back ouside the imposing stone building. But this time I was prepared. The nerves of the previous week were now excitement and anticipation.The conversation with Remus McCabe had troubled me a little at first, but after a while it seemed obvious he was making a fuss about nothing. McCabe's rather irritating mannerisms would try anyone's patience. And what was so unusual about a secretary typing an article for a new reporter? If anything, I felt a sympathy for Pal rather than the older man.

It was a warm afternoon and as usual I was wearing the white cotton dress and the white shoes and gloves which I wore each

Sunday to choir. I looked, I think, as pretty as I will ever look. Prettier. I had, my father said, a perfect complexion and I used only a little lipstick and sometimes, though not on this occasion, a touch of eye shadow. My figure was good and I had nice legs and I was happy and excited inside and that always shows through. The footpath was almost deserted and I quickly checked my appearance in the little compact mirror I carried in my purse. I did look pretty. My hair was shoulder length and wavy and my reflection was smiling back at me. When I tried to look serious I found I couldn't. My lips wouldn't relax. I popped the compact back into the purse and, as I approached the glass door, I caught a flash of myself when Joe pulled it open. I was still smiling.

"Yes, I do know the way, Joe," I said and as soon as the words were out I could have bitten my tongue. His welcoming grin threatened to subside. "But of course I'd always be glad of an escort," I said quickly and the grin came instantly back into place.

"If I was thirty years younger, miss . . ." he said. "I really shouldn't leave the lobby." He walked with me across the marble floor. "But the least I can do is get you the lift."

He pressed the button and I glanced up as usual at the inscription engraved in gold letters above the lift: "Freedom of the press is indivisible and cannot be limited without being lost—Thomas Macaulay." I always repeated the words over to myself while I waited for the lift. They had a fine, heroic ring.

Joe pulled the door open and I stepped inside. But, just as the doors closed and I reached for the button, they suddenly slid back. Someone else entered.

For a moment I didn't recognise him. He was so thin and gaunt. His face was parchment white and there were dark rings around his eyes. A crimson scar split his forehead and disappeared into his hair which was uncombed and untidy and there were lines at his mouth. His jaw muscles stood out and I could see them straining with pressure. His shirt was frayed around the collar and his suit looked as though it hadn't been pressed for a week or more.

But the thing which really struck me was the way he had aged. He looked not two years but ten years older than when I had last seen him. It was impossible to believe that he was actually a year younger than me.

He barely glanced at me. He slammed his thumb on to the button then moved to the back of the lift. I didn't take my eyes off him. He was a stranger. But it was him, unmistakably. Yet how could he have aged so much? What had he been through? What was the matter with him? Why hadn't they told me? Remus McCabe had called him the kid. But he was no longer a kid. I had to say something quickly, speak

182

to him and hear the familiar voice. But what? Dear Mother, what?

He stared resolutely ahead, his eyes fixed on the door in front of him as the lift ascended then braked gently at the third floor. I had to break the silence before it stopped.

"Hello, Palmer," I said. "Don't you remember me?" In the quietness of the lift it sounded unnaturally loud and harsh.

"What?" He stared at me and there was such a fierceness in his eyes that I half expected him to slap me across the face. I felt that somehow I almost deserved to be slapped.

"Bronwyn," I prompted. "Brolie Cassidy."

He continued to stare. Then the words registered and his expression slowly changed. The furrows above his eyebrows flattened and his green eyes focused on me. He encompassed me with them and I could watch him registering every detail as though committing it to memory. His face relaxed some more.

"Of course I remember you," he said. But his voice was so soft and quiet I had to strain to catch the words. The lift stopped but neither of us made a move to open the door.

"I heard you were working here," I said. "I heard it last week . . . two weeks ago from your father. Then last week, when I brought the sermon around, Remus McCabe said you'd be here today." The words were pouring out of me and there was nothing I could do to stop them. "I bring the sermon from St Stephen's every week and Mr Cranborne takes some sentences out of it for his column." I stopped and still he stared.

"God's messenger," he said.

I expected him to smile with the words and I smiled in response but his expression didn't change.

"I suppose so," I said. "I mean, it's a funny way of looking at it . . . Mr Cranborne . . . I mean, not really . . ." I stumbled to a halt. Then remembering, I said hastily, "Palmer, I'm very sorry about your mother. I went up to the shop to see you when I heard but . . . we went to her funeral . . ."

"I wasn't there."

"No."

The silence that followed lasted for only a few seconds, I suppose, but it seemed forever. My response, prompting a reply, was left hanging.

"Well," I said finally, I moved to open the door but he reached out before me and dragged the metal lattice screen back, then held the heavier outside door open for me. "I should deliver the sermon," I said as I passed close to him.

The faint wisp of a humourless smile just touched his face making me suddenly aware of the double meaning in my words. "To Mr

Cranborne," I said but it was lost in the rattle and slamming of the lift doors as he followed me down the passageway. I could hear his footsteps on the hard floor. It sounded as though he was limping.

As I made my way through the desks I was aware of only one sensation, the relentless stare that I could feel piercing me from behind. If I spoke with Douglas Cranborne then I have forgotten what was said. But as I walked back I saw Pal and Remus McCabe in the glass office. Pal was twisted round in his chair and they were both looking at me. I was certain that McCabe had said something about me and Pal was looking around towards me in response.

"Hey." It was John Lavelle. I was glad of the distraction. It would give me a moment to think. "That's a worried look for a cathedral girl on a Sunday." Lavelle was smiling.

"Hello, John." I changed direction but as I did I was aware of a movement in the office and Pal came quickly through the door and intercepted me.

"You have something of mine," he said. His voice was cold and hard.

"Yes. I'm sorry." I fumbled at the catch on my purse. "Remus McCabe gave it to me last week. I was bringing it back."

John Lavelle came towards us. "What's up?" he said.

"Stay out of it, Lavelle," Pal said and the friendly expression on the police roundsman's face froze for an instant then puckered into a frown.

"What do you mean . . ."

Pal ignored him but by then I had the white pages out of the purse and I handed them over. "I thought it was very good," I said, but even to me the words sounded defensive and hollow and inadequate.

"Thank you," he said, whether for the meagre compliment or for the story's return I couldn't tell. He left abruptly and returned to the glass office.

"What was that all about?" John Lavelle said.

"Oh nothing." I could feel myself close to tears. I wanted to run to the door, to the lift, to the street, anywhere. There were voices raised inside McCabe's office. I glanced past John and saw Pal standing on one side of the desk staring down at Remus McCabe, whose fat face seemed on the point of bursting. Then the rush of tears came back behind my eyes and I was walking quickly down the corridor. John Lavelle's voice pursued me. "What the devil is going on . . . damn it . . ."

Joe the doorman said something but it didn't register. The street was nearly deserted and I walked for a long while before I reached the bus stop. All the while I was thinking that life should be like one of those films that runs backwards so that if there is a part of it that seems wrong, the film maker can cut it out and replace it with another scene. I wanted desperately to be able to do it again. To forget that the meeting had occurred. To have a second chance. If only I could, I would make it all different. I would be prepared. It would be different.

AFTER that first meeting I expected never to see him again. By the time I reached home I had already thought of two or three perfectly good excuses for not having to return to the *Courier-Mail*. There were plenty of others in the choir or the congregation who could do it. Monsignor Guy and the others wouldn't press me.

I had made another decision too. It was time for my foolishness to stop. Time I came to my senses and acted my age. Time I realised there was nothing, and could be nothing, between Pal Lingard and myself. That was the rational thing to do, the only rational thing. I would put him behind me, get him into proper perspective as simply an adolescent obsession, a part of growing up. The thought itself was a help. It put a distance between us and the distance, I knew, would grow the longer I kept my resolution.

But then, late that evening, he telephoned. Connie answered it and I could hear her from the lounge room laughing and chatting and I thought it must have been one of her many admirers. She had them by the droves. Ever since she was sixteen there was always at least one boy and usually two or three on a string. I wasn't jealous of her, at least not in the usual way. I think I envied her exuberance and her vitality but the boys she had in tow were always such dumb-bells they could hardly excite jealousy, at least in me.

She was flushed when she came back into the room. "It's for you," she grinned. "A surprise."

And I was surprised, not so much that it was Pal but at the gentle tone of his voice, the pleasure in his laugh, the genuine interest with which he questioned me, the sincerity of his apology. The fierce, gaunt, self-absorbed figure of the afternoon might never have existed.

It confused me and thrilled me and when he asked if he could take me to dinner the following evening I probably accepted far more quickly and eagerly than I should have. But when it was over and I was back in the lounge with the family, and after Connie had had her joke about my rather breathless appearance, I felt I could analyse and see the reason for his strange attitude of the afternoon. I saw it as part loneliness, part shock at seeing me again, but most of all the distaste he must have felt at my invasion of his privacy, my talking with Remus McCabe and reading his story behind his back. I had never felt happy about it and my intuition was right.

187

He had no car, so rather than bring him all the way out to St Lucia I met him outside the restaurant. He was waiting on the footpath and he smiled at me through the crowd as I approached and came a few steps towards me.

"I hope you haven't been waiting long," I said.

"It was worth it," he said and his smile broadened.

I relaxed immediately. He was just the way he had been on the phone—pleasant and charming and interested. His appearance was still a little disconcerting. The skin seemed to be stretched taut over his cheek bones and there was an unnatural brightness to his eyes, as though he was suffering from a slight fever. But, apart from that, he was much more like the Pal Lingard I used to know than the stranger I had met in the newspaper building.

The restaurant was a new one I had never been to before, a little place in Albert Street where you had to go downstairs from the footpath and there were candles on the tables and New Australians—Italians or Greeks—as waiters. It was rather dimly lit and there was soft music playing gently in the background.

A waiter led us to our place and almost immediately there were drinks in front of us—mine was a martini, the first I had ever tasted—and Pal was talking.

I have no memory of what he said. I cannot recall a single phrase. All I remember is that as he talked I sat opposite him looking into his face, oblivious to everything else around me. He made pictures with his words, pictures and scenes, some funny, some desperately sad, some exciting and filled with action and drama, but in every case completely compelling.

He interrupted himself to order for us and the meal passed very quickly. I think he barely touched his and concentrated instead on the wine. Then I was talking too. Suddenly I felt the words coalescing into fine phrases and witty asides and I was joining him. He was drawing me out of myself and whole thoughts sprang into my mind and I was able to send them out across the table to him.

But then, just as suddenly, he was silent. It was as though he had thrown a switch. His face was expressionless. My words and thoughts were not penetrating and I was floundering. I tried to smile at one of my own remarks but his expression remained unchanged. He wasn't listening. I was no longer a person but an object and I heard my voice fading into silence.

"Pal, is there something wrong? Did I say something . . ."

"What?" His face cleared. A tight smile stretched his lips and his eyes refocused but with what seemed a conscious effort.

"No," he said. "On the contrary. I was just thinking how lovely you look. Do you know, I haven't taken a girl out for . . . almost as

188

long as I can remember."

The awkward moment passed and we resumed our conversation but for the rest of the evening I was unable to recapture the exhilaration and carelessness I had felt, the complete self-confidence of those few moments.

He took me home and in the back of the taxi we sat close together. I was wondering all the while if he would kiss me when we reached my home. But instead he made some little joke when we got to the front door and came inside for a minute to say hello to my parents. He stayed only a short while as he had kept the taxi waiting but I felt he made an excellent impression on my father.

I suspect that my father, like many accountants and others who spend their working lives enmeshed in balance sheets, had a deep curiosity, almost an awe, of someone who was able to express himself in an artistic way. Anyway, he was very jolly and hearty with Pal after the inevitable awkward moments at the beginning when both mother and father offered their condolences.

Later when I was in bed I went over every single moment of the evening a dozen times and each time was better than the last. The small incident dissolved into nothing and I went to sleep with the image of him sitting across from me, his hands moving expressively as he talked, the light burning in his eyes and that soft modulated voice creating pictures and scenes in the air around us.

After that we met at least two or three times a week for dinner when he was working the day shift and later, when he was moved to evening work, we had lunch together nearly every day. He had a very small flat in New Farm then and on Saturdays I would usually go there to help him clean it up and do his laundry. It was always a shambles when I arrived. He was then, and forever after, the untidiest person I have ever known. His clothes were strewn about the room, his suits crumpled in corners, the dishes piled in the sink and invariably in the refrigerator there were at least two half-filled bottles of sour milk. I could never understand how he could bear to come home to such a mess.

"I never see it," he said.

"But you must, Pal. Can't you smell the milk? Can't you see the mould on the cheese? And what are you going to wear to work tomorrow? There's absolutely nothing left that's wearable. Nothing."

His answer was to change the subject.

But it gave me pleasure to look after him in this way and to keep some kind of order in the apartment. I wanted to do more. Apart from the meals we had together I knew he wasn't eating properly or regularly. There seemed always to be something else on his mind,

189

some reporting job or an idea for a story, I thought, which was more important to him.

Only twice in three months did he come home to dinner and neither occasion was really successful. He agreed only after I really pressed him and both times he seemed subdued and preoccupied. Of course, Connie and Mary made a fuss of him but my mother was reserved and I'm sure he was aware of it. I knew that the difference in our religions was the cause of her attitude but I felt it best to say nothing, at least for the time being.

It was almost the same with Pal. He made no reference to it but I knew it was there. Whenever the conversation threatened to lead us in that direction he changed its course to other less divisive channels.

In a sense, I was happy to avoid it. That way we could just enjoy each other's company and keep the relationship uncomplicated. But it wasn't that simple. Every time I was with him, every day I was alive it seemed, I was coming closer to him, becoming more dependent on him, more a part of him. Each new day began with a thought of him and each evening ended the same way. It was as though he had wrapped himself around me like the fine silk of a cocoon and the thing inside was changing with a beautiful inevitability into something grand. We had so quickly, I thought, passed over the normal barriers and inhibitions people erect around themselves that I was sure in my soul that one day we would be married. Nothing less would satisfy me. Nothing else was really possible for me. And I was sure from his attitude and his words that the same idea was in his mind. Not perhaps the all-encompassing emotion, the love, that I felt for him but it was there—a communion, a depth and an intensity of feeling.

So I knew I had to face the question and I had to ask Pal to face it too. But before I did, I had to be clear in my own mind. What would I do if he refused to change his religion? I might have wondered vaguely what my answer would have been if he had asked me to break away and give up my faith. But I was sure that he had no strong allegiance to the Methodist Church. In fact, from his evasiveness I began to hope that he held no deep personal commitment either way. And if that were true, I felt he would see my point of view and understand the importance of it to me. I dwelt upon that hope in the quiet hours at night when I lay in bed conjuring up visions of the way it might be, then agonising over the alternatives if he would not make the effort, if he became obdurate and thoughtlessly wilful. I tried to banish such thoughts but they kept returning to haunt me. And all I could do finally when my imagination turned nightmarish was to pray to God and the Blessed Mother for the courage to face it. I dared not pray for intercession. To do so would be to reveal a hesitancy in my own conviction and determination. I had to find the strength within myself

190

to set down my own values and stick to them.

Once I actually started to produce a balance sheet, a kind of emotional ledger so that I could see the problem on paper and calculate the results of all the possibilities. But of course I abandoned it incomplete. How could I ascribe a numerical value to love or to faith. I tore it up. And that solved nothing.

Then there was the physical attraction I felt for him, and it too was fraught with complications and contradictions. When I think of the way he was then, the word respectful comes to mind. But that doesn't really describe his attitude. He was gentle yet intense. He was masterful and confident yet deferential whenever he seemed to sense a hesitancy on my part. When he kissed me I was suddenly filled with such powerful, overwhelming emotions that I was afraid of them and of what was happening to me. I didn't trust myself to keep control. Logically, of course, I knew exactly what was happening. But emotionally I was so undeveloped then that the sudden presence of this great tide of emotion within me frightened me terribly and I shrank away from it.

He was considerate. He let me catch my breath.

But despite the complications, I was happy. Vividly happy. When I was with him I felt I was living a different life from the one I had known. More intense; more exciting. The smallest details of living had a new importance, a new reality. I was even happy when I worried about him. I actually had someone to worry about. Someone I loved.

But my worries were serious too. I knew he was drinking too much. Not when he was with me, but the evidence was all too obvious when I went to his flat on Saturday mornings. I said nothing but I was afraid that he might be damaging his health. He was still terribly thin and there was always a tension in him, a brittleness, as though his nerves were stretched tight with the effort of his work and his writing. I tried to comfort him and distract him but that seemed only to make it worse. He was like that on the night I went to my first journalists' party. I had heard about the parties he went to after work but I had never been with him and I had the feeling that he didn't really want to take me.

But nothing was planned about that evening. I had gone to see a film with Connie at a theatre not far from the *Courier-Mail* and on an impulse I decided to call by the newspaper to say hello to him on our way home.

Apparently it was a quiet night for news and the reporters were sitting around at their desks talking and arguing when we arrived. Pal was off in one corner typing laboriously with two fingers and we had to pass by the others to get to him. Some of them recognised me and called out to me and Pal looked up. For a moment he stared vacantly at us then he frowned and pulled the paper out of the typewriter, shoved it into a drawer and came to meet us.

"This is a pleasant surprise," he said. "Hello, Connie."

"I hope we didn't interrupt you. We can wait until you finish," I said.

"No. It's just an idea I had for a feature. It can wait till tomorrow."

"We've been to see *The Entertainer*. We thought you might have time for a cup of coffee."

"Sure. It's nearly knock-off time anyway. What did you think of the film? It's good isn't it."

"I'm sure Brolie thinks so," Connie said. "She cried for the last half hour."

"Did she?" Pal grinned. "How about you?"

"Not likely."

"I'll just go and ask the chief of staff if I can leave," he said. As he was moving away, James Wilson Jenner caught him.

"Hey, you want to go to a party?"

"Nope."

"I do," Connie said.

Pal turned back to us. There was an edge to his voice. "What about you, Brolie?"

"I don't know. What kind of a party?"

"Just a party," Jenner said.

"Where?" Pal asked.

"Uncle's."

"Isn't he on tonight?"

"No, Lavelle just called him. He's expecting us."

"Thanks anyway, Wilson . . ."

"Oh come on, Pal, don't be a grump," Connie interrupted.

He looked steadily at her and for a moment I sympathised with her. Then he smiled. "Okay, you win."

"We'll just stay a little while," I said. "I'll call home and tell them we'll be late."

"All right."

We crowded into Jenner's car—Connie in the front with him and another reporter, Pal and myself in the back squeezed between Harry Mesmer the sports writer and Suzy Lindeman from the Women's Page. I hadn't met either of them before and once or twice as we drove I tried to make conversation with them but everything I said seemed to fall on empty air and my words sounded trite and naïve. So I stayed quiet and just listened as they spoke across us. I could make very little sense of what they said. They talked in a kind of shorthand and I felt completely excluded.

The party was quiet at first. Remus McCabe seemed much less boisterous in his home surroundings—a cluttered but well furnished flat at Kangaroo Point—and was a very easy-going host. Not that his guests made great demands on him. They simply stacked their beer into his refrigerator when they arrived then served themselves until it was gone. His only contribution seemed to be a great slab of cheese that lay skewered by a carving knife in the centre of a battered cedar dining table which had been drawn into the lounge room for the occasion.

Almost immediately after we arrived, Connie was led away to a corner by Wilson Jenner and John Lavelle and I saw very little of her for the rest of the evening. For a while I sat on a big comfortable lounge with Pal and just listened to the reporters talk.

At first the conversation was about other journalists whose names meant nothing to me. But then they began to speak about public figures, people whose names featured almost daily in the news and whose reputations for decency and honesty I had always taken for granted until then. But as they spoke, these people became almost unrecognisable. They talked about their nasty personal habits, their selfish motives and their finangling and manipulating with such complete matter-of-factness that there was just no room for disagreement. And this was the case, not only with people who might be suspect, like politicians, but with everyone—doctors, academics, philanthropists, businessmen—everyone. It was sometimes difficult to follow because they referred to them either by their Christian names or by slang names like "the little Hitler" and it wasn't until I whispered to Pal that I understood whom they meant.

But then I was shocked. It was as though another world existed, a completely different world where the normal values of life were just unknown and I suddenly felt that almost everything I read each day in the paper was little more than a fraud, a trick to beguile an innocent public. But I think what disturbed me most was that the journalists seemed to have no sense of outrage at the shoddiness and the trickery they talked about. In fact, I began to get the feeling that they rather relished it, that even though they were being used by all these self-seeking people they almost enjoyed it, that in a sense they were part of it, co-conspirators, and that seemed to give them a sense of superiority which I found rather horrible.

I felt out of my depth and even a little angry. I was terribly tempted to break in sometimes and ask them if the person they were discussing was really so bad, why didn't they write about it in the paper. Why didn't they expose him? Wasn't that what newspapers were for? Wasn't that what Lord Macaulay was talking about in his motto in their foyer? But of course I didn't. I saved it up to ask Pal later. I was rather relieved that he didn't seem to be part of the conspiracy.

In fact, the attitude of the others towards him was even more interesting than their talk. Because he'd been at the paper only three months he wasn't privy, as the more senior reporters were, to that tawdry, behind-the-scenes' world, yet they made no attempt to exclude him from their conversation and patronise him the way they did with the other comparative newcomers. On the contrary, they seemed eager to involve him, to have him join them in their cynicism. They made jokes about his long sojourn in the bush but the cracks were good-natured and obviously designed not to offend but simply to get a laugh. He laughed with them and played the country hick a little for effect but there the joke ended. Nothing went too far and there was, I'm sure, a wariness in their treatment of him, an unwillingness to press too deeply.

There was something else in their attitude too which at the time I didn't quite understand but which afterwards I was able to adjust to proper perspective. I believe it was half envy and half respect. And its cause was undoubtedly his writing. I suspect that most journalists are frustrated authors, that most of them never quite discard the belief that their work is just a preparation for something better, for the big book, the novel that will take the country by storm and lay fame and fabulous riches at their feet.

This was true even of Pal but with him there was an important difference. He was being published as a writer before he became a journalist and of course it was not long afterwards that *The Boy Who Found O'Halloran* was produced. But even in those very early days he was, if not established, then certainly on his way to gaining a reputation for his creative work.

With some of the older men, like Kevin O'Dea, the chief reporter, and Harry Mesmer, this rankled. The idea that a 21-year-old not yet out of his cadetship should have achieved more than they was anathema to them. Of course, with others like Remus McCabe and Dick Morely, Arthur's son, who was probably Pal's only real friend on the paper, the reaction was quite different. To Remus, I think, he represented a kind of vicarious link to the creative world and his successes became very important to the older man.

Dick was different again, and it was at that party that I first met him. He came and sat on the couch with us. He was four or five inches shorter than Pal. His face was as round as the sun and when he smiled, which was often, he reminded me of a child's pumpkin mask at hallowe'en. The grin stretched in a big curve from cheek to cheek and there was no other thought behind it but simple pleasure. He was utterly unaffected by the cynicism and the touch of malice which amused the others. He was far from the carefree innocent that his

194

appearance suggested, but he simply paid such worldliness no heed and allowed it to pass him by. There were better things.

But the quality which drew the two of them together was, I think, Dick's capacity to deflate a situation, to find some small whimsy which would act as a safety valve to the gathering tension and the single-minded intensity that drove Pal beyond himself. Dick was the infallible antidote.

Of course, none of this could even have been guessed at at that first party. As the time passed and the beer flowed, the conversation became louder and the jokes broader. Pal drank his beer quickly but the only effect it seemed to have on him then was a greater animation in his voice and his gestures and even that was probably unnoticeable unless you watched him closely. He smiled and joked with the others but there was a conscious reserve, a tension and an inhibition which I was coming to recognise. I felt he was consciously holding himself back and even rehearsing his words before he let them out, gauging their effect in advance. I had only two or three glasses but that was enough to make me a little light-headed so I stopped.

Then it was time to go. We went looking for Connie and found her still entangled in muted talk with Wilson Jenner. They were in the kitchen and Pal called from the doorway.

"All set?"

"Are you going already?"

"Yes. Come on. We'll get a cab at the corner."

"But it's early, Pal. It's not even 1.30."

He turned to me. "What do you think?"

Before I could answer, Jenner came towards us.

"It's all right. I'll take her home."

Pal ignored him and waited for my response. "It's up to you," I said. "She shouldn't be too much later or they'll worry." It suited me if she stayed. It meant we could be alone.

"We won't be long," Jenner said.

Pal shrugged and we made our way back through the empty beer bottles to the door, calling goodbye as we went.

"You're not worried about her, are you?" I said as we reached the street. "Is Wilson . . . you know?"

"It's not Wilson I'm worried about."

"Connie?"

He was silent. "Connie can look after herself," I said. "In fact she's probably had more practice at it than I have."

"Really?"

It was a beautiful clear night and I took his hand as we walked.

"Yes, really. She's been going out for years now. There's always someone around the house or on the phone to her. Still, you can't blame them, I suppose. She is attractive. She's vivacious. She's fun to be with. Unpredictable. A bit wild. No, I'm the little innocent of the family. Or hadn't you noticed?"

"To tell you the truth, you had me fooled. I thought you were both women of the world and it was only the lovely Mary who kept you all on the straight and narrow."

"Misty? Yes, well you're half right. I don't think there's anyone in the world as angelic as Misty. But she is lovely, Pal, isn't she?"

"She's okay."

"No, I'm serious. She's only fifteen but she's one of the most beautiful creatures I've ever seen. And it isn't just her looks, Pal, she's beautiful all through. She has that special quality . . . don't you see it? I'm sure you do, you must."

He made a grunting noise which could have meant yes or no. We had reached the main street by now and the headlights of the cars brushed over his thin face. He was staring at some point in the darkness across the street.

"Mother thinks she will enter the church," I said. "She's probably right. She has a purity, a quality you can't really define . . ."

He turned abruptly to face me. "Brolie, for Godsake!"

I stepped back a pace. My heel twisted in a crack in the cement footpath and I staggered a little.

"What is it? I don't understand . . ."

"Just stop it. Please."

"What? Pal, what did I say? About Mary becoming a nun? Is that it?"

"No. No, that's not it. It's you. Can't you see that? I don't care if Mary becomes a nun or an astronaut or a trapeze artist. And I don't really care if Wilson Jenner takes Connie away in his car and they aren't seen again for the next six months. Connie's great; Mary's beautiful with a special quality no one can define. All right. But I'm not interested in Mary or Connie. I'm with you and I care about you . . . I . . ."

I stared dumbly at him. "Pal, I'm sorry, it's just that . . ."

"And for Godsake stop apologising."

"Pal, I can't help it. If it annoys you I'm sorry . . ."

"You see."

I could feel myself losing control. My eyes were burning and there seemed nothing I could say.

"I didn't know. I didn't know. I didn't mean to." I was crying in earnest now. He stepped towards me and his arms came around my shoulders. I put my forehead on his chest so he wouldn't see my face.

"Now, now," he said gently. "Don't cry, Brolie. Let's get that cab and go to my flat. It's on the way."

"Pal, it's late."

"Yes, but this is important." He waved at a taxi then held the door open for me. "Besides, I still haven't bought you that cup of coffee."

"Coffee?"

"Yes, isn't that what you came to the office for?"

When we reached his flat, I made some instant coffee while he cleared a space on the night-and-day for us to sit. But when I joined him there the coffee had to wait. I don't know whether it was the beer or whether his harsh words after the party affected me. Perhaps both. But whatever the cause, when he kissed me I felt enfolded, enclosed in darkness yet adrift, set free to be acted upon and affected without troubling about the cause or the result. The real world outside no longer mattered and in the darkness there was only sensation and feeling. His lips and his hands and his body were not separate parts as they touched me. They were one. They were the wind pushing me further and further from my mooring place and the wind was its own shelter. It was around me and inside me too. It relaxed me yet moved me giddily about, then rose some more and pushed me faster and faster through the blackness, faster and faster until suddenly I became aware of it and was afraid. The speed of it, of myself, frightened me and I panicked. I fought it. It was an alien, unwelcome force now. His hand was on me bunching to a fist to work my legs apart and expose me.

"No!" I opened my eyes. Pal was above, looking down at me. There was no expression on his face.

"Yes," he said.

"Please. Please, Pal don't." I pushed his hand away and forced myself almost to a sitting position but with my legs draped awkwardly apart. His hand stayed in contact with me but it was unpleasant now and he could see that.

"Please," I said.

He withdrew the hand and stared at me silently for a long while.

"Pal, I'm . . ."

"No. No apologies remember."

"I remember. But still . . . Oh God, Pal, I love you." I pulled his head down to my shoulder. "It's just me, Pal. I'm sorry but there's nothing I can do about it. No matter how much I want it, no matter how many other people are doing it, I just can't, that's all. And we could talk about it all night and it wouldn't make the slightest bit of difference."

"Why?"

"Because it wouldn't alter a thing. I wouldn't . . ."

"No, I mean why not."

"Because . . ." I took a deep breath. "I suppose because it's wrong."

"Not before marriage, is that it?"

"Not exactly. Yes. I suppose it is. But is that so bad, Pal?"

He stared at me for a long while. "No, I guess not." Then he broke away and went into the tiny bathroom off the lounge. Waiting for him, I finished my coffee and washed the cups. I looked at the time. It was nearly 2.30. I had to call my parents. Connie would surely be home by now and they would be up worrying about me. I lifted the receiver. I was just dialling the first number when I became aware that he was back in the room. I started to speak but stopped when I looked at him.

He was quite motionless yet there was something hard and implacable in his attitude. His eyes were not quite focused, as though he were looking past me and through me to a point on the other side of the room. Yet I felt there was nothing else in his vision or his mind but me. And suddenly, even as the expression changed and he came alive again I knew where I had seen it before, that same look, the same impersonal, withdrawn, unfeeling expression. The first night we had been to dinner together. I had been speaking, talking to him and telling him about myself and it was there.

And there were other times too. I hadn't registered them before or, if I had, they were too minor and fleeting to remark upon. But suddenly they came back to me: another dinner in another restaurant; in the foyer of a theatre; walking together in a park by the river; and that time in the coffee shop in Queen Street when I had just left the table to go to the ladies room and I turned quickly to go back for my purse. But then it was instantly replaced by a warm smile and I thought it must have been my imagination or an unusual pattern of shadow flashing across his face in the artificial twilight of the lounge.

It was the same now. The coldness was gone without a trace and his eyes encompassed me. I was still tempted to say something, to ask him if there was something about me, something that troubled him and forced him away inside himself, but there was no easy way to say it and the thought died in the rush of emotion as he spoke.

"Brolie, would you marry me?"

"I don't know," I said.

"I mean, if I asked you. If I went out to see your father and got his permission then took you off to Lennons and after a magnificent dinner I went down on one knee and asked you to marry me. What would you say?"

His tone was soft and serious but there was something in the words that told me this was not just a roundabout way of proposing. He was asking me a question. He wanted information. But it was more than that too. I felt as if he were testing me and that my answer was

198

important to him not just for its own sake but because in some undefined way it would tell him something about himself and about us. It frightened me. I had no way of knowing what he was seeking, what kind of assurance or encouragement or even challenge was implicit in the question.

"I don't know," I said again.

"Why? Is there something you don't like . . . my job . . . my writing . . ."

"No."

"What then?"

He came towards me, his eyes never leaving my own, and he touched me gently on the arm. His hand was cold and when he saw my reaction he rubbed it softly against my skin until it became warm.

"I don't know." A third time I heard the words and they flustered me. "It's the first time you've mentioned it. I haven't thought about it. No, that's not true. I suppose I have a little. But there are so many things, Pal. Things we have to talk about."

"What, for instance?"

I took another deep breath. "Well, for one thing, religion."

He took his hand from my arm and turned away towards the couch. I followed him. We sat apart.

"Yes," he said. His voice was even softer now. "What about it?"

"Well, I'm sure my family would want me to marry in the Church. I know they would. It's important to them."

He nodded and his eyes found mine again. I could see nothing behind them, no hint of what he was thinking, no reaction at all.

"What about you? Is it important to you?"

"I wouldn't want to hurt them, Pal."

"That wasn't the question."

"No, I know it wasn't but . . . yes," I said. "It is important to me."

"I see. So important that you wouldn't go through with it? You'd say no."

"I don't know. Yes. Pal, you're not being fair. I don't know what I would say." I tried to break the seriousness of the moment. I wanted time to collect my thoughts. I smiled at him. "You aren't being fair, you know. You want to know all the answers before you ask the questions."

His brief smile didn't reach his eyes. "Not all the answers, Brolie. I want to know those things that stand between us. What else is there?"

"Pal, my religion doesn't have to stand between us. You make it sound as though there's nothing that can be done, that we're trapped and there's no way out. It doesn't have to be like that at all."

"So you didn't mean what you said. You could marry me no matter what your parents or your priest said."

"Outside the Church?"

"Yes."

"No, I couldn't, Pal. Don't you see. If I married you at a registry office or in some other church I wouldn't feel married. I wouldn't be married. I wouldn't be happy that way. I couldn't be. I belong to the Church. It's not just something I do on Sundays for the sake of my parents. I believe in it and I always have. Don't you remember the arguments we used to have on the bus about it? Can't you see that I'd never be happy if I went against my own beliefs, if suddenly one day I just threw it all out the window and said: 'That's it. I'm finished with it.'

"It's not like that. I'm not like that. It's a part of me and I happen to believe it's an important part. And if you loved me you would never ask me to give it up . . ." I could feel myself coming close to tears again.

"Brolie . . ."

"No. I have to tell you. You haven't said anything about what you feel, what you believe. You used to talk about it all the time but now it's something you seem to put aside. And you've never said that you love me. Oh, you've said other things but never that and it's important to me . . . it's important to any girl, any woman . . ."

"All right!" He jumped up from the couch, away from me. We were both quiet for a long time.

Then he said, "I understand."

He came back towards the couch. "What would I have to do?" he said.

"When?"

"Any time. What would I have to do to make it right for us to be married in the Catholic Church?"

"Do you mean it?"

"I'm asking you. What's the procedure?"

"I'm not sure. I'll have to ask Monsignor Guy or Father O'Hanlon." The words were rushing out of me. "I think you have to take instruction. I'm sure they would do it. I think you'd like the Monsignor best. No. Perhaps Father O'Hanlon. He used to take Scripture at St Mary's. Do you remember I told you about him once. He's at the cathedral now. I told you, didn't I? I think there are five lessons, or maybe it's eleven. I'll have to make sure. Oh Pal, are you sure you want me to? . . . Are you sure it's what you want? . . . Oh dear, I think you have to sign something. If there are children they'll have to be . . . I mean if we do decide to get married and there are children . . ."

"Brolie, let's drop it for the moment. We'll talk about it again after you've spoken to Father . . ."

200

"O'Hanlon."

"Yes. When will you see him?"

"Tomorrow. No, today. Look at the time. Pal, I'll have to go."

"All right. Let's go and get a taxi."

"There's no need for you to come all the way out to St Lucia," I said. "It'll cost you a fortune."

"I don't mind."

"No, you stay. Save your money."

He looked at me.

"No, I didn't mean that . . . I . . ."

"Yes. It's all right. Call me tonight."

When I reached home the house was in darkness, much to my relief. I was undressing quietly when Connie came into my room.

"Where have you been?"

"The flat. Did they say anything?"

"No, I told them we were together."

"Thanks. See you in the morning."

"Can't we talk for a while? Don't you want to know what happened to me?"

"No. It's late. Go to bed."

Just then the phone in the living room rang. I raced to it before it woke my parents.

"Hello, Pal, is it you?"

"Yes, I . . ."

"What is it?"

His breathing came harshly over the line, then: "Nothing, goodnight." The phone went dead. I tried to call him back but I couldn't get through. The line was engaged. Then when it rang there was no answer. I went back to my bedroom and tried to sleep.

That day I went to the cathedral at lunchtime and talked for nearly an hour with Father O'Hanlon. I wasn't looking for him especially. I would have been just as pleased if I had found Monsignor Guy but he was in the bishopric so Father O'Hanlon and I sat in the choir stalls and he explained it to me.

At first my heart sank. He talked of a ceremony "behind the altar" with the vows taking place in the vestry while the congregation sat out front and waited for us to emerge. It sounded horrible.

But that was only if Pal refused to become a Catholic. If, after instruction, he was converted, we could be married before the altar, in the church and before God. And then too there would be no need for the declaration that our children would be baptised and brought up in the Church.

Would he, Father O'Hanlon, be prepared to give the instruction?

"I'd be delighted." he smiled. "If you say he's the right man,

201

Brolie, I'll do anything I can. I hope you'll be very happy."

"Thank you, Father, I'm sure we will."

Twice during the afternoon I tried to call him at the *Courier-Mail* but no one could find him. He was probably out on a job, they said. I tried again after dinner but still with no success. Finally, Remus McCabe came on the line.

"What have you been doing with my star reporter, Miss Cassidy?" he said.

"I don't know what you mean. Is he sick? What's happened?"

"You haven't heard from him?"

"No. I've been trying to call him all afternoon. Someone said he was out on a job."

"No, he called in sick this morning apparently. Have you tried him at home?"

"No, I'll do that now."

I dialled his number but there was no answer. I tried again in half an hour. By now it was nearly ten o'clock. I was just about to hang up when his voice came on the line. It was muffled, as though I had woken him from a deep sleep.

"Pal, is that you? Are you all right?"

"Who's this?"

"Who do you think? It's Brolie. Remus McCabe said you were sick."

"I am. I'll call you tomorrow."

He was gone. I stood looking at the phone in my hand. He was gone. I wasn't so much angry as afraid. I didn't understand. Perhaps he was really sick. Perhaps he was in pain. I couldn't leave it like that. I started to call his number again but halfway through I stopped. He did say he would call me. If he wanted to talk he knew where I was. And now was no time to be pressing him and intruding if he wanted to be alone. I replaced the phone again. He would call me if he needed me.

A dozen times during the night I thought I heard that first small tinkle a phone makes when the connection is made. I stiffened when I heard it, ready to leap out of bed and run to it when the ring came. But it never did.

The morning was almost unbearable. I wanted desperately to call him but if he was sick I didn't want to wake him. In the afternoon I called the office first to see if he had reported for work but no one had heard from him. They weren't expecting him. By three o'clock I had raked up enough courage to call the flat. It rang and rang but there was no answer. After that I called on the hour every hour until six but with the same result.

By then I was totally bewildered. It all seemed utterly inexplicable unless he was seriously ill. But no. That couldn't be the case. If he had needed help he would have called.

I went into my father's office. I hadn't mentioned any of my news to him yet though I'm sure he had a good idea of the situation. He knew my feelings for Pal and if he was able to make the change I was quite sure my father would be pleased to have him as a son-in-law. Even if he wasn't able to change . . . No; I put that possibility firmly out of my mind. I simply couldn't tell how he would react. Much better not to worry about it.

Of course, the events of the previous two days were completely unknown to him. I had no intention of saying a word until it was settled between us.

He looked across and smiled as I entered. He was a handsome, rather distinguished man with greying hair which at the end of the day always looked just as neat and smart as when he finished combing it in the morning. He was standing beside his desk packing some papers into a brown briefcase.

"I'll be with you in a moment, dear. Are you ready to go?"

"Almost." I closed the door after me. We were the only ones left in the office at that time but I liked it better with the door closed. His room was soundproofed against the clacking of typewriters and with the door closed I felt sealed inside, secure and safe from the problems of the outside world.

My father's personality too had a similar effect. Beside him I always felt my worries were only half as serious as I had imagined them. He had a special way of putting things in perspective. He did it, I think, by giving credit for maturity and judgment even when it wasn't there. He would never make my decisions for me but instead force me to see the various alternatives and come to my own conclusions. It was his way and he had used it with me and my sisters from the time we were very small.

"Why the frown?" he said and suddenly without expecting it my resolution crumpled and I was telling him everything that had happened: the party, the late night talk with Pal, my conversation with Father O'Hanlon and then Pal's strange behaviour. It all tumbled out. I hadn't realised until I began just how much the silence of the past two days had affected me.

He sat on the side of the desk and listened quietly until I had finished. Then he came around to me.

"Brolie, you've been very quiet about this. Is it really serious?"

"Yes, I think so," I said. "I didn't want to worry you with any false alarm, Dad. I wasn't even planning to tell you tonight but I just can't imagine what's wrong with him; why he hasn't called; why he won't answer his phone."

203

"What would you like to do? How about if I run you down to his flat now. Would that help, do you think?"

"No."

"I wouldn't embarrass you by marching in on the fellow and demanding an explanation, you know."

"No, of course not. I wasn't thinking that. But I don't want him to feel I'm pushing him, that suddenly . . . oh, I don't know. I only want to do what's best."

"Well, if you're worried about him it's not going to get any better with you sitting at home waiting for the phone to ring."

"I know that."

"Then what do you propose?"

"I don't know. What do you think?"

"I think your intuition is probably right," he smiled. "He's probably sorting himself out, adjusting to his new . . . circumstances. He has a very big decision to make and he probably just wants some time alone to weigh it all up."

"Dad, do you think he's the one? Would it make you happy if we were married?"

"If it makes you happy then of course I'd be pleased. He seems to be a very talented young man. Frankly, I had hoped you might wait a little longer but I have a lot of confidence in you, Brolie. You've always been the steady one in the family. If you're sure, then you'll certainly have my blessing."

"I am sure."

"Then I'm sure you'll work it out. You have your mother's determination when it comes to something important like this. You'll work it out. Now come along or we'll both be in trouble."

After dinner I lay on my bed analysing his words and trying to find some comfort in them but it was strangely absent. His offer to take me to the flat immediately and his description of Pal as "talented" rather than fine or good were far from reassuring. Anyone could be talented. It was hardly the first quality he would look for in a son-in-law. And yet . . . the whole situation was new to me; I had never talked with my father about the possibility of marriage before and he had never mentioned it even in the light-hearted, half-joking way other fathers did. Maybe he resented Pal. Maybe he wanted it to fail.

As the minutes passed I found myself becoming angry—angry with myself, with Pal, with my father, my family, with the whole business of being dependent on someone else, out of my own control.

Or was it that? Perhaps it was just the opposite. Perhaps I was angry because the one on whom I was so dependent was away from me and unreachable.

Finally, at nearly eleven o'clock I could bear it no longer. The night stretched endlessly ahead. My thoughts were turning nightmarish again. I had to do something; anything was preferable to the torture of just waiting for the phone to ring.

My father was in his study working on the papers he had brought home.

"I'm going to the flat," I said.

He looked up. "Are you sure that's wise?"

"Yes."

"All right, Brolie. Take care. Don't be too late. Your mother won't sleep until you come home."

"Will you tell her where I've gone."

"Yes."

From the road, the only window I could see was in darkness. I thought of asking the taxi driver to wait but then it was too late. The car was moving away down the quiet street.

It was a fairly new brick building, two storeys high with a concrete landing on the second floor connecting the flats at that level. I climbed the stairs, knocked on his door and waited. Nothing. I knocked again. I could hear the sound echoing on the other side of the door. I lifted my hand for a third attempt when the door swung open with such suddenness and violence that it startled me. A voice, Pal's voice but muffled, the way it had been on the phone said, "Come in, Brolie."

I couldn't see his face in the darkness. "Pal, are you all right?" I followed him into the dark room. Automatically, I reached for the light switch at my left.

"Leave it off."

I checked my movement. "Why? What is it? Pal, I don't understand." It was taking me a long time to adjust to the darkness of the flat. I could just see his outline in front of me. Then it disappeared. The door slammed of its own accord and his voice came quickly on top of it.

"Sit on the couch. It's just behind you."

"Where are you? Why can't we turn the light on? Pal, what's been happening?" I was aware of a strong, sickly sweet smell in the room. It was overpowering. Rum.

"Pal, have you been drinking? Are you drunk?"

"Yes to the first, no to the second. I've been drunk, though, several times in the last twenty-four hours. Or is it forty-eight? It doesn't matter. I'm not drunk now."

"Then let me turn the light on, please. I don't like sitting here in the dark. I want to see you." I rose from the divan and reached towards another switch.

205

"No! Sit down!" His shout cut into me, frightening me. I jerked back into my former position. But his next words were soft. "I prefer it like this, Brolie. I want to talk to you and I don't want any distractions. I don't want to see your face or your body or this room or anything else. I want to talk to you and I want you to listen to every word . . ."

"It's just that . . ."

"Please."

There was a long silence. I could just see him across the room. He moved and I heard the sound of ice hitting against the side of a glass then the glass being placed on the table near him. When he spoke his voice was firm and clear, not muffled the way it had been when he opened the door.

"Brolie, no matter what you might think now," he said, "you don't know me very well. I know you think you do, but it's not true. The person you know, the Pal Lingard you know, is a kid of thirteen or some smartaleck Grammar boy, or maybe even a journalist. Or something else you can label. But whatever it is, it's not me. It's not the person I know. It's someone else that lives only in your mind. It's not me."

Again he was silent. I was tempted momentarily to interrupt and contradict him but I was a little afraid of his reaction and it suddenly occurred to me that what he was saying might be true.

"After tonight," he said, "you might prefer it that way. I wouldn't blame you in the slightest. In fact that's the only sensible thing for you to do. Just walk away. Just cut your losses and walk away. You won't have lost a thing, I assure you, because you won't have had anything to lose. The Pal Lingard you've been going out with and being with and falling in love with just doesn't exist. You won't have lost a thing."

"Pal, I don't understand you."

"Of course you don't. I'm sorry." He paused. "Brolie, have you ever thought about loneliness? No. Of course you have. Everyone has at some time or other. It's the most terrifying thing of all, isn't it? The most frightening thing in the whole damned world. It frightens me to think about it, to talk about it, even to admit that it exists. But it does exist. It's there. I don't remember a time in my whole life when I wasn't aware of it. No, that's not true. Not quite true anyway. I remember a time . . ." He chuckled and the sound startled me. "Do you know, when I was a kid, oh I suppose thirteen, nearly fourteen, I wasn't really lonely until then. From the time I was six or seven, if I was on my own, far away from everyone and I belched, or worse, if I, ah, broke wind, I used to say, 'Pardon me. Excuse me.' I'd say it out loud because Jesus was with me. He was beside me, watching over me.

He would have heard it so, naturally, being a well-mannered kid and not wanting to offend, I excused myself.

"But then something happened, and I grew up a little, I suppose, and Jesus was no longer there. It happened quite suddenly. Jesus was gone and I was alone. Lonely. Completely alone and lonely. It was a terrible, terrifying feeling.

"Then I discovered that I wasn't alone after all. There was my mother. Perhaps if I had had brothers and sisters it might have been different. I might have been different, not so bound up in myself. I don't know. But suddenly she was there. She had always been there but I hadn't realised it, not consciously anyway. I wasn't quite alone after all.

"What I'm talking about, Brolie, is not just having a close friend, someone who cares for you, though I don't recall that I had one anyway. I mean someone who is always there, someone who's so joined to you, who's so much beside you that no matter what you're doing or what you've done that person is with you. You could be a thousand miles away but the distance doesn't matter a damn. She's there. She's with you, a constant referral point, something to judge the world and yourself by. Something inside you. Do you understand that?"

"Yes."

He laughed again but there was no pleasure in the sound.

"I remember something. Perhaps it was a poem on *Kindergarten of the Air*. And the announcer, a woman with a pretty voice, said, 'A mother is someone who knows all about you but loves you just the same.'"

"I think it was a friend," I said quietly. " 'A friend is someone . . .' "

"Was it? Perhaps you're right. But a friend can't know all about you. A friend only knows those things you want him to know. I always thought of it as being a mother because mothers know all about you, all the secrets, all the bad things."

I saw his arm move and there was the sound of drinking.

"You know, when I was out in the bush she used to send me books. Once a fortnight there'd be a letter and two or three books. Every kind of book imaginable. And this went on for three years. Three years, as regular as clockwork. She had an arrangement with a man at the Queensland Book Depot and every other Monday she'd call in and select two or three out of a little pile he'd made for her. The hut I lived in on The Place was overflowing with them, bursting at the seams.

"But the interesting thing was that after the first few months I noticed that they'd been read before they were sent. A dust jacket would be a little frayed or a page corner would be turned over. I asked her about it and she confessed—it was a kind of confession the way she put it—that she'd started to read them before she posted them. Then there were pencilled notes on the margins and she started talking about them in her letters.

"She wasn't an educated woman. I think she left school when she was fourteen. But the judgments she made were completely unanswerable. She could cut through all the guff and camouflage and nail down an argument or tear it apart in two or three words. Towards the end I was looking forward as much to reading her comments as to the books themselves. And then she was gone. Just like that. One moment she was there, and the next, dead." He was silent for a moment. "Dead." Another silence.

"Damn it! Dead!" He shouted so loudly and sharply I caught a scream in my own throat and in the next instant his glass smashed against the wall at the other end of the room but with such force that I caught some of the spray.

"Pal, don't," I cried. "Please." He didn't appear to hear me. He seemed to be half out of his chair.

"Just torn away. Ravaged. Then torn away from life and thrown into the dirt to rot. With no reason, no possible reason. The great God, the dispenser of all good things, just took it into his divine, magnificent head to wipe her out, to send her back to the grubs and the maggots. And they wanted me to be a part of it. Not my father, but the others. You should have heard them. The minister. You should have been there and heard his mouthings, his obscene, disgusting mouthings. God has taken her to Him, he said. We cannot hope to know the mysteries. We must learn to accept them and to put our trust in Him. I should go to the funeral. I should pay my respects. Pay my last respects. Play the game. Go along with the whole stupid, useless, demeaning charade. All good children together, following His ways, being grateful for His mercies. Well, I wouldn't do it. Damn Him. Damn Him. I wouldn't!"

I was shaking inside. I was afraid but I wanted to touch him. I moved to go to him. "Pal . . ."

"No," he said. "No, stay away from me, Brolie. And don't waste your sympathy on me. There's something else. You'd better listen carefully. Do you remember what I said to you when I first met you at the office?"

"I remember everything."

"Then you'll know the words I used: 'God's messenger'. Do you remember that?"

"Yes, I think so."

"Well, I meant it. That's exactly what you looked like when I saw you that day. All white and clean and filled with the shining light."

"That was because . . ."

"And I hated your guts. I hated everything you represented. Everything you stood for. I wanted to take your pretty face and push it against a wall. Push it and push it until it bled. And then, when I heard what you'd been saying about me and I remembered those anxious, brimming eyes, I had an idea. A magnificent idea sprang to mind. You were the way. My own sacrificial lamb. What a thought it was. I nearly wet my pants just thinking about it. I could barely wait until you got home to call you up. But then I thought it would be good tactics to let you sweat a while. And it was. I was right. It was easy. You were half in love with me to begin with. All I had to do was show you a little attention—not too much, mind, just enough—and you'd come in the rest of the way. And when you were all the way in, the way you are now, or rather the way you were when you came here, all I had to do was let the axe fall. Perhaps not even that. Something better. I could just walk away and you'd never know. You'd tear yourself apart wondering what went wrong, what you did or said that turned Prince Charming off and you'd never know. You'd never know."

His voice was breaking with the strain and I could feel tears streaming down my cheeks. I wasn't conscious that I was crying but I could feel the tears.

"Pal . . ."

"Wait. There's more. You haven't seen your friend Natalia lately, have you?"

"Nata? No, I . . ."

"There's a good reason. She's been avoiding you. I think, strangely enough, that she's got a conscience. She doesn't want to face you when she knows she's sleeping with your, what shall I say, your intended. How's that?"

"Oh Lord."

"She doesn't want to face you. She can't bear to look at you. And neither can I . . . it's no good, Brolie . . . neither can I . . . I can't let you see me . . . damn it . . . damn it."

His words were coming in bunches between great shuddering breaths.

"I tried . . . and now I've got myself so fouled up . . . and you . . . none of it's your fault. You're the only decent thing . . . it's been months and there's been no one, not a soul . . . God, I'm sorry . . . I'm more sorry than I can tell you, Brolie . . . you didn't deserve it. You didn't deserve it."

He stood up and smashed his fist against the plaster wall. It made a soft sound. He did it again and again. "Damn it . . . damn it . . ."

209

I went to him. He tried to push me aside but I wouldn't go. I held him. I held him as tightly as I could and he swayed against me. I held him as we moved across the room to the divan. I held him as we half fell on to it. I held him and kissed his face until he was still. Then I undressed for him and I held him close and helped him as he entered me. I bit my lip to stop the pain and I pushed my face into his chest as it happened. I thought it would never end but I stayed and I held him until he was finished.

"I won't let you go," I said.
   It was quiet in the room and I listened to his breathing.
   "I can't be a Catholic."
   "It doesn't matter."
   "I don't know what I am."
   "It doesn't matter."
   His breathing was strong and deep.
   "I love you," he said.
   "Yes."
   "Brolie, will you marry me?"
   "Yes."
   "Oh God. Do you know what it's going to be like? Do you have any idea?"
   "Yes."
   I made the divan into a bed. I called my father and told him I would not be coming home. In the night Pal woke up only once. He kissed me and went back to sleep. In the morning I was waiting for him when he awoke and we made love again. He was very gentle and the pain was easier to bear.
   That day I went home and got my clothes. My mother was there and she tried to prevent me from going. She was crying when I left. I had thought she was going to strike me.
   My father and Connie came to the wedding which was held in a small, bare room at the City Hall. Pal's father came and Dick Morely was his best man. I had bought a new hat, a green one, the same colour as his eyes. It was very dusty in the room and the man sounded as though he had said the words many times before. There was a white scar on his cheek and it moved when he spoke. I kissed Mr Lingard and my father and Connie and Dick and we went back to the flat alone.

WE WERE married for seven years, but I don't think of it as a movement of time, as a changing thing from one month or one year to the next. In my mind and in my memory it is one experience and I have to delve into it consciously to separate the incidents and to trace the various threads of our lives, of his life, from that beginning to the end. I have to pull it apart and try to put them down as they happened. But inside me it is not like that. It is just there. It is a hundred different images, or a thousand, all piled on to each other and all transparent so that if I look at one I can see a dozen more and then more still. And I am afraid again. I am afraid of it happening.

I can see him talking softly to his son, our son, Clem. I can see him and hear him rampaging and swearing at an empty room. I can hear the sound of applause in the theatre and I can see him walking nervously on to the stage and I can hear his first words: "I don't believe it." And then the stillness that followed.

I can hear his drunken ramblings after too much rum and I can smell his breath as he moved on top of me. I can hear the frightened, sad words when all he wrote was being rejected and rejected and rejected again. I can hear the words he said after he had been with her. I can hear the pleasure and the pride and the pain. And the anger. I can hear the anger and the confusion and the frustration. It is all just there. It is so clear, so intense that as I write I feel it happened only an hour ago. Or perhaps it is happening still.

I suppose that through it all there are separate threads that make up at least parts of the whole. His writing is one, his journalism another. There is our life together. Adele Champion. And then, overlaying them all, there was our son. The others mixed and intertwined but that, at least for him, was outside the rest. The Little Boss, as he called him, was somehow kept apart from the rest of his world. Even from her.

Ten days after we were married she came down from the country. She called Pal the day she arrived and the next evening we went to dinner with her at Lennons. She came down to the foyer of the hotel when Pal called her room and she looked very beautiful, very assured and at ease.

211

"What have you been doing with him?" she said to me. "Haven't you put some flesh on his bones yet?" She smiled as she said it and Pal laughed with her. In fact they laughed together most of the evening.

For a while they talked about people they knew in the country. I learned that Adele's daughter, Marcia, was engaged to be married to a young grazier named Tom Reed; that Humphrey Baggett was still the same; and that everyone wanted to be remembered to him. They talked at some length about Boss and The Place and Pal said he would write to Boss the moment he got home. I thought at one stage that he was going to go back and see the old man for a few days but after some discussion they decided it was better to leave well enough alone, that his going back could do no real good and might even make matters worse. Besides, there was no way he could get time off from the paper.

Then Adele said, "This must be terribly boring for you, Bronwyn. I'm sorry. Let's talk about something else."

I hadn't been bored. I wanted to learn all there was to know about his life in the west. But the names and places and incidents were never put in context for me and I kept missing the point.

"No, it's all right," I said. But her mind was made up.

"Tell me about your writing," she said and for a while Pal talked about things he wanted to do.

"But what are you doing now?" she said.

"It's been a bit mixed up," he said. "Other things . . ." he looked young when he smiled.

She turned to me. "Brolie, it's up to you. You have to see that he gets his head down and does some real work. You took on a mighty big job when you married this young fellow. I hope you realise that."

"I do."

"Of course you do, dear. And I know you won't let me down. I'm depending on you."

After that, Pal went several times to see her at the hotel at night when he finished work and they had lunch together. I was always invited to the lunches too but I wasn't able to go. I had found another job in the Valley much closer to the flat and it was too far for me to go all the way uptown in an hour.

She stayed for two weeks and he was happier than I had seen him. The night she left he came home very late and sat up in the kitchen until it was almost light. The next evening he began to write in earnest some of the things he had mentioned at the dinner. She had bought him a portable typewriter and he worked on that.

I always waited up for him, even when he stayed behind at the office or went drinking with the other reporters. I wanted to be awake when he came in so that I could talk to him. I was up when he arrived

212

home that night and began work on his story. He told me to go to bed and I lay there for a long time listening to him tapping on the typewriter. When he came in I asked him about the story but he said he was tired.

After that first visit she came down every three or four months and stayed for at least a week. Then, when he finished writing *O'Halloran* she stayed for nearly five months. She invested a lot of money in it. She persuaded the Playhouse group to produce it and she had a hand in the production herself.

Bill Duncan, Pal's colleague on the newspaper, reviewed it on opening night at Albert Hall. Adele insisted that Pal wait at the party she threw at Lennons for the cast until the papers were delivered and by the time they came it was very late and Pal was drunk. When he read the review he went out to find Bill and fought with him at Uncle's place. He stayed out all night and when he met him again the next day at the office they fought again and Arthur Morely threatened to fire him. Pal stayed home for three days and played with Clem. By then the play had closed and he went back to work.

For six months he wrote almost nothing. Then one evening with absolutely no warning he came home and began to write an hilariously funny story about a young playwright whose first effort was an utter disaster. He worked on the story for two weeks and I could hear him from the bedroom chuckling as he wrote. As with all his writing, he wouldn't show me a line until it was published and it drove me nearly mad lying there listening to the tapping and the chuckling and the hooting.

When I did read it I thought it was like his own story but broadened so that it had appeal to people who had never heard of *O'Halloran*. Arthur Morely had given him the name of an agent in America and he had sent four or five stories to him before he had started the play. Only one of them had been published and that in some obscure mid-western magazine. But this one, "Opening Night", was published in *Esquire*. When the cheque came he went out and bought so many toys and books for Clem that it was almost impossible to walk through the living room.

A few months later he began work on *Untamed Land*. He worked on it for nearly two years and in the last four months he left the paper so he could concentrate on it full-time. I was able to go back to work then and he looked after Clem. When it was finished, Adele came down from the country again.

When he left work he had been with the *Courier-Mail* for nearly seven years. Most of the time I think he enjoyed it and that part of it was

213

good for me too. He often brought Dick home for dinner and those times were full of laughter and the wildest ideas for making the *Courier-Mail* a "real" newspaper. They were full of ideas and I knew what they meant and the people they talked about. Very occasionally the other reporters would come after work too but it was best when it was just the three of us.

One of their ideas—I say theirs but it was really Pal's—was for a series of articles to show what life was really like away from the city. One would be on a picnic race meeting on one of the big cattle stations on the Barkly Tableland, another on a shearing muster in the far west, another on the Kingaroy peanut harvest, another on the Barrier Reef, but all of them written, Pal said, "at people level".

"You've got to be able to smell the dust," he said. "You've got to make them see the sweat and feel it running down their faces. You've got to fill it up with flies and wind and the smell of things cooking."

"That's right," we said.

"That's what newspapers are for. To tell the whole story. A real newspaper . . ."

"That's right."

Mr Morely agreed and Pal was given the job.

It took him away from home a lot but I didn't really mind. For those first few days and nights when he returned after a week or ten days in another part of the state we were a little strange to each other. There was a sense that we were meeting almost for the first time. And he loved the land so much. He loved it and he talked to me about it.

The stories that came out of the trips attracted a lot of attention and comment. I think they, more than anything else, established him as a journalist and gave him the opportunity to start the column. The column was Dick's idea and for a while they took turns at writing it and submitting it to John Harris, the features editor, trying to sell him on the idea. It was a little like the other plan except that instead of encompassing the whole state they wanted to concentrate on Brisbane.

"There's half a million people in this town," Dick said. "There's thousands of off-beat stories, things that would really grab a reader. Now you take, just for example, eggs."

"Right," Pal said. "Eggs."

"Yeah. Eggs. I think there's something pretty funny about eggs."

"You do."

"Sure I do. You just think of it. Think of an egg. Brolie, go and get an egg and put it on the table."

"I can think about it without . . ."

"No, you wait."

I did as I was told. The egg wobbled a little on the formica table top.

"See," Dick said. "You think it's funny too, don't you?"

"No."

"Well why are you laughing then?"

"I'm not laughing at the bloody egg."

"You are. Look at it. Look at the shape of it."

"I'm looking at it." Pal held his hand over his mouth.

"Brolie, get another one."

The two eggs wobbled at each other.

"See what I mean. He's killing himself."

Pal swayed in his chair. "Okay, you win. But you'll have to write it. I'm not going to write about eggs."

The next day Dick went to the Egg Board and the day after he wrote the story. "You should have seen them," he said. "Millions of them. Millions of eggs all around me."

But then Dick was sent to Canberra to cover the parliamentary session and Pal had to carry on the campaign alone. It was then that John Harris agreed. When Dick came back he was transferred to the *Sunday Mail* and there was no time for him to research and write stories for the column as well. The column was called "Off Beat" and it became very popular. For a while, Pal was afraid that Dick might resent its success and he was hesitant about the subject until one night Dick said, "Listen, I don't mind that you pinched my column if you'll just do one thing."

"What's that?"

"Write a story about chickens."

"Chickens?"

"Right. There's something pretty funny about chickens . . ."

Those were the good times. I was included. And he was relatively relaxed. With his work on the paper there wasn't the same intensity, the same pressure as with his other writing. There was still time for him to talk to me and sometimes, when he hadn't been drinking, he would make love to me very quietly and gently and I would feel as though my whole soul was filled and straining to contain the beauty of it.

But when he was writing he was completely different. I felt there was no love left in him, that he drained himself when he wrote and all his attention and human feeling seemed to go into his writing, into the people and the world he was creating. There was nothing left for me or for anyone else. Except, of course, little Clem. For him there was always enough.

It was nearly two years after we were married before I fell pregnant with Clem. That first period had not been an easy time but I remember it very clearly. I said I had found another job but that

215

wasn't quite true. My father had found it for me. He wanted me to stay with him but I knew it wouldn't work. If I was with him every day the time would come inevitably when there would be recriminations and hurtful things would be said. I knew that I had hurt him deeply and if I had to look at him every day and watch him as he tried to keep the anger and the reproach out of his voice it would be bad for us both. The other way I could telephone him as often as I wanted and we could keep in touch.

At first we were very cautious when we talked, but then one day he said, "Brolie, just tell me one thing: Why?"

"I told you at the time," I said.

"Not really. There are ways. You know as well as I do . . ."

"No," I said. "My answer's the same. If I marry in the Church it will be the proper way. Not like that."

"But surely . . . is that likely?"

"I don't know."

But I did know. I think I knew from the moment Adele Champion walked down those stairs into the foyer of the hotel. I knew then. And I knew when I learned that I was pregnant. I knew Pal would never agree to having him baptised. I knew.

Several times when I was talking to my father I asked if I could come home and see my mother but he advised against it. I called her twice but it was difficult to talk to her. Every silence felt like a demand for an apology and even after I apologised it was still there.

I went to the cathedral too and I tried to talk with Father O'Hanlon the way we had that day in the choir stalls. But it was different now. He tried to be understanding and kind but he made me feel that suddenly I was an outsider, not really a stranger, but an outsider, which in one way I suppose I was. After that I didn't go back. I went to the church nearby. I couldn't take communion.

Of course, I didn't talk about any of this to Pal. I knew that if I did he would become angry.

Connie was a help. She came to see us at least once a week and I got all the family news from her. At first she seemed rather awed by it all and I think I gained a place in her estimation for courage and rebelliousness which was quite undeserved. We had never been really close but my marrying Pal under those circumstances changed our relationship and we became the best of friends. After a while I think she understood.

Connie was the first person I told about the baby. I had meant to wait until Pal got home but she came over after dinner and I was so excited at the news it was almost the first thing I said to her.

"Are you sure?" she said.

"Certainly I'm sure. The results came back this afternoon."

"Have you told him? Have you told Pal?"

"No, and don't you say anything if you're still here when he arrives."

"No, I won't. But I want to see his face when you tell him."

He was very late. Connie had called home twice to let them know they shouldn't worry. But she was determined to stay until he came.

When he finally arrived I knew at once that he'd been drinking. He had a slightly feverish look and he laughed loudly when he came into the room.

"Aha," he said. "Now here's a beautiful sight for the thirsty traveller. Two for the price of one." He came over and kissed me lightly on the cheek, then turned to Connie. "Now pucker up, you beautiful beast and I'll test the merchandise." He kissed her on the lips. For a moment she seemed to return it then she squirmed away and giggled.

"Pal, don't . . ."

"Mmmmmm." He licked his lips. "That was good. Let's have another one." He advanced towards her but she backed away.

"Pal, stop it."

"No. It's too late now. You've lit the fires, wench. Ha!" She dodged around a chair but he was too quick for her. He grabbed her arm. "In a single bound he was by her side," he said. "He tore the thin veil from her body." He pulled her towards him and as he did I saw his hand close over her breast.

"No, Pal." She pulled away from him. "Please."

"Ah well," he shrugged. "You can't win 'em all."

She came over to me. "You'd better go," I said quietly.

"All right." She gathered her purse from the table.

"Connie, you're not going, are you? Just give me a minute to water the horses. You're not going. Don't be crazy. Just wait a minute." He went to the bathroom.

"I'll call you tomorrow," I said to her.

He came out of the bathroom. "Now, where's the flashing-eyed vixen?"

"She's gone," I said.

"Gone? Not because of me, I hope."

I said nothing.

"Now, Brolie, that's just absurd. What did she think I was going to do, rape her?"

"No, Pal."

"What then."

"Nothing. It doesn't matter."

217

"It does matter. It's absurd."

"Do you want something to eat? If you don't, then I'll go to bed."

"Oh God, it's martyrdom time again. Welcome, one and all, to the land of injured innocence. On your right, if you look carefully, you'll see the Crass Villain. No, don't put down the windows of the bus, ladies, you never know with Crass Villains, can't trust 'em an inch. And look, there she is, Miss Injured Innocent herself, standing, as is her wont, in a shaft of sunlight . . ."

"Pal, please don't. Not tonight."

"She speaks. Did anybody hear the words? Did anyone catch the gilded phrases falling trippingly from those virginal lips? No? Fear not, ladies. They will be repeated. Of that you can be sure. I know them by heart, dear souls. Not tonight, she spake, and Crass Villain, once again . . ."

"Pal, no." I ran into the bedroom and shut the door.

After a while he came in. He undressed and climbed into bed. I was still wide awake.

"Brolie?"

"Yes."

"I'm sorry."

He touched me on the back and I turned to him.

"I'm really sorry."

"It's all right. It's just that tonight of all nights . . . Connie waited because she wanted to see your face when I told you."

"What? Told me what?"

"Pal, I'm going to have a baby."

I felt him tense. Then he sat up in bed. He said nothing for almost a minute. Then he said: "A son."

"The test came back today," I said.

He got out of bed.

"Oh shit." He walked back and forth at the end of the bed. "Jesus Christ," he said. "A son."

"Well, there's no way . . ."

"Christ. Jesus Christ." He left the room and went into the living room. I listened to him pacing for a while then I joined him.

"Pal, it's all right about Connie. She's not a child any more."

"Who?"

"Connie."

"Oh yes. Brolie, go back to bed."

"Are you coming?"

"No. I'll be in later."

I listened to him for a long time but then he was quiet and I fell asleep. When I woke in the morning, he was sleeping in a lounge chair. I went across to him and kissed him. He stirred and I felt him

218

come awake and return the pressure of my lips. Then suddenly he pulled away.

"What is it?" I said. "What's wrong?"

"It is true, isn't it?" he said. "You are pregnant?"

"Yes," I smiled, "but that doesn't mean . . ."

"Yes, of course. Brolie, I've got some work to do. What's for breakfast?"

It was the same throughout the whole time I was pregnant. Whenever I was affectionate he found some excuse. He changed the subject. He never admitted that he did it consciously and purposely but after a while it was obvious. He kept me at a distance.

At first I thought he was just being over-protective and it was appealing and a little flattering. But it wasn't that.

Then I thought since he so quickly became involved in the writing of *O'Halloran* that it was the work, the writing that was involving him and draining him. That might have been a small part of it but I think he consciously sought the writing as a release, a substitute. Not once during the whole period did he make love to me.

It was very confusing and hurtful. It made me feel ugly and in a way I began to resent the thing inside me. It was keeping us apart. It was denying me the only thing I really wanted, not in the physical sense of course, but emotionally. He withdrew from me and he watched me as though I carried something that belonged to him alone, that was no part of me at all. When he did things for me around the flat, when he moved my chair or carried groceries I felt like some stupid, weak child that couldn't be trusted to look after itself.

I began to hope desperately that it would be a girl. I know they say a daughter always loves her father best and I suppose it's true but he was so insistent that it would be a boy, a son, that I knew it would shock him to have a daughter and it would take him a long time to adjust to it. And by then she would have been mine, too. I wanted it to be a girl and I wanted her to look like me. And if my hopes and prayers had come true he would have grown to love her, I know. She would have been ours. I would have been included.

When he came to see me after it was over, he said, "You're just wonderful, you know that? You're magnificent. You did it." There were tears in his eyes. "Magnificent. Can I hold him?" He dug the little bundle out from under the crook of my arm. "Magnificent," he said. But now he was talking to the child.

"I'm glad, Pal," I said. "I'm glad it's a boy."

"Oh yes. Did you ever doubt it?"

"I'm glad you're happy."

"Just look at him. He's the one. Here, you take him. Keep him warm. Is it time for his feed?"

"No, not yet. Are you really happy?"

"Of course I am. When do you feed him?"

"Soon, I think."

"Well, I'll leave you to it." He kissed me on the forehead. "Take care of him."

"I will," I said.

I tried for days to feed him but I wasn't able to and he had to go straight on to the bottle. I tried and tried but there was nothing I could do. Then he lost too much weight and had to stay in the hospital after I was ready to be discharged. Pal said nothing, but I knew what he was thinking. He went to the hospital alone to pick him up when he was better and ready to come home. I wanted to go too but he left without telling me and when they came back together in the taxi he pretended we had talked about it and I hadn't said anything about going.

It was worse than it had been. He made me feel like a housekeeper. He shouldn't have done that.

I was putting the pin into his little nappy and I was doing it the proper way. I had my fingers underneath the pin, between his skin and the nappy, but then something happened. Perhaps he had some wind and he cried out; he squealed as though the pin had gone into him. It hadn't. It only sounded as though it had. Pal pushed me aside. He didn't say anything. He pushed me aside and sat holding the baby and looking at me. Then he put him to bed himself.

It was good when Dick came around. Those were happy times. I was always sorry that Dick and Connie didn't get on better together. It would have been nice if they had been able to get married. One time we were sitting around the kitchen table talking about the *Courier-Mail* and Dick told me to go and get an egg and put it on the table. Pal laughed so much I thought he would burst. Even after Dick was gone he was still laughing.

For a while I stayed home from work and looked after little Clem, the Little Boss as he called him, and we would sit in the sun and I would watch him while he played on the blanket. Then I went back to work and Pal looked after him in the mornings and when he went to work in the afternoon he dropped him off at the nursery and I picked him up from there on my way home in the evenings.

Pal came straight home after work. He was deeply involved in *O'Halloran* and he stayed up very late and often I was able to sleep

220

through the early morning feeding time. I would mix the formula before I went to bed and it would be there waiting when Clem woke up. All Pal had to do was heat it up and test it in the inside of his forearm to see that it wasn't too hot. But after a while he mixed it too.

Later, when they were in rehearsals, Pal would take him to the theatre and he would sit in the stalls. Not for *O'Halloran* but *Untamed Land*. By then he was nearly four and he was a very beautiful child. He had Pal's colouring and the greenest green eyes. They were really the best of friends. I thought of them sometimes as my two men. I bought Clem a little cap which fitted close to his head. It had a tiny peak that came down over the forehead and just covered the scar.

Once I took a day off work and went to the rehearsals too. When I came in they had been going for more than an hour and Clem was sitting quite still in the first row of seats watching the action on the stage. I sat beside him and we watched together. Pal was at the side of the stage sitting on a chair with the script on his knee. He waved when he saw me and when the scene was finished he came down to us.

"Enjoying it?" he said.

"Yes. Is Clem always so good? Does he just sit here?"

"No. Sometimes he's a pest. Aren't you, Boss?" He gave him a playful chuck under the chin.

"No," Clem said. "No, I'm not."

Then Adele joined us.

"This is a surprise, Brolie. How are you feeling?" she said.

"Fine," I said. "Just fine."

"Good. What do you think of the play?"

"I've only seen a small part of it."

An actress whose name was Jane MacAuliffe came over. "Hello. You must be Mrs Lingard," she said. "I'm Jane."

"How do you do."

"Jane plays the daughter," Pal said.

"I see." She was blonde and very pretty.

"Isn't he the most gorgeous thing," she said. She sat beside me and took Clem on her knee. "Are you going to give Jane a big kiss today?" She snuggled him against her cheek.

"I think we should be getting back to work," Adele said.

"Okay," Pal said. "What are you going to do, Brolie? You're welcome to stay and watch."

"Yes. I'll stay for a little while," I said.

They went back to the stage and I stayed for the start of the next scene, then I went to a cinema until it was lunchtime. I called Connie and we had lunch together.

"You're looking wonderful," she said.

My father asked me to go back and work for him. I told him no. I wanted to but I knew it was better that way. And after Pal sold the story to *Esquire* there were many others. Not to that magazine but to others in America that paid very well so there was no need for me to go to work.

One truly wonderful night was when Mr Cunningham came down from the country. Pal had a day off and he met the old man in town during the afternoon and brought him home for dinner. He telephoned me from the hotel and I went out and bought the finest steaks I could find. They were both very happy and flushed when they arrived. Little Clem was still up and by then he was walking. Mr Cunningham took him on his knee and little Clem looked up at him and ran his hand over the rough chin then giggled when it tickled him.

After Pal put him to bed we sat around the lounge and Boss told us the news.

"I should be ashamed of myself, I suppose," he said. And even though he growled the words and his hair was so white and his face all lined with the sun, he looked like a young boy.

"Come on, Boss," Pal said. "It's the best thing that could have happened and you know it."

"She's a good woman. I'll say that for her. And she's got the place looking like a new pin."

"How did it happen?"

"Oh I knew the family. She had to sell the property when her husband died, to pay the probate. That was a few years ago now. She was living on her own in Roma—kids all grown up—and I ran into her one day when I went in to a Masonic meeting. We got talking and one thing led to another and she agreed to come out to the place as housekeeper. Then . . . well, it seemed better this way. She's a good woman, son."

"Of course she is. She must be. You look like a frisky young colt."

"Hah. Cut that out, now. You could do with a bit of condition yourself if the truth be told." He looked at me. "With a beautiful young woman like Brolie here and with meals like the one we had tonight I don't understand it. What's he doing to himself, Brolie? More of that bloody writing, I suppose."

"He works very hard," I said.

"Hah. You call that hard work. You should have seen him . . . well, I suppose it is when you think of it. I wanted to come down and see your play, son. But it was crutching time and I just couldn't get away."

222

"I'm glad you didn't," Pal said. "It was a flop."

"It was about old John Harrigan, wasn't it?"

"Yes. It was based on that. On the search."

"Yes, Adele told us all about it. It's the only thing she talked about for months. I'm sorry it didn't go better for you."

"Not to worry. There's always a next time."

"Yes. And there's always a place for you on Wilderwood. I want you to know that. And you too, Brolie. Come out and see us and stay with us for a while. Get a bit of really hard work under your belt. It'll do you the world of good."

"Thanks, Boss," Pal said. "We might just do that. '

"You go to work on him, Brolie," he said. "Anyway, I'd better be going. I just wanted to let you know the score. And you don't have to worry when . . . you know. You'll be well looked after."

"Don't talk about it, Boss."

"I just wanted you to know."

"That's enough, Boss. You'll live to be a hundred and you know it."

The old man grinned. "I just might do that too," he said. "Now you come out and see us, both of you. All three of you."

We never did. I wish we had but there were so many other things Pal had to do there just wasn't time. I've never seen The Place. And now, of course, it's impossible.

There was another dinner too. But it wasn't as good as that. It was somewhere in the city and the man from J. C. Williamson's, the theatre people, was the host. He fascinated me because he was the absolute image of Father O'Hanlon. All through the meal I couldn't take my eyes off him. They were talking about *Untamed Land* and he said, "It's the best we can do."

"It doesn't seem fair," Adele said. "Why should it have to prove itself in Brisbane of all places with unknowns? Why not let us have name actors to begin with?"

"Mrs Champion, you should know how much it costs to put on a play like this one. We're in business. We could have just said no and stuck with that musical. It's a guaranteed money-spinner. But it's company policy to encourage Australian . . ."

"*Untamed Land* will make money."

"It might." He turned to Pal. "And that's why we're prepared to give you a chance. I think it's very fair. If we get good houses here and it looks as though it might be a goer in the South then we'll back you all the way. As it is, I think you'll agree we're giving you a big opportunity."

Pal nodded. "I'm very grateful. But wouldn't it make more sense to start with a reasonably big name? Someone like Ed Devereaux."

"Do you know what Devereaux would cost?"

"No, I . . ."

"And he's in London at the moment, anyway. We couldn't get him. Not for Brisbane anyway. Not for something that might fold in a few days."

"It's not going to fold," Adele said. "And you know it."

The man said nothing.

"It's completely different from *O'Halloran*," she said. "It's a winner. I know it is."

"Well," the man said, "I'm afraid it's the best we can do."

When it was time to go, I took a taxi home. Pal and Adele wanted to talk some more about the deal before Pal decided. When we said goodbye to the man, I said, "You know, you remind me terribly of someone I used to know. A priest."

"Really," he said.

Connie was at home baby-sitting with Clem. She often did that.

After the baby was born Pal didn't drink nearly as much as before. Sometimes he'd go for a long time without any at all but then suddenly one day he'd come home quite drunk, for no apparent reason. I could never tell when it was going to happen.

He cut his finger on one of Pal's old razor blades and I was bathing it. I had to bathe it and the water had to be hot. I told Pal that but he didn't understand. He said he could hear him screaming from a long way down the street when he came home. But that wasn't true. Perhaps the water was a little hot but it had to be hot to kill the germs. He claimed he couldn't even see the cut but it was there all right. And it was his fault. He shouldn't have left his razor blades around.

It was the same with the rose bush. You can't watch children all the time. We had moved to the big flat by then. Pal liked it much better. It overlooked the river and he sat on the balcony watching the river for a long time. Sometimes he wrote on the balcony but in the afternoon the wind came up and blew the pages about so he came inside. Adele had taken a flat in the next block and he said it was more convenient that way. There was a garden in the front and there were roses. Mrs Baxter who lived on the floor below us talked to Pal and told him it looked as though I pushed Clem into the roses. It was a lie. She was an old woman and after that I never spoke to her.

In the book Pal bought for me before I had the baby it said that after it was over and the baby was born you didn't remember the pain. No

224

matter how bad it was, the memory of the pain just vanished. It wasn't true. It was something written to help you through that time. You could think, "When this is all over I won't remember any of it." It wasn't true.

The woman near me had so much milk that they had to use a little machine and even then she had pads under her bra so that it wouldn't come through and stain her nightie. If she had agreed, then it would have been all right and nobody would have known. There were thick blue veins around her nipples and her child made a noise when it suckled her.

When I was in the hospital a minister came around and when he got to my bed he asked me what my religion was. He was carrying some magazines and I would have liked to read one. But when I said I was Roman Catholic he just walked away and kept the magazines. I saw him another time and I said something to him. He went away and then the doctor came in and talked to me.

The priest at my church spoke through his nose. I don't remember his name but he didn't like me. I could tell from the way he looked at me. I sat in the back of the church and watched the others as they took communion. They looked at me too.

On the opening night in the J. C. Williamson's theatre which used to be called His Majesty's and was changed to Her Majesty's, I had the best seat in the house. Right in the front row. The seat beside me was for Pal but he couldn't be there. When it was over I heard the rumble at the back of me. It was like an avalanche and I thought all the seats were falling down and rushing towards me. But it wasn't that. When I looked around all the people were getting to their feet and they were clapping and calling out.

Sometimes we had heart-to-heart talks and Pal would sit opposite me and look me in the eyes and say some things that were just not true. They were his idea, these heart-to-heart talks, and I would try to please him by waiting until he was finished before saying anything. But sometimes he would talk such nonsense that I wouldn't have the patience to just sit there listening.

Bill Duncan had left the paper and gone home to England by the time *Land* was produced so David Winterbottom reviewed it. He called it a phenomenon and his review said, "Australian plays never make money. This one will." I thought Pal was going to cry when he read it.

"But it still has to prove itself," Adele said. "It has to be drawing good houses for at least four weeks. At least."

"I thought it was very good," I said. But other things were happening around us and I don't think Pal heard.

Connie came very often to stay with me when Pal was late. She sometimes read Clem a story before he went to sleep. Pal said it was a good idea. She would be company for me. But we didn't talk very much because by then we had a television set and it seemed silly to have it on and then spend all of our time talking.

Pal said the book proved that it was all right for married couples to make love like that. I told him it only proved that the writers were basically obscene and I won that argument very quickly.

Once I went back to the cathedral on a Sunday. It was very beautiful and the priest who preached the sermon sounded so much like Monsignor Guy that I made a complete fool of myself by staying back after it was over and asking him for the notes. It was an absolutely stupid thing to do and I didn't tell anybody about it. But somebody must have told because that week my mother came to visit me and she metioned it. It was nice to see her and talk to her. She looked older than I had remembered her.

Those weeks of waiting and watching the attendances at the theatre were terrible for Pal. And for me too. But then, as the days passed and the people kept coming to see it, he became happier and he began to smile again. And drink a little.

"It's Sydney or the bush," he said. "And by God it looks as though it's going to be Sydney."

He was full of plans about finding a nursery school somewhere in the inner city.

"Somewhere near Hyde Park or the Domain," he said. "I could pick him up after school and we could walk in the park."

"Yes," I said. "He'd like that."

"And what about you, Brolie? What would you do?"

"Are you sure you'd want me to come?"

"Certainly, if you'd like to."

"But do you want me to come?"

He was quiet for a while, then he said, "Yes. I do. It might do you the world of good."

"Is she going?"

"Who?"

"Adele. Is she going?"

"I don't think so. I think she's going back to Morgandale."

"Are you sure?"

"We haven't talked about it, but I'm pretty sure. Dammit, Brolie, we're not talking about Adele. We're talking about you. What are you going to do?"

"I don't know."

"Well, when you've made up your mind, just let me know."

Seven years.

It's very strange, but I remember the first part so much better than the last. And then, that evening of the party after the closing night, I remember hardly anything at all. I know it was held on the stage behind the curtain after everyone had left, that it was terribly crowded and there were many speeches. Everyone was shaking his hand. Dick was there and we talked for a little while. So were all his other colleagues from the *Courier-Mail* and Mr Morely gave one of the speeches.

Early in the evening, Pal put his arm around me and said, "Brolie, pack your bags. We're going places." He was laughing. "Just the two of us?" I said. "You betcha," he said. "Just the two of us." That's what he said. "You betcha." But then I didn't see him until nearly everyone had gone. And then we didn't talk at all.

That man was there, the one who looked so much like Father O'Hanlon. He waved in my direction and I smiled and waved back. But then I looked behind me and saw that he was waving at someone else.

Pal's Story
III

THE HOUSE lights dimmed then faded completely and for a long moment before the curtain rose the theatre was in complete darkness. In the darkness and the silence that accompanied it, he was suddenly intensely aware of the audience, the crowd of individuals blended and melded for an evening into some corporate thing larger than the sum of its parts, more volatile, more emotional, more malleable, more expectant, more naked and primitive than any of its component parts. He felt the power of the thing, the identity, and it drew him towards it, surrounded him with its ambience and drew him inwards to its great childlike heart where he could partake of it and be it. Every night was the same. Every evening for the past eight weeks he had felt the same pull, the same smothering power, and always for an instant he had gone with it, allowed it to take hold, felt its core, and then like an interloper unmasked in a crowded room, he had withdrawn in haste. He was not part of it. He was outside it. This thing, this audience, had formed and come together not to encompass him but to judge him. And every night the quick realisation chilled him and scared him and voided his belly.

Then the curtain rose. It never rose fast enough. It rose slowly and he willed it to move faster, to show it all, to grab the audience quickly and hold its attention, to allow his people to say their first words and begin the engagement. It wasn't until that happened, until the first two or three speeches were done and the connection was established and ready to grow, that he was able to begin to relax. But the first scene was good. He knew that now. It was as good as anything in the play. It would intrigue them. It would hold them and it would give his people room to breathe, to establish themselves with sureness and unhurried strength.

At last it was all the way up. At the right of the stage was the verandah of an old country homestead, a good solid verandah with three steps leading to the front yard. At the left front a gnarled and pitted kurrajong tree gave shade to a long, slatted bench with a curved backrest and iron bindings. Between the house and the tree, upstage and facing the audience, was a five-strand wire fence with netting at its base. And beyond the fence, for as far as the eye could see, was the land. The harsh, brown, bitter land.

It was good. It was stark, but calm. Then Hector Bannerman came

230

on to the verandah. Hector Bannerman was not the character's name but Palmer always thought of him by that name. He was taken from life. He was lifted as best he knew how and placed whole upon the stage. Hector Bannerman began to speak. The audience moved forward in their seats and Palmer Lingard, who had written the words, leaned back in his. It was beginning. It was under way.

For a short while he listened to the words but he knew them so well they were like the echo of his own mind. He tried to stop his mind, to retreat even further from the scene and as he did another familiar thought swept into him. He looked around him with his mind and he marvelled at it. He heard the sound of the play in the distance and the wonder of it swept into him. The power of it. The joyous, mind-bending pleasure of it. His play. His creation. His mind, his Self was on the stage and they had all come and paid their money to share a part of it with him. And to judge him. Don't forget that, he said. Don't forget that.

The woman beside him touched his arm. For once, he hadn't been aware of her.

"Is she here?" she whispered.

"Yes," he said. "I spoke to her."

"Are you going down to sit with her?"

"I'd like to but I can't. It's too close. I can't sit there."

"Do you want me to?"

"Yes, please."

"Is it all right, do you think?"

"Yes, I think so. I'm sure of it."

"All right. I'll go after the first act."

"Fine."

He started to settle in his seat but she touched him again.

"It's another good house."

"Yes."

"I'm so glad for you." She squeezed his hand and he returned the pressure briefly.

"I think the publicity helped."

"You're not going modest, are you?"

He grinned at her. A reflection from the hot, white light of the stage touched her hair and gave it a sheen.

"No, Adele."

"Good." He saw the whiteness of her answering smile and turned back to the play.

The whole cast was on stage now. Hector Bannerman, his wife, their two sons and Lucy, their adopted daughter. After Bannerman himself, hers was the most important and demanding role. They had taken her in after her parents had been killed in a flood. They had been townspeople and she was only twelve when it happened. Now she was eighteen and it hadn't rained since and the drought was taking everything. The remaining sheep were dying in the paddocks; the money was gone and the property was mortgaged and mortgaged again. Hector Bannerman was trying desperately to keep his family together but it appeared that the drought would finally take them too. Soon, one by one, they would have to go from the land and the property until he was left alone. Lucy would be the last to go. She was the most dependent of them all upon the place and yet she felt in some mystical way that she was the cause of it all. She hated the rain so much that she knew it would never come while she was there. But she couldn't go. She couldn't leave it. She was tied to it. In the end he would have to force her, and it would break her heart. Then he alone would stay and he would fight to the end.

There were only five in the cast but the review had said there were six. And it was true. There was the land itself. He had the review practically by heart.

"The Land is there as a great, brooding presence from almost the first moment of the play," it said. "And with every succeeding scene it becomes more pervasive, more tangible, more powerful. This has the paradoxical effect of at once diminishing the 'other' characters through its sheer size and passive strength and yet increasing their stature and their dimensions by the magnitude of their struggle—to survive, simply to survive upon it until the day comes when the land can be 'tamed'."

He repeated the words with satisfaction and pride. When he was writing he hadn't thought of it in exactly those terms. But in the early days of rehearsal he had become more aware of it and he had rewritten part of the last act to capitalise upon it and give the act dramatic power.

Adele Champion leaned close to him again.

"They're really putting everything into it tonight."

"Yes. Do you think they know?"

"Probably. You know what Derek's like. All directors are the same."

He nodded. He hoped they didn't know. He wanted to be with them when they were told that they were not going to be replaced; that they, and not some "name" players, were going to take *Land* to Sydney and then on to Melbourne. The men, especially Dan Eviston who played the lead, would be delighted and the women, Jane MacAuliffe, the daughter, and Beth Henderson, the wife, would say "Darling" and he would be able to count to five before they reached the second syllable.

He liked them all. They had had their squabbles, especially at first

232

when the actors were working themselves into their roles; but then, as he watched the characters come to life and as the picture in his mind adjusted itself to the confines of the stage, he felt an immense empathy with them, an irrational, overwhelming gratitude that they were giving substance and reality to his words.

With Derek Clayton, the director, it hadn't been quite the same. Derek, with his frill of grey, curly hair and his busy mannerisms was basically a bloody meddler and there had been some monumental battles over both the staging and the dialogue. But in the end they had worked together and in places Clayton's experience and pro-fessionalism had made for positive improvements. He could see that now.

It was Clayton's idea that the original cast be retained for the southern season when J. C. Williamson's had made their decision. At first, Palmer had objected. J.C.W.'s had promised name actors in the south and Clayton was a J.C.W. man. It smelt as though they were trying to wheedle their way out of the extra expense. But then they had talked and finally Palmer had agreed. The Queenslanders fitted their roles perfectly by then. In his mind they had become the people he had created and he couldn't visualise anyone else playing any of the roles. They *were* the characters. Anyway, in the final analysis there was really nothing he could do about it if the J.C.W. people insisted.

Besides, he liked them, all of them. Off stage they made him feel old. Mature. And that served to remind him that it was possible. At twenty-eight he was a writer of plays that people came to see.

Well, if not plays, then one play. And there would be others. Already there was the outline of another and perhaps it too would be an advancement, an improvement on the present work, the way *Land* had improved on the rawness of *O'Halloran*.

O'Halloran. How he used to cringe at the word. Even the thought of it used to curl his toes and set him fidgeting and squirming in his place. Then his jaw would set and he would look around him for some escape, some focus for his anger. It was better now. He could see the way it was—raw and undisciplined, a great lumbering beast of a play that charged forward from the opening scene to the final curtain without ever deciding what it was charging at.

Involuntarily, he glanced at the woman beside him. She had been there through all of it. Right from the beginning in that other world in the bush. It seemed so far away now; so different. She was different too. In the city she always seemed smaller, more vulnerable than he had remembered her. But always she was there when he needed her. When he had been lashing out at the world like a young fool and hurting only himself, she had picked him up and put him back into

233

the business of living. She had been there when he had begun *O'Halloran* and she had been beside him when it was finished. She had believed in it. She had believed in him, in his talent, and she had fought and argued and persuaded until others had believed in it too. And she had been there on opening night when the review had arrived in the *Courier-Mail* and they had read it together, that clever crack about the enthusiasms of middle age and the young playwright. He had looked at her face and seen the pain, the sudden collapse of her defences. Then he was somewhere else . . .

McCabe's bulk stood between him and the tall, urbane Englishman standing back from the door holding his drink in one hand and a brown cigarette holder in the other.

"Palmer, for Christsake go home," McCabe was saying. "You'll wake up the whole bloody neighbourhood."

"Well, let me in. I don't give a stuff who I wake."

"No."

"Send him out then. Come out here, you pommy shit. Come on, you gutless fart, get out here and say it to my face."

Then Duncan's voice from inside. "Go away, Lingard. You're in the real world now, not some piss-ant little country village. Go back and cry on your angel's shoulder . . ."

"Uncle, for Christsake, let me through."

"Pal, leave it alone. And you too, Bill. Jesus wept."

"Well send him on his way. Come back when you're sober, Lingard. In the meantime, push off like a good boy and sleep it off. You never know . . ."

The sentence was never finished. He ducked under McCabe's arm and began to throw the punch from three yards away. Bill Duncan's glass sailed high in the air, almost touching the ceiling before it dropped to the floor. He was bending over, readying himself to jump on the other man when McCabe and another reporter caught him from behind and together pushed him out the door.

He had gone straight to the main road and caught a taxi back to the hotel. By the time he reached it his wrist was badly swollen but there was very little pain. He guessed he must be drunk. The pain would come when he sobered but that was a long way off. For now, he just wanted to see Adele. He had to see her. He had to tell her what he had done; that it was all right. He had made it right.

He knocked on her door with his left hand and it opened immediately. She was in her nightdress and over it was a green silk robe.

"Adele," he said. And then he stopped. He looked at her face and there were streaks through the make-up on her cheeks, little patterns that glistened in the light of the hallway.

"Adele . . ."

"Come in." A light was burning beside the big bed. A cigarette smouldered in an ashtray just beneath the light.

"I found him. I found the sod . . ."

"I don't want to hear."

"Adele, are you all right? You sound strange."

"Pal, why did you come back?"

"Here?"

"Yes. Why did you come back here."

"To tell you. I came to tell you."

"Did you think it would make any difference?"

"Telling you?"

"Yes. What difference would it make?"

"None, I suppose, but damn it . . ."

"You should have gone home to your wife. To Brolie."

"I couldn't without telling you."

She turned away. "Do you want a drink?"

"Yes."

She went to a table and poured the drink into a glass then added water almost to the brim. He watched her move about the room. The silk robe was unfastened and the nightdress underneath was transparent when she moved near the light. She handed him the drink then sat on the bed. There was a stab of pain in his wrist. He took a long swallow of the drink and it gradually subsided.

"Adele, I'm very sorry," he said.

She looked at him then turned away and retrieved her cigarette from the ashtray.

"About the play?"

"Yes, what else. Isn't that bad enough? Jesus Christ, it was a mess wasn't it."

"It wasn't your fault."

"Of course it was. The damn thing just didn't work. There was no point to it. It was full of mistakes. It was boring. It even bored me at the end. I just wanted the bloody thing to finish."

"No, it was my fault," she said. Her voice was lifeless. "I should have known. It just wasn't ready. Perhaps you weren't ready. I don't know. It doesn't matter."

"Adele, what if we got a script now? There should be a copy here. I could go through it and prune some scenes. I marked some places down . . . if I started now it could be done by midday or so and by tonight . . ."

"No."

"Adele, damn it, what's wrong with you? Aren't you interested? I don't understand you."

235

"Don't you?"

"No."

"Pal, keep your voice down, please. We don't want to get evicted from the hotel, do we? That would look good in your paper. Ageing patron of the arts and young playwright turned out for . . . or is it patroness. Yes, patroness."

"Is that it? Is that the problem, that smartaleck bloody crack. I told you about that. You don't have to worry about it . . ."

"Yes, dear. You told me. You went riding off into the night on your white horse and you slew the dragon and now you've come back to claim your reward."

"Adele, it's not like that at all."

"Isn't it? While you were out in the night making a fool of yourself I've been lying here thinking it all out. Mr Duncan, or whatever his name is, could have been a little more subtle but at least he was clear." She brushed a hand across her face. "I suppose I should have had more sense."

He said nothing.

"Still, there's no fool like an old fool." She stood and faced him. "Pal, do you know how old I am? I'm forty-two years old. And what are you, twenty-four, twenty-five? And yet I come racing down here leaving my husband and my daughter just to charge around Brisbane like some schoolgirl . . . some stupid, idiotic schoolgirl let off the leash for the first time, and all for a . . . for a damned fool who wouldn't know when to come in out of the rain, who has a wife who loves him, a family, and who tears off into the night thinking he can solve everything by hitting some clever journalist and knocking him down. Of course he was right. And if you weren't so . . . so damned young, you'd know it too."

"And the play?"

"Oh, the play. Yes, of course. The play. Can you imagine? I was forgetting the play. You see that proves it, doesn't it. It couldn't have been the play at all."

"Please don't."

"Why not? Everyone else knows it. Everyone else has forgotten the play too. There's a much better story than a search for some grubby little half-caste . . ."

"Bugger it, stop it!"

"Dear God how I'd like to." She turned away from him. "Dear God how I'd like to." He took her arm but she pulled away.

"Adele, is there a script here? If you've got a copy I can go to work on it. I can make it better. You can call a rehearsal for this afternoon and I can explain it. I can fix it. I know what the mistakes were and there's a way. If I can rearrange the second act . . . Adele, are you

236

listening to me?"

She turned and there was a new expression on her face. Her eyes glittered in the light. "Are you going home?"

"No. Didn't you hear . . ."

She shrugged out of the robe and let it fall behind her.

"You're staying?"

"Jesus Christ." The short nylon nightdress stood out from her body and the neckline fell to the tops of her small breasts.

"What's wrong, Pal? Isn't it what you expected? Don't you like looking at me? Don't you want to touch me?"

"Yes."

"Then what are you waiting for?"

"Not like this."

"How then?" She crossed to the bed and lay on it near the lamp. "Is this better?"

Her nipples made dark shadows and the nightdress rode up on her thighs. He took a pace toward the bed.

"Adele . . ."

She put a finger to her lips. Then she said, "Come over here."

He sat on the side of the bed not touching her. "Now, take off your coat. Here, let me help. Now the tie." Her fingernail scratched his neck as she took hold of the tie. "There, that's a little better. Now, put your arms around me."

"There's something . . ."

"Later."

He held her awkwardly. "Palmer, tell me I look young and beautiful."

He said nothing.

"Is it so hard? Is it so much to ask?"

"No."

"Then say it. Please say it."

"You're very beautiful. You're young and you're beautiful and you're all the things . . ."

"No, that's enough. Now kiss me. Just kiss me."

He bent his head to hers. When their lips touched she moved suddenly and he felt her legs wrapping around him and pulling him in to her. Then she was fumbling at his clothes and he was helping her. No one spoke.

Afterwards, he dozed and she woke him. She was running her tongue up and down his stomach and her hand was feathering over him. She moved down to him and straddled him.

The next time it was light and she was naked. She was rubbing her body on his, pushing her nipples into his mouth and groaning with each movement. Her eyes were closed and as he entered her she

237

gasped and raked her fingernails down his flanks.

"Harder," she said. "Harder. I want more, more, more." Then she cried out and Palmer crushed her body against his and thrust again and again until he was finished.

They flopped back on to the bed and he slept.

When he awoke, he was instantly aware of the pain in his wrist. She was dressed and sitting on a chair near the bed watching him. He held the wrist with the other hand.

"Is it painful?"

"It's all right."

"Go to the bathroom and run some cold water on it."

When he came back he went over to her but she leaned away from him. "Pal, sit down. We have to talk."

"I know."

"No, not about that. You want to make a confession, don't you? About Marcia."

He looked at her.

"There's no need," she said. "I know all about it. I knew almost from the beginning."

"And the baby?"

"The abortion. Yes, I knew about that too. We may not be very much alike, Pal, but she is my daughter. We talked and we decided. I was the one who spoke to Peter Barrett. I drove her there and I waited for her and drove her home again."

"You never mentioned it."

"Why? What was the point? It was over and done with. She wasn't right for you. She would never have fitted in here, with your work, your writing . . ."

"Such as it is."

"Just listen to me." She paused. "Pal, what happened last night, today, is never going to happen again."

"Between us?"

"Yes. Never again."

"Why? Are you sorry?"

"No." She looked away, then back to him. "No, I'm not sorry. I'm glad it happened. It had to happen. There were a hundred reasons why it had to happen. It was there, inside both of us whether you realised it or not."

"Of course I knew."

"It shouldn't have been but it was. On my part because, well, you represented something, someone I've always wanted, something I almost had once. There was a man . . . no, that's not important. It may just have been that you're young and I'm . . ."

"Adele, please, there's no need."

238

"There is. It has to be said. It happened and I'm not sorry but it isn't going to happen again. It's done now and we can forget about it."

"It doesn't work that way."

"Then we'll make it work. Don't you see? This whole fiasco with *O'Halloran* wouldn't have happened if I hadn't been so blind, if I hadn't mixed up the play itself with other things, if I hadn't wanted to play Lady Bountiful with you and give you your toy as a nice present."

"Is that all it was?"

"No. No, it's not all." She stood up from the chair, found a packet of cigarettes on the bedside table and lit one. He watched her blow the stream of smoke. It looked like a giant blue ice cream cone lying on its side.

"It was . . . do you remember what Arthur Morely said that time in his letter about your stories? Potentially, he said . . . do you remember? Potentially they were very, very good. There was vitality and strength but I should buy you a blue pencil to cut away the unimportant things. And that's what we forgot with *O'Halloran*."

"I could still do it."

"No. It's too late now. After tonight or tomorrow night we'll close."

"It might be different tonight."

"No, Pal. First night audiences in a small community like this are terribly important. Once the word gets around, and with that review, there's really no chance." She paused. "And frankly, I'm not about to throw good money after bad."

"Christ."

"Anyway, that's not really important. The important thing is for you to forget about it. To learn from it and then forget about it. Put it behind you and go to work on something else, something new."

There was a long silence in the room. He felt the ache in his wrist and he was glad of it. His throat was closing up.

"Ah shit," he said.

She sat on the side of the bed and touched his hand. "Do you want me to go?"

"No," he said. "No, I must. What's the time?"

"Nearly lunchtime. I called Brolie while you were sleeping. I told her you came back to the hotel and I got you a room."

"What did she say?"

"Not very much."

"I see. Is the baby all right?"

"She didn't say. I didn't ask."

"No, of course. Where are my clothes? I must go home and change.

239

I have to work."

"At the paper?"

"Yes."

"Pal."

"Yes?"

"It will be better now. Believe me."

"If you say so." He put on his trousers.

"I do. It might even be better for you at home. With Brolie."

"Adele, do you have any idea what you're saying?"

"No, I'm sorry. I shouldn't have said that."

"No."

At the door, she took his hand. "Are you coming tonight?"

"I don't know. Probably not."

"It will be better," she said.

Later, when he had returned to the newspaper building, Bill Duncan was standing in the foyer waiting for the lift. There was a large strip of white sticking plaster across his bottom lip.

"Look, Bill . . ." he had said, but that sentence had remained unfinished . . .

He shook his head to dispel the memory and moved in his seat.

"What is it?" Adele whispered.

"What? Nothing. I was just thinking."

"What?"

"Oh, that you're pretty special."

She smiled again in the darkness.

On stage, Kerry, the eldest son who had been to university, was talking about the future; about the way it might be, with satellites charting the weather patterns, with scientific cloud seeding, with the rivers turned back from the coast, with the miracle pasture seeds, the deficient soil elements sprayed and ploughed back into the earth. A green land, green and flowering and rich.

The family listened and Lucy watched the sky.

But he was right, he thought. She *was* special. She had made it work. And he hadn't helped at all, especially in those weeks and months after *O'Halloran* folded and she had returned to the city twice and called him about his new work. There was no new work. But the memory of that night stayed with him and he tried to make it happen again. She had rebuffed him sharply and it had hurt.

Gradually he had changed and partly at least she was the cause of the change. When they were together she was more relaxed, more friendly, more equable and this had an effect upon him, probably the effect she intended. She was still desirable but somehow the illicitness and something of the challenge was missing and in her presence there

240

was no posturing, no tension.

Then, when he began work on *Land* he sent scenes, then acts and finally the completed play to her. It helped him to know there was someone waiting to read his work. It forced him at the end of a long day and in the mornings before work to go back to the typewriter, to write some more, to get it down. She was his audience and the scenes he carved on to the paper were designed to hold her attention, to tell her the story, to involve her and grab her emotions and show her, through Hector Bannerman, how the spirit of a man could withstand everything that nature, the land, could throw against him. He could withstand it and he could win. But it was the struggle more than the winning which gave him his dignity and his strength. His determination never to capitulate to the sightless, random forces of nature, to keep his love for the land and never to walk away from it despite the pain and the deprivation of those who loved him and depended on him.

This was the message, the theme, of the play and as he wrote it the strength of the words and the action and the struggle seemed to flow back into him as though he were writing to himself and learning from the power which dredged his brain and guided his fingers. And, as the writing progressed and her reactions came back to him in long, meticulously worded letters, the direction of the work became clearer and he went back to the early scenes and wrote them again.

Finally, when he felt it was done, she came down and they went together to the producers. Not to the Playhouse group this time but to "The Firm", the biggest Australia had to offer.

He remembered vividly the first confrontation with Roy Fadden, J.C.W's Queensland manager, the words and the look of utter incredulity when she made her demands, the gut-paralysing fear he had that Fadden would laugh at them and turn them away. But he hadn't laughed.

"I think he was too shocked to laugh," Pal said as they left the building.

"Just wait until he reads it," she said.

They waited a week, then he called and they returned.

"Sorry," Fadden said when they were seated. "It wouldn't go."

"Why not?" Adele said.

"Look, I'll grant you that it's got a certain strength to it, but the subject . . . you can't expect a city audience to come along and listen to a two-hour lecture about how rough things are in the bush. There's only a limited theatre audience in any city. And they want to see the big shows, the ones they know about, the musicals that have made it on Broadway and in the West End. You know that, Mrs Champion. If they're going to go to a play it's got to be by someone they know,

241

Tennessee Williams or Osborne or Albee."

"If a play's good enough, people will come to see it," Adele said, "and it doesn't matter a tinker's damn who wrote it. Look at *Summer of the Seventeenth Doll* and *One Day of the Year*. They weren't by Williams or Rattigan or whoever else you said. Ray Lawler was practically unknown before *Doll* was produced."

"That may be so, but I'm sorry. I've read it very carefully and I'll have to say no."

"Have you shown it to anyone else?"

"No."

"Will you?"

"Adele," Palmer said, "I think he's made up his mind."

"No. I asked you a question, Mr Fadden. Will you send it to Melbourne and ask for a reading?"

"I'm sorry . . ."

"Very well, I will. I'll write to John McCallister tomorrow. Today. And I'll be delighted to tell John that I showed it to you first and you turned it down after one superficial glance at it."

"John?"

"Yes. John McCallister. He is still your general manager, isn't he? He was when I last talked to him."

"You know John McCallister?"

"Of course. That's why I came to J.C.W.'s first."

Palmer watched as their eyes locked. Adele didn't flinch. Finally Fadden turned back to the script on his desk.

"Look, I'll tell you what I'll do. Just to satisfy you, I'll send it to Melbourne myself."

"And what will you say about it?"

"I'll have to say I'm very doubtful about its possibilities."

"No. If you do that, it won't get a fair reading."

"Mrs Champion, what do you want?"

"If you can't recommend it, and I don't see why you can't, then you should say nothing at all. Just address it to John McCallister from you and leave the rest to him."

Fadden paused. "All right," he said. "But I can assure you there's very little chance . . ."

"We'll have to see, won't we?"

"Very well. I'll send it today."

"Thank you." Adele took a notepad out of her purse. "Do you have a pen, Mr Fadden? I want to write a note to John."

Fadden passed over a fountain pen and Adele scribbled a few lines, addressed an envelope and after Fadden had the script wrapped, tucked it into the package. Then Fadden dictated his own note and that went in too. It was non-committal.

Then had come the waiting. Adele went back to the property and Palmer sweated for three weeks until Fadden called with the news that John McCallister himself was coming to Brisbane the following week and wanted to see him when he arrived. He had called Adele in Morgandale immediately and she had been there when the distinguished ex-actor had told them of the company's decision.

He took them to lunch at his hotel in the city and after endless preliminaries announced that The Firm had decided to take a gamble; to give him a chance. There were a number of changes which they thought could help the play but they were only suggestions and he was sure Palmer would see their value.

"Nothing major, I hope," Palmer said.

"No, no, no." McCallister said. "Details. Details. The sorts of things you can fix during rehearsal."

Palmer nodded.

The rest of the luncheon was a blur. He listened sporadically as Adele and McCallister talked of old friends, but mostly he was locked inside himself tasting the thrill, repeating to himself over and over again that it was happening. He was actually sitting there at a table with John McCallister himself and they were talking about his play. His own work. And all the time and agony he had put into the writing of it were gone without a trace. He couldn't remember them, even when he tried.

But they didn't mean a damn. The only thing that mattered was the result. His play. How could they be so casual about it? How could he just sit there? Why didn't he stand on the table and cooee it across the dining room? Why didn't they all run down Queen Street shouting at the top of their lungs? His play.

When they were outside in the sunlight, he could restrain himself no longer. He took Adele by the arms and jumped around the crowded footpath.

"Jee-sus," he said and laughed aloud.

"Pal, for goodness sake."

"But Adele, it's magnificent. Bloody magnificent."

"Yes. Now, come on, calm down."

"Never. Isn't it fantastic?"

"Yes."

"And you seemed to enjoy yourself too. You didn't tell me you knew him that well."

"Do you know, Pal, I only met him twice. It was in London after the war and I was with my husband. I honestly think he had me confused with someone else."

"Really?"

"I didn't know half those people he was talking about. I honestly think he thought I was someone else entirely."

"Oh no. That's beautiful."

"And he was just too vain to admit it."

"Oh dear." They laughed together and Pal saw smiles on the faces of the footpath crowd as they passed.

The euphoria lasted only a few days. It was left to Roy Fadden to spell out the fine print of the agreement and he did so at a dinner a week later. Not only would the play be cast locally but only local set and costume designers would be used. It would open at His Majesty's certainly, but after only three months and in the off-season, the Brisbane winter when the city's theatregoers traditionally preferred their comfortable lounge rooms and television. If, and only if, it drew good houses for an extended season would the company take it south.

After the dinner, Palmer and Adele stayed behind in the dining room.

"I just don't understand it," Palmer said. 'They're the ones who stand to lose money doing it this way. It seems like an absurd false economy. If you want to make money, you've got to be prepared to spend it."

"Yes."

"Do you think this is their way of backing out of it? That they want us to say no?"

"Possibly. But I don't think so. I think they're genuine but at the same time they're worried that if they really went all out with a top money production initially, and it failed, they'd be that much worse off."

"But the chances of it failing are higher this way."

"Yes, I know what you're saying, Pal, but you know, if the play's good enough and the acting is good enough, these other things really don't matter very much."

"So you think we should agree."

"Don't you?"

"Of course I do. It just seems crazy, that's all."

There were other problems. The changes to the script which McCallister had mentioned were relayed through Roy Fadden and Derek Clayton even before Clayton sprang his own ideas and they sounded much more like demands than suggestions. Palmer had to fight line by line and scene by scene to retain the original. But with a few tolerable exceptions he won his battles.

Then in the thousand and one decisions required for set design, staging, lighting, costuming and casting, Derek Clayton and Roy Fadden virtually closed him out. More battles ensued and with Adele brandishing her mythical intimacy with John McCallister like a torch, he forced his way back into the inner counsels.

244

It was an absorbing time. Absorbing and frustrating and exhausting and immensely thrilling. Though there were times when it took on a dreamilke quality, as though he were wandering lost in a huge jigsaw puzzle where none of the separate pieces bore any possible resemblance to their fellows and the pattern he sought had faded from memory. And time was pressing. There was never "a whole month to go"; it was always expressed the other way: "only four weeks"; "only a fortnight"; "only three days".

On the day of the opening he was in a kind of hysterical despair.

"A mess," he said in the taxi as he sat between his wife and Adele on the way to the theatre. "A catastrophe. I have created a catastrophe. Did you hear that, driver?"

"What?"

"I said I've created a catastrophe."

"Good for you."

"It hasn't happened yet. It's going to go off in about three hours. No, God, look at the time. Can you speed it up a bit?"

"Nope."

"It doesn't matter. It'll wait till I get there. But then, oh ho, just wait till then. Refugees will come staggering out of the wreckage, dazed and bleeding inside. It's a good place for you to be, mate, if you want a lot of work tonight."

"Where?"

"Outside His Majesty's."

"When?"

"Any time. Any time from eight o'clock on. There'll be a steady stream, the walking wounded, dazed and bleeding inside."

"Can't park there."

"Never mind. They'll probably stagger as far as the Edward Street rank."

"Do you ladies know what he's talking about?"

"Yes," Adele said between giggles, "but only vaguely."

"He's not one of those Vietniks, is he?"

"No, I don't think so."

"He's not going to blow up the place then?"

"Only metaphorically."

There was a silence.

"Jesus," Pal said. "It really is going to be a mess."

He stayed in his seat during the first performance for less than a minute. He couldn't sit. He couldn't even stand still. He walked back and forth at the back of the theatre, then into the lobby, then ran back knowing that in his absence the scenery had fallen and the actors had all forgotten their lines. He couldn't stand to watch it and he couldn't bear not to.

245

The house was only three-quarters full and the applause after the first two acts sounded forced, almost obligatory. He stayed away from the lobbies between acts and went backstage instead. He didn't want to see their faces until it was done. Backstage, he was ignored. The others seemed to be just as restless and unnerved as he was. He tried to speak to Derek Clayton but when he opened his mouth there was nothing he wanted to say. He smiled at the cast and the stage hands indiscriminately but they passed him without a word.

The third act was worse. He spoke the lines with the actors but their reading seemed false to him, overpitched then underplayed but never the way he wanted it. They were destroying it. The audience was hating it. They were only staying because it was less embarrassing to wait it out than to walk out now.

Then suddenly, as he stood at the back of the seats in the final minutes of the play as Hector Bannerman, alone on the stage and on the land, flung his challenge into the silence and the space around him, as he told of the love and the hate that bound him to the land, as he strode with a man's stride upon it, as he stood unconquered, unbeaten, without wealth, without family, with nothing left but his own will, he was suddenly back inside the play, within the character, sharing his pain and his strength. He was caught up. He was on stage, but it was no longer a stage, it was a piece of arid land a thousand miles away and the wind was rising. And when the thunder cracked he answered, as Hector Bannerman did, with his own cry of defiance. And, like Hector Bannerman, he stood and waited.

The burst of sound was all around him. The curtain was falling and the sound was buffeting him and filling him. It was around him and inside him and filling the air. They were applauding. They were clapping and applauding and here and there people were standing up and when the curtain rose they were shouting and calling and clapping and someone was propelling him down the aisle towards the stage. The curtain was going up and down and the whole cast was beckoning him to come on. Lucy had him by the hand and was pulling him across the stage into the light which was driving into his eyes so that beyond it there was only darkness and sound.

Then the sound stopped. They wanted him to say something, but what? Dear Christ, his mouth was so dry it wouldn't open. He stared into the darkness.

"I don't believe it," he said. The silence was palpable now. Overwhelming. "But I thank you just the same."

There were a few chuckles, then silence.

"I thank you because you came and because you stayed." He paused. "You know, if only someone would boo I'd be able to say, I agree with you, sir, but who are we against so many." In the laughter,

246

he said, "I'm sure that fellow had it all set up before it happened." The dryness was gone now and through the light the audience was becoming visible.

"I suppose that in a sense I've been talking to you all night and I've said what I had to say." He paused again.

"I'm sure you realise that something like this is not the result of just one man's effort. There are many others, too numerous to mention individually. But there is one person who is in the audience tonight, and without whom this play, such as it is, could not have been written. Hers has been an extraordinarily difficult, long-term job, and without her help and her encouragement it would just not have been possible. I'm going to ask her to come on stage. This is really her night just as much as mine. Ladies and gentlemen, Mrs Adele Champion."

He had watched her walk quickly down the aisle. The clapping had broken out again as he bowed and she curtsied. Then they had backed away from the lights; the curtain began to fall but the clapping and the lights persisted . . .

He was back in the theatre and the people around him were clapping again. The lights were coming on and she was sitting beside him. The first act was over.

HE FOUND his wife in the crush of the lobby. She was standing by herself near a group he had noticed at the theatre before. They turned inwards as he passed them and he heard a man say, "That's him." He grinned to himself. He was tempted to say something to them but his wife was watching him as he approached.

"Enjoying it?"

"Yes, of course."

"Good."

"But it's lonely down there by myself, Pal. Are you coming to sit with me now?"

"No, it's too close for me. I need to be further away . . ."

"That's what you said on opening night."

". . . but Adele's going to join you."

"I see."

"You don't mind, do you? If you'd rather be on your own . . ."

"Where's she been sitting? With you?"

"Yes."

"Well, if she's going to move, why can't I come and sit with you?"

"No reason at all, Brolie. Except that you won't have a very good view."

"That doesn't matter."

"Don't you want to see it?"

"Yes, but I want to sit with you."

"All right. I was planning to take a walk this act and blow out the cobwebs." He smiled. "I've seen it before, you know."

"Were you really going, or is it something you just made up to avoid me?"

"Of course not. I'll come back with you for a little while and then I'll go for my walk. It's going to be a long night tonight. A bit of fresh air will do me good."

"Can I come with you?"

"Where?"

"When you go for your walk. Can I come with you?"

"Jesus. I thought you wanted to see the play."

"I can see it any time."

"Well, you can see me any time too."

"Can I, Pal?"

"Brolie, for Christsake, will you stop it."

"Stop what? I only want to be with you."

"Look, if I go for a walk it's because I want to be on my own. I want to get away from people and just walk and think and talk to myself for half an hour."

"Is that what I am? Just 'people'?"

"No, damn it." He was suddenly aware that heads were turned and the group nearby was listening. He lowered his voice. "Brolie, will you please, just for once, let me do what I want to do without having to explain how and when and why. Will you just let me be."

She said nothing.

"We'll be together for the rest of the evening. We'll be together at the party afterwards. We'll be together when we go home. We'll be together tomorrow morning when we both wake up."

"In a way, we will."

"Brolie, that's the start, do you know that? You always start with those words. 'In a way we are together.' Do you know what comes next? I'll tell you. 'But not really together.' Not really together . . ."

"Well it's true." Her voice cut through the murmur of conversation in the lobby. The group near them started to move away.

"Come with me," he said. He took her elbow and they walked quickly back into the theatre. He sat beside her in the aisle seat of the back row.

"Now look," he said. "I'll sit here with you until after the first scene. Then I'll go for my walk. Then I'll come back and sit here with you again. All right?"

"It doesn't matter."

"Okay. If it doesn't matter, I'll leave you now and go for my walk now and you'll be here when I come back."

"Where's Adele?"

"I don't know where Adele is. I think she probably went for a leak. If you like I'll go and check the ladies room and let you know. How's that?"

"That's not funny, Pal."

"No, dear. None of it's funny." He stood up and looked towards the front of the theatre. "I thought so. Adele's waiting down there for you. Do you want me to tell her to come up here and sit with you till I get back?"

"No."

"All right." He started to move away then turned back to her. "Did Connie come?"

"When?"

"Before you left. Did Connie come to mind Clem?"

"Yes."

"Was he comfortable?"

"Yes. She was reading him a story. He wanted you to do it."

"Yes, I wanted to too, but I couldn't get out of it. It was like a madhouse here this evening."

She said nothing.

"I might just slip out and see he's okay. It'll only take ten minutes in a taxi. There's not much on the roads this time of night."

"I'm sure Connie can look after him."

"Yes, I am too."

"What does that mean?"

"Nothing. I'll see you later."

The bell rang just as he left the seat and he had to wait until the crowd passed the passageways before he could clear a way through to the lobby. As he went down the steps he felt his arm held.

"Hey, it can't be that bad."

He looked around. Arthur Morely was grinning. "They tell me it gets better."

He grinned in return. When Arthur smiled it was impossible to do otherwise. "Hello, Arthur. Hello, Mrs Morely."

"You're not much of a recommendation for your play, my boy, walking out in the middle. Or did I miss something?"

"No, there's more to come. And it's right what they tell you. It must be. I read it in the *Courier-Mail*."

"And that's going to cost you some day too, young Lingard." He turned to his wife, a handsome woman whose mischievous sense of humour almost matched her husband's. "Did you hear what happened, dear? Poor old Dave Winterbottom came into my office and fell on his knees. He said, Arthur, please send somebody else. Think of what happened last time. I'm too old to review a Lingard play."

They laughed and Mrs Morely said, "But you hardened your heart and sent him anyway."

"I had to, dear. The only other reviewer on the paper was me and I'm even older than Dave." They laughed again.

Palmer said, "I've been meaning to call in and thank you."

"For sending old David?"

"No. For the other."

"Oh, don't thank me. I wanted to suppress it. Sentimental rubbish. But I was outnumbered. Remus McCabe, Suzy Lindeman, and when my own son turned against me there was nothing else for it."

"Right." Pal was still grinning. "Well, thanks anyway. Please don't miss any more of it. You're coming to the party afterwards?"

"Yes, we'll be there. Come on dear, we'd better go in. He's getting that combative look in his eye."

Palmer was still smiling when he reached the footpath. What a thoroughly delightful man. And how he enjoyed life. For Arthur it was an exquisite meal in a magnificent restaurant delivered a course at a time, each one surpassing the last with fresh surprises and delights. And there was all the time in the world to savour it. Nothing took from the pleasure.

Momentarily Palmer remembered the great tram depot fire. Even in a fast-breaking story like that, when half the General Room was pouring out copy, when three and four pages were being pulled apart between editions and reset with new leads, new pictures, new sidebars, Arthur had stood in the eye of the storm enclosed in a belt of calm making a dozen crucial decisions on detail while still managing to hold perspective, to see it as others might in a week or a month's time. And to savour it; to be moved by it.

And when the final edition was locked in and the others staggered home exhausted, he had sat down and written a beautiful homely piece about Brisbane's wretchedly uncomfortable, inefficient, traffic-blocking, ugly old trams with the drivers who wore strange Foreign Legion caps and the conductors who carried babies up and down the high steps for their mothers and some who whistled and had a patter to go with their ticket selling; the comradeship of little groups who always travelled together in the same seats that faced each other; and the schoolchildren who stood up for their elders, once in a while, and tried to fool the conductors with yesterday's tickets, and never succeeded. And how they were now gone. The politicians on the council would win the battle and the trams would never be replaced. Buses, where you paid at the door then buried your head in a newspaper, would take over and it would be a damned shame. Something would be lost.

It was the same gentle, human touch that had made Arthur's daily column the paper's best-read feature. It was the same quality that he had passed on to Dick, his son. Both of them seemed to find in life a texture that others were unaware of until they read about it. After the tram piece, everyone mourned their passing. Without it, Pal was sure, they would have gone unnoticed.

He turned into the footpath traffic and walked to the Edward Street corner. There were no cabs on the rank and the light said "Walk", so he kept going. He would walk down to Creek Street and then double back. By then he was sure to find a taxi. He would make the short ride out to Toowong and look in on Clem. If he was still awake he'd read him a story or make one up as he went along. He thought of his son, then of his wife, and shied away from the thought.

He was passing the G.P.O. on his right and he glanced automatically across the road to the old newspaper building, now converted into an office block. The paper had moved to a new glass and brick factory in Bowen Hills where the operation could be run more efficiently and the two papers, the *Courier-Mail* and the afternoon *Telegraph* could be printed on the same presses and money saved.

The move had been an accountant's decision and in that sense it had been successful. But when they left the old stone building they left something else behind. Like the old trams, it was inefficient and ugly and the delivery trucks snarled the traffic. It was all of those things. But it had character. It had tradition. And when you sat in the General Room after all the others had gone, sat amongst the debris and the crumpled paper and the old wrist-busting typewriters and listened to the soft mutterings of the police radio band on the roundsman's desk and felt the gentle vibration of the presses in the basement pounding out the hundreds of thousands of freshly printed newspapers there was a sense of belonging. You weren't alone. Echoes of the drama and the conflict which had gone before were still present. It was the same in a theatre when the cast and the audience and all the others had left. It was the same too in a shearing shed the day after cut-out, especially if the race for gun shearer had been close. The same echoes quivered in the air. The same ghostly sounds.

He stopped and leaned against the post office for a moment, then turned and walked back slowly toward the taxi rank.

The new building had none of that. Fluorescent lighting gave it an artificial glare. The General Room spread across half the block and dissipated the atmosphere. The walls were all hospital green and the telephones the same colour, and he was glad he had left.

If the play did well in the south they would be able to live on that for a while. And if money was still tight he had the shares Boss had signed over to him when the old man had remarried. A wedding present in reverse. He had sold some of them to buy the new apartment but the rest were there if necessary.

He wouldn't go back. He couldn't. When he saw them all tonight at the party he'd say goodbye and they'd all get sentimental and full of booze and it would be good. Then someone would say, "Jesus, Pal, you're breaking my heart", and they would all laugh and it would be over. Who would it be? Probably Kevin O'Dea. Kevin O'Dea with his big pot belly and his silver hair, his red face and the blood of Irish kings that ran in his veins and was spattered over the dining room of the Hotel Royal in the famous O'Dea-McCabe grudge match after the Jetstar joke.

God, the Jetstar joke. The summer of '66 and the Federal elections only days away, with the Holt Government looking safe but always the outside chance that Arthur Calwell could come from behind. The

Vietnam election, with Holt All the Way With L.B.J., while Calwell wanted the troops out now. Arms and armaments being debated across the country and at the heart of the debate the F-111, the controversial fighter-bomber the Government had ordered from America three years before but which still hadn't been delivered. "The greatest thing with wings since angels," said Holt's Defence Minister. "It'll never get off the ground, it should be broken up for ploughshares," Calwell retorted. And rumour everywhere that in a stunning final coup the Government would take delivery and fly half a squadron over the capital cities in the week before the election.

A quiet Sunday afternoon in the General Room: Remus McCabe ensconced in the glassed-in office handing out the assignments; Kevin O'Dea in one of the sound-proof booths at the side of the room but with the door slightly ajar so that the other reporters can hear. A piece of copy paper to crumple over the mouthpiece of the telephone as he is connected to McCabe who casually locks the receiver between his shoulder and his ear and continues his writing.

"Hello, is that the *Courier-Mail*?"

"Yeah."

"Amberley Air Base here." The accent is clipped. "Squadron Leader Paddington."

"Yes, Squadron Leader. How can I help you?"

"Well, thought you'd like to know we'll have some new arrivals this afternoon. In about an hour actually."

"Really. I can't hear you too well. There's a bit of static."

"Oh, sorry about that. Probably the radio. We're in touch with them now."

"Who?"

"What?"

"Who? Who are you in touch with?"

"What? The Americans. Thought you'd like to know. We've got these F-111's coming in."

"What!" McCabe stands. "Lavelle, for Christsake get in here. Take this call."

John Lavelle, the police roundsman, ambles towards the office.

"I've got a three car prang, Uncle. I was just leaving."

"I don't care what you've got. Hello, Squadron Leader, are you there?"

"Still here. Look, I was wondering. I've got them on the radiophone. Would you like to talk to them?"

"Talk to them! Yes, yes. Lingard, get in here with your notebook. Where's O'Dea? Jesus."

"Putting you through now."

"Jetstar leader, Colonel Calaban here."

253

"Hello, Colonel. This is McCabe, *Courier-Mail*." McCabe's accent is more American than the "American's". "Lingard, Jesus, get the extension."

"McCabe, you say?"

"'s right, Colonel."

"Well now, you sound like a hometown boy . . ."

Crackling, then another O'Dea voice. "Jetstar three to Jetstar leader. I've got a problem."

"Who's that?"

"That's my wingman, McCabe. Jetstar three, this is Jetstar leader. What is it?"

"I don't know, sir. I'm losing altitude. The gyro's doing crazy things."

"What did he say?" McCabe's accent is becoming broader still. "This goddamn static."

"We have a problem. Can you handle it, Jetstar three?"

"The dials are all screwed up. I can't hold her. I'm going to have to eject."

"Jesus wept." McCabe is walking around his desk. "Oh Jesus, Lingard, Lavelle, are you getting this? Oh my God. Colonel, are you there?"

"McCabe, this is Jetstar leader, we're coming over land. I'll have to cease transmission."

"Oh God. Colonel, where are you? This bloody static. Colonel, can you hear me? Is he going down? What's happening? Please state your position. State your position."

"My position? Why, I'm thirty feet southwest of you." O'Dea's red face appears around the corner of the booth. "Hah, hah, hah." . . .

Palmer was still laughing to himself as the taxi pulled in to the kerb. He gave the driver the address and closed the door.

"You're looking pleased with yourself."

"Yeah. Well, there's the good and the bad."

"You're so right, mate," the driver said.

He listened half-heartedly as the driver talked. His mind wandered. He would miss the paper. It had been good to him, and good for him too. Good for his writing, good for his understanding of people under pressure. It had given him the opportunity to travel and to be present at moments of drama and heartbreak and triumph. And it had given him friends; but closer than friends, fellow travellers in the best sense of the phrase. Wherever he went, in the provincial cities and the country towns, when he met other reporters, men or women, they had an immediate bond, a shared attitude, never stated but real. The attitude of the outsider, the interested spectator, the sceptical

254

observer. But more than that. You didn't just observe. Unless you allowed yourself to be affected by what you saw, unless you could place yourself inside the action, you could never really understand it; you couldn't write about it. At least not well.

It was only now, as his decision to leave the paper took root in him, that he could see it as it was. Now he was crossing the line. Now, in place of the restrictions of column inches, there were the confines of the stage but the stories he told were his own stories, his deadlines were set within him though their pressure was just as demanding. But, subtly, he was breaking from the pattern and from the assumed comradeship of journalism. And once he crossed the line and became a source of news, however minor, he knew how difficult it would be to go back.

He had felt it the night David Winterbottom had come to talk to him about *Land*. Everyone knew him as "old" David. He was no more than forty-five but the description fitted him naturally. A slight figure of impeccable neatness, his suits were of heavy, dark worsted even in the summer months and his shining white collar sat close to his veiny neck, the narrow knot of the patternless tie protruding like an extension of his Adam's apple. His full head of dark hair was parted just above his ear and brushed straight across in the style balding men affect to cover the shine. He seemed to be preparing his acquaintances for a day, never distant, when he would have to use the same subterfuge. He was grey complexioned, clean shaven and precise. His manner was the courtly manner of an old man who has lived daringly and come to terms with a well-worn prostate. His conversation was invariably formal yet without artifice. Palmer remembered an occasion in the Royal late one afternoon when he was drinking with Dick Morely. David had joined them and ordered his regular half-scotch and water, sipped it with pleasure and confided, "You know, as civilisation becomes more complicated, they invent these little assistances to see us through. Thank God."

On the evening David came to the theatre, Palmer was in the lobby before the performance watching the attendance. It was ten days after the opening and he was scared. Advance bookings were running low and the numbers seemed to be falling each night. If something didn't happen soon, he feared the management would close it and decide against the southern tour. Nothing had been said yet. It was still paying its way. But for how much longer no one could say. Adele had gone back to Morgandale promising to return in a couple of weeks when J.C.W.'s would make their decision. She was confident it would still be running then, but he was starting to believe she was over-optimistic.

He had talked to Dick about it and to Jane MacAuliffe and anyone

255

else who would listen, as though by talking about it the worry would be lessened by having others share a part of it. But that seemed only to intensify it. As he listened to his own words it grew and took on a greater certainty for having been expressed. He was scared.

"Just the man I wanted to see," David said as Palmer went across the lobby to him. "How's it going?"

"Tonight looks all right, Dave, but I'm starting to get a little panicky."

"So I hear. Is there somewhere we can talk?"

"Sure, we can use the manager's office. What about?"

"Oh, Arthur has an idea. Let's go inside."

The office was empty. Palmer went to the small bar in the corner but it was locked.

"Fadden's around somewhere. If you'd like one, I'll find him and get the key."

"Later," David said. "Let's talk first."

"All right."

They settled themselves in the easy chairs at the end of the room opposite the desk.

"Now," Palmer said. "What's Arthur's idea? I'm all ears."

"Not very sensational, but I think it's a good one. Apparently you told Dick about the rather extraordinary agreement you have with Williamson's."

"Yes?"

"This business of opening on a shoestring here and, if you prove yourself in Brisbane under these conditions, they'll take it south to the money markets."

"Yes, I mentioned it."

"It's true?"

"Yes."

"Good God. Whatever possessed you to agree to such a thing?"

"David, I'd have done anything to get the bloody thing produced. I'd have acted in it myself if they'd asked me, painted the backdrop, swept the bloody theatre, anything."

"Quite. And how much are they paying you?"

"For the rights? The Queensland season?"

"Yes."

"I'd rather not say."

"I see. It's like that. Well, I won't press you."

"You're not going to write it, are you?"

"Yes and no. I'll tell you Arthur's idea. We know that J.C.W.'s took a risk and more power to them for that. At least they had the courage to put an Australian play on stage. But the whole thing's so bloody half-hearted that we wonder if they're not just using you to make their alley right for Government subsidies if those magical things ever materialise, or for self-publicity—you know, the Australian company supporting the Australian playwright and so on—and we think it's fair enough for us to print it."

"Christ."

"You don't mind, do you?"

"I don't know. What if they object? They might close on the spot and never touch another thing I write."

"They might, but I hardly think so. Besides, that's not the end of the idea."

"God, there's more?"

"Yes, but I don't think you'll object to this. I'll write the first story tonight, a straight news story about the fact that a play about Queensland, written by a Queenslander—under an extraordinary agreement concocted by a southern company—stands or falls on the response of a Queensland audience. How's that for a bit of aggressive parochialism?"

"Do you have to say 'extraordinary'?"

"Perhaps not. But something like that. Then, in the next few days I'll talk to the principals, Dan Eviston and Jane MacAuliffe, maybe Derek Clayton—that should keep J.C.W.'s on side—and yourself, and we'll run the series on the Op. Ed. page."

"Jesus."

"I think it'll help."

"Help. It's fantastic. But why?"

"Well, first off it's a valid news story. Local boy makes good and all. And for the rest, I think Arthur feels you started a little behind the eight ball and it's only fair to weigh in on the side of the downtrodden for once."

"And you?"

"Pal, old boy, the downtrodden aren't my cup of tea. I'd simply like them to see the wretched play. My review doesn't seem to have helped very much."

"No, that's not true."

"Oh, perhaps with the theatrical set. But there just aren't enough of them in this godforsaken place. This way we might induce a few of the great unwashed to leave their idiot boxes and expose themselves to a little culture for once."

Palmer smiled. "I'm not sure it's a cultural experience."

"Palmer, you wouldn't know what it was. You only wrote it. Leave the reviewing to your betters."

Palmer laughed and David Winterbottom permitted himself a smile.

"Now, let's make a time," he said.

257

"What for?"

"The interview."

"Oh hell, I suppose you have to."

"Of course. That's what it's all about. No coy virgining now, it doesn't become you."

Palmer grinned. "Okay, come out to the flat tomorrow if you like."

"Right, now about this agreement . . ."

"Is this the street, mate?"

"Yes, that big place on the left."

"Okay." He paused. "Overlooks the river, does it?"

"Yes."

"Must be a good view."

"Yes it is. Would you mind waiting? I won't be too long."

"Suit yourself, mate. There's not much work around till the picture crowds come out."

He went inside the building, pushed the lift button, then decided to use the stairs instead. He ran the eight flights and was breathing hard when he reached the door of his flat. It locked automatically and his wife had the key so he knocked. Connie opened the door. "Pal, what's the problem?" She pulled the door wider. At twenty-seven she had become a beautiful woman. Dark haired like her sisters, blue-eyed and with finely sculpted lips that parted easily to smile and reveal strong white teeth. But now there was a look of concern on her face which brought wrinkles and little furrows above her eyebrows.

"No problem." She should be married with a family of her own, he thought and realised he had the same thought every time he saw her. But she rarely mentioned any prospective suitors and the men she had brought once or twice to the flat seemed to have more money than sense. Still, he was grateful she was there and that she came so often to stay with them, particularly in the last few weeks.

"I was restless," he said. "I had to rush away early tonight and I thought I'd just look in on the boy. Is he awake?"

"No, he's sleeping now. He was snuffling a little while ago and I went in, but he was just dreaming I think."

"Could be. Or maybe he rolled on his face."

"I don't think it gives him any pain any more. It's just uncomfortable."

"If he rolls on it the brace pushes into his cheeks."

They walked together through the living room to the child's bedroom. There were two beds in the room. When she stayed over, Connie used the spare bed and in the days after the accident Palmer had slept there to be on hand if he woke.

The accident had occurred three weeks ago, the night Roy Fadden had told him the company's decision to go ahead with the southern tour. By then it had been a foregone conclusion but it still gave him a tremendous thrill to hear it despite Fadden's grudging tone. He had called and told his wife then he and Dick and Adele and Jane MacAuliffe had gone off for celebratory drinks at a weird, discotheque in Elizabeth Street. For an hour they had shouted themselves hoarse then Jane suggested they go back to her flat. Adele left them and Dick and Palmer stayed at the flat until Palmer took Dick's hint and called a cab.

When he reached the flat there was light shining under the door. He fumbled with his key at the lock and the door swung open.

"Pal, there's been an accident," she said. "The doctor's here."

He pushed past her into the bedroom. The doctor was working on the child who was crying softly. There was blood all over the sheets. Palmer was instantly sober.

"Jesus, what happened?"

"No need to panic," the doctor said. "I've stopped the bleeding and I've given him something to ease the pain but I think we should take some X-rays. You can do it in the morning or we can take him now, whatever you like."

"Now, of course. But what the hell happened?"

"Your wife said he must have fallen out of bed on to the parquet floor. I think he must have been standing on the bed when he fell. He gave himself a terrible thump on the face. I think the nose may be broken."

"Standing on the bed at three o'clock in the morning?"

"He was probably still asleep. Your wife said he's subject to nightmares."

"Christ Almighty. Well, let's go. Quickly. Do you have a car? I'll call a taxi. Jesus."

"Better if I call you an ambulance."

"Then please do."

When the ambulance arrived, his wife said, "I'll come too."

"No. You're not dressed," he said.

He travelled in the back of the ambulance to the hospital and waited while the X-rays and other tests were taken and analysed, then brought the child home about lunchtime. The nose was broken and they had fitted a plastic brace in the shape of a nose but open at the end so his breathing wouldn't be impaired.

"You see," Palmer said, as he and Connie bent over the bed. "He's got it a little twisted. He must have rolled over on to his stomach."

He tried to straighten the brace but the child stirred. In the midst of his delicate features and the silky auburn hair, the brace was a gross,

259

clownish mask. Palmer felt a knot of anger twist in his stomach.

"Let's leave him," Connie said. "He's all right now."

"Okay."

"Would you like a cup of coffee? I just made one for myself."

"Fine."

He sat in the living room while she went into the kitchen. Through the glass doors and between the metal railings of the balcony he could see the river and in the distance the light of the St Lucia-West End ferry.

"I can't stay long," he said. "I've got a taxi waiting."

"Coming right up."

She handed him the cup then sat in another chair facing him.

"You can take my car if you like."

"No, it's all right. I shouldn't be away long."

"Does Brolie know you're here?"

"Brolie? Yes, I told her."

"She was afraid she might not be able to find you at the theatre."

"She found me."

"Did you talk to her?"

"Of course, I just told you . . ."

"No, about the other, going to Sydney. I think she's afraid you don't want her to go with you."

The knot doubled and redoubled on itself then lashed like a whip in his belly. "I told her I wanted her to come . . . How many times . . ."

"But did you mean it?"

"I don't see . . . what is this, Connie? Did she ask you to run a third degree on me?"

"Of course not."

There was a silence and he looked at her. In the past there had always been a touch of the kid sister in her attitude to his wife. But now there was a new element, almost as though the roles had been reversed. His thought was confirmed when she spoke again.

"Pal, I'm getting worried about her."

"In what way, Connie?"

"I don't know. In the last few months she's become terribly vague. She forgets things and sometimes . . . Pal, did you know she went back to the cathedral?"

"What? No, I didn't think she'd been to church since we moved here. But that's not so terrible."

"No, not if that's all it was. But she went to see the priest afterwards and demanded that he give her the notes of the sermon."

"What for?"

"She wanted to take them to the *Courier-Mail*."

"Good God." He stood. "To the *Courier-Mail*? I knew nothing about it. What happened?"

"Apparently she was very insistent. Luckily, one of the women in the choir was there and she told Father James, the priest, who Brolie was. He got in touch with my parents and my mother came to see her."

"Where?"

"Here."

"She came here? When? Why wasn't I told?"

"Pal, I thought it was best this way. You know, you and my mother . . . well, I arranged it at a time when I knew you'd be out. I thought it might help."

"Connie . . ."

"No, let me finish. It was about six weeks ago, just after the play opened. I arranged it for a Wednesday afternoon when you wouldn't be here and I took the afternoon off work and brought mother myself. I think Mummy was glad of an excuse to come. She hasn't been too well lately and it's been a long time, nearly seven years. But she was terribly nervous, and so was I. I didn't say anything to Brolie beforehand. You know, I wanted it to be a surprise. But when we came she acted as though she didn't really care. I mean, she was polite and everything but she was so casual about it they might have been meeting for a regular weekly afternoon tea. Mummy was terribly upset. She didn't understand at all. She seemed to think Brolie didn't care, but I'm sure that's not true. In the past Brolie often talked about seeing her. I thought it would help."

"What about your father?"

"He doesn't seem to realise . . . he says I shouldn't have interfered. She talks to him on the telephone every now and again and he refuses to believe there's anything wrong. He was terribly angry when he found out."

"I see. Is that all?"

"No, there have been other things. Sometimes when I come here and you're out at the theatre or somewhere I'll stay the whole evening and she won't say a word. Just hello and goodbye. It's not like her, Pal. It's not natural."

He walked over to the glass doors and looked up the Milton reach toward the lights of the city. He sipped his coffee but it was cold.

"No, it's not natural," he said.

Connie crossed the room and stood beside him. "That's why I asked you about Sydney. I'm afraid that if you don't really want her with you it will only get worse."

"I won't leave her here with Clem."

"Well, I was thinking that if I took some holidays, perhaps Brolie and I could go away together, to Surfers Paradise or perhaps the

North Coast."

"Would she go?"

"If you talked to her, she would. If you explained . . ."

He turned to her. "Connie, we're going to have to talk some more. Perhaps when we get home tonight. No. It would be better when Brolie's not here. We'll have lunch tomorrow."

"All right."

"I'm not sure she'd go, no matter what I said."

They walked together across the carpeted room to the door.

"I suppose you think I'm a first class shit," Palmer said.

"No, I . . ."

"If Brolie's having a hard time . . ."

"Pal, I'm not a child any more. I know the way it is."

"Do you?"

"A little anyway. Perhaps you are partly to blame. Perhaps more than that. I don't know. I'm not blaming you."

"Thank you for that." He paused. "You know, sometimes . . ."

"Yes?"

"No, it doesn't matter. I must get back to the theatre. We'll talk tomorrow."

The taxi driver was sleeping when Palmer reached the car.

"Sorry to keep you waiting."

"That's all right, mate. It's your money."

They drove in silence until they reached the top of Queen Street near the Victoria Bridge. Suddenly he had to get out. The taxi was a prison, a cell, closing in on him, forcing him back upon himself. He had to get out.

"Anywhere here'll do."

"I thought you wanted His Majesty's."

"I'll walk."

"Okay."

He paid the fare and began to walk down the main street. There were very few people on the footpath. Some kids; a few window shoppers; and walkers, perhaps like himself, searching desperately for comfort in the simple act of moving, so that with every step a new set of figures and patterns met the eye and kept the mind occupied.

But the street was like an old, worn pullover to him, so familiar and so often used that it had moulded its shape to his. There was no mystery in it, no distraction. Every soft angle and threadbare patch had its own small history but he had been there before too many times for it to interest and involve him.

Impulsively, he stopped and turned back toward the bridge. Across the bridge and in a broad, tree-filled park by a school something had happened, something not relevant, not connected with Connie's words, not part of the fear that gnawed at him now. An instant in a nightmare that was more welcome now than it had ever been. It would distract him and hold the fear away.

That time . . . He was sitting under one of the trees, very late at night. He was alone except for the bottle in his hand, the half-empty bottle that spilled its sweet contents on his face when he tilted it. It was a cold night, like tonight, and the others, the scum, had built themselves a fire under another tree twenty or thirty yards away. There were five of them and they had a bottle too. They were passing it from hand to hand, each one watching the others to see that only one swallow was taken. He had been watching them for a long time. It was the second bottle and it must be nearly empty by now. Two of them were women, one fat and the other old and stringy. The fat one was the talker, the life of the party. Every so often she would stand up and dance a little in the firelight, her head tilted back, her arms encircling an old dream, singing without words the same phrase of a song. His mind supplied the words involuntarily: "When you are in love, it's the loveliest night of the year . . ." And when she stumbled near the fire the others said something and one of the men grabbed her hand and pulled her down near him. It was flirtatious. "Oooo," they said, like children in a schoolyard. Then they all laughed except for the one with the bottle. He watched them and he thought again of God and of his mother and of the abortion. The deaths. Then one of them, a man, left the firelight, coming towards Palmer with his hands moving at his crotch. He tried to stop but his momentum carried him forward and his foot struck something on the ground. He fell silently, unnoticed by the others, and Palmer heard the sound in the man's throat as he struggled first to stop the piss running in his trousers and on to his legs, then as he lay back and let it flow, let it flow out of him and on to him while his neck relaxed, allowing his head to fall back on to the soft grass. For a long while he didn't move. Then he turned on his side and reclined his head on his shoulder. The others looked off into the darkness in his direction but no one came. Palmer stood up from his tree and went over to him. The man's hat had fallen off and tufts of white hair sprang out from his scalp in the darkness. Palmer bent and put his hand on the slack throat but the stench was too strong so he stood and carefully placed his shoe on the neck. Then he leaned forward on the shoe, applying his weight slowly, intently. So intently that he didn't notice the woman, the fat one, breaking from the circle and coming towards him. Then he heard her shout. He looked up and she was near to him. The body beneath his shoe moved sluggishly and there was a sound when he took it away and began to run . . .

263

That time . . . at the El Morocco, they were dancing with each other, mother and daughter, the kid no more than twelve and the mother as old as a crow. Dancing while he and the Aborigines and the fat girls with beehive hairdos laughed and applauded, then clapped some more as he joined them, dancing with both of them, steady on his feet, the crow delighted with his youth, the kid resentful. Then home together to the little flat and the crow saying, "Wait, wait till the kid goes to sleep." The kid in the same bed, watching and pushing his hand away as he grabbed at the small hairless cunt. Watching with big eyes as the crow groaned beneath him. Wanting her mouth, pushing the crow on to the floor then feeling her slaps as the kid's teeth burned into his neck.

That time . . . In the Albert Street Methodist Church, the minister had only just begun the sermon. "Nonsense," he shouted. The hush and all the faces craned around. "What you are saying is utter bullshit." "Sir, if you wish to speak to me after the service . . ." "I wouldn't speak to you, you hypocritical shit . . ." "Sir, you are drunk. You are defiling the House of God." "Bullshit. Do you hear? What he's saying is a great fucking load of bullshit." "I am asking you to leave." "And I am asking you to stop filling these people's minds with bullshit." "Will somebody help this gentleman out." "Don't touch me." "Would somebody call the police." "Get away from me." "Please." "B u l l s h i t."

That time. That time and this. They were connected. Connie's words connected them. His wife connected them. There was no place in his mind that she wasn't there waiting for him, waiting with those big hurt eyes that demanded and demanded. Demanded that he fill the gap that had been left in her, the great black hole burned into her by her religion. Demanded that he take the place of her church, her family. Demanded that he weld her into his mind so that every thought was of her, every waking moment just one more chance to be with her.

"Dick," he was saying, "I just can't fuckingwell do it." They were walking the streets. Where was he? In Elizabeth Street.

"Steady on, old son."

"You don't know what it's like. She won't listen. There are some things I want to write. I don't have any bloody choice in the matter. It's a private thing. It's inside. It's not sharable, but it's there. It's mine and she resents it. She hates it. She hates everything that can't be shared with her. I'm busting a gut trying to get this play finished and she just won't leave me alone. I sit down at the typewriter and in ten minutes she's calling from the bedroom. 'Pal, your little wifey's waiting. Come to bed, Pal. Come to bed, Pal.' You think it's funny; try living with it. And the absurd thing is that she doesn't like it. She

264

uses it but she hates that too."

"What?"

"Sex. It's a weapon. It disgusts her but she uses it until it's got to the stage where I can hardly bear to touch her."

"I think you're being a bit rough on her. Whenever I'm there . . ."

"Oh yes, everything's fine and dandy then. We're together then, really together, she says. But do you know what that means? It means that there is just no space, no room for me to move an inch without her too."

"Christ, Pal, you married her."

"Yes." He paused. "Yes, I did. And I probably shouldn't be talking like this. But sometimes I build up such a bloody head of steam it's either talking to you or getting pissed."

"And speaking of getting pissed, what about a beer?"

"I can't. I'm writing."

He grinned. "You make it sound like Lent."

"It is. There are things you have to give up."

"It can't be easy on her you know."

"I know it. She reminds me of it every day. Every waking, fucking day."

"Now don't get steamed up again. How's the Little Boss?"

"Ah, now you're talking. You should have one, Dick." (There are screams in the distance. He is running towards them.)

"A kid?"

"Yes. Preferably a boy. You wouldn't like to be bored for half an hour, would you?" (The child's face is red. There is steam coming from the bowl.)

"Trouble is, I'd have to get married."

"Well, there is that. But they make a lot of things worth while." (He pushes her away, plunges his hand into the bowl. It is scalding. It is boiling.)

"Maybe one day."

"Good." ("He cut himself. I had to kill the germs. It had to be hot. It's not too hot. Look, I'll put my own hand in. See.")

"Dick, I have to go home." (Long stinging stripes from the rose thorns down his back and on his arms: "How did it happen?")

"What's the rush?"

"Act three." ("He must have fallen. He was playing with his ball.")

"How's it coming?"

"Well." ("Mr Lingard, you'll excuse me for being a Nosey Parker, but I thought you ought to know.") "It should be finished in about a week." ("It's not true, Pal. It's just not true. He's my son too, you know.")

"And then?"

"I'll have to talk to my business manager, Adele." ("How could he fall so hard? His bed's only two feet from the floor." "The doctor said, the doctor said, the doctor said..."

"No!" He shouted the word and beat a fist into his palm. He looked around. He was at the Albert Street intersection. The theatre was only a hundred yards away. There were people near him, looking at him. He avoided their eyes and walked on.

Yes. Face it. Face it. It's true. What Connie said fits the pattern: It's so obvious; plain as the nose on your face, the twisted clown's nose on your son's face. It's her only weapon, the only one she has left, the only way she can get your attention. You've taken the rest. You've taken the affection, the sharing, the attention, the love.

No.

Yes. You've kept it to yourself. You've hugged it to yourself. And the little left over you've given to others. To Adele, to Dick, to little Clem.

No, it's not like that. I tried. I tried but she was smothering me.

But that's why you married her. She fawned on you, idolised you.

No. I loved her.

You loved yourself. It was all you had in common.

I tried.

What about Adele?

That's finished.

What about the others? What about all those one night stands. What about Kay and Joyce and Carrie and Jane?

They don't count. It was impossible with her.

Did you try?

Yes, I bought a book. I talked to her. She wouldn't listen.

Did you try?

I have to write.

Did you try?

I have to be myself.

Did you try?

Yes.

Did you try?

No!

Good. Face it. Will you try now? Will you make an effort?

Do you know what she's done? You saw his face.

Don't blame her.

Who then—myself?

Yes.

No.

Will you try?
Leave me alone. I don't think I can. I don't think I can.
Will you try?
Yes. Yes. Yes. Fuck it, yes.

He walked into the lobby. She was waiting inside. He couldn't go in.
He opened the door to the manager's office.
    "Hello, Roy."
    "Lingard. Come in. Your wife was looking for you."
    "How long to go?"
    "About half an hour. Where've you been?"
    "I went for a walk."
    "Going in?"
    "No, I thought I might have a drink with you."
    "Sure. Help yourself."

THE STAGE was a babble of noise. Now that the journalists had arrived, the crowd was overflowing into the wings and they were packed three deep around the small portable bar set up in the corner. It was a strange mixture. Aside from the reporters, there was the theatre crowd, "opinion leaders" the J.C.W. people said had to be cultivated; the group Adele had persuaded down from Morgandale for the occasion: Marcia and Tom Reed now married with twin daughters, Humphrey and Mrs Baggett, the Parkinsons, Boss with his bride and looking younger even than the last time he had seen him, the McIntyres; then the cast, showered and changed now into mufti but still performing; and there, over in a corner by himself, his father. His wife's hand was becoming heavy on his arm.

"Brolie, I must go and say hello to Dad. He's looking lost."

"You said we could talk."

"We will."

"About Sydney? You don't want me to come, do you? You still haven't told me what Connie said."

"I said later. Maybe I won't go either. There's no real need for me to go. There's no more writing to be done."

"You have to go. You told me."

"They want me to. Look, we'll talk about it later."

"But you said. 'Just the two of us', you said."

"I know. And that's the way it's going to be. But we need to talk. Now, do you want to come and say hello to Dad?"

"If you like."

"Are your parents here? I asked Adele to invite them."

"I don't know."

"Come along then."

"No, I'll stay here. I can see Dick. I'll talk to him."

He threaded his way through the crowd, hands touching him as he passed, smiles, compliments and from Boss a good natured wave.

"Good to see you, Dad."

His father smiled. "Don't see too much of you these days."

He let it pass.

"Enjoy the play?"

"Wasn't as good tonight as it was last week."

"You've been before?"

268

"Oh, once or twice."

"I haven't seen you. You didn't say anything."

"I don't suppose my opinion's worth much."

"It is to me."

"Well, I thought it was good. Better than some of the things you see on TV these days."

Palmer grinned. "Thanks."

"I'm just sorry your mother wasn't here to see it. She'd have been very proud, son."

Palmer said nothing.

"Still, I suppose we have to believe that she knows. I sometimes get the feeling, in the shop you know, that . . . ah well, that's enough of that. We can hope anyway, can't we? But she'd have loved a night like tonight, all these people standing around saying nice things about you."

"Yes."

"Still, you can't have everything."

"Dad, how are things at the shop?"

"Just the same. In fact, it's better than it used to be. People are getting sick of that bloody supermarket. They want a bit of personal service."

"And you're just the man for it."

"I tell you, son, I've noticed one or two around here tonight I wouldn't mind giving a bit of personal service to."

"Hah. There's life in the old dog yet. Have you seen Boss? Isn't it amazing?"

"Yes, I talked to him before. She'll kill him, that woman."

"At least he'll die happy."

He saw a frown crease his father's face and the older man looked away then back to him. "What about you, son? How are things at home?"

He paused. "No complaints."

"Good. Now, what about introducing me to one or two of these little dollies. Look, that one there."

"Jane?"

"Yes, she's a bobby dazzler, isn't she."

"Did somebody call me?" She turned towards them.

"Yes, Jane, come and meet my father."

"For you, darling, anything." She kissed him on the cheek and turned to his father. "Aren't you proud of him? Isn't he gorgeous?" She put an arm around his waist.

"Cut it out. You'll have me shot. Now, be a good girl and say hello to Dad."

Her expression and manner changed instantly. It was a characteristic that always amazed him, the speed of it, the sureness with which the new role was assumed.

"How do you do, Mr Lingard. I hope you don't mind. We're all terribly excited tonight."

"About going south?"

"Yes, the whole thing, it's just too wonderful."

"Well, you don't have to worry. I thought you were very good."

"You did? Why, thank you. That's the nicest thing . . ."

Palmer moved away. Dick and Brolie were standing together and he started in their direction. As he did, Tom Reed crossed his path with Marcia on the other side. Tom looked uncomfortable in his dinner suit and in this company. He had put on weight and the hair at his temples was touched with grey flecks below the permanent indentation made by his hat. Marcia too had gained weight. But it was still well distributed and the dress she was wearing pushed her breasts into even greater prominence. He hesitated. Then he brushed away the memory and said, "Hey, Tom."

"Here he is. We've been looking everywhere for you. How are you, you old bastard?"

"Great." They shook hands. "It's good to see you, Marcia." He leaned forward and kissed her on the cheek.

She smiled. "You too, Pal."

"How long's it been?" Tom said. "A bloody dog's age."

"Nearly eight years," Marcia said.

"That's right. Lot of water passed under the bridge since then, eh," Tom said. "And speaking of water, it's a bloody dry argument. How about a grog?"

"I'll see what I can do."

"No, I'll get them. You look after the filly till I get back."

"No. This is my show. What'll it be?"

"Anything wet, mate."

"The same."

When he returned with the drinks, Tom said, "Well, here's to it."

"Right." They drank.

"We haven't met your wife," Marcia said. "Is she here?"

"Yes, I'll get her." He looked through the crowd. She was standing in the same place. Dick was gone but another reporter, John Lavelle, was beside her.

"Brolie," he called, but his words didn't reach them. He moved towards them. "Back in a minute, Tom."

He had almost reached them when a noise from the other end of the room interrupted him.

"Ladies and gentlemen." God. It was Kevin O'Dea. What now?

"Ladies and gentlemen, if I could have your attention." He was

270

standing on a prop used in some earlier play. It looked like a winner's stand, the type they used at athletic meets. His coat was open and one of his shirt buttons undone revealing a dazzlingly white strip of underbelly. Palmer moved closer.

"I understand that before we arrived tonight there were some speeches. Mr McFadden told you . . . What? Sorry. Mr Fadden told you some good news. I have some good news too." The crowd was quiet. Palmer sipped his drink.

"My news is that I'm not going to make a speech. Hah. Hah." There were a few chuckles. "As you might have guessed, I'm a reporter on the *Courier-Mail* and I just want to say to Pal Lingard—Is he here?—Ah yes, on behalf of myself and the other blokes, good luck to you." There was scattered applause.

"And all I can say is, it's just as well he'd gone into the playwriting business because he wasn't much of a bloody reporter. Hah, hah, hah.

"No, the real reason I stood up was to introduce someone who is going to say a few words. Ladies and gentlemen, Mr Arthur Morely."

He stood down from the podium and Arthur Morely took his place. In contrast to the reporter, Arthur looked the very essence of elegance in his black dinner suit and with the stage lights above glinting on his grey hair. The crowd quietened and he smiled.

"Those of us who write for our living," he said, "always welcome the opportunity to put away the typewriter and talk instead. It's much less complicated." He paused. "And afterwards you can always deny it and say you were misquoted."

There was some laughter from the journalists.

"But, I'm sure that what I say tonight will never find its way into a newspaper. It had better not or there will be trouble, I can assure you." More laughter from the journalists and some of the others.

"Now, I want to do some thanking. I'm sure Palmer won't mind if on his behalf I thank J. C. Williamson's for having the courage to produce the play in the first place. Perhaps they got a little help that they weren't expecting but a newspaper can only report facts. And the simple fact was that they took a chance on an unknown, and a Queenslander to boot, and I think they're to be congratulated for it.

"Of course, if the play wasn't any good, all the free publicity in the world wouldn't save it. You all saw it tonight—some of you, I think, not for the first time. I'm rather ashamed to admit that it was the first time for me.

"Which brings me to my second thankyou. It is to the man who wrote it. Pal, thank you on behalf of us all for a really first class piece of work." The applause was louder this time. Palmer felt a space growing around him. People seemed to be moving away from him. He looked around for his wife but he couldn't see her in the crowd.

"I have no doubt at all that it will succeed in the South. And I say that for two reasons. The first, of course, is the play itself. But more important than that, you know, this fellow has discovered the secret of success. The reviewers down there just won't be game to pan his play. They know if they do he'll be after them with the meanest right hand in the business." He waited for the laughter to subside.

"I'd like to get a little more serious." He put his hand into his coat and drew out two sheets of paper.

"A long time ago, Palmer Lingard made a very bad mistake." In the silence, Palmer felt his palms tingle and took a sip of his drink. The glass was empty. He looked around to the bartender and held up his glass. The man nodded.

"He won the heart of my secretary." Only the journalists responded. Palmer relaxed. "For those of you who don't know her, I'd better tell you that Miss Mavis Calloway retired a couple of years ago at sixty-five, so take that worried look off your face, Brolie.

"I don't know how it came about, but Mavis was always a notoriously bad judge of character. But whatever, when he first came to the paper and, I might say, for an unconscionably long time afterwards, he couldn't type, and since no one could read his handwriting he had a problem. He solved it by forming a clandestine relationship with Mavis. In other words, she did his typing for him on the quiet. And, I might tell you, most of the things she did for him had absolutely nothing to do with his newspaper work.

"But I don't suppose that matters now. I can see you're all wondering what the devil this is all leading up to. Well, it's this. Mavis came to see me a couple of days ago. She'd been to see the play and she wanted to give me something she'd typed for him about six years ago. She wanted me to return it to him through my son, Dick, who's been his partner in crime since he returned to civilisation . . ."

"Steady on, now." It was Tom Reed.

Arthur smiled but made no response. ". . . and I have it in my hand now. I'm going to return it to him. But first I'm going to read it to you. When Mavis gave it to me she said, Mr Morely, this is where it started', and having seen the play I think she was probably right. Let me read it to you."

He unfolded the pages then took out a pair of horn-rimmed spectacles from another pocket. His voice was soft: "'I will tell them the way I feel about it; about the land,'" he began. "'When I go to the sea, I will say, and I stand and face the breaking waves with the miles of clear, empty water beyond, it is as though the whole world is at my back. There is nothing before me. It is all behind and I can feel it and see it with my mind. I know that if I turn around I will see through the mountains the great, flat, red, open plains of

272

the gulf, cut through with river courses, rimmed with dark green mangroves near the coast, and where in flood time the alligators thrash to the high ground and fight free of the current to crowd with other reptiles on the small knolls, and with frightened stupid cattle who will blunder into them in the darkness.

" 'I will see the Namatjira purple of the hills around Cloncurry and the small herds of goats that feed and jingle bells in the outskirts of the towns. I will see Mt Isa and the giant smokestacks of the outback and I will hear the harsh accents of the blond miners.

" 'Then the dust will come and I will see it dark and fearsome on the horizon, dark and growing stormy and closer and redder and closer still until it is all around me, until it is the air I breathe. It is the air itself.

" 'And south, the dry, brittle, pale grasses and the precious mint-green grasses and the ocean of burry sheep and the closeted white flock rams. I will see the wheat and the oats and the maize and the barley pushing back against the westerly. Then nearer to the mountains, fat lambs and fattening cattle, the silky hides of stud stallions, the ripening apples and citrus of Stanthorpe and the southern Downs.' " He paused.

" 'Across it all there will be the land. The black, the red, the brown, the white, the grey, the sharp, stony, rich, harsh, strong, flinty land gouged with flood, cracked and baked with the dryness and the heat, lashed and pounded by the tropic storms that rage in from the sea. I will tell them about that land, my pride in it, my pleasure in its struggle, the way it fights and makes men work and tests their stamina and gives them strength. For the people and the land are one, inseparable, acting and reacting upon each other, struggling in hate and love and becoming one.

" 'And that strength is contagious. It passes from the solitary man far out there on the awesome, lonely plains into the small towns, the bigger towns, by word, by story, by wire and print into the selfish city itself. And it enriches us all. We feel the harsh, hot breath of it and it enriches us. We partake of it.' " Another pause.

" 'And I will tell them of my fear: That one day the land will be tamed and it will give up its bounty willingly, automatically, like the dull-green, sluggard, pretty fields of Europe. And then the men upon it will be weakened and cheapened and there will be no struggle and no conquest and little pride. They'll be feasting on a whore. They will be lessened in spirit.' "

He stopped. There was a long moment of silence as he folded the pages. His voice was quiet when he spoke again.

"It's a strange message but I think all of us here in this place understand it. Those of you who work the land will know it, and the

273

rest of us who travel over it and write about it will understand it. It's not very sophisticated, not clever, perhaps not even original. But that's by the way. The point is that he did it. He took this concept and he brought it to life for us. He gave us an insight into an aspect of our life and our history and our humanity which we didn't have before and all of us, whether we like it or not, whether we agree with it or not, will have been changed a little by having been exposed to it. And I am sure, absolutely sure, that it will be understood not only in Queensland but right across Australia. And if it ever gets performed outside this country, and I hope it does, then it will show others something of the way we are and the forces that mould our character.

"Personally, tonight has been a good night for me. Some of you may not know this, but about seven years ago an old friend of mine brought a very bedraggled, sad looking character along to my office and said, 'Arthur, he's got something.' " He smiled. "I didn't doubt it for a moment. I thought it might have been rabies." More laughter interrupted him. "But you all know Adele Champion and she can be pretty persuasive when she gets an idea into her head. Well, this turned out to be one of her better ideas and I agreed to take him on.

"Kevin said he wasn't much of a reporter, and of course he ought to know. He's not much of a reporter either." Remus McCabe applauded loudly. "But all I can say is: He didn't do a bad reporting job tonight and if he has any more stories he wants to tell, then I'll be standing in line to see them . . . and I'll probably have Kevin O'Dea pushing in ahead of me."

The crowd laughed and clapped as Arthur held out the pages to Palmer and he came forward to accept them. Then the country people called, "Speech, speech" and Arthur Morely stepped down to give him room on the podium. There was a quiet, then Kevin O'Dea called out, "Keep it short, Pal." He grinned as the others laughed.

"I must be an exception," he said finally. "I'd much rather write than talk."

"Come off it," from O'Dea.

"It's true. And it's a strange thing. When I listened to Arthur reading those words just now, I remembered the occasion when I wrote them but I didn't remember the writing itself. When I heard them I thought, 'Well, I'm damned. Did I write that? Yes, of course I did.' And it's the same with the play, with *Untamed Land.* I sometimes sit in the audience and I know that I wrote it, that it's a part of me, that it's what I believe, and yet there's something else involved.

"I thank you, Arthur for the kind things you said but I feel as though there was more to it, that I don't really deserve the credit, that almost my only part in it was having the pig-headedness to keep going back to the typewriter, once I finally learned to type, until it was done, that those of us who write have simply learned a trick, that there is in us, all of us, what I think of as a Presence, and the trick . . ." He looked down into the crowd. Heads were averted. Here and there people were whispering to their neighbours. He could feel the journalists' restlessness. He went on quickly. ". . . is just to learn through practice to summon it, then keep a tight rein on it. All of which means that I thank you all very much indeed even though I don't deserve it. Thank you."

As they clapped he stepped down from the winner's stand and towards a group of reporters.

"Never heard so much bullshit in all my life," Kevin O'Dea said with a grin splitting his big Irish face. He stuck out his hand: "Good on you, Pal. When do you leave?"

"Thanks, Kev. We go in about a week. Christ, I'm dry." He turned and found the barman at his side. "Thanks a million."

John Lavelle pushed towards him. "Who's that old bugger over there with the bird?"

"Where? That's my father."

"He seems to be doing all right for himself. Listen Pal, the next time you write a play you want to make sure there's more women in it. This is ridiculous."

Palmer laughed and moved away. Arthur Morely and his wife came up to him. "Palmer, we're off. Nice party, but there comes a time . . ."

Palmer gripped his hand. "Arthur, thank you for everything."

"No thanks necessary."

"No, I mean it."

"You just look after yourself and that family of yours. How is the boy now?"

"Fine. I'd better go and find Brolie."

"Good." They moved to leave. Palmer looked through the crowd for his wife. Others were leaving too but through the movement he saw her at the end of the stage. Tom and Marcia waved to him as they left. Boss came towards him. They shook hands.

"Won't keep you now, boy. Come and see us at the pub tomorrow. Can you get away?"

"Sure. After lunch?"

"Okay."

He took a few steps nearer. Suddenly Adele was beside him.

"Where have you been?" he said. "I haven't seen you all night."

"Pal, I have to talk to you."

"Well, here I am."

"No, not here."

"Adele . . ."

275

"Please, Pal." Her eyes were moist and the grip on his arm trembled a little.

"All right. Where?"

She led him back the way he had come, off the stage and down a dirty corridor at the side of the dressing rooms. She opened the nearest door. There was no one in it and she led him inside. The room was furnished like all the house dressing rooms: a built-in cupboard on one side, a small couch, and, at the centre of the wall opposite the door, a chair and vanity table topped by a mirror. A tube of fluorescent lighting ran along the top of the mirror.

"What is it?" he said. "Can't it wait till tomorrow?"

"No, I'm going back in the morning with Tom and Marcia."

"Didn't John get down? I didn't see him at the party either."

"No. Pal, are you listening to me? I said I'm going back."

"I heard you, Adele. You've decided."

"Yes. I'm not going to Sydney."

"I'm not sure that I am either."

"What? Don't be silly. You have to go. It's important for you to go. The experience is important. We've talked about it. I thought it was decided."

"I want to, Adele, but there's Brolie."

"What about her?"

He paused. "I don't want to talk about it."

"You know I came back and sat with her this evening. Where were you?"

"I went out to see Clem, then I went for a walk trying to sort things out."

"Pal, there's nothing between you and her sister is there? Connie."

"No, of course not. Whatever gave you that idea?"

"Your wife gave me that idea. She talked through the whole of the third act. The people around us were getting angry at the finish. I thought I was going to have to take her outside."

"Good God." He sat on the couch. "What did she say?"

"Nothing specific. But she gave me the impression she thought something was going on between you two."

"Adele I swear to you."

"I believe you, dear . . ."

"It's just not true."

"I said I believe you. I meant it."

"The point is: will she? Dear God what next?" His body suddenly relaxed and he leaned back on the couch. "You see what I mean? How could I take her to Sydney when she's like this. And I certainly couldn't leave her behind. I think the best thing might be to go to the beach somewhere and have a holiday. Just the three of us."

"You could always come out to Morgandale."

"No, I don't think that would help."

"Because of me?"

"Partly. No, I don't know. I don't really want to go back to The Place with the new set-up."

"She'd make you very welcome. She's really very nice, Pal."

"Yes, but I don't want to go."

Adele sat on the couch near him. "So," she said, "either way, this is it."

"I don't understand."

"This is goodbye, Pal."

"Goodbye?" He looked at her. The thought wouldn't penetrate.

"Yes. I'm going back to Morgandale to stay. When I come down in the future it will be with John, with my husband."

"But what difference . . ."

"And when you write another play, I'll be there with Arthur Morely and the others standing in line at the box office, but that's all. I mean it."

"Hell, what are you talking about?" He stood up. "What's got into you?"

"Pal, you don't seem to realise that I have a marriage too. I have a husband who's not getting any younger, a husband I love and who needs me."

"But surely that doesn't mean you have to give up . . ."

"Give up what? You? Just think about that for a moment. How would you like it if your wife spent half her time running around looking after someone else's affairs?" She stood up from the couch and walked over to the vanity table. "Answer me, Pal. How would you like it?"

"Not too well, I suppose; but is that the point?"

"Yes. It is the point. It's the whole point."

"And what if I tell you I need you. There are so many things, Adele . . ."

She turned to him and took one of his hands in both of hers. He looked down at her hair, then at her face as she turned it up to him.

"If you said that," she said softly, "I think you'd be telling the truth. You'd believe it. But it wouldn't really be true. You don't need me any more. Pal, you've made it. There's nothing more I can do for you. You're there."

"One play. One season with a bloody lot of help from others."

"Stop it. Be honest now. You know you're good. You know there'll be others. You know this is just a beginning."

"Adele, I don't know what to say."

"You've said it already. You said it on opening night before a

277

whole crowded theatre. You gave me that moment. It was all I could have wished for, standing up there, being with you, listening to the crowd. It was perfect, Pal. Don't spoil it now by trying to prolong it when it's passed."

He felt her quick breathing as she pressed his hand to her chest. A dozen thoughts sprang to mind, words he could use to persuade her, to hold her, to keep her from leaving. He rejected them all. Still she looked at him, her eyes glistening in the light from the mirror. It was true. It was time, once again, to move on. Another movement, another parting. All of life seemed to be encompassed in those two phrases. Nothing stayed. Nothing remained. Only the memories and the scars, and trophies. He bent his head and kissed her gently. It was passionate yet chaste. It left him unaroused. And when he pulled back and looked at the tears falling down her face his feelings were paternal. He wiped them away with his thumb and felt gratified when she smiled. She was a small child he had found in a playground, left behind by the others.

"We'd better go back," he said.

"Yes." She broke away and turned to the mirror. "You go. I'll just fix my face and we'll have a last drink and all go home."

"Fine."

Only the diehards were left, two or three men from Morgandale and some of the reporters. They stood near the bar and Dan Eviston was reciting "The Man from Snowy River". He looked for his wife but couldn't see her. He walked over towards the group.

"Dick," he said.

"Hey, Pal. We thought you'd gone."

"Have you seen Brolie?"

"Not for a while. Didn't she find you? I thought she went looking for you."

"No, I haven't seen her. When was this?"

"Couldn't say. About twenty minutes ago, I suppose. Great party, Pal. Come and have one."

"I'd better find her."

"Okay. Don't be long."

He walked back across the stage toward the dressing rooms. There was a toilet there, somewhere near the stage door.

"Pal, thank God I found you. The man at the door wouldn't let me in. What is it? What's wrong?" She ran towards him.

"Connie! Jesus Christ, what are you doing here?"

She stopped. The question didn't seem to register.

"Is it Clem?" he said. "What happened?"

"Pal, I don't understand."

"It's clear enough. What are you doing here? Why are you here?"

"But she called. She said you wanted me. It was urgent."

"I wanted you? Damn it, who called? Brolie?"

"Yes. She said you wanted me right away. Something had happened. She wouldn't say what. She hung up. I tried to call back but it was engaged. I didn't want to come but she said it was an emergency. Pal, what is it?"

"Wait. Just wait and let me think for a moment." His head felt fuzzy from the drinks and the talking and the noise. "The Man from Snowy River" had become "Eskimo Nell" and Kevin O'Dea's voice was penetrating his thoughts, confusing them.

"When did this happen?"

"About twenty minutes ago. I came as quickly as I could."

He looked at her. "Oh Christ," he said. "We have to go. Come on. Quickly. Where did you park the car?"

"Just outside."

"Then come on. Fuck it, Connie, run."

She trailed after him as he bashed through the front doors and through the lobby into the street. "Run, bugger it, run."

"I'm going as fast as I can. What is it?"

"Which one is it?"

"You know my car. The Volkswagen. There."

"The keys?"

"Here. Are you sure you want to drive?"

"Get in, for Christsake."

The key wouldn't go into the ignition switch. He pushed it hard. It was upside down. He turned it around and it slid in easily. He turned it and the engine started. He felt the sweat break out on his chest and shoulders as he rammed it into gear and accelerated away from the kerb. The lights were red at the Albert Street intersection. He didn't hesitate. A car coming towards him on the right skidded in a squeal of brakes.

"Pal, you'll kill us. Be careful."

He said nothing and concentrated on his driving. The back wheels slid sideways as he rounded the bend on to Coronation Drive then the small car leapt forward as he pushed the accelerator to the floor.

"What's wrong with you? What's happening?"

"Clem," he said. He focused on the broken white line in the centre of the road. The strips became smaller and dashed under the hood of the car like pellets fired from a gun.

"She wouldn't hurt Clem. Is that what you're thinking? For God's sake speak to me."

The car was going into a drift. He fought the wheel, eased back slightly on the accelerator then pushed down hard as it came out of

279

the turn. The Toowong swimming baths flashed by on the right and he saw the lights of the television studio on his left out of the corner of his eye. The broken line had changed. Now it was continuous, two lines, no overtaking. Remember that. No overtaking. No overtaking.

He changed down to third, then second, as the right angle of the Glenn Road corner came fast and hard on his left. The engine screamed and he pushed it harder through the corner. A car was parked in the road just back from the corner. He saw it but it was too close. He couldn't avoid it. The Volkswagen belted and scraped along the side of it, throwing him away from the steering wheel. He pushed a hand against Connie and righted himself. He caught a glimpse of her face. Her mouth was open as though she was screaming but he heard no sound. The car was still moving. He was back in control. Only a hundred yards to go. The apartment building was lit at the front by a single lamp. The car twisted as he hit the brakes and he was out of it and running before it had stopped. He tripped on the guttering but picked himself up and burst through the glass doors into the lobby.

The steps came easily. They disappeared under his feet. The steel railing was smooth on his hand as he pulled himself upward. Eight flights. Every flight ten steps. The door was in front of him. Key. No fucking key. She had the key. He beat on it with the side of his fist.

"Brolie!" he yelled. "Brolie, it's me, Pal. Open up, Brolie!"

The door opened. He started towards her to push her aside, to push her away. Then he stopped.

She was smiling. A bright innocent smile. She was glowing. Her eyes were dancing in the light. She looked pretty, relaxed. She was wearing a hat, a green hat. It looked familiar but he couldn't remember where he'd seen it. She was carrying a suitcase in her hand but the catch had come undone and the clothes had fallen out, leaving a trail from the bedroom to the door.

He looked beyond her. A breeze was blowing in from the river and the translucent white curtains that covered the glass doors to the balcony were billowing out and she was framed between them.

"We can go now," she said. "I'm all packed."

He felt Connie brush past him. He saw her run to the child's bedroom then back and through the curtains to the balcony. She was coming back towards him. Her mouth was open again but he still couldn't hear the scream.

"We can go now."

EPILOGUE

THE MAN stood holding the grey steel rail of the bridge with both hands, his body bent forward as he looked down through the pale shadowless light of the false dawn to the slow movement of the river below.

"It is my right," he said. He was unsure whether he had spoken the words aloud. It is my right. It is my possession. It is what I have. (They were filing out of the crowded funeral parlour. They were following the man who was struggling with the small casket.)

It is the right of any man. The right to decide. The right to die. It is that and that alone which gives him his dignity. It is that which the preachers and the priests cannot abide, the one act which holds the key to their destruction. (He tried to hoist the plain brown box on to his shoulder. The others shouted in fear and stepped towards him. He shouted back at them. He controlled it. They fell back.)

They, the preachers, live upon it, upon the fear of it. And if a man asserts himself he strips them of their robes and their panoply and their power. They can never forgive him. They write words into the mouths of their gods, damning him, damning him eternally. There is no appeal. (The grey suited man opened the shining black doors and the other man, the man who was carrying it, lowered it on to the silver bars.)

They are wise. They must maximise the fear. They must play on the fear which is their daily bread. For once it goes, once the fear goes, they are naked and human, with no special knowledge, no message worth the learning. (The car started very gently and moved on cushions over the street. Faces on the footpath turned, shining faces sobered suddenly with fear. Good faces, sympathetic faces.)

And once the fear is gone they can no longer usurp the rights of men. They can no longer grip them and bind them to their fantasy. They can no longer crowd and pen them, draft them through races to assuage their own doubts, brand them and emasculate them to feed their own powerfulness. (An old man near a telegraph pole removed his hat and placed it across his chest. A baker's van fell back from the window, the driver flushed with embarrassment.)

They can no longer speak to presidents and men of good sound mind and ability. They must fly back to the shadows where the witches have gone, and the golden calves and the wood nymphs and the scorpions and the scarabs. (The car stopped as gently as it had begun. The man remained determined. It slid out easily along the silver bars and the steps were not too difficult.)

And people will wonder how it could have been that such a few fanatics could ever have held the sway they held. How a thousand generations could have lived demeaned, in bondage to a fear, and no man had the courage just to say, I am very young. I happened only yesterday. I can barely see beyond my hand, but what I see and what I know belong to me, become me. (The belt moved slowly with barely a sound and the blue curtains with golden tassels parted to let the coffin through. Parted and fell back when it passed. The furnace spat and roared and god perished. It happened long ago.)

It is my right. I assert my right. A fear is there but it is a fear of falling. And yes, there is another. I admit there is another buried there, an old, old fear. Old as childhood, old as darkness, old as questions, old as man.

But it is beatable!

A man can beat it.

And a man can muster what's left inside and look it over and find a place for pride; can see some place unsullied and care for it and build upon it. Build and struggle and build again.

Build and find the strength to move again. Build and move and fight and build again. Build and weep and purge and learn and forgive nothing. Forgive nothing. Not even in others.

I assert my right. And I waive it.

The man took his hands from the grey steel rail. It was warmer where he had touched it. He walked along the narrow footpath, back the way he had come.